THE WRITINGS OF
BEATRIX POTTER

A HISTORY OF
THE WRITINGS OF
BEATRIX POTTER
INCLUDING UNPUBLISHED WORK

BY
LESLIE LINDER

The Potter Family Crest

FREDERICK WARNE & CO LTD: *London*
FREDERICK WARNE & CO INC: *New York*

© Frederick Warne & Co Ltd
London, England
1971

ƒ 2 8 JUN 1971

LIBRARY OF CONGRESS CATALOG CARD
NO 78–145549

ISBN 0 7232 1334 8

Printed in Great Britain
Text and Photos by W & J Mackay & Co Ltd, Chatham
Picture Letters and The Sly Old Cat section by
Lowe & Brydone (Printers) Ltd, London
1671.870

CONTENTS

Contents

Contents

PART THREE

MISCELLANEOUS WRITINGS

Contents

LIST OF ILLUSTRATIONS

Colour Plates

Illustrations

Illustrations

Black and White Plates

Illustrations

Illustrations

Illustrations

Illustrations

Illustrations in the Text

ACKNOWLEDGEMENTS

This book on the writings of Beatrix Potter could not have been prepared without the help and co-operation of the many people who have so kindly contributed information about Beatrix Potter's books and her other writings, and who have made available many of her letters, manuscripts and other relevant material.

Amongst Beatrix Potter's friends who have supplied personal recollections of her life and writings, I should like to thank Miss Margaret Hammond and the late Miss Cecily Mills, who were her close personal friends and next-door neighbours at Sawrey for more than twenty years; also the late Capt. K. W. G. Duke, R.N., and the late Mrs. Mary Stephanie Duke, who, when living at Castle Cottage, Sawrey, allowed me access to all Beatrix Potter's private portfolios and papers.

Thanks are also due to Mrs. Joan Duke for making available material which has helped considerably in the preparation of Part 3 of this book; and to Mrs. F. W. Gaddum for her co-operation and help. I am indebted to Mrs. N. Hudson (*née* Nancy Nicholson) too, for lending the manuscript of *The Oakmen*. I am also grateful to Mr. Tom Storey, the late Mrs. Storey, Mrs. Freda Jackson, the late Mrs. J. E. Brockbank, and other residents in and around Sawrey, who told much about Beatrix Potter.

The late Mrs. Susan Ludbrook, who for many years was Curator of Hill Top, gave me constant help from 1951, when I paid my first visit to Hill Top, until a few months before she died in March 1970. I owe her much for the help and advice she gave. I am also grateful for information about Beatrix Potter, which she passed on to me from time to time, through her contacts with visitors and people living in and around Sawrey.

Others who have helped with recollections of Beatrix Potter and her books, are Miss Lucie Carr (the 'Lucie' of *The Tale of Mrs. Tiggy-Winkle*), and in particular, Mrs. James Boultbee (the 'Winifred Warne' to whom *The Tale of Two Bad Mice* was dedicated), who never tired of answering questions about Beatrix Potter and about the members of the Warne family. Help has also been received from the late Mrs. Berkeley (*née* Louie Warne) and the late Mrs. Sturgess (*née* Nellie Warne).

I should also like to thank Mrs. Thwaites (*née* Hilda Moore), and her sisters Miss Marjorie Moore and Miss Joan Moore for their very warm welcome, when on recent visits they gave first-hand recollections of Beatrix Potter in the days when she was writing her picture letters and her books.

Much help has come from America. The late Mrs. Bertha Mahony Miller, founder of *The Horn Book Magazine*, generously lent her collection of personal letters from Beatrix Potter, which contained information about her writings from 1930 onwards; Mrs. Charles Cridland (*née* Margery McKay) lent the letters which

Acknowledgements

Beatrix Potter had written to her father Alexander McKay, Beatrix Potter's American publisher, together with a copy of her Fairy Caravan 'Explains'; and Mrs. Richard Stevens sent a copy of the delightful set of verses about 'The Wanderings of a Small Black Cat'. I should also like to mention Miss Elizabeth Booth, who gave me information about *The Tailor of Gloucester* contained in a letter she had received from Beatrix Potter; and her friend Mrs. Ann Henisch who told where Beatrix Potter probably got the idea of squirrels sailing on rafts, which she used in her Squirrel Nutkin story.

I should like to thank the Rev. O. G. Lewis, who until recently lived close to Eastwood, Dunkeld, for giving information as to the most likely origin of the name 'McGregor' in *The Tale of Peter Rabbit*.

I am also grateful to Miss Rumer Godden who read through the typescript and gave much helpful advice.

To the National Trust I am indebted for allowing me access to their Beatrix Potter papers and manuscripts at Hill Top, and for their ready co-operation and help at all times.

Mr. Bruce Thompson, who when on the staff of the National Trust frequently met and discussed the Trust's affairs with Beatrix Potter, has also given valuable assistance in connection with her Fairy Caravan writings, and with those associated with the Lake District. Thanks are also given to Mr. L. E. Deval who made many useful suggestions in regard to the first three Appendices.

Special thanks are due to Mr. Cyril Stephens of Frederick Warne & Co. Ltd., who put at my disposal the firm's very large collection of letters from Beatrix Potter, and allowed me to examine their original manuscripts and other Beatrix Potter items. In addition I would express appreciation to Warnes for the time they spent in looking through old records to find how many copies of the first editions of Beatrix Potter's books were printed, and the approximate dates of printing; and to their editor Miss A. M. Emerson for helpful suggestions when reading through the typescript.

It would not be fitting if I did not pay tribute to Margaret Lane's fine biography, *The Tale of Beatrix Potter*, for the inspiration I have received from this book.

I should like to record with appreciation the considerable help I have had from my sister Miss Enid Linder, who has been responsible for many improvements in the text and arrangement of this book, and who has taken the colour photographs of Hill Top and of other places associated with Beatrix Potter's books.

In closing I should like to thank the Executors of the Heelis Estate for their permission to print the hitherto unpublished work of Beatrix Potter; and to Frederick Warne & Co. Ltd., for the care they have taken in the preparation of this book.

L. L.

INTRODUCTION

Beatrix Potter was born on July 28th 1866, and died on December 22nd 1943 at the age of seventy-seven.

The Writings of Beatrix Potter, together with *The Art of Beatrix Potter*, which was published in 1955, give a detailed study of her work in the joint capacity of writer and artist. These two books were largely inspired by Margaret Lane's biography *The Tale of Beatrix Potter*, written in 1946.

With a desire to learn more about her work, I set out on May 17th 1951, on a three-day visit of exploration to the little village of Near Sawrey where Beatrix Potter had lived, and quite by coincidence found myself staying at Ginger and Pickles', no longer a shop, but still bearing signs of the past, with the magnificent weather-vane on the chimney, as seen in one of the pictures at the end of *The Tale of Johnny Town-Mouse*; and the notice-board on the side of the house bearing the name of the original owner, John Taylor, to whom *The Tale of Ginger and Pickles* was dedicated.

It was my first visit to Hill Top, and those three days were an inspiration. I had the privilege of being invited by Capt. K. W. G. Duke to have tea at Castle Cottage, the home of Beatrix Potter after her marriage, where I was shown some of her original drawings in their hand-made portfolios. He also took me round the village and to Hill Top, and I saw for the first time some of the actual settings of the book pictures. The interior of Hill Top had changed little since Beatrix Potter portrayed it in *The Roly-Poly Pudding*; neither had the garden as depicted in *The Tale of Tom Kitten*, nor the farm where Jemima Puddle-Duck lived.

In that short time it was not possible to examine all the treasures at Hill Top, but I had seen enough to realize that more should be told of Beatrix Potter's work, both as artist and writer.

The following year a meeting was held at Warne's London Office, and it was decided to plan a book of Beatrix Potter's drawings and paintings, to be called *The Art of Beatrix Potter*. The late Mr. W. A. Herring agreed to help in the selection of the drawings, and the late Anne Carroll Moore of New York, for many years a close personal friend of Beatrix Potter, was asked to write an Appreciation.

It was Mr. Herring who many years ago had supervised the production of all Beatrix Potter's *Peter Rabbit* books, and he remembered her quite well, and told of the days when she would drive up to Bedford Court in her carriage, and how they discussed the printing of her books. Although over eighty years of age at the time, he went to the office several days a week, and during the whole period of our work in planning *The Art of Beatrix Potter*, no detail was too small or insignificant to command his keen interest and undivided attention.

Introduction

In May 1952 we spent ten days together in the village of Sawrey, staying at Ginger and Pickles', and making a survey of all the Beatrix Potter material in the area, with the full co-operation of Capt. Duke and the National Trust, who owned Hill Top.

When Mr. Herring rested in the afternoons, I would visit some of the settings used by Beatrix Potter for her books. As a special privilege, I was allowed to roam wherever I wished over Hill Top Farm and into Jemima's wood. For a short time each evening Mr. Herring and I would walk together to the sign-post just behind Hill Top Farm, where one road leads round the far side of Esthwaite Water to Hawkshead and the other to Lakeside, in which setting Alexander and Pigling Bland may be seen in the frontispiece to *The Tale of Pigling Bland*. If Mr. Herring were not too tired we would continue our walk down the hill and stand on the stone bridge overlooking Esthwaite Water, which was rebuilt in 1906 with stone from Beatrix Potter's own quarry.

As we sat at meals in the little front room of Ginger and Pickles' we saw a notice-board across the road, and this attracted Mr. Herring's attention—'I have seen that board somewhere,' he kept on saying, and eventually we found that it was the notice-board in *Ginger and Pickles*, on which Sally Henny Penny announced her 'Opening Sale'.

Ginger and Pickles' stands at the centre of the small group of cottages which makes up the heart of the village of Near Sawrey. Here at every turn one is reminded of pictures in the books which have their setting in Sawrey.

Across the road is the garden of Buckle Yeat where Duchess stood when she read her invitation from Ribby. Behind is the post office meadow across which Ribby walked when she fetched butter and milk from the farm. Facing the lane that runs alongside the meadow is the attractive doorway of the old post office which Beatrix Potter used as a model for the doorway of the house from which Duchess set out with her basket containing the veal and ham pie. Round the bend of the road, a little beyond Duchess's garden, stands the Tower Bank Arms; and beyond it the stone wall at the bottom of Hill Top garden, on which Tom Kitten sat with Moppet and Mittens, close to the wicket gate and the garden path leading up to the house.

Before leaving Sawrey we called at Lakefield Cottage, Ribby's home, where many years ago Duchess had lived. Duchess was Mrs. Rogerson's pedigree Pomeranian, and the late Mrs. Brockbank, her daughter, told us of her recollections of Beatrix Potter, and related some anecdotes about Duchess. We were also shown Ribby's larder, and the wall-cupboard in the sitting-room where Duchess had looked for the pie made of mouse.

Some of the older inhabitants of Sawrey still remembered Beatrix Potter in her younger days, going round the village with her sketch book, sketching everywhere in the village—even inside the cottages.

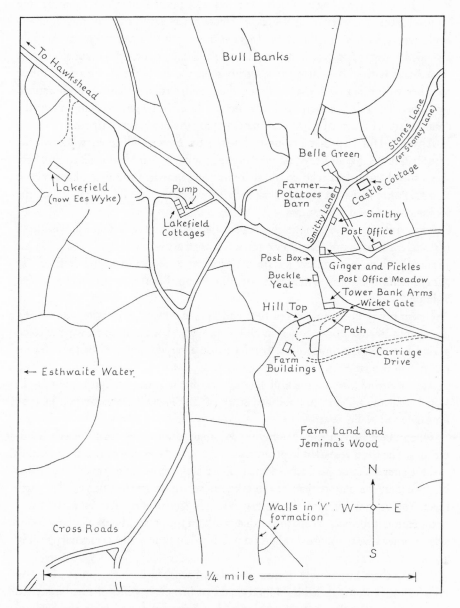

Map of the village of Near Sawrey showing Hill Top and other places associated with Beatrix Potter's books

Introduction

It is interesting to find that some of the background scenes in Beatrix Potter's books have been photographed by her father, Rupert Potter, for example, the Squirrel Nutkin scenery on the shore of Derwentwater and some of the Cumberland scenery in *The Tale of Mrs. Tiggy-Winkle*. Just as Beatrix Potter carefully inscribed many of her drawings with the title and date, so he, with meticulous care, signed and dated his photographs, writing on the back the name of the place together with other details, and adding the familiar rubber stamp 'Photographed by Rupert Potter'. We were told how he would often be seen walking along the country lanes, followed by his coachman carrying the camera and tripod.

It was at Hill Top that I came to know Mrs. Susan Ludbrook, who was the custodian there. At our very first meeting the previous year I had realized that here was a friend and helper who would spare no pains in telling me all she knew about Beatrix Potter and who would show me all the treasures at Hill Top in which she took such pride and interest.

This visit to Sawrey made me realize that not only was there a wealth of material for a book on Beatrix Potter's work as an artist, but every justification for another book on her work as a writer. Therefore, as soon as the final draft of *The Art of Beatrix Potter* was within sight of completion, I started work on the present volume.

I spent my summer holidays of 1953 and 1954 in Sawrey, classifying and sorting the various Beatrix Potter papers at Hill Top, with Mrs. Ludbrook always at hand giving help and encouragement. Later I made a careful appraisal of the relevant material in Beatrix Potter's private portfolios.

When sorting through the Hill Top papers, different manuscripts came to light —including the hitherto unpublished story of *The Faithful Dove*, written in 1907 for Louie and Nellie Warne.

One cannot study these manuscripts without admiring Beatrix Potter's handwriting. The most remarkable penmanship, however, was that of her code writing —sheet after sheet of perfectly formed cipher writing, some so small that in one instance there were more than fifteen hundred words on one side of a single quarto sheet. This code writing is fully dealt with in *The Journal of Beatrix Potter*, and I will not mention it further, except to say that work on the present book was put on one side in order that the Journal might be published in time for her centenary in July 1966.

During these memorable summer holidays I worked in the room at Hill Top which Beatrix Potter called the Library, and sat in a chair which she had inherited from her grandmother Potter, writing at her baize-lined card table and making copies of the various manuscripts and other papers. Sometimes I was allowed to take the papers away so that I could continue this work in the evenings.

I felt that Beatrix Potter must have realized that one day someone would write

Enid Linder

The village of Near Sawrey

Hill Top, Sawrey, in the late spring

Enid Linder

The path leading up to Hill Top

Enid Linder

View from the doorway of Hill Top

Enid Linder

Rhododendrons beside the carriage drive at Hill Top

Enid Linder

A garden in Smithy Lane, Sawrey

Enid Linder

Sheep in the meadows around Sawrey

Enid Linder

A May evening in Sawrey

Left to right: Miss Cecily Mills, Miss Margaret Hammond, two of
Beatrix Potter's closest friends, with Mr. Leslie Linder

Enid Linder

about her, and about the Hill Top she loved so much, for when she had sorted through her Hill Top possessions she had been preparing the way by writing little notes on slips of paper. These notes were sometimes attached to the backs of pictures, sometimes slipped into books or placed with papers of special interest. In a parcel containing her personal copy of *The Tailor of Gloucester* manuscript and some other papers, there was a small slip on which she had written, 'None of these papers must be destroyed. H. B. Heelis, Oct. 43', just two months before she died, and probably the last of her written instructions at Hill Top.

Mrs. Storey, who was at that time living at Hill Top, told how Beatrix Potter loved her old home even more than Castle Cottage, where she lived after her marriage in 1913, and how in later years she would often come to arrange and sort her treasured possessions. 'She liked to come and go unnoticed, and to be left quite alone with her memories of the past; and I would never come into that part of the house when Mrs. Heelis was there,' said Mrs. Storey, 'although on cold, dark winter afternoons, I often wanted to bring in cups of hot tea or cocoa to warm her.'

From her earliest years Beatrix Potter had had the desire to write. In 1912 she said, 'I was cram full of stories including one or two novels when I was a small child! (much more so than now) only I could not for the life of me get them out. I did, however, compose elegant hymns in imitation of Dr. Watts (which have disappeared).' In her teens she began to keep an almost day-to-day record of her activities in the code-written journal, which she kept until she was thirty.

At twenty-six she began to write her picture letters to children, which were the bases of her first books.

The Writings of Beatrix Potter gives the history of her published work and also includes some of her unpublished stories and essays.

In describing her methods of writing, Beatrix Potter told Mrs. Bertha Mahony Miller, 'I have just made stories to please myself because I never grew up! . . . . I think I write carefully because I enjoy my writing, and enjoy taking pains over it. I have always disliked writing to order; I write to please myself . . . My usual way of writing is to scribble, and cut out, and write it again and again. The shorter and plainer the better. And read the Bible (*unrevised* version and Old Testament) if I feel my style wants chastening. There are many dialect words of the Bible and Shakespeare—and also the forcible direct language—still in use in the rural parts of Lancashire.'

In speaking of her children's books she said, 'I think the great point in writing for children is to have something to say and to say it in simple direct language.' Of their final preparation she tells us, 'I polish! polish! polish!—to the last revise.'

Towards the end of her life Beatrix Potter wrote, 'I think the art of essay writing is—to balance the main theme by ruthless cutting no matter whether the incidents sacrificed are pretty or not.'

Whatever may be said of her later works, they are all inspired by the love of writing; and although in 1934 Beatrix Potter told Mrs. Miller, 'I am written out for story books, and my eyes are tired for painting', to the very end she took pleasure in writing.

Mrs. Mary Duke, who sometimes stayed at Castle Cottage, told how Beatrix Potter in later years would often slip away to her room upstairs where all was quiet, and her thoughts would go back to the past—to the fell and rough lands, to the flowers and patches of bog and cotton-grass, to the hills which she would never climb again, and she would scribble fragments of prose and verse, writing on any odd scrap of paper. The following verses were found after Beatrix Potter's death amongst her papers at Castle Cottage:

> I will go back to the hills again
>   That are sisters to the sea,
> The bare hills, the brown hills
>   That stand eternally,
> And their strength shall be my strength
>   And their joy my joy shall be.
>
> There are no hills like the Wasdale hills
>   When spring comes up the dale,
> Nor any woods like the larch woods,
>   Where the primroses blow pale,
> And the shadows flicker quiet-wise
>   On the stark ridge of Black Sail.
>
> I will go back to the hills again
>   When the day's work is done,
> And set my hands against the rocks
>   Warm with an April sun,
> And see the night creep down the fells
>   And the stars climb one by one.

How fitting it is that one of these last fragments of writing should be a poem about her beloved Lakeland Hills!

LESLIE LINDER

St. Just
Buckhurst Hill
Essex
Spring 1971

PART ONE

LETTERS TO CHILDREN

1
Picture Letters

Picture Letters

When Beatrix Potter was nearly seventeen, Annie Carter, who was just turned twenty, came to Bolton Gardens to be her companion and to teach her German. They had many interests in common and used to go for long walks in the London parks. They became devoted to each other, and when a year or two later Miss Carter married and became Mrs. Moore and went to live at Bayswater, Beatrix Potter kept in close touch with her.

It was at Bayswater that her first child, a boy, was born and called Noel because he arrived on Christmas Eve. The other seven children were born at Number Twenty, Baskerville Road, Wandsworth Common, to which Mrs. Moore moved shortly after Noel's birth, and where she lived for the rest of her life.

Over the years Beatrix Potter visited her frequently. It was a red-letter day for the Moore children when she came to tea, for she arrived in a smart carriage and pair with a coachman on the box. Sometimes the carriage waited outside the house until the visit was over. On these occasions she often wore a straw hat with velvet ribbons tied under her chin.

The Moore family say she was pretty and gay, with sparkling blue eyes. Her voice was quiet and soft, though slightly higher in pitch than average. When she told of some amusing incident she gave a little twist to her mouth which, combined with a smile, they found quite fascinating.

She brought cages of white mice to show them; she used to open the door of the cage and let the mice run around the drawing-room floor, which their mother did not seem to mind. Sometimes she brought lovely party frocks from Woollands in Kensington for the two younger children, Hilda and Beatrix, who were called the 'baby Moores' because there was a gap of six years between them and the rest of the family, which consisted of two boys, Noel and Eric, followed by Marjorie, Winifrede (or Freda), Norah (at one time called Bardie because when she was very small she could not pronounce her name properly), and Joan. The youngest child, Beatrix, was named after Beatrix Potter, who was her godmother.

Beatrix Potter became very fond of the children, and in September 1893, when five-year old Noel became ill, she sent him a letter all about Peter Rabbit and his adventures in Mr. McGregor's garden. The letter was a great success and during the years that followed, many more picture letters were sent.

To Eric she sent a letter about the adventures of Pig Robinson, and to Norah a letter about the adventures of Squirrel Nutkin. Other picture letters were sent to Freda, sometimes spelt Frida, and to Marjorie, sometimes spelt Marjory.

Marjorie Moore tells how her mother used to read these letters to them, and because her own were so precious she tied them up with yellow ribbon. Beatrix

Potter learned from Mrs. Moore how much the children loved them and this probably gave her the idea of writing books for children, some of which were based on these letters.

Beatrix Potter's picture letters are full of delightful sketches, and descriptions of the animals she loved; they also tell about her holidays at the seaside, and in Wales, Scotland, and elsewhere.

THE MOORE CHILDREN

Most of Beatrix Potter's picture letters were sent to the Moore children, and as it is of interest to know the age of the child when the letter was received, their dates of birth are given below:

Noel Christian	December 24th 1887
Eric	November 23rd 1888
Marjorie Kathleen	January 3rd 1890
Winifrede Cecily (Freda)	January 8th 1891
Norah Constance (Bardie)	July 13th 1893
Joan Elsie	August 31st 1896
Hilda May	May 31st 1902
Beatrix (Baby)	November 3rd 1903

Mrs. Annie Moore, their mother, was born in 1863; she married in 1886; and died at Wandsworth in 1950.

Eastwood Dunkeld
Sep 4ᵗʰ 93

My dear Noel,
I don't know what to
write to you, so I shall tell you a story
about four little rabbits
whose names were—

Flopsy , Mopsy   Cottontail

and Peter

They lived with their mother in a
sand bank under the root of a
big fir tree.

'Now, my deers', said old Mrs Bunny
'you may go into the field or down
the lane, but don't go into Mr McGregor's
garden.'

Flopsy, Mopsy & Cottontail, who were good
little rabbits went down the lane to gather
blackberries. but Peter, who was very naughty

ran straight away to Mr McGregor's garden and squeezed underneath the gate.

First he ate some lettuce, and some broad beans, then some radishes, and then, feeling rather sick, he went to look for some parsley; but round the end of a cucumber frame whom should he meet but Mr McGregor!

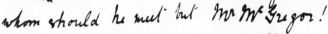

Mr McGregor was planting out young cabbages
but he jumped up & ran after Peter waving
a rake & calling out 'Stop thief'!

Peter was most dreadfully frightened &
rushed all over the garden, for he had
forgotten the way back to the gate.
He lost one of his shoes among the cabbages

and the other shoe amongst the potatoes.
After losing them he ran on four legs &
went faster, so that I think he would

have got away altogether, if he had not
unfortunately run into a gooseberry net
and got caught fast by the large buttons
on his jacket. It was a blue jacket with
brass buttons, quite new.

Mr McGregor came up with a basket which
he intended to pop on the top of Peter,
but Peter wriggled out just in time,
leaving his jacket behind,

and this time he found the gate,
slipped underneath and ran home
safely.

Mr McGregor hung up the little jacket &
shoes for a scarecrow, to frighten the
black birds.

Peter was ill during the evening, in consequence
of over eating himself. His mother put him to
bed and gave him a dose of camomile tea,

but Flopsy, Mopsy, and Cottontail
had bread and milk and blackberries
for supper.   I am coming
back to London next Thursday, so
I hope I shall see you soon, and
the new baby   I remain, dear Noel,
yours affectionately
           Beatrix Potter

Pendennis Hotel
Falmouth
March 25. 94

My dear Eric

.. there are a great many ships
here some very large ones. there is one
from Norway, and a French one unloading
at the quay.   Some of the sailors
have little dogs, and cocks and hens
on the ships.   I have read about the
owl & the pussy cat, who went to sea in a
pea green boat, but I never saw anything
of that kind till today.

I was looking at a ship
called the Pearl of Falmouth
which was being mended
at the bottom because
it had rubbed on a
rock, when I heard
something grunt!

15

I went up a bank where I could see onto the deck & there was a white pig with a curly tail walking about. It is a ship that goes to Newfoundland & the sailors always take a pig I daresay it enjoys the voyage, but when the sailors get hungry they eat it. If that pig had any sense it would slip down into the boat at the end of the ship & row away.

This is the captain & the boatswain & the ship's cook pursuing the pig. The cook is waving a knife

and fork. He wants

to make the pig into sausages!

This is the pig
rowing away from
the sailors, it is
squealing because it
sees the knife & fork.
This is the pig
living on Robinson
Crusoe's Island.
He is still
rather afraid of the cook & is looking for the
Ships through a telescope.
This is the same pig
after he has lived ten
years upon the island;
he has grown
very very fat and the
cook has never found him.

Aug 8th 96.

LAKEFIELD,
SAWREY,
AMBLESIDE.

My dear Eric,

My little cousin Molly
Gaddum has got a squirrel
who has 2 baby squirrels in
a hay nest,
you cannot
think how
pretty. They are not much bigger
than mice yet. They live in
a box in the hay loft, + one day

18

Molly opened the
lid and Mrs
Squirrel jumped
out. They had such a business
to catch her. Jim her brother
has 2 jack daws
which sit all day
on a stick in a corner, I think
they are not very interesting, he
wishes to give me one. He has
also got a hedge hog
& some gold fish.
There are plenty of hedge hogs here
in the fields, they come out in the

evening. So do the rabbits, there are
two black ones in a field near
the house.

Our coachman brought his cat in
a basket. It mewed
dreadfully amongst the
luggage, but I think it is
enjoying itself. It sings songs
with the
gardener's
cat, which is grey, + the farm cat,
which is white with a black tail.
There is a very pretty yellow colley

20

dog, it is so

clever with the sheep,
it drives them right & left, which
ever way it is told and never
bites them. Sometimes it comes in
at our dining room window & shake
hands. We have got a
tame owl
he eats
mice, he sits with a tail
hanging out of his mouth.
I remain yours aff.
Beatrix Potter

March 6th 97

My dear Walter

Thank you for your nice letter, but I am sorry to hear about poor Frisky. Another squirrel I knew died lately. It was a grey American squirrel and lived 8 or 9 years. The lady who had it says red squirrels do not live so well in cages as the grey ones.

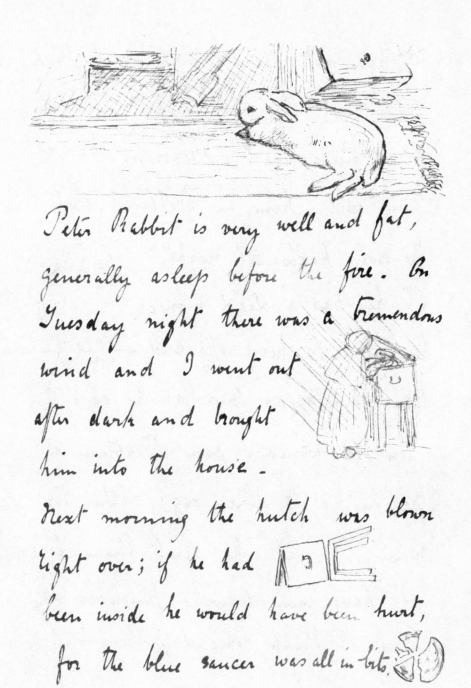

Peter Rabbit is very well and fat,
generally asleep before the fire. On
Tuesday night there was a tremendous
wind and I went out
after dark and brought
him into the house.
Next morning the hutch was blown
right over; if he had
been inside he would have been hurt,
for the blue saucer was all in bits.

I have not heard much about Jack
lately but the owl is said to be a
great nuisance. Bertram has got
them with him in Scotland and
the owl hoots all night.
If he has a dead mouse
he bites it's head off and
then shouts as loud as he can.

An old woman gave Bertram a
present of 5 dozen eggs, rather too
many to eat, he sent them to us.
I have been drawing funguses very
hard, I think some day they will be

put in a book but it will be a dull one to read. We have had one little fungus like red holly berries. it had only been found once before in Scotland. I am glad you have got a nice dog, ours had the cramp very badly in the cold weather; he falls down when he is walking. We have got 4 canaries, I hope they will lay some eggs. A friend of mine has got a savage dormouse, it bites something like the prick of a pin. It lost half its tail by accident, it seems to have spoiled its temper. I remain yr aff Cousin

Beatrix Potter

LINGHOLM,
KESWICK,
CUMBERLAND.

My dear Noël,

    We have got a trap for catching minnows, which is amusing.

It is made

of perforated zinc. I did not believe it would answer, but my brother tied a bit of string to it, put some bread inside and

          watched.

        The minnows

came all round snuffing and at
last one old fish found the way
in at the end, and all the others
followed. I should think there were
50 or 60 inside when it was pulled
out of the water. We use them
for bait for larger fish, trout
and perch. The fishing is not
very good in the lake; the groom,
who drives my pony, catches more
than anybody.
He is always at it. One day the
otter hounds came round the lake

to hunt, they did not find an
otter and we have never seen one,
as they only come out at
night. I went out in our boat
& watched the
dogs. The men
wade about with long poles.
There is a lady who lives on an
island on the lake who told me
some curious things about animals
swimming. She had a cat which
she did not want, so she gave
it to some one in Keswick, but a

week afterwards it came back into her
house dripping wet!

Also when her nuts are ripe, squirrels
appear on the island, but she has
not seen them coming.   There is an
American story that squirrels go down
the rivers on

little rafts,
using their
tails

                                for sails, but
I think the Keswick squirrels must
swim   I must write to Eric next time
I hope you are quite well again. I remain
dear Noel yrs aff —
       Beatrix Potter.

Waverley hotel
Dumfries Aug 23rd 95

My dear Marjory,
I was so much pleased
to get all your nice little letters,
I intended to have written to you
sooner but I have been travelling
about so much I have always
been too sleepy. You will have
to look on the map for the places.
My brother and I left Keswick
on Tuesday 16th came through Carlisle
to Dumfries, then to Kirkcudbright
then to Stranraer & Belfast, back

to Stranraer to Ayr & Dumfries. We
shall go home tomorrow or Saturday.
I have seen so much I shall have
to pick out things to tell you about.
One day we were on the train at
Castle Douglas
and there
was a great
sheep fair. Three old farmers got into
the railway carriage with a big brown
& white colley. One said "I never take
a ticket for him, he will go under
seat!" and sure enough the dog hid
himself in a minute, without being
told to do so. Directly we had started
he came out & sat up. The carriage door

was locked, so when the old man wanted
to get out at his station he got out
of the window You would
have laughed to see
how nicely the dog
jumped after him.
Another farmer
has just gone past this house
driving six pigs, so I suppose there
is a fair today in Dumfries.
When we were out we met one driving
a big flock of lambs; two of them
were so tired they could not go on,
so the poor little things were left
lying in a corner with
their legs tied.
The farmer would pick them up as he
went home.

I have just been laughing till I cried,
there is a very solemn american gentleman
with his wife and daughter staying
in the hotel, + he has just sat
down on a chair which came to
pieces quite flat.

Everybody screamed

with laughter, but he never said
nothing. I don't think any
Englishman could have been so dignified
I was very much amused at your Mamma
saying she felt like a rag; I have
felt like one too!
like a very dirty
pocket handkerchief, they
don't give one much water for washing
in Scotch hotels. I remain dear
Marjory, yr aff. Aunt Beatrix Potter.

16 Robertson Terrace
Hastings
Jan 13th 99.

My dear Marjorie,

The last time I wrote to the boys I was at Hastings. I went home on Dec. 28th but I did not like the cold weather in London so I came back here, with a servant. I am feeling much better and I shall go home next

Monday. There are some
other people in the lodgings
who have such a funny cat,
a Manx cat,
from the Isle
of Man, where
they have no tails. It runs
about in a curious way, I
think it has longer legs than
an ordinary cat. It peeps into
my room but I cannot catch
it, but I always know when
it is there because it wears a bell.

There are some little goat
carriages on the Parade, they
would be just the right size for
Baby; one of the goats is very
pretty, I
saw him
eating his
dinner one day
out of a nose bag, just like a
horse's nose bag, only very small.
He has a long beard, but it
was tucked inside. There are

a great many carriages, one fat
old gentleman always amuses
me, he has the very smallest
grey ponies in little blue & red
coats.

My pony must be having a lazy
time, I shall come and see you
some day when it is fine.
yrs. aff. Beatrix Potter.

Derwent Cottage
Winchelsea
Jan 26ᵗʰ 1900.

My dear Frida,

I am staying in such a funny old cottage; it is like the little mouse-houses I have often drawn in pictures.

I am sure_(when I am half. asleep)_that it is a mouse-house, for Mrs Cooke, the landlady, and her family go to bed up a sort of

ladder stair-case, and I can
hear them scuffling about
upon the rafters just above
my head! The ceiling of
my bed-room is so low I
can touch it with my
hand, and there is a little

lattice window
just the
right size
for mice to 
peep out of. Then there are
cupboards in the walls, that
little people could hide in,

and
steps
up and
down
into 
the rooms, and doors in every
corner; very draughty! I wish

it would stop raining and be
bright and fine; I don't think
my brother & I will stop more
than a week if the weather does
not mend. We came here last
Wednesday. I have been for 2
long walks, it is pretty country, &
on nearly
every hill there is
a windmill, spinning round
in the wind and rain.
I am dear Frida yrs affectionately
Beatrix Potter.

January 26ᵗ 1900
Derwent Cottage
Winchelsea.

My dear Marjory,

I shall write to you and
Frida, for I suppose the
boys have gone away to school
by this time; I wonder
if they have got boxes like
we used to have

I wonder if I have spelt
your name right this time!

If I have not, you will
say I ought to go to school
too, and learn
out of a big
spelling book.

I expect when I see you again,
you and Frida will have grown
so big I shall
not know you!
I believe I 
haven't seen you since last
July, it is quite shocking.
It is all because of my poor old
pony being dead; when I want

to drive to Wandsworth in the
big carriage; my Mamma
wants to drive
the other
way;
and when your Mamma
wanted to call at Bolton
Gardens at Christmas, I
could not ask her to come,
because we had influenza in
the house. I hope you
did not have ~~time~~ a visit

from him.
he is a dis-
agreeable old
person!
I have been very well, but my
brother and Cox had it rather
badly.   I daresay Bardy
is big enough now to want a
letter, so I must not put any
more nonsense into this letter, or
I shall have none left for her.
Good bye dear Marjory, from
yrs aff. Beatrix Potter.

2 Croft Terrace, Tenby
April 24ᵗʰ. 00.

My dear Marjory,

It is quite time for me to
write to you, I generally send
a letter from the sea-side at Easter
and I am going home on
Thursday 26ᵗʰ. It has been so hot
lately, the only cool place is on
the water in a boat. I go
out every morning and I generally
tell the boat man to row close under
the cliffs so that I can watch the

birds. The rocks are a tremendous height, as high as a church, and quite straight from top to bottom in many places, but sometimes there are little ledges half way up with wild cabbages growing on them, & at the top where there is soil there is a row of rabbit-holes. What a very funny place for cabbages & rabbits right up in the air! My boatman says he has sometimes picked up poor dead rabbits that have

tumbled off; but as long as they
don't go too near the edge
— or if they have a
little railing — it is
a very nice safe
place, for nobody
can
possibly
get near them,
r their little
cabbage gardens.
They have wall flowers too, just like
the garden wall flowers only they are
all yellow   Another thing that is

very convenient is the coal. I can see
it like black lines between the cracks
in the cliffs, and little bits of it
fall down onto the sand, so if Mrs
Bunny picks some cabbage leaves for
dinner she can light a little fire
and boil the pot. yrs aff.
Beatrix
Potter.

Tenby
April 24th oo

My dear Frida,

I went a long way in a
boat one day to see puffins who
live on an island. They are black & white birds with
very large red bills. They are
considered very silly,
and look something like parrots
that have tumbled into the water,
but they behave in a very sly way.
They never take the trouble to
build nests, but live in rabbit holes

They look for a nice hole and
drive the rabbits out. They do

not live here in the winter but
arrived about a fortnight since, it
must be most annoying to the
rabbits to see them landing. There
are little rabbits by this time, lots
of them, all
comfortable in
bed, I am
sure they
don't give up

their holes without a fight!

I don't believe either rabbits or puffins are able to hurt much, but the puffins always win and take possession of the best holes. I don't know what

becomes of the rabbits; perhaps they go and live with the jackdaws, who are much more polite, They walk about

bobbing their heads as if they were
bowing. I notice the rabbits & jackdaws
live close together
quite
nicely.

The jackdaws go into holes
in the rock exactly like little square
doors. I am very sleepy with
going on the sea in the wind. With
love to all of you from yrs aff—

Beatrix Potter

Miss Potter is sitting upon her book at present & considering!
The publisher cannot tell what has become of it.

53

Lingholme, Keswick
Sept 25th 07.

My dear Norah,

There are such numbers of squirrels in the woods here. They are all very busy just now gathering nuts, which they hide away in little holes, where they can find them again, in the winter.

An old lady who lives on the island says she thinks they come over the lake when her nuts are ripe; but I wonder how they can get across the water? Perhaps

they make little rafts!

One day I saw a most comical little squirrel; his tail was only an inch long; but he was so impertinent, he chattered and clattered

and threw

down acorns

onto my

head

I believe that his name was Nutkin
and that he had a brother called
Twinkleberry,
and this is
the story of how
he lost his tail — —

There is a big island in the
middle of the lake, covered with woods,
and in the middle of it stands
a hollow oak-tree which is the
house of an owl, called Old
Brown.   One autumn when the
nuts were ripe, Nutkin and
Twinkleberry, and all the other

little squirrels came down to the
edge of the lake and paddled across
over the water to Owl Island to
gather nuts.   Each squirrel had
a little sack with him, and a
large oar, and spread out his tail
for a sail

They also carried with them an
offering of 3 fat mice for Old
Brown, which they placed upon a
stone opposite his door.

Then Twinkleberry and the other
squirrels each made a low bow,

and said politely — "Old Mr Brown,
will you favour us with permission
to gather nuts upon your island?"

But Nutkin, who was excessively
impertinent in his manners, jumped
up & down, and shouted —

"Old Mr B.! riddle-me-ree?
Higgledy piggledy
   Here we lie,
Pick'd and pluck'd,
   And put in a pie:
My first is snapping, snarling, growling,
My second's industrious, romping, prowling.
   Higgledy, piggledy,
   Here we lie,
   Pick'd and pluck'd
   And put in a pie!"

Now this riddle is as old as the
hills. Mr Brown paid no attention
whatever to Nutkin.

The squirrels filled their bags and
sailed away home in the evening.

The next morning they all came
back again to Owl Island; and
Twinkleberry and the others brought
a fine fat mole, and laid it on
the stone in front of Old Brown's
door, and said —

"Mr Brown will you favour us
with your gracious permission to
gather some more nuts?"   But

Nutkin, who had no respect, danced
up & down, and sang —
    "Old Mr B! riddle-me-ree?
        As soft as silk,
        As white as milk,
As bitter as gall, a thick wall,
And a green coat covers me all!"
- - - - - - - - - - - -

Mr Brown made no reply to the
impertinent Nutkin.

    On the 3rd day the squirrels came
back again and brought a present
of 7 fat minnows.

But Nutkin who had no manners
danced up & down, and sang —

"Old Mr B! riddle me ree?
As I came through the garden gap,
Who should I meet but Dick Red-cap,
A stick in his hand, a stone in his throat
If you'll tell me this riddle
I'll give you a groat!" — — — — — — — —

Which was very absurd of Nutkin, because he did not possess 4 pence; even if Mr Brown had taken the trouble to answer.

The fourth day the squirrels came with a present of 6 large beetles for old Brown. But Nutkin danced up and down and sang as rudely as ever —

"Old Mr B! riddle-me-ree?

Flour of England, fruit of Spain,
Met together in a shower of rain;
Put in a bag tied round with a string,
If you'll tell me this riddle,
I'll give you a ring! "
- - - - - - - - - -
which was rediculous of Nutkin,
because he hadn't got any ring to
give to old Brown.

The fifth day the squirrels came
again and brought a present of a
comb of wild honey. It was so
sweet that they licked their fingers
when they put
it down upon
the stone.

But Nutkin danced about, as saucy

63

as over and sang —
  "Old Mr B! riddle-me-ree?
  As I went over Tipple Tine,
  I met a flock of bonny swine;
    Some green-lapp'd
    Some green-back'd,
They were the very bonniest swine,
That e'er went over Tipple Tine!
Hum-a-bum, bum, buz. 3·3·3 3·3 —
  — — — — — — — —

Old Brown turned up his nose in
disgust at the impertinence of
Nutkin. But he ate up the honey

The sixth day, which was Saturday,
the squirrels came for the last time.
They brought a parting present for
Old Brown, consisting of a pie with
4 & 20 black birds.

But I am sorry to say that
Nutkin was more saucy and excited
                              than ever.

He jumped up and down and sang
"Old Mr B! riddle-me-ree?
Humpty Dumpty lies in the beck,
with a white counterpane round his neck,
All the king's horses, and all the king's men,
Can't put Humpty Dumpty
together again!"

Now old Mr Brown took an interest
in eggs; he opened one eye and shut
it again; but still he never said
nothing.   Nutkin got more
and more excited —

"Old Mr B. riddle-me-ree?
Hick-a-more, Hack-a-more,
On the king's kitchen door;
All the king's horses,
And all the king's men,
Couldn't drive Hick-a-more, Hack-a-more
Off the king's kitchen door!"
— — — — — — — — — — —
And Nutkin danced up and down
like a sunbeam; but old Mr
Brown never said nothing.
        Then Nutkin began again —

"Old Mr B.! riddle-me-ree?
(Nutkin bounced up & down and
clapped his paws)—
"Old Mr B.! riddle-me-ree?
Arthur O'Bower has broken his band,
He comes roaring up the land;
The king of Scots, with all his power,
Cannot turn Arthur of the Bower!"

Nutkin whisked and twirled and made
a whirring noise like the wind, and
flicked his bushy tail right in the
face of old Brown's whiskers.
Then all at once there was a
flufflement and a scufflement
and a loud "Squeak!!"

The squirrels scuttered away
into the bushes. When they came

back and peeped cautiously round
the tree — there was Old Brown
sitting on his door step, quite still,
with his eyes closed: as if nothing had
happened.

But Nutkin was in his waistcoat
pocket!!!

That is the end of the story. Old
Brown carried Nutkin into his
house, and held him up by the
tail, intending to skin him; but
Nutkin pulled so hard that his tail
broke in two, and he dashed
up the stair-case, and escaped out of
the attic window.

And to this day, if you meet
Nutkin up a tree, and ask him a
riddle, he will throw sticks at you,
and chatter his teeth, and scold,
and shout — "Cuck cuck cuck cuck
Cur-rrr"!

Yours aff. Beatrix Potter

My dear Louie

This is Mrs Potts & McCannon,

the farmer's wife
giving medicine
to a calf.

It was dreadfully ill last week.
First the farmer gave it cow-
-medicine, then we gave it a
whole bottle of chalk-mixture
then I bought half a pound
of arrowroot & it had it for
gruel. Then it was so very ill

it had to have brandy! It is
getting quite well again. It was
so good taking medicine, it took
it out of a horn we put-
the horn into its mouth & poured it
down. The big cart-horse has got
tooth ache; I am considering
about doctoring him next, but he
might bite! There is a colley dog.
& a white puppy and a little brown puppy!
and Mrs Cannon is
going to get 5 cats to catch the rats,
because they eat the corn. I am so
glad you like school you will be
able to write letters soon
Your aff. Aunt B

2
Miniature Letters

Miniature Letters

Beatrix Potter's picture letters of the '90s were the delight of the children to whom she sent them. After that came her books. Then she had a new idea—her Miniature Letters—which are believed to have been written between about 1907 and 1912.

These miniature letters were sent to the children of the Moore family, to the 'Lucie' of *The Tale of Mrs. Tiggy-Winkle*, and to Lucie's small sister Kathleen, and also to the Warne children. Others were sent to Master Drew Fayle, and to Master John and Miss Margaret Hough. Each letter was shaped and folded to represent an envelope. It was addressed, and there was a tiny little stamp drawn in red crayon.

Some were posted in a miniature mail-bag inscribed with the letters G.P.O. which Beatrix Potter had made herself. Others were sent in a toy tin post-box, enamelled bright red. 'Some of the letters were very funny,' she wrote. 'The defect was that inquiries and answers were all mixed up.' In a letter to Harold Warne, dated December 23rd 1907, there is a reference to these miniature letters which reads, 'You will find some curious correspondence in Louie's post office. I am not sure whether it is rather over the heads of the children.'

These letters, written as from some of the animal characters in the books, throw delightful sidelights on their doings, and tell us more about them. We learn that some of Mr. Jeremy Fisher's friends thought he should take a wife—and that Mrs. Tiggy-Winkle was always getting her washing mixed up, much to the discomfort of her clients. One or two of the letters tell us something about Miss Potter herself.

It is too much to hope that all the miniature letters Beatrix Potter wrote are reproduced here, for as they were sent to children it is more than likely that some have been lost or destroyed, but as Beatrix Potter kept her own copies of many of them, it is believed to be a fairly representative collection.

PETER RABBIT

Mrs. McGregor, Gardener's Cottage.

Dear Sir,

I write to ask whether your spring cabbages are ready? Kindly reply by return & oblige.

Yrs. truly,

Peter Rabbit.

Master P. Rabbit, Under Fir Tree.

Sir,

I rite by desir of my Husband Mr. McGregor who is in Bedd with a Cauld to say if you Comes heer agane we will inform the Polisse.

Jane McGregor.

P.S. I have bort a new py-Dish, itt is vary Large.

Master Benjamin Bunny, The Warren.

Dear Cousin Benjamin,

I have had a very ill written letter from Mrs. McGregor she says Mr. M. is in bed with a cold will you meet me at the corner of the wood near their garden at 6 this evening? In haste.

Yr. aff. cousin,

Peter Rabbit.

Master Drew, Kylimore.

Dear Master Drew,

I am pleased to hear you like Miss Potter's books. Miss Potter is drawing pigs & mice. She says she has drawn enough rabbits. But I am to be put into one picture at the end of the pig book.

Yr. aff friend,

Peter

x x

x x x x x   x x x x

SQUIRREL NUTKIN

Mr. Brown, Owl Island.

Sir,

I should esteem it a favour if you would let me have back my tail, as I miss it very much. I would pay postage.

Yrs. truly,
Squirrel Nutkin.

Mr. Old Brown Esq., Owl Island.

Dear Sir,

I should be extremely obliged if you could kindly send back a tail which you have had for some time. It is fluffy brown with a white tip. I wrote to you before about it, but perhaps I did not address the letter properly. I will pay the postage.

Yrs. respectfully,
Sq. Nutkin.

Old Mr. Brown Esq., Owl Island.

Dear Sir,

I should be exceedingly obliged if you will let me have back my tail, I will gladly pay 3 bags of nuts for it if you will please post it back to me, I have written to you twice Mr. Brown, I think I did not give my address, it is Derwent Bay Wood.

Yrs. respectfully,
Sq. Nutkin.

The Right Honourable Old Brown Esq., Owl Island.

Sir,

I write respectfully to beg that you will sell me back my tail, I am so uncomfortable without it, and I have heard of a tailor who would sew it on again. I would pay three bags of nuts for it. Please Sir, Mr. Brown, send it back by post & oblige.

Yrs. respectfully,
Sq. Nutkin.

Hilda

Beatrix

Two miniatures of the Moore children, painted by their aunt, Miss Rosa Carter, and given to Beatrix Potter. They now hang in the doll's house at Hill Top

Four of the Moore children
Left to right: Marjorie, Norah and Winifrede
(Freda), with Joan in front

O. Brown Esq., M.P. Owl Island.

Dear Sir,

I write on behalf of my brother Nutkin to beg that as a great favour you would send him back his tail. He never makes—or asks—riddles now, and he is truly sorry that he was so rude. Trusting that you continue to enjoy good health, I remain,

Yr. obedient servant,
Twinkleberry Squirrel.

Master Squirrel Nutkin, Derwent Bay Wood.

Mr. Brown writes to say that he cannot reply to letters as he is asleep. Mr. Brown cannot return the tail. He ate it some time ago; it nearly choked him. Mr. Brown requests Nutkin not to write again, as his repeated letters are a nuisance.

While this correspondence was going on Squirrel Nutkin was in contact with Dr. Maggotty to see if medical assistance could restore his tail.

Dr. Maggotty, The Dispensary.

Dear Dr. Maggotty,

Having seen an advertisement (nailed on the smithy door) of your blue beans to cure chilblains, I write to ask whether you think a boxful would make my tail grow? I tried to buy it back from the gentleman who pulled it off, but he has not answered my letters. It spoils my appearance. Are the beans very strong?

Yrs. truly,
Sq. Nutkin.

Sq. Nutkin Esq., Derwent Bay Wood.

Sir,

I have much pleasure in forwarding a box of blue beans as requested. Kindly acknowledge receipt & send 30 peppercorns as payment.

Yrs.
Matthew Maggotty, M.D.

Dr. Maggotty Esq., M.D. The Dispensary.

Sir,

I am obliged for the box of blue beans. I have not tried them yet. I have been wondering is there any fear they might make me grow a *blue* tail? it would spoil my appearance.

Yrs. truly,
Sq. Nutkin.

Sq. Nutkin Esq., Derwent Bay Wood.

Sir,

I do not think that there is the slightest risk of my beans causing you to grow a blue tail. The price per box is 30 peppercorns.

Yrs. truly,
M. Maggotty, M.D.

Dr. Maggotty.

Sir,

I am sending back the box of blue beans, I think they have a very funny smell & so does my brother Twinkleberry.

Yrs. truly,
Sq. Nutkin.

TWO BAD MICE

Mrs. Thomas Thumb, Mouse Hole.

Miss Lucinda Doll will require Hunca Munca to come for the whole day on Saturday. Jane Dollcook has had an accident. She has broken the soup tureen and both her wooden legs.

Miss Lucinda Doll, Doll's House.

Honoured Madam,

Would you forgive my asking whether you can spare a feather bed? The feathers are all coming out of the one we stole from your house. If you can spare another, me & my wife would be truly grateful.

Yr obedient humble servant,

Thomas Thumb.

P.S. Me & my wife are grateful to you for employing her as char-woman I hope that she continues to give satisfaction.

P.P.S. Me and my wife would be grateful for any old clothes, we have 9 of a family at present.

Mr. T. Thumb, Mouse Hole.

Miss Lucinda Doll has received Tom Thumb's appeal, but she regrets to inform Tom Thumb that she has never had another feather bed for *herself.* She also regrets to say that Hunca Munca forgot to dust the mantelpiece on Wednesday.

Miss Lucinda Doll, Doll's House.

Honoured Madam,

I am sorry to hear that my wife forgot to dust the mantelpiece, I have whipped her. Me & my wife would be very grateful for another kettle, the last one is full of holes. Me & my wife do not think that it was made of tin at all. We have nine of a family at present & they require hot water.

I remain honoured madam,

Yr. obedient servant,

Thomas Thumb.

Mrs. Tom Thumb, Mouse Hole.

Miss Lucinda Doll will be obliged if Hunca Munca will come half an hour earlier than usual on Tuesday morning, as Tom Kitten is expected to sweep the kitchen chimney at 6 o'clock. Lucinda wishes Hunca Munca to come not later than 5.45 a.m.

Miss Lucinda Doll, Doll's House.

Honoured Madam,

I have received your note for which I thank you kindly, informing me that T. Kitten will arrive to sweep the chimney at 6. I will come punctually at 7. Thanking you for past favours I am, honoured Madam, your obedient humble Servant,

Hunca Munca.

MRS. TIGGY-WINKLE

Mrs. Tiggy Winkle, Cat Bells.

Dear Madam,

Though unwilling to hurt the feelings of another widow, I really cannot any longer put up with *starch* in my pocket handkerchiefs. I am sending this one back to you, to be washed again. Unless the washing improves next week I shall (reluctantly) feel obliged to change my laundry.

Yrs. truly,

Josephine Rabbit.

Mrs. Rabbit, Sand Bank, Under Fir-Tree.

If you please'm,

Indeed I apologize sincerely for the starchiness & hope you will forgive me if you please mum, indeed it is Tom Titmouse and the rest of them; they do want their collar that *starchy* if you please mum my mind do get mixed up. If you please I will wash the clothes without charge for a fortnight if you will give another trial to your obedient servant & washerwoman,

Tiggy Winkle.

Mrs. Tiggy Winkle, Cat Bells.

Dear Mrs. Tiggy Winkle,

I am much pleased with the getting up of the children's muslin frocks. Your explanation about the starch is perfectly satisfactory & I have no intention of changing my laundry at present. Nobody washes flannels like Mrs. Tiggy Winkle.

With kind regards, yrs. truly,

Josephine Rabbit.

Master D. Fayle, Kylimore, Co. Dublin.

Dear Drew,

I have got that mixed up with this week's wash! Have *you* got Mrs. Flopsy Bunny's shirt or Mr. Jeremy Fisher's apron? instead of your pocket handkerchief— I mean to say Mrs. Flopsy Bunny's apron. Everything is all got mixed up in wrong bundles. I will buy more safety pins.

Yr. aff. washerwoman

T. Winkle.

Master D. Fayle, Kylimore.

Dear Drew,

I hope that your washing is done to please you? I consider that Mrs. Tiggy Winkle is particularly good at ironing collars; but she does mix things up at the wash. I have got a shirt marked J. F. instead of an apron. Have you lost a shirt at the wash? It is 3 inches long. My apron is much larger and marked F.B.

Yrs.
Flopsy Bunny.

Mrs. Tiggy Winkle, Cat Bells.

Mr. J. Fisher regrets that he has to complain about the washing. Mrs. T.W. has sent home an immense white apron with tapes instead of Mr. J. F's best new shirt. The apron is marked F.B.

Jan. 22. 1910

Mrs. Tiggy Winkle, Cat Bells.

Mr. J. Fisher regrets to have to complain again about the washing. Mrs. T. Winkle has sent home an enormous handkerchief marked 'D. Fayle' instead of the tablecloth marked J.F.

If this continues every week, Mr. J. Fisher will have to get married, so as to have the washing done at home.

MR. JEREMY FISHER

Master D. Fayle, Kylimore.

Dear Master Drew,

I hear that you think that there ought to be a 'Mrs. J. Fisher'. Our friend is at present taking mud baths at the bottom of the pond, which may be the reason why your letter has not been answered quick by return. I will do my best to advise him, but I fear he remembers the sad fate of his elder brother who disobeyed his mother, and he was gobbled up by a lily white duck! If my friend Jeremy Fisher gets married, I will certainly tell you, & send a bit of wedding cake. One of our friends is going into the next book. He is fatter than Jeremy; and he has shorter legs.*

Yrs. with compliments,
Sir Isaac Newton.

* Mr. Jackson in *The Tale of Mrs. Tittlemouse*.

Master Drew Fayle, Kylimore.

Dear Master Drew,

I hear that you are interested in the domestic arrangements of our friend Jeremy Fisher. I am of opinion that his dinner parties would be much more agreeable if there were a lady to preside at the table. I do not care for roast grasshoppers. His housekeeping and cookery do not come up to the standard to which I am accustomed at the Mansion House.

Yrs. truly,
Alderman Pt. Tortoise.

Master D. Fayle, Kylimore, Co. Dublin.

Dear Master Drew,

In answer to your very kind inquiry, I live alone; I am not married. When I bought my sprigged waistcoat & my maroon tail-coat I had hopes . . . . But I am alone . . . If there were a 'Mrs. Jeremy Fisher' she might object to snails. It is some satisfaction to be able to have as much water & mud in the house as a person likes.

Thanking you for your touching inquiry, Yr. devoted friend,

Jeremiah Fisher.

Master Drew Fayle, Kylimore, Co. Dublin.

Dear Master Drew,

If you please Sir I am a widow; & I think it is very wrong that there is not any Mrs. Jeremy Fisher, but *I* would not marry Mr. Jeremy not for worlds, the way he does live in that house all slippy-sloppy; not any lady would stand it, & not a bit of good starching his cravats.

Yr. obedient washerwoman,
Tiggy Winkle.

MR. ALDERMAN PTOLEMY TORTOISE

Mr. Jeremy Fisher, Pond House.

Mr. Alderman Ptolemy Tortoise
Request the pleasure of
Mr. Jeremy Fisher's
Company at Dinner
on Dec. 25th
(there will be a snail)

R.S.V.P.

Mr. Alderman Ptolemy Tortoise, Melon Pit, South Border.
Mr. Jeremy Fisher accepts with pleasure Alderman P. Tortoise's kind invitation to dinner for Dec. 25.

Sir Isaac Newton, The Well House.

Mr. Alderman Ptolemy Tortoise
Request the pleasure of
Sir Isaac Newton's
Company at Dinner
on Dec. 25th
(to meet our friend Fisher)
R.S.V.P.

Mr. Alderman P. Tortoise, Melon Pit, South Border.

Dear Mr. Alderman,
I shall look forward to dining with you on Dec. 25th. It is an unexpected pleasure as I thought you were asleep. No doubt the melon pit is proof *against* frost. I am nearly frozen in the well house. Our friend Fisher was taking mud baths at the bottom of the pond when I last met him.
Yrs. faithfully,
I. Newton.

THE PIE AND THE PATTY-PAN

Mrs. Duchess, Belle Green.

My Dear Duchess,
If you are in, will you come to tea this afternoon? but if you are out I will put this in the post & invite cousin Tabitha Twitchit. There will be a red herring, & the patty pans are all locked up, do come.
Yr. aff. friend,
Ribby.

Mrs. Tabitha Twitchit, Hill Top Farm.

Dear Cousin Tabitha,
If you can leave your family with safety I shall be much pleased if you will take

tea with me this afternoon. There will be muffins and crumpets & a red herring. I have just been to call on my friend Duchess, she is away from home.

Yr. aff. cousin,

Ribby.

Mrs. Ribstone Pippin, Lakefield Cottage.

Dear Cousin Ribby,

I shall be pleased to take tea with you. I am glad that Duchess is away from home. I do not care for dogs. My son Thomas is well, but he grows out of all his clothes, and I have other troubles.

Yr. aff. cousin,

Tabitha Twitchit.

Mrs. Ribstone Pippin, Lakefield Cottage.

My dear Ribby,

I am so sorry I was out, it would have given me so much pleasure to accept your kind invitation. I had gone to a dog show. I enjoyed it very much but I am a little disappointed that I did not take a prize and I missed the red herring.

Yr. aff. friend,

Duchess.

MR. SAMUEL WHISKERS

To Samuel Rat, High Barn.

Sir,

I hereby give you one day's notice to quit my barn & stables and byre, with your wife, children, grand children & great grand children to the latest generation.

signed: William Potatoes, farmer.

witness: Gilbert Cat & John Stoat-Ferret.

Farmer Potatoes, The Priddings.

Sir,

I have opened a letter addressed to one Samuel Rat. If Samuel Rat means me, I inform you I shall *not go*, and you can't turn us out.

Yrs. etc.

Samuel Whiskers.

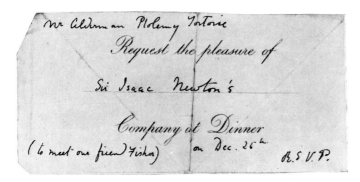

Mr Alderman Ptolemy Tortoise
Request the pleasure of
Sir Isaac Newton's
Company at Dinner
(to meet our friend Fisher) on Dec. 25th. R.S.V.P.

My dear Duchess,
      If you are at home and not engaged
will you come to tea tomorrow? but if you
are away I shall put this in the post and
invite cousin Tabitha Twitchit. There will
be a red herring, & muffins & crumpets.
The patty pans are all locked up. Do come.
      yr aff friend Ribby —

Examples of Beatrix Potter's Miniature Letters
Beatrix Potter kept a record of her miniature letters, and often varied the wording
when sending them to children. This explains why the above letter to Duchess
differs slightly from that in the text

The mail bag made by Beatrix Potter in which miniature letters were sent to Hilda and Beatrix Moore

Mr. Obediah Rat, Barley Mill.

Dear Friend Obediah,

Expect us—bag and baggage—at 9 o'clock in the morning. Am sorry to come upon you suddenly; but my landlord William Potatoes has given me one day's notice to quit. I am of opinion that it is not legal & I could sit till Candlemas be-cause the notice is not addressed to my proper sur-name. *I* would stand up to William Potatoes, but my wife will not face John Stoat-Ferret, so we have decided on a midnight flitting as it is full-moon. I think there are 96 of us, but am not cer-tain. Had it been the May-day term we could have gone to the Field Drains, but it is out of the question at this season. Trusting that the meal bags are full.

Yr. obliged friend,

Samuel Whiskers.

TOM KITTEN AND THE PUDDLE-DUCKS

(Private) Master Tom Kitten, Hill Top Farm.

Sally Henny Penny at Home at the Barn Door

Dec. 24th.

Indian Corn and Dancing

Master T. Kitten, Miss Moppet & Miss Mittens Kitten.

Miss Sally Henny Penny, Barn Door.

Dear Henny,

Me and Moppet and Mittens will all come, if our Ma doesn't catch us.

T. Kitten.

The Puddle-Duck Family, Farm Yard.

Sally Henny Penny at Home at the Barn Door

Dec. 24th.

Indian Corn and Dancing

Mr. Drake Puddle-Duck & Mrs. Jemima & Mrs. Rebeccah

Miss Sally Henny Penny, Barn Door.

Mr. Drake Puddle-Duck and Mrs. Jemima accept with much pleasure, but Mrs. Rebeccah is laid up with a sore throat.

Mrs. Ribstone Pippin, Lakefield Cottage.

Dear Mrs. Ribby,

Can you lend me a red flannel petticoat to wear as a comforter. I have laid up with a sore throat and I do not wish to call in Dr. Maggotty. It is 12 inches long, a mustard leaf is no use.

Yr. sincere friend,
Rebeccah Puddleduck.

Mrs. Rebeccah Puddleduck, Farm Yard.

Dear Beccy,

I am sorry to hear of your sore throat, but what can you expect if you will stand on your head in a pond? I will bring the flannel petticoat & some more head drops directly.

Yr. sincere friend,
Ribby.

GINGER AND PICKLES

Messrs Ginger & Pickles—Grocers—in account with Miss Lucinda Doll. Doll's House

4 thimblefuls of brown sugar	@ 2d	=	1	farthing
6 „ „ white ditto	@ 2d	=	$1\frac{1}{2}$	„
3 tastes stilton Cheese	@ 1/3 per lb.	say $\frac{1}{10}$ farthing		

$2\frac{6}{10}$ farthings—$2\frac{1}{2}$d (about)

with Messrs G & P^s comp^ts & thanks.

Miss Lucinda Doll has received Messrs Pickle & Ginger's account, about which there is some mistake. She has lived for some months upon German plaster provisions & saw dust, and had given no order for the groceries mentioned in the bill.

Miss Lucinda Doll,
Doll's House.

Messrs Ginger & Pickles beg to apologize to Miss Lucinda Doll for their mistake. The goods were selected (& taken away from the shop) to the order of Miss Doll. But Messrs Ginger & Pickles' young man had his doubts at the time. The messenger will not be served again.

MR. BENJAMIN BUNNY AND HIS WIFE
FLOPSY BUNNY

Miss M. Moller, Caldecote Grange, Biggleswade.

My dear Miss Moller,

I am pleased to hear that you like the F. Bunnies, because some people do think there has been too much bunnies; and there is going to be some more!

My family will appear again in the next book; and Cottontail is put in because you asked after her, which me and Cottontail thanks you for kind inquiries and remembrance.

Yrs. respectful

Flopsy Bunny

Dear Madam

My wife Mrs. Flopsy Bunny has replied to your inquiries, because Miss Potter will attend to nothing but hatching spring chickens; there is another hatch chirping this evening. And she is supposed to be doing a Book, about us and the Fox; but she does not get on; neither has she answered all her Xmas letters yet.

Yrs

B. Bunny.

CHRISTMAS GREETINGS FROM
MRS. FLOPSY BUNNY AND HER FAMILY

Master John Hough, 88 Darenth Road, N.W.

Dear Master John Hough,

I and my Family (6) are writing to you because Miss Potter has got no stamps left and she has got a cold, we think Miss Potter is lazy. I think you are a *fine big* boy; my children are *small* rabbits at present.

Yrs. respectfully,

Mrs. Flopsy Bunny.

Dear Master John Hough.

I wish you a Merry Christmas! I am going to have an apple for my Christmas dinner & some celery tops. The cabbages are all frosted but there is lots of hay

Yrs. aff.

First Flopsy Bunny.

x x x x x x x

Dear Master John,

I wish you the same as my eldest brother, and I am going to have the same dinner.

Yrs. aff.

2nd. Flopsy Bunny.

x x x x x x x

Dear Master Hough,

I wish you the compliments of the Season. We have got new fur tippets for Christmas.

Yrs. aff.

3rd. (Miss) F. Bunny.

x x x

Dear Master John,

I have not learned to rite prop perly

Love from

4th. (Miss) F. Bunny.

There is just a scribble, and a few kisses from the 5th Miss F. Bunny; and a scribble and a few kisses 'with his love', from the 6th Master F.B.

COCK ROBIN AND MISS JENNY WREN

Miss Jenny Wren, The Nest, Beech Hedge.

Dear Miss Jenny,

Will you accept a little cask of currant wine from your trusted friend Cock Robin! The carrier will leave it at the garden gate.

Cock Robin Esq., The Holly Bush.

Dear Cock Robin,

I thank you kindly for the little cask of currant wine. I have worked a new little scarlet waistcoat for you. Will you dine with me on Christmas day on the parlour window sill?

Yr. aff. friend,

Jenny Wren.

Jack Sparrow, The Eaves.

Dear Jack Sparrow,

 I have overheard that Jenny Wren & Cock Robin are going to eat their Christmas dinner on the parlour window sill. Lets all go and gobble up the crumbs. Bring Dick Chaffinch and I'll tell the Starlings.

Yr. friend in mischief,
Tom Titmouse.

THE ANTS AND THE CRICKET

The Cricket, Buckle Yeat.

 The little Red Ants under the door stone present their compliments to the cricket at Buckle Yeat & how is he feeling this bitter cold weather? The little Red Ants have heard that Miss Potter would rather like a cricket on the hearth. But they cannot say that she is nice to ants; she poured boiling water on them out of a kettle and has had it on her conscience ever since!

The Little Red Ants, Hill Top Farm.

 The Cricket at Buckle Yeat sings his compliments to the little Red Ants & he is as merry & warm as a cricket in this wintry weather. But he says to the kettle from the hearth he wouldn't like boiling water!

PART TWO

BOOKS—
PUBLISHED AND
UNPUBLISHED

3
The Peter Rabbit Books

The Tale of Peter Rabbit
1901-1902

It was at Eastwood, Dunkeld, a dower house on the Atholl Estate beside the river Tay in Perthshire, that a picture letter was sent to Noel Moore. This letter, dated September 4th 1893, was the origin of *The Tale of Peter Rabbit.*

Many years later, in a letter written to Mrs. Miller in 1940, Beatrix Potter gives interesting sidelights on the setting of the story and on Mr. McGregor. She writes:

> I have been asked to tell again how Peter Rabbit came to be written. It seems a long time ago, and in another world. Though after all the world does not change much in the country, where the seasons follow their accustomed course—the green leaf and the sere—and where nature though never consciously wicked has always been ruthless. In towns there is change. People begin to burrow under ground like rabbits. The lame boy for whom Peter was invented more than forty years ago is now an air warden in a bombed London parish.
>
> I have never quite understood the secret of Peter's perennial charm. Perhaps it is because he and his little friends keep on their way; busily absorbed in their own doings. They were always independent. Like Topsy—they just 'grow'd'—Their names especially seemed to be inevitable. I never knew a gardener named 'Mr. McGregor'. Several bearded horticulturalists have resented the nickname; but I do not know how it came about, nor why 'Peter' was called Peter. It is regrettable that a small boy in church once inquired audibly whether the Apostle was Peter Rabbit? There is difficulty in finding or inventing names entirely new, void of all possible embarrassment.
>
> A few of the animals were harmless skits or caricatures, but Mr. McGregor was not one of them and the backgrounds in Peter Rabbit were a mixture of locality.
>
> The earlier books (including the late printed Pig Robinson) were written in picture letters of scribbled pen and ink for real children; but I confess that afterwards I painted most of the little pictures mainly to please myself. The more spontaneous the pleasure, the more happy the result. I cannot work to order; and when I had nothing to say I had the sense to stop.
>
> I do not remember a time when I did not try to invent pictures and make fairy-tales—amongst the wild flowers, the animals, trees and mosses and fungi—all the thousand common objects of the country side; that pleasant unchanging world of realism and romance, which for us in our northern clime is stiffened by hard weather, a tough ancestry, and the strength that comes from the hills.

Other recollections of *The Tale of Peter Rabbit* are contained in a letter to Mr. Arthur Stephens of Frederick Warne, written in February 1942, in which Beatrix Potter tells how 'Peter was so composite and scattered in locality that I have found it troublesome to explain its various sources. If the vegetable garden and wicket gate were anywhere it was at Lingholm near Keswick; but it would be vain to look for it there, as a firm of landscape gardeners did away with it, and laid it out anew with paved walks etc. . . . The lily pond in Peter was at Tenby, South Wales. The fir tree and some wood backgrounds were near Keswick. Mr. McGregor was no special person; unless in the rheumatic method of planting cabbages. I remember seeing a gardener in Berwickshire extended full length on his stomach weeding a carriage drive with a knife—his name I forget—not McGregor! I think the story was made up in Scotland . . . Peter Rabbit's potting shed and actual geraniums were in Hertfordshire [at Bedwell Lodge, near Hatfield].'

The gardener in Berwickshire with whom she had associated Mr. McGregor, was in fact the gardener at Lennel near Coldstream, where the Potters spent the summer of 1894—but as this was a year *after* the Peter Rabbit story letter was written, it could not have been the origin of Mr. McGregor. It was at Lennel, on October 10th 1894, that Beatrix Potter wrote in her Journal, 'We were somewhat nettled during the last week by the activity of that idle person Mr. Hopkirk, the gardener, who made a frantic effort to get the place straight for his own employer after our departure. I have seen him lie flat on his face in a gravel walk, to weed with a little knife.'

In actual fact the Peter Rabbit picture letter was written in Mr. Macgregor's garden! for this was the name of the tenant who sub-let Eastwood to the Potters in 1893.

A few years after the Peter Rabbit letter had been sent to Noel, it occurred to Beatrix Potter that she might make a little book out of the story, and she wrote to ask if Noel had kept the letter, and if so could she borrow it? Noel *had* kept the letter and was glad to lend it to her.

First she made pen-and-ink copies of the drawings on some folded sheets of thin paper, but they showed through on the reverse side so she started all over again, this time using notepaper. From this copy Beatrix Potter rewrote the story in a stiff-covered exercise book and prepared forty-two pen-and-ink drawings to illustrate it, which were tucked into corner slots cut in the pages of the book. It was called 'The Tale of Peter Rabbit and Mr. McGregor's Garden, by H. B. Potter.' In addition to the black-and-white drawings there was a coloured frontispiece, showing Peter in bed, and his mother, Mrs. Rabbit, giving him a cup of camomile tea.

Canon Rawnsley, a founder member of The National Trust, who was a friend of the family, became interested in Beatrix Potter's idea to make this story letter into a book. He offered to help her find a publisher and to submit the manuscript on her behalf.

During 1900 the story was sent to at least six publishers, from whom, one by one, it was returned with or without thanks. On March 13th 1900, in a picture letter to Marjorie Moore, Beatrix Potter told her she did not think her Peter Rabbit story would be made into a book this time. 'The Publisher is a gentleman who prints books, and he wants a bigger book than he has got enough money to pay for! and Miss Potter has arguments with him . . . I think Miss Potter will go off to another publisher soon . . . she would rather make two or three little books costing 1/– each than one big book costing 6/–, because she thinks little rabbits cannot afford to spend six shillings on one book.' The text of this letter was accompanied by a drawing of two little rabbits looking in a book-shop window, with one shilling each, and mother closing her purse.

Five weeks later, in a postscript to another picture letter, this time sent to Freda Moore, Beatrix Potter told her, 'Miss Potter is sitting upon her book at present and considering! The publisher cannot tell what has become of it.'

By 1901, however, there seemed no immediate prospects of finding a publisher, so Beatrix Potter made up her mind to have the story printed privately, and got in touch with a London printer called Strangeways & Sons, of Tower Street, Cambridge Circus, W.C., who had been recommended to her by her friend Miss Woodward of the Natural History Museum.

Canon Rawnsley, on the other hand, was still trying to get the Peter Rabbit story published. In September 1901 he wrote again to Frederick Warne & Co., one of the publishers who had previously been approached and had courteously declined to accept the book, offering them as an alternative his own version of the story, written in verse, to be illustrated by Beatrix Potter's drawings.

On the title page of his manuscript were the words 'The Tale of Peter Rabbit, written and illustrated by Beatrix Potter, done into rhyme by Canon Rawnsley', and by way of decoration, there was a silhouette of Peter.

The same size was used, and the story began:

> There were four little bunnies
> —no bunnies were sweeter
> Mopsy and Cotton-tail,
> Flopsy and Peter.

> They lived in a sand-bank
> as here you may see,
> At the foot of a fir
> —a magnificent tree.

and after proceeding, verse upon verse for some forty-one pages, ended with the moral:

> They sat down to tea
> Too good mannered to cram
> and ate bread and milk
> and sweet blackberry jam.

Eastwood, Dunkeld
It was while staying here in 1893 that
Beatrix Potter wrote the *Peter Rabbit*
story letter to Noel Moore

Enid Linder

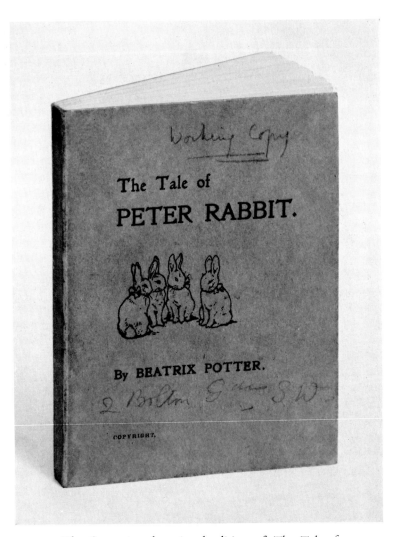

The first privately printed edition of *The Tale of Peter Rabbit*, with flat back, December, 1901 (Marked 'Working Copy' and used when planning Warne's edition)

First he ate some lettuces
and some French beans,
And then he ate some
radishes;

Beatrix Potter's 'Working Copy' of her privately printed *Peter Rabbit*.
The previous picture was crossed through, and the corresponding text
transferred to the following page as shown

The door in the wall at Camfield Place, Hertfordshire,
beside which Peter stood when he asked the mouse
the way to the gate

Enid Linder

And thought as we all
　　think by far the best way
To do what we're told
　　and our mothers obey.

Frederick Warne & Co. in their reply to Canon Rawnsley on September 18th preferred the simple straightforward text of Beatrix Potter, and told him, 'As regards the letter-press, we think there is a great deal to be said for the simple narration . . . though there are many good ideas in your verses which might be introduced with advantage.'

They hesitated as to the advisability of accepting the book, saying, 'moreover we are persuaded that to make the book a success it is absolutely necessary that the pictures should be coloured throughout', adding, 'Miss Potter seems to think the colour would be uninteresting.' She had told them, 'I did not colour the whole book for two reasons—the great expense of good colour printing—and also the rather uninteresting colour of a good many of the subjects which are most of them rabbit brown and green'; and summing up they said, 'as it is too late to produce a book for this season, we think it best to decline your kind offer at any rate for this year.' So for the time being nothing further happened.

It is clear that Frederick Warne & Co. had given careful consideration to the acceptance of *Peter Rabbit,* for in order to provide a practical lay-out for printing, they had gone to the trouble of marking with an 'E' the drawings which they considered should be eliminated without interfering with the story. There were 42 drawings in Beatrix Potter's manuscript. 'In our opinion', they wrote, 'the book would be best cut down to 32 pictures only, and each of these should be reproduced in colour.'

In the meantime Beatrix Potter was making progress with her privately printed edition. The coloured frontispiece had been produced by the recently introduced three-colour process, and Hentschel of 182, Fleet Street had made the required set of colour blocks and sent her 500 impressions. This was about twice the number required for the first printing, but Beatrix Potter was probably considering the likelihood of a second printing.

For the black-and-white illustrations she had 42 zinc blocks made by the Art Reproduction Company of Fetter Lane, E.C., excluding the block for the cover picture which was dealt with later.

The size of the book was to be in accordance with her own ideas of what a child's book should be like—small enough for little hands to hold, and printed on stout paper. The size she first suggested was $5 \times 3\frac{3}{4}$ inches (127 mm $\times$ 95 mm), which was the size of the manuscript she had sent to Warnes. The page was eventually made 135 mm $\times$ 103 mm, and due to the printing arrangement, it was only possible to include 41 of the 42 pictures which had been prepared.

The story was very like Noel's letter, except that it was longer, and there were more illustrations. On alternate pages a few lines of simple text faced each picture. The book was bound in paper boards cut flush, and the cover was of a subdued shade of grey-green on which there was a drawing of four little rabbits. The pages were unnumbered.

On December 16th 1901 this first privately printed edition of 250 copies was ready. Besides giving these books to her relations and friends, Beatrix Potter was selling them for the modest sum of 1/2d.

The Tale of Peter Rabbit (she had omitted 'and Mr. McGregor's Garden'), proved a success from the very first, and within a week or two Beatrix Potter decided to have a second impression of 200 copies in a slightly better binding with a rounded back. There were two or three changes in the punctuation, and a few changes to the text; also, in this second printing, the date 'February 1902' appeared on the title page, which had hitherto been undated. The cover was olive-green.

Apart from the small changes in punctuation, the alterations to the text were as follows:

(Page numbers are counting from the first page of text)

Page	First Printing	Second Impression
51	She shook her head at him. Peter began to cry again.	She only shook her head at him. Peter began to cry again.
57	He went towards the tool-shed again, but suddenly there was a most peculiar noise—scr-r-ritch, scratch, scratch, scritch. Peter scuttered underneath the bushes. Then some one began to sing 'Three blind mice, three blind mice!' It sounded disagreeable to Peter; it made him feel as though his own tail were going to be cut off: his fur stood on end.	He went back towards the tool-shed, but suddenly, quite close to him, he heard the noise of a hoe—scr-r-ritch scratch, scratch, scratch. Peter scuttered underneath the bushes and hid. Then some one began to sing 'Three blind mice, three blind mice!' It sounded disagreeable to Peter: his fur stood on end. It made him feel as if his own tail were going to be cut off. But nothing happened;
59	After a time, as nothing happened, Peter came out, and climbed upon a wheel-barrow, and peeped over. The first thing he saw was Mr. McGregor hoeing onions. His back was turned towards Peter, and beyond him was the gate!	so presently Peter came out and climbed upon a wheel-barrow, and peeped over. The first thing he saw was Mr. McGregor hoeing onions. His back was turned towards Peter, and beyond him was the gate!

Before the first privately printed edition was ready Frederick Warne & Co. had reconsidered their previous decision, and, since Beatrix Potter was willing to prepare coloured illustrations throughout, they decided to accept *The Tale of Peter*

Rabbit, subject to a satisfactory agreement being drawn up with regard to royalties. They wrote to her as follows:

To Miss Potter

December 16th 1901   London

Dear Miss Potter,

I must apologize for not having written to you earlier with reference to the 'Bunny Book'. I am now writing to Cumberland as I find I have mislaid your London address. I am sorry the estimate which I based on a first edition of 5,000 copies, did not turn out very well, as I find it only shows a possible royalty for author and artist of 1d per copy, which would amount to about £20 on this first edition. On subsequent editions, we should be able to pay 3d per copy royalty. If you would care for us to go on, on this basis we shall be very pleased to produce an edition of 5,000 copies at our own risk, in colours as we suggested. Of course we cannot tell whether the work is likely to run to a second edition or not, and therefore we fear it might not provide a reasonable remuneration for you. It is possible we might be able to issue the book at a slightly higher price, so as to yield a better royalty. We will look into this, if you wish it, but we think that the book would not be half so saleable at a higher price than 1/6d. Will you kindly let us hear what you think about the matter, so that we may come to a definite decision about it.

Yours faithfully,
Frederick Warne & Co.

To Frederick Warne & Co.

December 18th 1901   2, Bolton Gardens

Dear Sir,

I was on the point of posting the book, when I received your letter of December 16th. I think Strangeways have printed it rather nicely. It is going off very well amongst my friends and relations, five at a time; I will spread it about as much as I can, especially in Manchester.

Had you decided *not* to go on with it, I would certainly have done so myself, it has given me so much amusement. I showed it this morning to some ladies who have a bookshop in Kensington, who wanted to put it in the window on the spot, but I did not venture to do so—though I would have been much interested.

I do not know if it is necessary to consult Canon Rawnsley; I should think *not*.

Speaking for myself, I consider your terms very liberal as regards royalty; but I do not quite understand about the copyright. Do you propose that the copyright remains mine; you agreeing to print an edition of 5,000, and having—as part of the agreement—the option of printing more editions if required? I must apologize for not understanding, but I would like to be clear about it. For instance who would the copyright belong to in the event of *your* not wishing to print a second edition? I am sure no one is likely to offer me better terms than 3d apiece, and I am aware that these little books don't last long, even if they are a success; but I should like to know what I am agreeing to.

97

I think it should certainly be kept down to 1/6, even if it took off my 1d. royalty on the first edition. I should be glad to call sometime at the office to hear what you decide about the coloured drawings. I still think the 3 colour photograph very nice, but I confess I had not thought of the plan of *brown* ink when I expressed such a strong dislike to black outlines—I have put a 'X' on some of the cuts which don't really seem to need alteration, but I am perfectly willing to re-draw the whole if desired.

I remain Sir,

yrs. sincerely,

Beatrix Potter

I have not spoken to Mr. Potter, but I think Sir, it would be well to explain the agreement clearly because he is a little formal having been a barrister.

It would appear that the colour process on which Warnes had based their first estimate was less costly than the three-colour process used by Hentschel for Beatrix Potter's Peter Rabbit frontispiece. Beatrix Potter wished them to use this three-colour process because she thought it would give the best results. Warnes therefore decided to prepare a further estimate and to reconsider their offer of December 16th.

In their letter of acknowledgement they wrote:

To Miss Potter

December 21st 1901   London

Dear Madam,

We have to acknowledge with thanks the receipt of your special edition of your quaint little book. It has been much admired by our representatives, who are just now home from their journeys, and we have no doubt that we should be able to do well with the coloured edition for next season.

With regard to the copyright, this would have to be ceded to us, but some clause could doubtless be inserted in the agreement by which in the event of our not deciding to issue a second edition, we would agree to transfer the copyright and blocks to you on payment of the original cost of the latter, or some agreed proportion thereof. You still seem rather to wish the plates to be engraved by the three colour process and we are therefore taking a new estimate. This will probably entail a considerable increase in the initial cost, but would we think give the most artistic result. We shall not have the particulars of this estimate for about a week, and we propose to write you again then fixing an appointment when perhaps you could kindly arrange to call and discuss with us the details of the agreement and form of the book.

With kind regards and wishing you all the compliments of the season

We are,

Yours faithfully,

Frederick Warne & Co.

P.S. We very much prefer your own letterpress to the verses by Canon Rawnsley.

By the end of the first week in January Beatrix Potter had not heard from Warnes about the new estimate, and we find her writing to them again, giving further information about Hentschel's three-colour blocks.

To Frederick Warne & Co.

January 7th 1902   2, Bolton Gardens

Dear Sir,

I send you another copy of Peter Rabbit—I did not remember to tell you when discussing Hentschel's blocks that the set I have got here in my possession seems to be particularly well finished.

I know a little about copper as my brother etches in it, and have some experience of printing—I work on stone myself but have never done coloured lithographs; but it is such an old-fashioned expensive method it would not have been of much use, even if I had been competent to work out my own drawings.

I think Hentschel would make the best job of it, if the money part of the business can be arranged, which I do not doubt it can be somehow.

I remain, Sir,
yrs. sincerely,
Beatrix Potter

The investigations into the additional cost of using the three-colour process took longer than at first expected, and it was not until May that Warnes submitted their revised proposals.

During the ensuing months, discussions took place on various matters relating to the book, as will be seen from the following correspondence:

To Frederick Warne & Co.

January 12th 1902   2, Bolton Gardens

Dear Sir,

I wrote to Hentschel to ask something about paint; and enquired at the same time about engraving very small blocks.

Two blocks can go inside their minimum of 20 sq. inch, and *if drawn on one sheet of paper* can be photographed together, with an extra 1/- each for dividing and mounting.

I work that out, 16 pairs at £3. 3 + 2/- for mounting = £52. — Their charge is 3/6 per sq. inch. I do not clearly understand whether they would be willing to photograph a larger number than 2 together, which might effect a further saving.

I did not mention your name, having no authority to write to them—

In case you have written to them and got a similar proposal I thought I would tell you I am quite willing to re-copy the drawings in groups if required. There is no use beginning to colour them until I know.

I was wondering, if you are too busy to attend to it at present, whether you would care for me to call at Hentschel's—without of course any authority to make a bargain—to find out what they mean by the 3/6?

The drawings must have ½ inch clear space round each; if a number could be photographed at once, and *if the ½ inch between is* NOT *charged for,* it would seem rather reasonable—under £40(?)

The £52 is less than I guessed; but more than your other estimate; but I thought you said Evans charged 4/6.

> I remain, Sir,
> yrs sincerely,
> Beatrix Potter

I calculated the blocks at their present size.

To Miss Potter

January 13th 1902   London

Dear Madam,

We have already made enquiries of Messrs Hentschel, and still wait further information from them, on receipt of which we will again write to you on the subject of preparing your designs for reproduction. We hope to have full particulars on Wednesday next, and we do not think it will be necessary for you to call at Hentschel's as suggested in your letter, as we shall be able to send you the necessary information to effect economy in making the blocks.

> We are, Dear Madam,
> Yours faithfully,
> Frederick Warne & Co.

*NDW**

To Miss Potter

January 17th 1902   London

Dear Madam,

Peter Rabbit

In further reference to your letter of 12th inst, we have now ascertained particulars of Hentschel's respecting the best method of preparing your designs to economise in cost of reproduction.

A saving can be effected by making two or perhaps three drawings on one sheet of paper, but to what extent depends upon the actual sizes of the blocks, and as we have not a copy of the book before us it is somewhat difficult to determine whether two or three drawings should be grouped. Also if it is your intention to prepare your designs with a view to reduction it would be necessary to have them drawn to reduce to the same scale.

The grouping arrangement could be very easily dealt with if we had the entire set of pictures, and we would suggest that you prepare the drawings *singly* and allow us to cut down the margin of paper and neatly mount them in groups whereby so doing, a saving can be effected.

* Some letters from Frederick Warne & Co. were initialled *NDW* (Norman Dalziel Warne).

With regard to the cost of the blocks, we are quoted the price you state, *viz.* 3/6 per square inch, but for separating the price quoted is 1/6 per block. The margin between each drawing is included in the calculation of square inches and is charged for.

We trust you will now be able to proceed with the drawings, but should you desire further information, we shall be glad if you would call and see us.

We are,
Yours faithfully,
Frederick Warne & Co.

NDW

To Frederick Warne & Co.

January 19th 1902   2, Bolton Gardens

Dear Sir,

I return the marked copy of Peter Rabbit—The present blocks are all within $2\frac{1}{2} \times 3$ (some being reckoned sideways). I find that 15 were reduced by $\frac{1}{3}$ and 17 by $\frac{1}{4}$.

I don't think this would signify, provided that the right sizes were mounted together in the way you suggest.

I suppose that you will not be doing anything just at present, with those already coloured. I think there was some paint used in some of them which would be better taken out before they are photographed.

The shapes of the zinc blocks, and also of the coloured drawings which you already have, were rather irregular.

Perhaps you will consider whether you prefer a variety of shape (within a certain size)—or whether you would like the backgrounds worked up to make a more uniform shape.

I shall be very glad to prepare the drawings in any way to suit your convenience: I will set to work to colour the others and will bring them to the office—

I cannot call this next week as I am going into the country, but I can get on with the work now that it is definitely decided which process is to be used.

I remain, Sir,
yrs. sincerely,
Beatrix Potter

I do not know if it is worth mentioning—But Dr. Conan Doyle had a copy for his children and he has a good opinion of the story and words.

Beatrix Potter was now planning the text and illustrations for her book. She was using one of the flat-backed privately printed editions as a working copy; on the cover she had pencilled 'Working Copy, 2 Bolton Gdns. S.W.'

First she looked carefully through the illustrations to decide which ones should be left out. Warnes had now restricted her to thirty, plus the frontispiece, so she had to take out eleven. These were crossed through in pencil, and the corresponding text transferred to other pages: in six cases to the following page; in two cases to the previous page; and in three, the text was deleted altogether—to be re-introduced two years later in *The Tale of Benjamin Bunny*.

The text which had been transferred was neatly written in ink on the appropriate pages, and the pictures which she decided to use were numbered 1 to 30. Beatrix Potter then hand-coloured three of the black-and-white illustrations—to see how they would look when coloured. On each picture she had lightly pencilled the reduction, $\frac{1}{4}$ or $\frac{1}{3}$, as a guide when preparing her new drawings in groups to facilitate block-making. Apart from the three pages of text which had been deleted, the text of the Warne *Peter Rabbit* was practically the same as that of her second impression of the privately printed edition. Only a few words were changed here and there, and an occasional paragraph omitted.

By the end of April good progress had been made with the preparation of the book, and the correspondence which follows covers many aspects of this work.

To Frederick Warne & Co.

April 25th 1902   2, Bolton Gardens

Dear Sir,

I think this is the drawing that Mr. Warne was looking for yesterday; the gardener seemed to be better in the drawing I brought yesterday, but I hope you will use which ever you like.

I have been wondering whether the rabbit on the cover ought not to face the other way, towards the binding; it would not take long to copy again—

I should like to take the opportunity of saying that I shall not be surprised or disappointed to hear that the figures work out badly for the first edition of Peter Rabbit.

I remain Sir,
yrs. sincerely,
Beatrix Potter

To Frederick Warne & Co.

April 30th 1902   2, Bolton Gardens

Dear Sir,

I am very sorry that I cannot call as I am going to Scotland to-morrow morning, my brother has made his arrangements and I don't want to miss travelling with him.

It is most provoking that I could not see the drawings before going, as I think I could very likely do them better there, as there is a garden—

Would you be so kind as to post me the two that are the worst? I should be very glad to try them again; any that you are not satisfied with—

The address will be Kalemouth, Roxburgh. I expect to be at home again in a fortnight and shall hope to call then at the office to hear what can be settled—

The book seems to go on of itself. I had requests for 9 copies yesterday from 3 people I do not know.

I remain,
yrs. sincerely,
Beatrix Potter

Peter Rabbit: 1901–1902

To Frederick Warne & Co.

May 2nd 1902   Kalemouth, Roxburgh

Dear Sir,

I have received the drawings and will do my best to make the alterations, I think they are all very reasonable criticisms.

My brother is sarcastic about the figures; what you and he take for Mr. McGregor's nose, was intended for his ear, not his nose at all.

I have written for some 'Albumen' and will set to work at once—

The people are very suitable here, if one was not afraid of them; especially the cook. If I cannot manage any other way, I will photograph her in the right position and copy the photograph—I never learnt to draw figures, but it is much more satisfactory to have another try at them and I am very glad that you have sent them back.

Believe me,

yrs. sincerely,

Beatrix Potter.

The rabbits will be no difficulty. I had exactly the same opinion about the one under the gate, and those with the kettle.

To Miss Potter

May 7th 1902   London

Dear Miss Potter,

We have now gone carefully into the estimates of *Peter Rabbit* and find that it will be necessary for us to produce a first edition of 6,000 copies. We propose to issue the book at 1/- net, with art paper cover as already submitted to you,—and at 1/6d net, bound in cloth. Initial expenses, as we feared, are rather heavy under the new method of producing blocks, and we should therefore have to ask you to allow us to have the first 3,000 copies of the 1/- edition, free of royalty. As regards the remainder, we propose to offer you a royalty of 10% on the published price. This would bring you in about $1\frac{1}{4}$d per copy on all 1/- copies sold after the first 3,000 and about $1\frac{7}{8}$d on all 1/6d copies sold.

If these terms will be satisfactory to you, you might let us know and we will have an agreement drawn up on these lines to submit to you when you return to London.

We shall be glad to have remaining illustrations for the book as soon as possible so that we may have samples in good time for our travellers.

With kind regards,

Yours faithfully,

Frederick Warne & Co.   *NDW*

To Frederick Warne & Co.

May 8th 1902   Kalemouth, Roxburgh

Dear Sir,

I enclose the drawings. I fear it is not of much use posting on Friday, but if any further alteration is required, you might have time to post them back here this week.

If there had been time, I should like to have copied a photograph for 'Mrs. McGregor'; I have taken a very suitable person but cannot develop it here.

I think if you would kindly—as you suggest—draw out a rough draft of the agreement, and allow me to call at Bedford Street in order to hear it explained, it would be the best plan.

The royalty upon the 1st edition of 6,000 which you offer in your letter of May 7th is quite as much as I expected.

I should wish, before signing an agreement, to understand clearly what arrangement it would imply about the copyright; and what stipulations would be made about subsequent editions if required.

I am very glad to hear that the book can be sold as cheap as 1/- net; I should think at that price a large number will sell.

I wish that the drawings had been better; I dare say they may look better when reduced; but I am becoming so tired of them, I begin to think they are positively bad. I am sorry they have made such a muddle of them.

'Peter' died at 9 years old, just before I began the drawings and now when they are finished I have got another rabbit, and the drawings look wrong.

I remain, Sir,

yrs. sincerely,

Beatrix Potter

In due course, the remaining drawings were sent to Warnes and the blocks made. On May 22nd Beatrix Potter wrote from Bolton Gardens saying, 'Perhaps you will kindly send a line when the proofs come, and I will call. I shall be very much interested to see them', adding in a postscript: 'If my father happens to insist on going with me to see the agreement, would you please not mind him very much, if he is very fidgety about things—I am afraid it is not a very respectful way of talking and I don't wish to refer to it again, but I think it is better to mention beforehand he is sometimes a little difficult; I can of course do what I like about the book being 36. I suppose it is a habit of old gentlemen, but sometimes rather trying.'

To Miss Potter

May 26th 1902   London

Dear Miss Potter

Many thanks for your note. As I thought you might like to look over the agreement quietly, I am sending you on a rough draft. I think it covers all the points we have discussed in our letters, and is based on the lines of a form issued by the Publishers Association. You will notice that Clause 6 gives you the right to re-purchase the work, in the event of our not wishing to risk further editions.

We have not yet received word from Hentschel's as to when the plates will be ready, but will let you know as soon as we receive proofs.

With kind regards,

Yours faithfully,

Norman D. Warne

P.S. As we have not made a copy of the agreement, we should be obliged if you will return same when finished with.

Peter Rabbit: 1901–1902

To Frederick Warne & Co.

May 27th 1902   2, Bolton Gardens

Dear Sir,

Does Clause 3—(which explains the amount of royalty)—refer to the first edition only, or to subsequent editions as well?

yrs. sincerely,

Beatrix Potter.

To Miss Potter

May 29th 1902   London

Dear Miss Potter,

Replying to yours of 27th, I unfortunately did not keep a copy of the agreement I sent you, as I thought you would preferably bring it with you when you wished to discuss it with us. As far as I can remember, in Clause 3, the amount of royalty refers not only to the first editions but subsequent editions. Of course you will quite understand that it is only the first 3,000 copies of the *first* 1/- edition which are to be free of royalty, on all subsequent you will receive royalty on the full number sold. If this is not quite clear in the agreement we can easily make it so when you call and see us.

Enclosed is the only proof at present to hand from Hentschel's. We have written hurrying them on with the three-colour blocks.

Yours faithfully,

Norman D. Warne

To Miss Potter

June 2nd 1902   London

Dear Miss Potter,

I am sending you herewith proofs of the first four blocks received for *Peter Rabbit* with the originals. I shall be obliged if you will return all to me, with your criticisms, at your earliest convenience. I hope the others will be coming shortly.

Yours faithfully,

Norman D. Warne

P.S. We shall want the originals back as well as the proofs to guide our printers.

To Frederick Warne & Co.

June 4th 1902   2, Bolton Gardens

Dear Sir,

I think that Mr. McGregor and the single figure have been done as well as they possibly could—The *blue* block seems rather heavy in the other pair, for some reason.

If you thought of asking them to do anything further to the blocks—I would suggest filing out the blackberry at the top right hand corner; and toning down the *blue* in the green, on the *left* side only, of the fir tree.

The ground between the middle rabbit and the blackbird might be lighter with advantage. They are such small points that if you are satisfied with the blocks I hope that you will not trouble about them, from my mentioning them.

I think they have done more work on the lighter pair; both upon the cucumber frame, and in filing the edges.

I like the fir-tree plate the least, but I think if that green could be taken down it would be much less confused.

Thanking you very much for sending them,

believe me,

yrs. sincerely,

Beatrix Potter

To Frederick Warne & Co.

June 8th 1902   2, Bolton Gardens

Dear Sir,

I put some white paint on the leaves behind the wheel barrow but it did not seem an improvement so I have taken it off again.

If I have put in too much on any of the others you would find that it is easy to wipe it off.

yrs. sincerely,

Beatrix Potter

By the end of June the Peter Rabbit colour blocks were finished and a set of proofs was sent to Beatrix Potter for her comments.

To Miss Potter

June 24th 1902   London

Dear Miss Potter,

I have at last received the remaining eight proofs of *Peter Rabbit* from Hentschels, and send you set herewith for your inspection. I do not think this lot are quite so satisfactory on the whole as the first, but I do not know that very much can be done to improve them. Perhaps you will make any suggestions you think fit as you did with the earlier proofs, when we will get them attended to.

We have also received from Hentschels the revised proofs of the earlier blocks. We have gone over these very carefully and find that they have carried out your wishes as regards alterations, very successfully on the whole. We are not therefore sending these again for your inspection.

We also send you in same parcel proofs in various coloured papers of the proposed cover design. We shall be glad if you would select say 2 colours from the specimens sent you. We have marked two on the back which we prefer ourselves, but are quite willing to leave the final decision to you if you like any of the others better. I send a placed copy showing how the letterpress would appear in the finished book. You will notice that I have not pasted in

Two sketches from life of Beatrix Potter's pet rabbit
Peter, drawn in February 1899

I AM sorry to say that Peter was not very well during the evening, in consequence of having eaten too much in Mr. McGregor's garden.

His mother put him to bed, and made some camomile tea ;

One of three pictures in Beatrix Potter's 'Working Copy' of her privately printed *Peter Rabbit* which she hand-coloured—no doubt to see how the pictures in Warne's edition would look, as they were to be in colour four of the plates, namely No. 29, 27, 23 and 20. This is because Hentschels have only sent me one proof of these, which I reserved for your corrections.

I shall be glad if you will kindly look over the letterpress and say whether it is exactly as you wish. Please let us hear from you as soon as possible, so that we may get the book complete in the printers' hands.

Yours faithfully,
Frederick Warne & Co.

NDW

To Frederick Warne & Co.

June 29th 1902   2, Bolton Gardens

Dear Sir,

The letter about the book cover came here after I had gone to Bedford Street. I did not understand I was to pick out 2 colours. I would choose the two that were marked, and if you at all prefer the brown, I think it looked very well. I liked the green a little better, but perhaps there are fewer brown books—They both went equally well with the colour of the rabbit—

yrs sincerely,
Beatrix Potter.

The final choice fell on grey and brown. The first proofs of *The Tale of Peter Rabbit* were expected in a few weeks, and Beatrix Potter was looking forward to seeing one.

To Frederick Warne & Co.

July 15th 1902   2, Bolton Gardens

Dear Mr. Warne,

If you send my rabbit book would you be so kind as to mark it to be forwarded, or else direct it to Ees Wyke, Sawrey, Lancashire? We go to the Lakes for 3 months tomorrow, and it would be a long time to wait. . . .

Beatrix Potter's letters were becoming more personal, and the rest of this letter is about a new idea—a book of Nursery Rhymes which she would try to do better than Peter Rabbit.

The printer's order for the first edition of *The Tale of Peter Rabbit* was placed on July 23rd, and in due course a set of proofs was sent.

To Miss Potter

August 16th 1902   London

Dear Miss Potter,

We send you herewith a first proof from press of the colour plates of *Peter Rabbit*, also a rough proof of the letterpress, showing you how it will fall. We shall be glad if you will kindly read this over, and see if it is all in order, before we finally go to press.

Our printers advise us they have found it rather difficult to register the blocks on the large sheet, but on the whole we think you will find they have not come out badly. We are going carefully over the sheet, with a view to getting them to improve the stock as they go along.

The plate slipped in, in front of the half title page, is the one we propose to use for pasting on the cover.

With kind regards,
Yours faithfully,
Frederick Warne & Co.

NDW

To Frederick Warne & Co.

August 17th 1902   Ees Wyke, Sawrey

Dear Sir,

I return the proofs of Peter Rabbit, the only alterations I would like to suggest—there is a full stop on page 27, where there ought to be a comma.

On page 75, it might read better if another line were crossed out, I have marked it in pencil; or if that is inconvenient you might print it 'straight across the *cabbages*'. The word 'garden' has come twice close together owing to some lines having been cut out.

The blocks do not seem to have registered quite exactly but the only two that seem really unpleasant are pages 65 and 74.

As long as it does not become worse, I rather like the effect in some of them; it makes them softer. I think your printer has succeeded much better with the greens than Hentschel did; I hope the little book will be a success, there seems to be a great deal of trouble being taken with it.

It is a disappointing summer for work out of doors, I cannot get on at all so far.

I remain,
yrs. sincerely,
Beatrix Potter

Beatrix Potter's copy in the ordinary 1/– binding is inscribed '1st Edition. Oct. 2nd. 02', and a copy of the 1/6d cloth binding, with Rupert Potter's book plate, bears the date 'Oct. 02'.

We are told that orders for the entire first printing were received prior to publication. The printers were Edmund Evans, The Racquet Court Press, Swan Street, London, E.C.

It is interesting to note that, according to Warne's records, the cost of labour, material, and royalty for the ordinary 1/– binding, was 5¾d per book—sheet and royalty 3$\frac{11}{16}$d, cover paper $\frac{3}{16}$d and binding 1⅞d.

In a questionnaire sent to Beatrix Potter in 1939, she recalled some of the details of the early printings of *The Tale of Peter Rabbit*, and wrote, 'There were two colours, both subdued inoffensive colours, used for binding the first impression of Peter. I have two more early impressions, still with the leaf endpapers, and the portrait of Mrs. M. (or myself) holding a pie. One bound in a stronger brown is either

2nd. or 3rd. printing. Another with a stronger green (I remember we couldn't match the two soft colours which I liked), this green one still has Mrs. McGregor and the leaf pattern endpaper and the word "shed" on page 51—I had marked it 4th. It must have been printed during 1903; before the date in 1903 when the Tailor and Squirrel Nutkin came out.'

After the fourth printing, the picture of Mrs. McGregor and the pie was removed, together with three other pictures including the cover picture, to make room for the new coloured pictorial end-papers, which were first introduced in the autumn of 1903 when *The Tale of Squirrel Nutkin* and *The Tailor of Gloucester* were first published.

Beatrix Potter's reference to this picture as being one of 'Mrs. M. (or myself)', is of interest. The drawing of Mrs. McGregor in the privately printed edition is of a rugged old country woman, and a similar, but coloured drawing was submitted to Warnes for *The Tale of Peter Rabbit*. They did not like it, and at the foot of the drawing wrote, 'We still do not like the old woman's face. Will you please have another try at this'. So possibly the young woman who appears as Mrs. McGregor on page 14 of Warne's edition is, after all, a caricature of Beatrix Potter herself, though not a very flattering one!

By 1907 the colour blocks of *The Tale of Peter Rabbit* had become worn, and in the autumn of that year they were renewed. In Beatrix Potter's copy of this printing, she wrote, 'New plates, Autumn 1907. Early copy, to be kept. H.B.P.' Also, on an inserted slip of paper are the words 'New blocks, first time of re-engraving. First printing—see p. 68.' On page 68 there is a different picture of Peter in the wheel-barrow and Mr. McGregor in the distance hoeing onions—both Peter and Mr. McGregor are drawn much larger. Also, the picture of Mrs. Rabbit pouring out Peter's camomile tea on page 81, is more pleasing than the earlier one. These two blocks were in use for six or seven years, after which replacement blocks were made from the first edition pictures.

It was unfortunate that Warnes did not copyright *The Tale of Peter Rabbit* in America when it first came out. The result was that in 1904 a pirated edition appeared, published by Henry Altemus & Co. It was the same format as the Warne edition, and the pictures and text were copied from the fourth printing of 1903. There was nothing Warnes could do about it, and later, more pirated editions of Peter Rabbit appeared. One of these contained puzzle pictures with hidden animals for the children to discover, while another was made up into a set of Peter Rabbit cut-outs.

From her writings in her Journal we learn more about her own pet rabbit, Peter. She taught him to do tricks, and there is a description of how two little girls came to tea and 'Peter Rabbit was the entertainment, but flatly refused to perform although he had been black-fasting all day from all but mischief.

'He caused shrieks of amusement by sitting up in the arm-chair and getting on to the tea-table. The children were satisfied, but it is tiresome that he will never show off. He really is good at tricks when hungry, in private, jumping (stick, hands, hoop, back and forward), ringing little bell and drumming on a tambourine.'

In one of her privately printed copies of *The Tale of Peter Rabbit,* Beatrix Potter wrote, 'In affectionate remembrance of poor old Peter Rabbit, who died on the 26th. of January 1901 at the end of his 9th. year. He was bought, at a very tender age, in the Uxbridge Road, Shepherds Bush, for the exorbitant sum of 4/6 . . . whatever the limitations of his intellect or outward shortcomings of his fur, and his ears and toes, his disposition was uniformly amiable and his temper unfailingly sweet. An affectionate companion and a quiet friend.'

The Tale of Peter Rabbit was one of the best loved of Beatrix Potter's books. In 1905 she wrote, with her picture letters in mind, 'It is much more satisfactory to address a real live child; I often think that that was the secret of the success of Peter Rabbit, it was written to a child—not made to order.'

Mrs. McGregor and the pie
This picture, intended for one of the coloured illustrations
in Warne's *Peter Rabbit*, was not used because they said,
'We still do not like the old woman's face. Will you please
have another try at this?'

Peter hiding under bush

This water colour, copied from a line drawing in the
privately printed *Peter Rabbit*, and illustrating the words
'Peter scuttered underneath the bushes', was not used in
Warne's edition because there was no room for it

Original book drawing for Warne's edition of *The Tale of Peter Rabbit*, first used in September 1907, when the blocks were re-engraved. After six or seven years, it was replaced by the earlier one

Four rabbits in their warren. Are they Flopsy, Mopsy, Cotton-tail and Peter?

The Tailor of Gloucester
1902–1903

In 1894 Caroline Hutton who was a remote cousin of Beatrix Potter invited her to stay at her home at Harescombe Grange, near Stroud, in Gloucestershire. Beatrix Potter, though almost twenty-eight years of age, had seldom been away from home on her own.

In her Journal she writes of this visit, 'I went to Harescombe on Tuesday the 12th. of June. I used to go to my grandmother's, and once I went for a week to Manchester, but I had not been away independently for five years. It was an event.

'It was so much of an event in the eyes of my relations that they made it appear an undertaking to me, and I began to think I would rather not go. I had a sick headache most inopportunely, though whether cause or effect I could not say, but it would have decided the fate of my invitation but for Caroline, who carried me off.'

Long after, when an old lady of eighty-six, Caroline Hutton, now Caroline Clark, remembered this first visit and wrote, 'I am always glad that in spite of her mother's objections I managed to get her to my old home. She said *B* was so apt to be sick and to faint; and I, regardless of the truth, said I was quite accustomed to all that; and of course she could do most things, quite long walks included, and very soon she made friends with my father who called her "The busy Bee".'

Beatrix Potter referred to this first visit as 'like a most pleasant dream', and in the years that followed she often stayed at Harescombe Grange.

It was during one of these visits that Beatrix Potter heard the story of the 'Tailor of Gloucester'. She tells us how she 'had the story from Miss Caroline Hutton, who had it of Miss Lucy, of Gloucester, who had it of the tailor.'

It was a strange story about a tailor who one Saturday left in his shop a waistcoat, cut out, but not made up. The following Monday when he returned he found it finished except for one button-hole, with a little scrap of paper pinned to the waistcoat, bearing the words 'no more twist'.

What really happened was told many years later by Mrs. Prichard, the tailor's wife. Every year there was a Root, Fruit and Grain Society Show at the Shire Hall, when the Mayor and City Corporation walked in procession from the Guildhall to the show. Attending this function was the first duty of a new mayor.

Mr. Prichard was on friendly terms with many of the councillors, and on such occasions he was extremely busy. On this particular occasion he was so overwhelmed with orders that he even asked one of the councillors if he could manage without his waistcoat so that he could make a very special one for the new mayor.

Work had been started on this special waistcoat; it was still unfinished and the show was imminent—Mr. Prichard was most concerned. When he left his shop that Saturday morning, the waistcoat was cut out and left lying on the board.

Mr. Prichard had two assistants who, realizing his concern over the waistcoat, and wishing to do their master a good turn, came back secretly to the shop that Saturday afternoon letting themselves in with some skeleton keys. They worked on until the waistcoat was finished—all but one button-hole—for they had run out of thread. Then they pinned on a little note bearing the words 'no more twist', and went home as secretly as they had come.

When the tailor returned to the shop on Monday morning, he could scarcely believe his eyes; *there* was the mayor's waistcoat—finished—all but one button-hole. The two assistants never said a word, and the tailor was completely mystified. He brought the waistcoat down and put it in his shop-window, with a little sign by it which read, 'Come to Prichard where the waistcoats are made at night by the fairies'.

When Beatrix Potter heard this story she was intrigued—all her life she had been charmed by the thought of fairies. Of her early childhood days at Dalguise in Scotland, she once wrote, 'Everything was romantic in my imagination. The woods were peopled by the mysterious good folk. The Lords and Ladies of the last Century walked with me along the overgrown paths in the garden.' At once she felt that she must make this strange happening into a story. She would change the fairies into little mice, but the mayor and the tailor should remain true to life.

When Beatrix Potter was driven into Gloucester she made sketches of some of the streets and buildings, and of the archway into the precincts of the cathedral. We are told how she sat on a doorstep in one of the streets of Gloucester in the hot, summer sunshine, sketching a *snow-scene* for her story! She also made background paintings of interiors of cottages in the neighbourhood: one of a bed with hangings, another of a dresser complete with coloured crockery. At Harescombe Grange she painted the coachman's little boy sitting cross-legged on the floor posed as a tailor; also slumped in a chair in front of an imaginary fire.

Back in London Beatrix Potter needed some first-hand information about a tailor's workshop, so one day when she was walking past a tailor's shop in Chelsea, she pulled a button off her coat and went inside. While the tailor worked at this small repair she was able to have a good look at him, his tools and the snippets and odds and ends which surrounded him, and later she made sketches of what she had seen. The tailor's shop was copied from a print of houses in old London city.

By December 1901 the story was finished, and written out neatly in a stiff-covered exercise book, including twelve water-colours based on some of the background sketches which Beatrix Potter had made—a Christmas present for Freda Moore.

The Tailor of Gloucester: 1902–1903

Christmas, 1901

My dear Freda,

Because you are fond of fairy-tales and have been
ill, I have made you a story all for yourself—a new
one that nobody has read before.

And the queerest thing about it—is that I heard
it in Gloucestershire, and it is true! at least about
the tailor, the waistcoat, and the

'No more twist'

There ought to be more pictures towards the end, and
they would have been the best ones; only Miss Potter was
tired of it! Which was lazy of Miss Potter.

yrs. aff. H.B.P.

The twelve water-colours in Freda's manuscript are briefly described in Table 1 at the end of this section, from which it can be seen that ten of these water-colours were later used as a basis for some of the illustrations in the Warne edition of *The Tailor of Gloucester*.

Beatrix Potter had woven many of her favourite rhymes and verses into Freda's story—the old Christmas verses sung by carol singers, and the rhymes recited by the little birds and mice and other animals; for according to an old tradition, 'all the beasts can talk in the night between Christmas Eve and Christmas Day in the morning'.

At the end of Freda's manuscript, she wrote a note on the origin of some of these rhymes, which reads, 'Some of the verses are the Scottish version (Chambers). Most of the rhymes are from J. O. Halliwell's collection.' She also explained some of the old-fashioned words she used in the story:

padusoy = padua soy—or soré— = silk of Padua.
taffeta   = a mixture of flax and silk.
lutestring = lustring = lustred or watered silk.
Robins   = Robings, old fashioned name for Trimmings—
           Hogarth's lady in frontispiece would wear a
           sacque trimmed with Gauze and Robins. She
           also wears a hoop or Crinoline.
           The gentleman carries his cocked hat under
           his arm and a pinch of snuff in his fingers.

December 1901 was an eventful month, for it marked the publication of the privately printed *Peter Rabbit*, and the decision by Frederick Warne & Co. to publish the coloured edition of *The Tale of Peter Rabbit* the following year.

Feeling that Warnes would be unlikely to undertake another book so soon, and that if they did so they would probably wish to cut out many of her favourite rhymes, she decided, in view of the success of *Peter Rabbit*, to have *The Tailor of Gloucester* printed privately—with coloured illustrations throughout. She therefore asked Freda if she might borrow the manuscript in order to redraw the pictures and copy out the story. In due course Freda sent her the manuscript, and some months later received the following letter:

July 6th 1902   Laund House, Bolton Abbey

My dear Freda,

I have kept your picture book a long time and I have not done with it yet; I had to copy out the pictures rather larger and it took me a long time—but you will get it back some day— I hope soon I shall have the new edition of the little rabbit book with coloured pictures—I have had the pictures to look at and they were very pretty, but not made up into a proper book yet.

I have been such a fine long walk this morning right up on to the top of a hill, where there was heather and lots of grouse. We could see a very long way, hills and hills one behind another and white roads going up and down from one valley to the next. There is a beautiful old church called Bolton Abbey about a mile off. Most of it is in ruins, but there is a little piece in the middle where they have service.

The river winds round about it and at the end of the lawn below the abbey there are stepping stones . . . such a width, I did not try to cross. I thought I should fall in. What a mess I have made with the ink! there is too much in the pot, and every one is talking at once.

I wonder how I am going to get to the station with my box, it is such a way! I hope your mamma is quite well, give her my love.

Your aff. friend,
Beatrix Potter.

Beatrix Potter now started to work seriously on her privately printed edition of *The Tailor of Gloucester*. She redrew ten of the twelve pictures from Freda's manuscript, omitting the one of Simpkin looking through the grating where the rats were holding their party; and for some reason or other she did not use the picture of the tailor sitting cross-legged on the floor, although it was later used in the Warne edition. She also painted six new pictures, making sixteen in all. (See Table 2 at the end of this section.)

Beatrix Potter worked carefully through her text and shortened it in places. Of the rhymes and verses, she shortened a few, deleted four, and added one. The colour blocks were made by Hentschel and the printing undertaken by Strangeways & Sons.

The format was of the same size as that of *The Tale of Peter Rabbit*, and the book was bound in pink paper boards, with a rounded back. On the cover there was a drawing of three little mice making coats. The date 'December 1902' appeared on the title page. The pages were unnumbered.

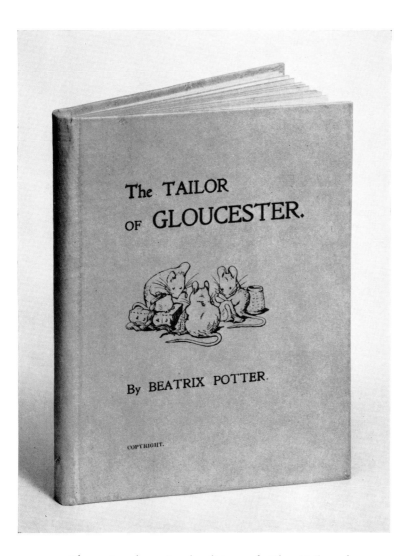

The privately printed edition of *The Tailor of Gloucester*, December 1902

The coachman's boy at Harescombe Grange, Stroud, posing as the tailor

f.

The Tailor of Gloucester: 1902–1903

By the beginning of December all was well in hand, and Beatrix Potter wrote to Norman Warne telling him about it; she also mentioned her squirrel book, which was being planned at the same time.

To Mr. Warne

December 1st 1902   2, Bolton Gardens

Dear Mr. Warne,

I will send you the little mouse-book as soon as it is printed; Hentschels have been very slow. Except the children's rough copy I have not shown it to any one as I was rather afraid people might laugh at the words.

I thought it a very pretty story when I heard it in the country, but it has proved rather beyond my capacity for working out. All the same it is quite possible you may like it better than the squirrels; things look less silly in type—

My opinion is that it is the best of them, but not as good as it ought to be.

I remain,

yrs. sincerely,

Beatrix Potter

By the middle of December the edition of five hundred copies was ready. Two of her father's copies are of interest—one bears the date Dec.18th '02, written on his ordinary book plate; in the other is his professional book plate, bearing the words 'Rupert Potter, Lincoln's Inn' in Gothic lettering. Although he never practised, Rupert Potter had been called to the Bar, and described himself as a barrister. In one of Beatrix Potter's copies of the privately printed *Tailor of Gloucester*, she wrote '500 copies, printed Dec.1902'. Norman Warne's copy was sent on December 17th.

To Mr. Warne

December 17th 1902   2, Bolton Gardens

Dear Mr. Warne,

I send the little book, I hope that at all events you will not think the story very silly. Two of the plates towards the end were intended for near to the beginning.

The colours for some reason seem better by gas light—but if it ever were reprinted I would be strongly inclined to leave out several of the illustrations and put in some new ones, of the cat. Also the words might be more compact.

I remain,

yrs. sincerely,

Beatrix Potter.

I don't think they have processed as well as Peter, but it is my own fault—I used Indian ink rubbed off a stick instead of the ink in bottles, for the outlines.

I undertook the book with very cheerful courage, but I have not the least judgement whether it is satisfactory now that it is done. I am afraid it is going to fall rather flat here—

In due course Norman Warne wrote a letter of thanks, and it appears that Warnes were now thinking seriously of publishing *The Tailor of Gloucester* together with the 'Squirrel' story, as will be gathered from Beatrix Potter's next letter.

To Mr. Warne

December 19th 1902   2, Bolton Gardens

Dear Mr. Warne,

Thank you for your letter about the mouse book; you have paid it the compliment of taking the plot very seriously; and I perceive that your criticisms are just: because I was quite sure in advance that you would cut out the tailor and all my favourite rhymes! Which was one of the reasons why I printed it myself.

I don't mind at all what is done with it in the future; we will see how it goes off this Christmas, and if it is a success it might be improved and reprinted someday. At present it is most in request amongst old ladies.

I will work a bit longer on the squirrel drawings before showing them again, the squirrel is getting tame and I think they will turn out well, it is a great improvement to draw some of them lengthwise.

I think my sympathies are still with the poor old tailor but I can well believe the other would be more likely to appeal to people who are accustomed to a more cheerful Christmas than I am.

With best wishes, believe me
yrs. sincerely,
Beatrix Potter

In describing her privately printed edition to a friend, Beatrix Potter said, 'I find that children of the right age—12—like it best; the smaller ones who could learn off the short sentences of *Peter* find this one too long. It has been a great amusement to me to draw it at all events.' She was amused also at the reaction of Sir J. Vaughan, late police magistrate, to the story, and told Norman Warne, 'He is very funny about the tailor; he says I ought to have punished Simpkin.'

The book was seriously reviewed in an unexpected quarter. We are told by Beatrix Potter, 'I have just been calling on my funny old tailor in Chelsea, and he says he has shown his copy to a traveller from *The Tailor & Cutter*, and he told him about my drawing his shop, and they had put in a *beautiful* review!'

In due course Warnes decided that they would publish both *The Tailor of Gloucester* and *The Tale of Squirrel Nutkin* in 1903, and Beatrix Potter now started to work seriously on the preparation of the Warne edition. As in the case of *The Tale of Peter Rabbit*, she first took one of her privately printed books and used this as a 'Working Copy'. A further two copies were used for 'cut-outs' to save rewriting some of the rhymes in her manuscript. These two copies were marked 'Imperfect'.

The Tailor of Gloucester: 1902–1903

On the title page of her working copy she lightly pencilled a quotation from Shakespeare:

> I'll be at charges for a looking-glass;
> And entertain a score or two of tailors.

> *Richard III*

The first page of text in the privately printed edition contained thirteen lines, and Beatrix Potter indicated by a numbered framework, that there were to be eighteen lines of text on each page of the Warne edition; she also intended the picture facing page 1 to be that of the gentleman and lady dancing—though later, it was used as the frontispiece.

Throughout her working copy there are faint pencil amendments to the text, and inserted between many of the pages are rough pencil sketches of the various pictures, indicating where they were to be placed. Some of the pictures Beatrix Potter did not intend to use again, and these were marked 'out'; she also made pencil notes against some of the paragraphs for which illustrations were needed.

Evidently with some regret, Beatrix Potter crossed through the eight or nine pages of text where she had described in detail how Simpkin wandered through the streets of Gloucester on the night of Christmas Eve, when all the animals were talking, and the carol singers were singing. This is the part of the story which contained the majority of her rhymes and verses—but Warnes had asked for 'cuts'!

Another of the 'cuts' included Beatrix Potter's picture of the rats' party in the Mayor's cellar. Referring to this picture many years later she wrote, 'In the privately printed edition of the Tailor there was a picture of the rats carousing in the cellar under the Mayor of Gloucester's shop—one of them drinking out of a black bottle —For the life of me I could not see why Mr. Warne insisted on cutting it out?'

Beatrix Potter now rewrote the story in a stiff-covered exercise book. She retained nine of the sixteen pictures from her privately printed edition, plus the picture of the little mouse sitting on the bobbin which became the cover picture, and eighteen new pictures were added, making a total of twenty-eight. Most of these may now be seen at the Tate Gallery, London.*

Some of the pictures in Beatrix Potter's manuscript were those she had removed from the previously mentioned privately printed editions, and they were pasted in —several were marked 'to be drawn again'. The remaining pictures, roughly sketched in pencil, were also pasted in, with an occasional word or two of explanation. Thus on the sketch of the tailor leaving his workshop, Beatrix Potter wrote, 'Cloth cut out on the table, tailor going out of door, mice examining the coat—too many mice.' Beneath the picture of the little mouse trying on a waistcoat, No. 15 in

---

* The missing drawings were lost during Beatrix Potter's lifetime.

the privately printed edition, which Beatrix Potter had now transferred to the beginning of the story, she wrote, 'I think I would draw this again better, more in style of the lady mouse—showing the clothes better', but Norman Warne wrote above the picture, 'Why re-draw this, very good. N.D.W.'; so it was not re-drawn! Against another picture, the one of the tailor lifting up the cups on the dresser, Beatrix Potter had written 'To be re-drawn *without* mice, and a more interesting kitchen.'

Only six of her rhymes were included in the Warne edition of *The Tailor of Gloucester*—of these, four appeared in both Freda's manuscript and in the privately printed edition, and of the remaining two, one was taken from each.

In a letter to Warnes on March 27th she wrote, 'I have been delighted to find I may draw some most beautiful 18th. century clothes at the South Kensington Museum. I had been looking at them for a long time in an inconvenient dark corner of the Goldsmith's Court, but had no idea they could be taken out of the case. The clerk says I could have any article put on a table in one of the offices, which will be most convenient'.

Many years later we hear a first-hand account of Beatrix Potter's work at the South Kensington Museum—which is now the Victoria and Albert Museum.

A visitor to Hill Top told the following story to Mrs. Ludbrook: 'When I left school at fourteen my first post was in the South Kensington Museum and Art Gallery which Edmund Potter, Beatrix Potter's grandfather, had helped to found. I was to train as a curator. On my first day there the Head Curator called me to him and said, "You see the young lady just entering the door. She is Miss Potter who writes children's books. I want you to make her your special care." By this time Miss Potter was well into the room.

'He drew me forward to meet her and introduced me to her, saying, "This is my assistant. She is to be your own special attendant. I have arranged a room for your use behind my own office, and given her the key of all the cases. She is to get out for your use anything you desire and when you have finished with it, she will put it back in the case and return the keys to me at the end of the day."

'The first things she asked for were the lovely embroideries which afterwards became the famous drawings in *The Tailor of Gloucester*. She found many more things of interest to her afterwards, but I only remember the drawings which she did from the beautiful embroideries I put out for her from the cases, perhaps because I was able to see them when they appeared in *The Tailor of Gloucester*.'

On April 8th 1903, just before visiting her cousin at Melford Hall, Suffolk, Beatrix Potter informed Norman Warne, 'I hope to do a good deal at the mouse book next week.' And on the 13th, from Melford Hall, 'I have been able to draw an old fashioned fireplace here, very suitable for the tailor's kitchen; I will get on with the book as fast as I can.'

Sketches of the Mayor drawn on the end-papers of one of Beatrix
Potter's privately printed copies of *The Tailor of Gloucester*

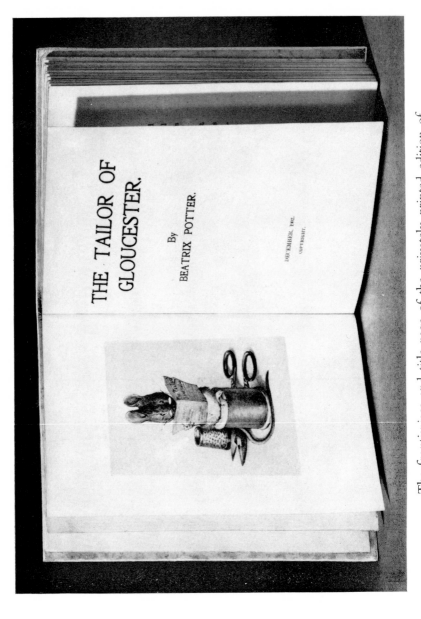

The frontispiece and title page of the privately printed edition of *The Tailor of Gloucester*

Again, this time from 6, West Terrace, Folkestone, on April 23rd she wrote in a postscript, 'I think I have done some rather good drawings for the mouse book but none quite finished yet'; and on April 30th from Folkestone, in another letter to Norman Warne she wrote, 'I only wish I could finish the drawings faster. I can do a good deal here, but shall be travelling again after the end of the week, which is a very vexatious interruption of work. I hope to bring some of them to Bedford Street the end of next week. I have done three quite different of mice, I think I can make the story more clear. I hope you will approve of those I have done. I have got some live mice.'

Beatrix Potter was still travelling, for on May 10th she wrote, 'I am going to meet my brother at the Lakes tomorrow . . . I did not expect to go away again, but I think I may come back Friday—But I will take the mice with me in case he wants to stay longer, so I can get on with them.'

At the end of May she went to stay with Caroline Hutton at Harescombe Grange, and on her return informed Norman Warne, 'I have nine drawings almost finished and I shall be glad to bring them on Thurs. afternoon. I think they may want touching up after you have seen them, but they can be ready by Monday. I wonder if you have a board with 4 mounted on it, including the tailor and the dresser?' And continued, 'I have had an amusing visit to Gloucester last week, I got a good deal of material in the way of sketches.' She also told how the tailor had now found out who did the sewing!

These drawings were evidently discussed and some further work done, for the following week Norman Warne wrote, 'Many thanks for sending down the new originals for *The Tailor of Gloucester*. We will have them put in hand, at once. I think the head of the cat is a good deal improved, also the colouring of the second candle light picture. I am returning herewith the four old originals which we had, and which I understand you wish to re-arrange.'

The third week in June the manuscript was finished and Norman Warne informed Beatrix Potter, 'We have to acknowledge with thanks, receipt of the M.S. of text for *Tailor of Gloucester*, and will have it set up in slip as you suggest.'

The drawings were now practically finished, and on June 25th Beatrix Potter wrote, 'Would it be convenient to you to look at the rest of the mouse drawings on Tuesday morning? . . . They might want touching up, but would be nearly finished.' A few days later she wrote, 'I wish the last drawings had been better; they have come back mounted. I will work on them tomorrow and post them so that you will get them Friday morning. I am quite sorry they are finished.'

Beatrix Potter spent the summer of 1903 at Fawe Park, Keswick, and while she was there an unexpected complication arose about the blocks. She wrote to Warnes immediately about it.

July 31st 1903   Fawe Park, Keswick

Dear Sir,

I think these are very good blocks; but I am much afraid they have cut away my black line round the plates? I am very much vexed if it is so; I think that one of the gateway is entirely spoilt by it. I relied on the line, to make the snow in the foreground look white. It is quite certain to look dirty against a white margin.

It is different when a thing is vignetted, but if there is an edge there ought to be a line, otherwise they look rotten; I asked particularly last winter if the line would be left.

I don't see how it can be remedied, but if there were time to get another of that one of the gateway I would gladly set the cost against one of the old blocks which you are taking over. That one is the most spoilt by it. I am really sorry. It is very unlucky because I think they are good blocks.

I did not notice if they had done it with the last batch, but I am afraid it is not unlikely, as I was very much puzzled why the street looked so different from the old illustration.

The black frame pulls them together and sends back the distance. I have blacked my own outline a bit more in case you think it worth doing again; but it was quite sufficiently black to show originally. The old one of the tailor's shop would be quite ruined if the line were taken away.

yrs. sincerely,

Beatrix Potter

This was Hentschel's fault, and they offered to make a new block of the gateway. Beatrix Potter was greatly relieved, and wrote:

August 9th 1903   2, Bolton Gardens

Dear Sir,

I am much obliged for yours of the 7th. enclosing Messrs Hentschel's. I was thinking afterwards I might rule the lines into my own copies. I hope I have not made too much bother about it. I think it is not unfair to let them make a new plate of the gateway; I only hope it will be as good as the first one.

When I took the first mouse drawings to Fleet Street myself, I asked particularly about having that black line—I did not see the same gentleman that was at your office, an older one, he said nothing whatever about my difficulty.

I think it is rather a lame excuse to apply it to part only of a set of plates—and it is not a bad check upon the register of the printing.

I suppose Mr. Evans won't take it off? I shall be much interested to see the cloth covers. I hope the little books will repay you for all this trouble.

Thanking you very much, I remain,

yrs. sincerely,

Beatrix Potter

In the letter of July 31st Beatrix Potter had referred to the old blocks which Warnes were taking over. These would be the nine three-colour blocks from her privately printed edition. For an unknown reason a new block was made for the picture of the little mouse sitting on a bobbin—to be used for the cover. When discussing the amount Warnes should allow her for the blocks, it is interesting to note that Beatrix Potter reckoned they had cost her £2 3s 9d each.

In due course the blocks were finished, the proofs corrected, and the books printed. Apart from the ordinary binding in paper boards, copies were also bound in a flower-pattern fabric—which is fully dealt with in the section on *The Tale of Squirrel Nutkin.*

It is interesting to recall that during the planning of the book, Beatrix Potter was at one time thinking of having decorations above and below her pictures—and some of these scroll designs were actually pencilled in on the illustrations of one of her privately printed copies. In another privately printed copy she has drawn pencil sketches of the Mayor, and some preliminary designs for her coloured pictorial end-papers.

In a presentation copy of Warne's edition of *The Tailor of Gloucester*, Beatrix Potter wrote in December 1916, 'This is my own favourite amongst my little books.' The *privately printed* edition, however, was the one she liked better, for in a presentation copy given to the late Mrs. H. D. Rawnsley in May 1918, we read, 'This is my favourite amongst the little books and I like this first edition because it contains more of the old rhymes (including the Christmas wedding day) which will serve for mid summer morning.'

Mr. Prichard, the tailor, died in 1934, and his tombstone bears the inscription 'The Tailor of Gloucester'—a fine tribute from the City of Gloucester to the memory of the tailor, and an honour to Beatrix Potter the writer of this children's classic.

Table 1

SCHEDULE OF WATER-COLOURS IN FREDA'S MANUSCRIPT

No.	Picture	Corresponding illustration in Warne's Tailor of Gloucester	
		Page number in earlier editions	*Page number in current editions*
1	He sat in the window of a little shop in Westgate Street	8	8
2	'After Hogarth' A gentleman dancing with his lady	frontispiece	frontispiece
3	The tailor sat down by the hearth	26	20
4	Lady mouse curtseying beside a tea-cup	32	24
5	He lifted up the tea-cup which was upside-down	29	23
6	Simpkin coming in door with the 'pipkin of milk'	41	31
7	Simpkin stood beside the four-post bed	50	36
8	Simpkin wandered about in the snow	56	40
9	The rats danced in the Mayor's cellar	not used	not used
10	Simpkin looks at the rats through a grating in the pavement	not used	not used
11	Simpkin in the snow outside the tailor's shop	59	43
12	Illustration for the rhyme 'Three little mice sat down to spin'	65	47

Table 2

SCHEDULE OF
WATER-COLOURS IN THE PRIVATELY PRINTED EDITION

No.	Picture	Corresponding to water-colour in Freda's M.S.	Corresponding illustration in Warne's Tailor of Gloucester	
			Page number in earlier editions	Page number in current editions
1	Mouse on bobbin reading *The Tailor & Cutter*	—	Cover	Cover
* 2	'After Hogarth' A gentleman dancing with his lady	No. 2	frontispiece	frontispiece
3	The tailor sat down by the hearth	No. 3	26	20
* 4	Lady mouse curtseying beside a tea-cup	No. 4	32	24
5	He lifted up the tea-cup which was upside-down	No. 5	29	23
* 6	Simpkin coming in the door with the 'pipkin of milk'	No. 6	41	31
* 7	Simpkin stood beside the four-post bed	No. 7	50	36
* 8	Simpkin wandered about in the snow	No. 8	56	40
9	The rats danced in the Mayor's cellar	No. 9	not used	not used
*10	Gentleman mouse bowing beside a tea-cup	—	35	27
*11	Simpkin in the snow outside the tailor's shop	No. 11	59	43
12	The little mice sitting upon the kitchen dresser	—	38	28
*13	Illustration for the rhyme 'Three little mice sat down to spin'	No. 12	65	47
14	The tailor came out of his cellar	—	74	52
*15	The mouse trying on a waistcoat	—	11	11
16	The mouse threading a needle, and mice in foreground working on waistcoat	—	47	35

* The blocks from these drawings were used for Warne's edition of *The Tailor of Gloucester*.

THE PRIVATELY PRINTED VERSION OF
THE TAILOR OF GLOUCESTER
(December 1902)

In the time of swords and periwigs and full-skirted coats with flowered lappets—when gentlemen wore ruffles and gold-laced waistcoats lined with padusoy or taffeta—there lived a tailor in Gloucester.

He sat in the window of a little shop in Westgate, cross-legged on a table from morning till dark.

All day long while the light lasted he sewed and he snippeted, piecing out his lutestring, and his silk, called pink persian.

And sometimes he used velvet brocaded with silver: for stuffs had strange names and were very expensive in the days of the Tailor of Gloucester.

Although he sewed fine cloth for his neighbours, he himself was very, very poor—a little old man in spectacles, with a pinched face, old crooked fingers, and a suit of thread-bare clothes.

At night he locked up his shop, and went home to a cellar kitchen. He lived there with his cat. It was called Simpkin.

One day in December the snow-clouds were low over Gloucester; it was cold and nearly dark.

The tailor worked and worked, and talked to himself excitedly. He was cutting out a cherry-coloured coat.

He measured the silk and turned it round and round, and trimmed it into shape with his shears; the table was all littered with cherry-coloured snippets.

'They are too narrow breadths for nought—except waistcoats for mice,' said the Tailor of Gloucester.

When the snow-flakes came down against the small leaded window-panes and shut out the light, the tailor had done his day's work; all the silk and satin lay cut out upon the table.

There were 12 pieces for the coat and 4 pieces for the waistcoat; and there were pocket flaps and lining, and buttons all in order. The gold braid was measured, and the gold and silver thread; everything was ready to sew together in the morning.

Nothing was to want but just one single skein of cherry-coloured twisted silk.

The tailor locked up his shop and shuffled home through the snow, mumbling to himself about the cherry-coloured coat.

He knocked, and his cellar door was opened by Simpkin, who said—

'Miaw?'

The tailor replied—

'Simpkin, we shall make our fortune. Take this groat (which is our last fourpence), and Simpkin, take a china pipkin: buy a penn'orth of milk, a penn'orth of bread, and a penn'orth of sausages. And, O Simpkin, with the last penny of our fourpence buy me one penn'orth of cherry-coloured twist.

'The Mayor of Gloucester is to be married on Christmas Day in the Morning, and he hath ordered a coat and an embroidered waistcoat. We shall make our fortune. But do not lose the last penny of the fourpence, Simpkin, or I am undone and worn to a thread-paper: for I have NO MORE TWIST!'

Then Simpkin said 'Miaw!' and took the groat and the pipkin, and went out into the dark.

The tailor was very tired and beginning to be ill. He sat down by the hearth, and rubbed his poor cold hands, and talked to himself about that wonderful coat:—

'I shall make my fortune—to be cut bias—but alack, I am worn to a ravelling—to be ready by noon of Friday, and this is Monday—to be lined with yellow padusoy—and the padusoy sufficeth; there is no more left over in snippets than will serve to make robings for mice—

'One-and-twenty button-holes of cherry-coloured silk—was I wise to entrust my last penny to Simpkin? Alack, I am undone; for I have no more twist!'

Then the tailor started, for suddenly, interrupting him, from the dresser at the other side of the kitchen came a number of little noises—

Tip tap, tip tap, tip tap tip!

'Now what can that be?' said the Tailor of Gloucester.

The dresser was covered with cracked plates and crockery, pie-dishes and pipkins, and pewter plates and grey-beard mugs.

The tailor crossed the kitchen, and again, from under a tea-cup, came those funny little noises—

Tip tap, tip tap, tip tap tip!

'This is very peculiar,' said the Tailor of Gloucester; and he lifted up the tea-cup which was upside down.

Out stepped a little live lady mouse, and made a curtsey to the tailor!

Then she hopped away down off the dresser, and under the wainscot.

The tailor sat down again by the fire, warming his poor cold hands, and mumbling to himself:—

'The waistcoat is cut out from peach coloured satin, and thread of gold embroidery is worked about the edge—tabby stripes and rosebuds in beautiful floss silk!—

'The braid is cut and measured and the thread of gold suffices—there is no more left over in ravellings than will serve to make hatbands for mice—to be done by noon of Friday, and I shall make my fortune—one-and-twenty button-holes—but —alack! I am undone, for I have no more twist!'

Then all at once from the dresser there came a chorus of little noises, all sounding together, and answering one another, like watch beetles in an old worm-eaten window shutter—Tip tap, tip tap, tip tap tip!

'This is very extraordinary!' said the Tailor of Gloucester.

He lifted two more teacups and a bowl and a basin, and the lid of the teapot and one or two mugs.

Out from under each stepped little live gentlemen mice, and made bows to the tailor! Then they hopped away down off the dresser and under the wainscot.

The tailor sat down again upon his three-legged stool close over the fire, and talked to himself about the Mayor of Gloucester and that cherry-coloured coat.

'The pocket holes are set about with thread of gold and silver, and much of it is laid upon the skirts of the coat—the skirts shall be stiffened with whalebone and horsehair—

'One-and-twenty button-holes of cherry-coloured twist—was I wise to entrust my last fourpence to Simpkin? Alack, I am worn to a shred and a thread-paper! Was it right to let loose those mice, undoubtedly the property of Simpkin? Alack, I am undone, for I have no more twist!'

The cellar door opened and in bounced Simpkin, with an angry 'Miaw ger-r-r-r-ruck!' like a cat which is much vexed.

There was snow in his ears, and snow upon the milk in the pipkin, and snow in his coat, at the back of his neck.

He set down the milk and bread upon the dresser, and looked at the tea-cups, and sniffed.

'Simpkin,' said the tailor, 'where is my twist?'

But Simpkin set down the sausages on a dish upon the dresser; he looked at the tea-pot and took off the lid.

'Simpkin,' said the tailor, 'where is my TWIST?'

But Simpkin slipped a little parcel into the tea-pot, and glared angrily at the tailor.

'Alack, I am undone!' said the Tailor of Gloucester.

All the night long the wind whistled and howled; it drifted the snow-flakes under the door.

And all through the night Simpkin hunted about the kitchen, peeping into cupboards and under the wainscot.

Sometimes he heard queer little tappings in the chimney, and from the top of the dresser, and behind the four-post bed.

And whenever the tailor mumbled and talked in his sleep, Simpkin said:—'Miaw ger-r-r-w-s-s-sch!' and made strange horrid noises, as cats do at nights.

When the sun rose next morning, like a big red ball, the snow was lying deep in all the streets of Gloucester. All the Vale of Severn and the hills on either hand were covered with a great white sheet. In the narrow streets people shovelled and scraped and dug out their door-ways, and the shovels made a cheerful clink! clink! upon the stones.

But nobody came near the little shop in Westgate, where the silk for the Mayor of Gloucester's fine new Christmas clothes lay spread out upon the table.

There were twelve pieces of the coat, and four pieces of the waistcoat; and nobody to sew them!

For the poor old tailor was ill with a fever, tossing and turning upon his four-post bed; and still in his dreams he mumbled: 'No more twist! no more twist!'

All that day he was ill, and the next day, and the next; and what should become of the cherry-coloured coat?

And when the bread should be finished, and the milk in the pipkin, what would become of Simpkin and the tailor?

Out of doors the market folk went trudging through the snow to buy their geese and turkeys, and bake their Christmas pies.

But there would be no Christmas dinner for Simpkin and the poor old Tailor of Gloucester.

Late at night upon Christmas Eve, Simpkin opened the door and came out, and crossed into the shadow over the way. The moon had climbed up over the roofs and chimneys; but there were no lights in the windows, and no sound of talking. All the city of Gloucester was fast asleep.

Up and down, in and out of the moonlight, all over the town went Simpkin, searching in vain for something to eat, and leaving a line of little round pit-pats wherever he went in the snow.

It is very, very silent on a winter night.

But all at once up above his head there was a whirring, buzzing sound, and the Cathedral clock began to strike the chimes; such a merry jangling noise of bells over the snow!

The jackdaws awoke in the tower and all began to shout, and all the cocks in Gloucester crowed together. Although it was the middle of the night, the throstles and robins sang; and before the end of the last echo of the chimes, the air was all full of little twittering music.

From all the roofs and gables and old wooden houses of Gloucester came a thousand little voices, singing the old Christmas rhymes—all the old songs that ever I heard of, and some that I don't know—like Whittington's bells.

Even poor hungry Simpkin sighed, 'Hey diddle diddle!'

For it is in the old story that all the beasts can talk in the night between Christmas Eve and Christmas Day in the Morning. (But there are very few folks that can hear them, or know what they say.)

First and loudest the cocks sang out:—

'Dame get up and bake your pies,
Bake your pies! bake your pies!
Dame get up and bake your pies
On Christmas Day in the morning.'

'Cock-a-doodle-doo!' shouted the cocks

'Oh, dilly! dilly! dilly! come and be killed!' sighed the hungry Simpkin.

And a little turnspit dog in a kitchen overheard him, and sang:—

'When she got there, the cupboard was bare!' and it looked up at the moon and laughed until it cried.

The icicles sparkled, and the sign-boards and carved gables of the houses showed clear like daylight; and everywhere the merry voices sang.

But Simpkin did not sing; he was too cold.

He wandered up and down in the snow.

And now there were lights and the sound of a fiddle in the garrets over the inn:—

'Fiddle, fiddle, fiddle
    Went the fiddlers three,
Fiddle, fiddle, fiddle, fiddle, fee!
    Oh, there's none so rare
    As can compare
With King Cole and his fiddlers three!'

'Hey, diddle, diddle, the cat and the fiddle! All the cats in Gloucester, except me,' sighed Simpkin.

In the stables the fat horses moved about in their stalls, and jingled the chains and rings.

'John Smith, fellow fine!
Can you shoe this horse of mine?'
'Yes, sir, that I can,
As well as any man!
Here a nail and here a prod,
Now the horse is well shod!'

'Ride a cock-horse to Banbury Cross!' grumbled Simpkin.

In the cellars under the Mayor of Gloucester's shop there was a fine racket! The rats were holding holiday, and dancing the heys, in and out amongst the casks and barrels. (For the Mayor was a grocer, at the sign of the Golden Candle).

Thumpetty thumpetty bump, danced the rats, and sang this ancient ditty of 'Uncle Rottan'. They were old English black rats: the brown rats had not come from Norway, in the days of cherry-coloured coats.

Simpkin listened, with his ear against the trap-door of the cellar.

> 'When he came to the merry mill-pin,
> Lady mouse are you therein?
>   Kitty alone, Kitty alone!

> 'Then out came the dousty mouse,
> I'm my lady of this house,
>   Softly do I sit and spin—'

> 'What shall we have to our supper?
> Three beans and one pound of butter—'

Simpkin grinned and listened.

> 'Lord Rottan sat at head o'th' table,
> Because he was both stout and able—'

'Mew, mew!' cried Simpkin very loud at the trap-door, and there was an interruption and the sound of broken bottles.

Then the rude squeaky voice began again close to his ear, on the other side of the boards:—

> 'Then did come in Gib our cat,
> With a fiddle on his back,
> Want you any music here?'

'Ger-r-r-miaw!' cried Simpkin, who could not bear it any longer, and came away. But all the rats sang at the top of their voices:—

> 'And he ate up all the good roast beef,
> The good roast beef,
>   The good roast beef,
> And he ate up all the good fat tripe,
>   The good fat tripe,
>   The good fat tripe,
> And his name was Aikin Drum;
> And he played upon a ladle,
> With a fi-fee-feedle-fum!'

Then Simpkin hurried away out of hearing of that disreputable company in the Mayor of Gloucester's cellar.

He went up the street in the moonlight, and listened to some much prettier singing, for the air was quite full of little twittering tunes. Under the wooden eaves the sparrows sang in their sleep:—

'Intery, mintery, cuttery corn!
Apple seed and apple thorn!'

And then they sang another song:—

'Little Poll Parrot
Sat in a garret
Eating toast and tea!
A little brown mouse
Jumped into the house,
And stole it all away!'

Another little voice chirped from over the way:—

'Upstairs and downstairs,
Upon my lady's window,
There I saw a cup of sack,
And a race of ginger!'

The starlings in the chimney stacks sang about Christmas pies and Little Jack Horner.

But a robin sang the prettiest song of all:—

'I had a little nut-tree,
Nothing would it bear
But a golden nutmeg,
And a silver pear.

'The King of Spain's daughter
Came to visit me,
And all for the sake
Of my little nut-tree!

'I skipp'd over water, I danced over sea,
And all the birds in the air couldn't catch me.'

And then they all sang at once from both sides of the street—

'Once I saw a little bird come hop, hop, hop!
So I cried: Little bird, will you stop, stop, stop?
And was going to the window
To say, How do you do?
But he shook his little tail
And away he flew.'

But is was all rather provoking to poor hungry Simpkin.

Particularly he was vexed with some little, little shrill voices from behind a wooden lattice. I think that they were bats, because they always have very small voices—especially in a black frost, when they talk in their sleep, like the Tailor of Gloucester. They said something mysterious that sounded like—

> 'Buz, quoth the blue fly; hum quoth the bee;
> Buz and hum they cry, and so do we!'

And Simpkin went away shaking his ears, as if he had a bee in his bonnet.

From the tailor's little shop in Westgate came a glow of light; when Simpkin crept up to peep in at the window it was full of candles.

There was a snippeting of scissors, and click of thimbles, and snappeting of thread.

And little mouse voices sang loudly and gaily—

> 'Four-and-twenty tailors
>   Went to catch a snail,
> The best man amongst them
> Durst not touch her tail;
> She put out her horns
> Like a little kyloe cow,
> Run, tailors, run! or she'll have you all e'en now!'

Then without a pause the little mouse voices went on again—

> 'Sieve my lady's oatmeal,
>   Grind my lady's flour
> Put it in a chestnut,
> Let it stand an hour—'

'Mew! mew!' interrupted Simpkin. The little merry voices tried another tune—

> 'Can you make me a cambric shirt,
> —Parsley, sage, rosemary and thyme—
> Without any seam or needlework?
> —And you shall be a true lover of mine?'

'G-g-r-r-r-miaw!' cried the exasperated Simpkin under the door; but the little mice only laughed—

> 'And then I bought
> A pipkin and a popkin,
> A slipkin and a slopkin,
> All for one farthing—

'And upon the kitchen dresser!' added the rude little voices.

'Mew! mew!' cried Simpkin at the key-hole.

'Hey diddle dinketty,' cried the little mouse voices.

'Hey diddle dinketty, poppetty pet!

The merchants of London they wear scarlet;

Silk in the collar, and gold in the hem,

So merrily march the merchantmen!'

'Mew! mew!' said Simpkin.

'Hark! hark!' answered the little mice—

> 'Hark! hark! the dogs do bark,
>
> The beggars have come to town,
>
> Some in tags and some in rags,
>
> And one in a velvet gown!'

They clicked their thimbles to mark the time, but none of the songs pleased Simpkin; he sniffed and mewed at the door of the shop.

But the key was under the tailor's pillow.

The little mice tittered and began again—

> 'Jack Sprat had a cat,
>
> It had but one ear;
>
> It went to buy butter
>
> When butter was dear!'

'Miaw!' scratch, scratch, scuffled Simpkin, jumping on to the window-sill, while the little mice inside sprang to their feet and sang together—

> 'Three little mice sat down to spin,
>
> Pussy passed by and she peeped in.
>
> What are you at, my fine little men?
>
> Making coats for gentlemen.
>
> Shall I come in and cut off your threads?
>
> Oh no! Miss Pussy, you'd bite off our heads!'

And then they all began to shout at once in little twittering voices—'No more twist! no more twist!' and they barred up the window shutters and shut out Simpkin.

But still through the nicks in the shutters he could hear the click of thimbles, and the little mouse voices singing: 'No more twist! no more twist!'

Simpkin came away home to the cellar, considering thoughtfully in his mind.

When he opened the door and went in he heard the poor old tailor snoring quite peacefully; he was fast asleep!

Then Simpkin went on tip-toe to the kitchen dresser, and took a little parcel out of the tea-pot, and looked at it in the moonlight.

When the tailor awoke in the morning, the first thing he saw upon the patchwork quilt was a skein of cherry-coloured twisted silk, and beside his bed stood the repentant Simpkin with a cup of tea!

'Alack, I am worn to a ravelling,' said the Tailor of Gloucester, 'but I have my twist!'

Out of doors the sun was shining on the snow. The tailor came out of his cellar, and hobbled along on the sunny side of the way, and Simpkin ran before him.

The starlings whistled on the chimney stacks, and the robins and throstles sang in the gardens—but they sang their own little noises, not the words they had sung in the night.

But the carol singers had come out again; for folks seem to have sung at all manner of times in the days of cherry-coloured coats.

And this is what they were singing:—

> 'I saw three ships come sailing by,
>   Sailing by, sailing by;
> I saw three ships come sailing by
>   On Christmas Day in the morning.
>
> 'And who do you think were in them then,
>   In them then, in them then?
> And who do you think were in them then,
>   On Christmas Day in the morning?
>
> 'Three pretty maids were in them then,
>   In them then, in them then;
> Three pretty maids were in them then,
>   On Christmas Day in the morning.
>
> 'And one could whistle, and one could sing,
>   And one could play on the violin;
> Such joy was at my wedding,
>   On Christmas Day in the morning!'

'Alack,' said the tailor, 'I have my twist; but no more strength—nor time—than will serve to make me one single button-hole, and this is Christmas Day in the morning! The Mayor of Gloucester shall be married this day, and where is his cherry-coloured coat?'

He fitted the key into the lock with a shaky hand, and Simpkin ran into the shop before him, like a cat that expects something.

But there was no one there! The boards were swept and clean; the pins were all picked up and stuck into the pin-cushion; the little ends of thread and the little silk snippets were all tidied away, and gone from off the floor.

But upon the table—oh, joy! the tailor gave a shout. There, where he had left plain cuttings of silk—there lay the most beautifullest coat and gold-brocaded waistcoat that ever were worn by a Mayor of Gloucester!

There was embroidery upon the cuffs and pocket flaps, and upon the skirts of the coat; it was cherry-coloured corded silk, lined with yellow padusoy; and there were one-and-twenty buttons.

The waistcoat was of peach-coloured satin, worked with rosebuds, and thread of gold and silver. Everything was finished except just one single cherry-coloured button-hole!

And where that button-hole was wanting there was pinned a little scrap of paper, and upon it were these words—in little teeny weeny writing:—

No more twist.

And from then began the luck of the Tailor of Gloucester; he grew quite stout, and he grew quite rich. He made the most wonderful waistcoats for all the rich merchants of Gloucester, and for all the fine gentlemen of the country round.

Never were seen such lappets, such cuffs, and such tabby silks and rosebuds! But his button-holes were the greatest triumph of all!

The stitches of those button-holes were so neat—*so* neat—I wonder how they could be stitched by a little old man in spectacles, with old crooked fingers, and a tailor's thimble.

The stitches of those button-holes were so small—*so* small—they looked as if they had been made by little mice.

Picture letter to Freda (spelt 'Frida') Moore

Harescombe Grange.
Nov 3ʳᵈ 97

My dear Frida,

I must tell you a funny thing about the guinea-hens here. You know what they are like, I daresay, grey speckled birds with very small silly heads. One day Parton, the coachman, saw them in the field, running backwards and forwards, bobbing their heads up (They say Pot Rack! Pot Rack! Pot Rack! Rack! 7 down 7 cackling. They were watching something white, which was waving about in the long grass. Parton could not tell what it was either so he went close up to it, 7 up jumped a

fox! It had been lying on its back
waving its tail.

I heard of another fox when I was at
Woodcote, which had gone to the
gamekeeper's & killed 4 hens & then
went to sleep in
the pig stye with
the pig. The
gamekeeper was so cross, he said the
people who had the foxhounds had let
loose some tame foxes, & they would not
stay in the woods. He ran for a gun but
mr Fox woke up.
yrs aff.
Beatrix Potter.

The Tale of Squirrel Nutkin
1903

In the summer of 1897 when staying at Lingholm, Beatrix Potter wrote a picture letter to Noel Moore telling him, 'There is an American story that squirrels go down the rivers on little rafts using their tails for sails, but I think the Keswick Squirrels must swim.'* And on September 25th 1901, also from Lingholm, she sent a picture letter to Norah Moore, telling her all about Squirrel Nutkin's adventures. This letter is illustrated by twelve pen-and-ink sketches, and we see the squirrels on their little rafts sailing across the lake to Owl Island, bringing presents to Old Brown.

Beatrix Potter was familiar with the beautiful Cumberland scenery around Derwentwater, for between 1885 and 1903 she had spent no less than six summers at Lingholm and one at Fawe Park, both of them near Keswick on the shore of Derwentwater. It was this Lakeland scenery that she used as background for *The Tale of Squirrel Nutkin*, where the little red squirrels frequented the wooded shore of the lake.

During the summer of 1901, in one of her sketch-books, Beatrix Potter painted pictures of Derwentwater and St. Herbert's Island, and of the wooded foreshore of the lake, some of which she used as backgrounds for *The Tale of Squirrel Nutkin*: Owl Island was, in fact, St. Herbert's Island. Another sketch-book of the same period is half filled with paintings of squirrels—entirely in brush-work. She also photographed one of the fine old oaks in the woods, and on the back of the print wrote, 'Old Brown's Oak, Lingholm, Derwentwater'.

By the beginning of 1902 the Warne edition of *The Tale of Peter Rabbit* and Beatrix Potter's privately printed edition of *The Tailor of Gloucester* were well in hand, so she began work on *The Tale of Squirrel Nutkin*.

The picture letter she had sent to Norah was borrowed and copied out on sheets of note-paper. This was marked '1st. Copy', but it was far more than a copy, for in the process of rewriting, Beatrix Potter had made extensive revisions to the text, shortening it in some places and lengthening it in others. She was still not satisfied with her revision, and we find small strips of paper pasted over the parts she wished to alter, with further revision to the text.

She then prepared a second draft, taking her first copy, and again rewriting it and amending the text. This time it was written in a paper-covered exercise book,

---

* Beatrix Potter was evidently referring to one of the stories by Mrs. Catherine Trail (Strickland), 1802–1899, of wildlife in the Canadian Forest, in which she tells of squirrels crossing the water on pieces of bark, using their tails as sails. See *Lady Mary and her nurse, or A peep into the Canadian Forest*, London, Arthur Hall, Virtue & Co. 1856.

with twenty-six rough sketches pasted in by their corners. In due course Warnes agreed to publish the story.

On two occasions Beatrix Potter put *herself* into her book pictures—once in *The Roly-Poly Pudding,* and once in *The Tale of Pigling Bland.* It is interesting to note that in the second picture in Norah's story letter, she has again drawn herself, this time beneath a tree, with Nutkin throwing acorns on her head, and the text in the second draft reads, 'I saw one most comical little squirrel; his tail was only about an inch long; but he was *so* impertinent, chattering and clattering and throwing down acorns onto my head'.

Beatrix Potter later deleted the first two pages of text, which included this reference to herself, and wrote a new beginning: 'Once upon a time there was a little red squirrel and his name was Nutkin . . .' Then a new idea came to her, and we find the following pencil note underneath: '? This is the Tale of a tail—a tail that belonged to a little red squirrel.' So the beginning of the story was gradually taking shape! Beatrix Potter always attached importance to her beginnings and endings. Another last-minute alteration was to change one of Old Brown's presents —from a pie containing four-and-twenty blackbirds, to a 'new-laid egg in a rush basket'. Against the picture of the pie she wrote, '? an egg instead'.

After receiving the manuscript, Norman Warne evidently suggested some 'cuts' and minor alterations, for in Beatrix Potter's letter of November 6th she wrote, 'I agree with you about the words of the squirrel book, it wants some leaving out and some dividing'; and again, in her letter of November 22nd from the home of her cousin at Melford Hall, Suffolk, 'The words of the squirrel book will need cutting down, to judge by the children here; I have got several good hints about the words —I only hope the gamekeeper will succeed in getting a squirrel before I leave on Monday. I did not find my friend's squirrels at all right when I tried to draw them.'

Apparently the gamekeeper was not able to procure a squirrel, for on January 17th 1903, in a letter to a friend, Beatrix Potter told her, 'I am trying to make a squirrel book at present, I have got a very pretty little model; I bought two but they weren't a pair, and fought so frightfully that I had to get rid of the handsomer —and most savage one—The other squirrel is rather a nice little animal, but half of one ear has been bitten off, which spoils his appearance!' She had evidently bought the squirrels soon after her return from Melford Hall, for on December 19th the drawings were well in hand, and she told Norman Warne, 'I will work a bit longer on the squirrel drawings before showing them again, the squirrel is getting tame and I think they will turn out well.'

On February 5th before leaving London for a visit to her uncle Burton's at Gwaynynog, Denbigh in North Wales, Beatrix Potter sent Norman Warne her proposed drawing for the cover—a picture of Nutkin dancing. 'I have done this in rather a hurry, if you think it requires more finish please send it to me at Denbigh. I thought it had better be strong and distinct for the cover.' Norman Warne liked the picture, but suggested that it should be contained in a circle. In replying, Beatrix Potter agreed with him: 'I will alter the squirrel, the circle is a good idea'; so she painted a new picture, saying in her letter, 'I enclose the drawing for the cover of Squirrel book. I hope it is more suitable. I have shortened the tail to get it inside the circle'.

By the end of March the drawings for *The Tale of Squirrel Nutkin* were almost finished—except that Beatrix Potter wished to do a little more work on the owls: 'I thought my owls very bad when I went again to the Zoological Gardens,' she said. A few days later, when sending Norman Warne the design for the title page, she wrote, 'I enclose the drawing for the title page. I brought the other drawings, but forgot to give them to you, so I will do a little more work on the owl and bring them with the patterns'—the patterns were of cover material for some special bindings.

In her next letter she told him, 'I have drawn No. 25 again, I could not get the owl right, and I thought we had rather too many from the same position, and this would be a variety.' Some weeks later she was still not satisfied with the owl drawing and wrote, 'I am going to meet my brother at the Lakes . . . I think *he* could very likely improve that owl, it is not worth a new block in its present form.' The drawings were finally finished and the rest of the blocks made.

It was the spring of 1903 when the question of special end-papers was first thought of. It occurred to Beatrix Potter, or possibly Warnes, that she might design some special pictorial end-papers for her books—on which the animal characters could appear.

There is reference to these end-papers in a letter to Norman Warne dated March 5th 1903, which reads: 'I have not made out an end-paper yet, so I will call again.' Beatrix Potter seems to have been in doubt as to whether Warnes preferred the end-papers to be black and white or coloured, for in her letter of March 20th she writes, 'I have got into a perplexity about the end-paper; those we looked at were all *line* blocks, but if Mr. Warne wants it to go through the press with the others —does he mean 3 colour blocks? Perhaps a line block could be printed once with one colour only, along with the others? I will do whatever sort you wish but one ought to know, because it is useless to do anything in fine pen and ink for half tone process; it cuts up the line, and there would be the tone all over the paper. I think you must have meant a line block.'

Apart from some preliminary end-paper designs, both coloured and uncoloured, which were roughly sketched out in one of the privately printed copies of *The Tailor of Gloucester*, the first design which Beatrix Potter submitted to Warnes was a pen-and-ink drawing for a line block. In composition it was similar to the end-papers of today, except that characters from only three books were included. It was finally decided, however, that the new end-papers should be coloured.

Beatrix Potter agreed to prepare a coloured end-paper design, though not without some misgivings. Her views are expressed in a letter to Warnes, dated March 21st 1903: 'I think if the design were for a cover or title page occurring once, it is very good. I am only afraid that when fully coloured and repeated four times it may look rather heavy for so small a book. I always think that an end-paper ought to be something to rest the eye between the cover and the contents of the book, like a plain mount for a framed drawing. At the same time (having let off my objections)—I daresay it will come out all right . . . I think if it were kept rather small or rather light coloured, it would look very nice.'

The coloured end-paper which Beatrix Potter then prepared was of the same composition as her line drawing, and the colouring was light and delicate. It was finished in a week, and on March 27th she wrote, 'I will call on Monday afternoon and bring the end-paper.'

The introduction of coloured end-papers presented no problems in the case of *The Tale of Squirrel Nutkin* and *The Tailor of Gloucester*, as these books had not yet been published, and the number of illustrations to be included could be chosen to suit the printing arrangement; but in the case of *The Tale of Peter Rabbit*, which had already been published—it meant that to retain the same printing arrangement, four of the original pictures would have to come out to make room for the new coloured end-papers. This was done in the fifth and in all subsequent printings of *The Tale of Peter Rabbit*.

In writing about these end-papers towards the end of her life, Beatrix Potter tells us, 'Squirrel Nutkin and Tailor of Gloucester 1903 had the end-paper of animals, for the first time—it was one page-of-design only—and was repeated 4 times=2 at the first opening and 2 at the end.' She also recalled that 'After Peter, the books mainly came out in pairs—Thus—Tailor of Gloucester and Squirrel Nutkin 1st. edition end-papers show Nutkin and a tailor [the tailor did not appear on the end-papers] as well as Peter. Next year the three were joined by the next pair of books+Two Bad Mice and Benjamin Bunny. Mrs. Tiggy joined them early on, but she was concealing the title of her book, until it was published.'

Beatrix Potter was also concerned with the styles of binding, and it appears that Warnes tentatively suggested the use of brocade for a de-luxe edition. Her grandfather's firm, Edmund Potter & Co. of Dinting Vale, Manchester, were one of the largest calico printers in Europe, and she felt certain that they would be able to offer some suitable patterns of brocade for these book covers. On March 12th 1903, Beatrix Potter sent Warnes some samples and wrote, 'I have been thinking

Beatrix Potter's fifth design in her series of coloured pictorial end-papers. It was first used in 1908, and Tom Kitten from her 1907 book was included amongst the animal characters

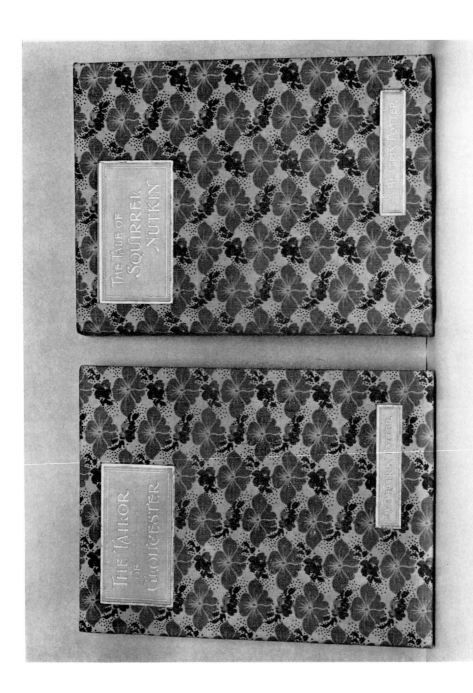

Two books bound in art fabric. The material came from Beatrix Potter's grandfather's printworks at Manchester. *The Tailor of Gloucester* and *The Tale of Squirrel Nutkin* were the only two titles bound in

about your mentioning brocade. I thought last year there was not sufficient difference between the two styles of bindings—that if the cloth binding had been more distinctly different, and pretty, there might have been more inducement to buy it. The difficulty would be to get the lettering to show on a fancy cloth. I don't mean to suggest that any of enclosed are suitable; I have a great quantity of samples but they are possibly out of stock, not having been to Manchester lately, but I should be amused to get another new bundle from the warehouse, if any chance of suiting. If they had any *pattern* suitable there would of course be no difficulty in getting E. Potter & Co. to print in any desired shade of colour or cloth . . . Perhaps you would keep the samples till I call again.'

Beatrix Potter was right—there had not been a great deal of difference between the two styles of binding for the first edition of *The Tale of Peter Rabbit*. The cloth binding had a picture and brown lettering on the cover, and it was not until 1904 that gold lettering and decorations appeared on the cloth covers.

On April 3rd Beatrix Potter informed Warnes, 'I had some extremely pretty patterns, but all very light coloured. I have written for a few more and hope to have them by Monday—The letter seems very obliging, but there are some questions I cannot answer. I thought I would bring all the patterns together, I shall be interested to hear if you like them.' She wrote again the following day: 'As the other patterns have not come yet and we are rather busy, I am sending these by post instead of calling—I am afraid the flowers are rather too wide apart in most of these except in the stripes which I don't much admire. I am sure that any colours which were guaranteed fast, would be reliable. The print which was used for a wall paper is as fresh as when first put up; and I have had many others exposed to the light for years.'

In due course the additional patterns to which Beatrix Potter had referred, arrived, but as she said, 'They are certainly less suitable than the old fashioned "Swiss" patterns and more expensive.' After receiving so many samples, she was now getting a little embarrassed since none of these appeared entirely suitable. She was about to pay a visit to Melford Hall, so she wrote to Warnes asking for some of the smaller patterns to be sent on to her there: 'I should be much obliged if you would post the small ones, which I have marked, *to me this week end* c/o Lady Hyde-Parker, Melford Hall, Long Melford, Suffolk, as I want to show them to her. I think I will probably get a piece for myself, which would be a way out of the difficulty, if it does not really seem suitable for the books . . .

'P.S. I cannot help thinking they must have some old "sprigs", if I happened to go to Manchester.'

When looking through the samples once more, Beatrix Potter came across one she liked, and on April 13th wrote to Warnes again saying, 'I am posting back the patterns to Bedford Street. I had overlooked those in the small packet, they are rather quaint, especially one like pansies.' It was this flower-pattern art fabric with the pansy design which was eventually chosen for the de-luxe bindings of *The Tale of Squirrel Nutkin* and *The Tailor of Gloucester*, both of which were first published in 1903. Beatrix Potter referred to these books as 'bound in a flowered lavender chintz, very pretty'.

As it was not practicable to print directly on to the art fabric, the title and author's name, which appeared on the cover, were printed in gold lettering on small panels of white vellum—there was no lettering on the spine.

The first proofs of the text of *The Tale of Squirrel Nutkin* arrived at the beginning of May. After examining these Beatrix Potter replied, 'Do you really wish to put in all those Mr's? Perhaps they strike me as being out of place because we had an aversion to the original (who was *not* an owl) and we always called him "Old Brown". The squirrels should address him as "Old Mr. Brown" to show extra politeness and it makes a change occasionally. I am afraid the page describing the tragedy will have to be altered because I altered the drawing. Except that very awkward looking division of Twinkleberry, I think the pages look well—very much better than I expected; I do hope the blocks will come out all right, I think it might make a nice little book.'

When correcting the proofs she pointed out, 'I have only written in pencil not being very certain how to do it, and also you may not approve of them . . .

'P.S. I think that division of Twinkleberry is rather unfortunate, the first time the name occurs in the book.' Warnes accepted this criticism and reset the type to avoid a hyphen in Twinkleberry.

Proofs of the blocks were soon to follow. In anticipation of these, Beatrix Potter had written, 'If the first proofs of the squirrel blocks are as bad as the first proofs of the mice were—they would be a shock.—I expect Mr. Evans will make quite a different job of it, as he did with the rabbits.' Although Hentschels produced excellent blocks, when it came to the prints, Beatrix Potter much preferred Mr. Evans's work. On May 10th commenting on Hentschel's first set of proofs, she wrote, 'I notice one page of proofs is *all* too green, another *all* too red, etc., so I think it is clearly the printer's fault. The blocks seem very fine in themselves and register all right.'

Two more sets of proofs arrived within the next fortnight; also some of her original drawings were returned. In acknowledging the first set, Beatrix Potter wrote, 'I received the drawings safely yesterday at Portinscale; I will make a new one of the owl, and go over the proofs carefully. The blocks are evidently capable of giving very good results; I don't like Hentschel's yellows and blues; but as they will not be doing the final printing, I should think there is not much object in complaining about their colours.'

Commenting on the second set of proofs, she informed Warnes, 'I like the blocks very much on looking them over carefully. I cannot help thinking that some of your criticism is directed against their disagreeable heavy blue. I don't think the backgrounds will be too dark with Mr. Evans' printing.'

The Squirrel Nutkin story was originally written for Norah Moore, and Beatrix Potter had just realized that the child's name did not appear anywhere in the book. Hoping it would not be too late, she drew attention to this fact: 'I have been a little sorry about one thing in the squirrel book; you said you thought there might be room to put in the child's name, but I entirely forgot when I looked over the proofs; perhaps there may be another edition some day. I remember there was a page with nothing but the title—I would have put, "The Tale of Squirrel Nutkin—a story for Norah", but it is my fault altogether. I quite forgot about it. I hope I have not made too many alterations.' However, it was not too late, and the dedication to Norah *was* included.

On June 8th Norman Warne informed Beatrix Potter, 'We are in receipt this morning, of the three new blocks for "Nutkin". I shall be glad if you will kindly go over these and suggest where lights are to be added. I do not think they are very good proofs, but I have no doubt Mr. Evans will be able to bring them up much better when we finally go to press. The proofs of the new end-paper block have not yet come to hand, but we will send them on as soon as they arrive.' Two days later the proofs of the end-paper block arrived, and Beatrix Potter was informed, 'The balance of the blocks with printed proofs have now been delivered so that we shall be able to start Mr. Evans to press as soon as we get this and the proofs returned by you yesterday.'

On June 22nd she was told, 'We hope to get the "*Nutkin*" book to press at the end of this week, so that you will probably be able to see perfect copies before you go away. We shall not be able to publish just yet awhile, as in order to secure the American copyright of the text, we must publish simultaneously with our American house, and they cannot possibly be ready till about three weeks after the edition is printed here.'

A month later, although they were not yet in the shops, Beatrix Potter received some advance copies of *The Tale of Squirrel Nutkin*, and in her reply she wrote, 'I am delighted with the copies of the squirrels which you have sent me. Mr. Evans' printing is very much better than Hentschel's . . . I like the grey binding, but they are both very pretty papers.'

The Tale of Squirrel Nutkin was an immediate success, and on August 30th Beatrix Potter wrote to Warnes saying, 'I am *delighted* to hear such a good account of Nutkin. I never thought when I was drawing it that it would be such a success—though I think you always had a good opinion of it. I should be glad to have a few more copies when convenient; it must be a troublesome business to distribute ten thousand.'

By September 1903 Beatrix Potter was beginning to receive letters of appreciation, and she wrote to Norman Warne telling him, 'I have had such comical letters from children about "Scell nuskin"—it seems an impossible word to spell; but they say they have "red" it right through and that it is "lovely"—which is satisfactory. I shall always have a strong preference for cheap books myself—even if they do not pay; all my little friends happen to be shilling people.'

Squirrel Nutkin's wood on the shore of Derwentwater

Enid Linder

Distant view of St. Herbert's Island, Derwentwater, where Old Brown lived

Enid Linder

Background study for *The Tale of Benjamin Bunny*
In the finished picture, old Mr. Benjamin Bunny is seen
'prancing along the top of the wall of the upper terrace
. . . smoking a pipe of rabbit-tobacco'

Background study for *The Tale of Benjamin Bunny*
The finished picture is of the cat who 'stretched herself, and
came and sniffed at the basket'

The Tale of Benjamin Bunny
1904

Beatrix Potter's books were now selling so well that it is not surprising to find Warnes asking for another story. Beatrix Potter wrote to them on July 8th 1903, saying, 'I had been a little hoping too that something might be said about another book, but I did not know that I was the right person to make the suggestion! I could send you a list to consider. There are plenty in a vague state of existence, and one written out in a small copy book which I will get back from the children and send to you to read', continuing 'I had better try to sketch this summer, as the stock of ideas for backgrounds is rather used up. I would very much like to do another next winter. I sometimes feel afraid that the Tailor and Nutkin are rather too ingenious and complicated compared with Peter Rabbit. Don't you think the next one ought to be more simple?'

A week later the Potters left London for Fawe Park, near Keswick, where they spent the summer of 1903. Fawe Park was a large country house overlooking Derwentwater, with a beautiful garden on the edge of the lake, which was ideal for sketching.

Just before she left Beatrix Potter wrote to Warnes telling them, 'I will make out a rough outline of the stories I know, and post it to you from Fawe Park, Keswick. I should not propose to work on any story while away, but if I knew what was likely to be chosen it would be a guide for sketching.' Soon after her arrival she wrote again: 'I think I will send the rabbit story as well when I have copied it out, perhaps Mr. Norman Warne might be amused to look over it when he comes back.'

'The Tale of Little Benjamin Bunny' as it was then called, was in a more advanced state than the other stories which she had referred to as being 'in a vague state of existence'. It was a continuation of the adventures of Peter. Now joined by his cousin Benjamin, Peter set out to recover his lost clothes from the scarecrow in Mr. McGregor's garden, having many adventures in the process. The principal character was named after Beatrix Potter's pet rabbit Benjamin, the forerunner of Peter.

Norman Warne had evidently chosen the rabbit story, for a few weeks later Beatrix Potter informed him that she was making good progress with the drawings, and on August 27th she wrote, 'I have drawn a good many sketches for backgrounds of rabbits already which is perhaps as well, as the rain has come here at last.'

On the whole, though, it had been a fine summer and she had been able to work industriously on her Benjamin Bunny backgrounds. Just before leaving Fawe Park, she wrote, 'We are going home the end of next week; it has been so fine I am half sorry; three months is always more than enough, but autumn is far away the best time at the Lakes . . . I think I have done every imaginable rabbit background and miscellaneous sketches as well—about seventy! I hope you will like them, though rather scribbled. I had a funny instance of rabbit ferocity last night. I had been playing with the ferret, and then with the rabbit without washing my hands. She, the rabbit, is generally a most affectionate little animal but she simply flew at me, biting my wrist all over before I could fasten the hutch. Our friendship is at present restored with scented soap!'

The majority of Beatrix Potter's backgrounds were paintings of the garden at Fawe Park. There was one of the pear tree from which Peter fell head first; one of the bed of lettuces which 'certainly were very fine' and we are told were 'Suttons Perfection'; a view of the little walk 'under a sunny red-brick wall'; and several drawings of the basket on which the cat sat for *five hours*, (*six hours* in the manuscript!). Also, there were various studies of plants, including onions, and even one of the earth on a flower-bed where she painted 'a great many odd little foot-marks all over the bed'. She had also half filled a small sketch-book with water-colours of the garden. In another sketch-book of the same period, there were paintings of cats—entirely in brush-work.

Back in London she settled down for the winter months to work on her new book. At first the drawings did not go as well as she hoped, for on November 6th we find her telling Warnes, 'I am afraid I am not making a good start yet with the rabbit book. I have been rather bothered but I hope it will come right; when will Mr. Norman Warne be coming back? and able to look over it.'

By the middle of February 1904, however, Beatrix Potter informed Norman Warne, 'I have nearly finished B. Bunny except the cat', and again at the end of March, 'I hope to send you the remaining rabbit drawings next week.' In her letter of April 6th she referred to these remaining drawings: 'There are eight more drawings, so there were twenty last time. One of these is not finished after all—the old rabbit jumping, unless I can do it before breakfast tomorrow. I thought I would post them all in case any others want altering—my address for a fortnight from tomorrow is Burley, Lyme Regis, Dorset. I am sorry to have not quite finished them but could let you have them by Monday morning, if you post them back to Lyme Regis at once. I don't know whether you will like the little rabbit for the cover? Is it good enough?'

When writing to Warnes from Lyme Regis, she referred to some redrawing which they had apparently asked her to do: 'I agree with all your comments— including the "*troublesome*!"—But I am only joking, it is much better to try to get them right. I think the snapdragon is much better for toning down and I have made those rabbits larger. The worst of copying drawings a second time is that I get so confused I don't know whether they are worse or better. Please don't hesitate to send them back if they are still wrong . . . There is a splendid view from this little house. It is at the top of the steep street and has a nice sunny garden. I have been able to sit on the verandah, so those "troublesome" rabbits have not kept me indoors. The weather has been delightful, quite hot in the sun. No. 6 is the one I am most doubtful about, the little rabbits have not much expression.'

In the drawing where 'the cat got up and stretched herself and came and sniffed at the basket', the cat had such an exceedingly large tail, that the accuracy of the drawing was questioned. In a letter to Warnes Beatrix Potter informed them, 'I was asked to pass a message to the publisher about the *tail* of the cat. Its owner wants you to be assured that the real tail is even larger. But if you think it looks exaggerated I will take it down. It belongs to old Sir J. Vaughan, late police magistrate, and he is so very feeble I am afraid he will never see the book.' Some years later the drawing was mislaid, and when preparing a new one she shortened the length of the tail!

The Tale of Benjamin Bunny and *The Tale of Two Bad Mice* were to be published simultaneously, and it was decided to include some characters from both of these books on the new end-papers. When submitting one of the revised designs, Beatrix Potter, with her customary modesty, wrote, 'I enclose the revised end paper, if it is not quite satisfactory in every particular, please send it back again. I am afraid my hand is rather shaky, or else the sketching makes one careless.'

Beatrix Potter prepared the text of Benjamin Bunny with great care, after having first tried it out on various children she knew. The story is written out in a paper-covered exercise book, in which the twenty-five pages of text are divided into short paragraphs, and eighteen pencil sketches are pasted in.

On the sketches there are notes to guide her when preparing the book pictures. Thus, for the picture of the pear tree Beatrix Potter has noted 'pear tree trained against wall', the falling rabbit being referred to as 'Peter'. Against the rough outline of her picture of the scare-crow we read, 'Benjamin emptying water out of shoes', and 'Peter trying to get on the jacket'. The next picture, which is of Peter and Benjamin amongst the onions, is only roughly sketched—there is a line pointing to 'Benjamin's handkerchief', while one of the two roughly sketched-in rabbits is marked 'Peter' and in the foreground is written 'Onions'. Underneath is a note which reads, 'The handkerchief will make a good bit of colour all through the book'—it was red.

As in her other manuscripts, individual words have been changed, and strips of paper pasted over parts of the text, with new wording written on them.

Typical examples of Beatrix Potter's corrections to the printed proofs are to be found in her letter to Norman Warne of June 16th:

p. 22 'conversed' (children like a fine word occasionally)
p. 51 'winked' instead of looked?
p. 64 'under*neath*' you crossed out neath. I think that
would a little alter the sense? by under*neath* I
mean an inside view.

The ending of the story had evidently been altered by Warnes, for Beatrix Potter made the following comment in her letter:

last page: 'they lived happily etc.' In the first place it is inexact, also rather a trite ending.

'When Peter got home to the rabbit hole, his mother forgave him because she was so glad to see that he had found his shoes and coat. Cottontail and Peter folded up the pocket handkerchief and old Mrs. Rabbit strung up the onions and hung them from the kitchen ceiling, with the branches of herbs and the rabbit-tobacco.'

If the above is too long—leave out C. Tail and Peter etc. and say 'and she strung up' etc. I would like the book to end with the word 'rabbit-tobacco', it is rather a fine word.

This Warnes agreed to do, and it was not long before a 'dummy' copy was ready, containing the pictures and text of *The Tale of Benjamin Bunny*, pasted up in their correct order. It was much liked, and Beatrix Potter wrote to Norman Warne, 'I think the proofs are very much better—The only one I don't like is the rabbit running along the path. *I* don't think anything can be done about it. It would be a pity to delay the printing to make a new block, and another block might be no better as it is a much-mended poor drawing. I think it will look much less patchy when printed with Mr. Evans' blue . . . When I showed the dummy book to my cousin, she picked out the rabbit running as a favourite! so perhaps you and I are over particular. I hope you will have a very pleasant holiday in August—and I hope I shall do a great deal of work before the autumn comes.'

No one could be more particular than Beatrix Potter about her written text, and the following examples show how she gradually improved her wording up to the time of publication:

Two paragraphs as originally written

When Mr. McGregor returned only 10 minutes later, he observed several things which perplexed him.

Especially he could not comprehend how the cat had shut herself into the green-house and locked the door upon the outside.

The first revision, with a new paragraph added

When Mr. McGregor returned about half an hour later, he observed several things which perplexed him; also he could not understand how the cat could have managed to shut herself up inside the green-house locking the door upon the *outside*.

Heads of Benjamin Bunny

August 1890

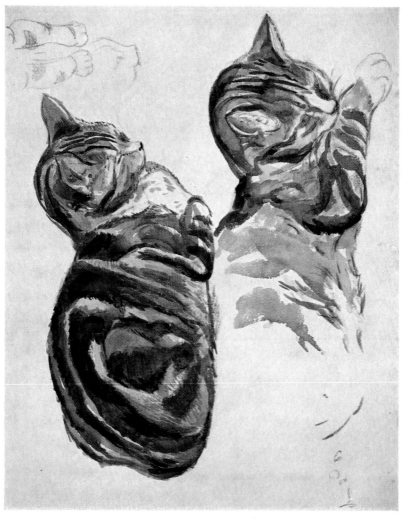

Study of cats for the picture of the cat who sat on the basket 'for *five hours*' in *The Tale of Benjamin Bunny*

It looked as though some person had been walking all over the garden in a pair of clogs—only the footmarks were so curiously little.

The final text

When Mr. McGregor returned about half an hour later, he observed several things which perplexed him.

It looked as though some person had been walking all over the garden in a pair of clogs—only the foot-marks were too ridiculously little!

Also he could not understand how the cat could have managed to shut herself up *inside* the green-house, locking the door upon the *outside*.

The Tale of Benjamin Bunny was now at the printer's, and Beatrix Potter was looking forward to seeing copies. On August 6th she wrote to Norman Warne from Lingholm, saying, 'I shall be very interested to see little "Benjamin". I tried to look over into the Fawe Park garden the other evening and got all over tar, he might well have had that adventure in addition to his other scrapes!'

Then, quite unexpectedly, a spelling mistake was found in her 'dummy' of *Benjamin Bunny*, and on September 12th Beatrix Potter wrote to Norman Warne asking him, 'Are you printing a large edition of Benjamin, does it seem to be liked? I notice muffetees is spelt wrong with an *a*; I know I do spell badly, but I cannot think how I overlooked it in the proofs.'

It was, however, too late to correct this mistake in the first two printings. In November Beatrix Potter wrote and asked, 'I wonder whether you are likely to be reprinting Benjamin Bunny and could alter two words . . . The two words are both on page 15—"Muffatees" to be altered to Nuttall's spelling, and "what *we* call lavender"—I think "we" might be printed in italics? It means that the rabbits call the plant tobacco—but *we* call it lavender. I had no idea that the little book would be reprinting already.'

So in the third printing, the word 'muffetees' was spelt correctly, and the word 'we' was put into italics. (In American editions no action was taken.)

It is of interest to note that several years later some of the original drawings were mislaid. In recalling this incident in December 1939, Beatrix Potter wrote, 'Some B. Bunny's were temporarily mislaid and I supplied three or four new ones, for fresh blocks, duplicates, very little different to the originals.'

With the exception of the picture where 'little Benjamin Bunny slid down into the road, and set off with a hop, skip and a jump', in which the figure of Benjamin was larger in the new picture, and also the drawing of the cat, whose tail had been shortened, the redrawn pictures were practically the same as the old ones.

About 1912 when translations into other languages were under consideration, all wording was omitted from the frontispiece and from the picture of Benjamin's aunt and the three little rabbits.

Of Benjamin Bunny, who was sometimes called 'Bounce', Beatrix Potter wrote, 'My first rabbit, Bounce, was exceedingly affectionate with myself; but suspicious, like a dog, of new servants or strange workmen in the house, at whom it would growl, the ordinary conversational noise being a low grunt.'

Amongst her papers at Hill Top is a photograph of Benjamin Bunny, and on the back Beatrix Potter has written, 'This is the original "Benjamin Bunny" (Commonly called "Bounce"). He was a very handsome tame Belgian rabbit . . . Benjamin was extremely fond of hot buttered toast, he used to hurry into the drawing room when he heard the tea-bell! He spent most of his time upstairs in a London house.'

In describing Benjamin's character in her Journal, she wrote, 'Rabbits are creatures of warm volatile temperament but shallow and absurdly transparent. It is this naturalness, one touch of nature, that I find so delightful in Mr. Benjamin Bunny, though I frankly admit his vulgarity. At one moment amiably sentimental to the verge of silliness, at the next, the upsetting of a jug or tea-cup which he immediately takes upon himself, will convert him into a demon, throwing himself on his back, scratching and spluttering. If I can lay hold of him without being bitten, within half a minute he is licking my hands as though nothing has happened. He is an abject coward, but believes in bluster, could stare our old dog out of countenance, chase a cat that has turned tail. Benjamin once fell into an Aquarium head first, and sat in the water which he could not get out of, pretending to eat a piece of string. Nothing like putting a face upon circumstances.'

The dedication page of *The Tale of Benjamin Bunny*, which reads, 'For the Children of Sawrey from Old Mr. Bunny', is of particular significance as it shows Beatrix Potter's growing affection for the village of Sawrey.

The Tale of Two Bad Mice
1904

The Tale of Two Bad Mice was written during a week's holiday at Hastings at the end of 1903, and it is one of three stories contained in a stiff-covered exercise book inscribed, 'Hastings, Nov.26th—Dec.3rd.' The stories are *Something very very NICE*, *The Tale of Tuppenny*, and *The Tale of Hunca Munca* or *The Tale of Two Bad Mice*.

The first was an early version of the story of Duchess and Ribby, but had a different plot; and the second was about a long-haired guinea-pig called Tuppenny, which later became Chapter 1 of *The Fairy Caravan*.

The third story was about two mice called Tom Thumb and Hunca Munca who lived in a doll's house. We are told by Margaret Lane: 'During Beatrix Potter's visit to Gloucestershire, two mice had been caught in a cage-trap in the kitchen of Harescombe Grange, and she had rescued them from the cook and brought them home and tamed them. She named them Tom Thumb and Hunca Munca.'

It was during this short holiday at Hastings, when it rained nearly every day, that Beatrix Potter occupied herself by planning these three stories. She hoped that Warnes would choose one of them to be published in 1904 together with *The Tale of Benjamin Bunny*. She was already making good progress with *Benjamin Bunny*, but liked to work on two books at a time.

On December 2nd she wrote to Norman Warne from 16, Robertson Terrace, Hastings, saying, 'I have tried to make a cat story that would use some sketches of a cottage I drew the summer before last. I believe I could make a pretty book of it—if the story is not too thin? There are two others in the copy book—the result of a *very* wet week here . . . The dolls would make a funny one, but it is rather soon to have another mouse book?', referring to *The Tailor of Gloucester*, which had only recently been published.

A week after receiving the copy-book, Norman Warne was still giving thought to her suggestions and wondering which story he would choose. In her next letter Beatrix Potter said, 'I cannot tell what to do about those stories; it would certainly be more amusing to do the one with toys and I would have liked to do whichever you prefer; the first one seemed easier to manage in some ways.' A few days later she told him she would be spending a week with her cousin at Melford Hall, adding, 'I shall try the new stories on the children there.'

While the cat story might have been easier to manage, and would have used up some of the background sketches of the cottage, they both preferred the story of Hunca Munca and the dolls; and it so happened that Norman Warne was at that time making a doll's house for his little niece Winifred Warne.

It was agreed that there *should* be another book for the 1904–1905 season, but for the time being Warnes delayed the final choice as to which story to use, and concentrated on the format. They thought the new book could possibly be similar in size to *Johnny Crow's Garden* by Leslie Brooke, which measured 215 mm × 150 mm, a book which Warnes had just recently published. Perhaps they were thinking of a remark Beatrix Potter had made a few weeks earlier, when she said, 'I think I am getting a little cramped with those small drawings; I want to put too much in them.'

The question of size was still under consideration when she wrote to Norman Warne again; this time definitely in favour of her *mouse book*, and the *ordinary* size: 'I am still puzzling about the larger book; I am inclined to the mice but it is difficult to spread them over so large a page as "Johnny Crow". They are more suited to the "Peter Rabbit" size as a matter of fact. I think you said that you should be out of town after Christmas; if you were likely to be away from London for long I should have liked to get the book settled before. I thought I might get them roughly planned towards the end of next week, if that would be time enough.'

Before finally deciding on the format, Warnes prepared a dummy in a slightly larger size, measuring 170 mm × 120 mm. It had been given the title 'The Tale of the Doll's House and Hunca Munca', and both pictures *and* text appeared on the same page. It was a curious dummy, pasted up with cut-outs from the text and illustrations of a copy of *The Tailor of Gloucester*—a regular patchwork—but it gave a general impression of what the finished pages would look like!

Although in an earlier letter Beatrix Potter had said, 'I would be glad to have the mouse book any shape you like', she really preferred the small size, and it was finally decided to print it in the ordinary format. 'I think I am glad that it is going to be the old size after all,' she wrote, 'we could not hope to do better'; and three weeks later when the title *The Tale of Two Bad Mice* was finally decided upon, 'I have not thought of any better name for the *Tale* of the two bad mice.'

To help Beatrix Potter in the preparation of the drawings Norman Warne made her a cage with a glass front, a ladder, and an upstairs nest for Tom Thumb and Hunca Munca to live in, so that she could observe the mice through the glass front when drawing them.

The doll's house Beatrix Potter used for her story was the one which Norman Warne had made. It stood on a broad stool in the nursery of Fruing Warne's home at Surbiton. It was very tall, and little Winifred found it difficult to reach up to the top storey.

The suggestion was made that Beatrix Potter should prepare some of her drawings there, but Mrs. Potter apparently objected, so Norman Warne offered to take photographs of the doll's house and to send them to Bolton Gardens. 'If you could photograph the door side of the house rather from the right, it would be a great

De-luxe binding for *The Tale of Two Bad Mice*,
believed to have been designed by Beatrix Potter

The contents of the Doll's House at Hill Top, used by Beatrix Potter for her pictures in *The Tale of Two Bad Mice*

assistance', wrote Beatrix Potter. When referring to these doll's house pictures many years later, Winifred Warne, now Mrs. James Boultbee, said, 'She did them very well, and although only working from photographs, the colouring was most accurate.'

Beatrix Potter wanted models from which to paint her doll pictures, and Norman Warne said he would find a flaxen-haired doll for Lucinda and a Dutch doll for the cook; he also promised to send her some doll's house food.

In addition, she needed a policeman doll, and knowing that Winifred possessed one, asked if she might borrow it. Winifred Warne, who was about four years old at the time, remembers how one day Beatrix Potter came to see them at Surbiton. 'She was very unfashionably dressed, and wore a coat and skirt and hat, and carried a man's umbrella. She came up to the nursery dressed in her outdoor clothes and asked if she might borrow the policeman doll; Nanny hunted for the doll and eventually found it. It was at least a foot high, and quite out of proportion to the doll's house.' Winifred was sad because she thought that she might never see the doll again—but in due course it was safely returned to her.

On February 12th 1904 she wrote and thanked Norman Warne for his offer of help, and apologized for not accepting the kind invitation to Surbiton. She also mentioned the progress she was making: 'When you have come back and can fix a time, I should like to show you the mouse book. I have planned it out, and begun some drawings of "Hunca Munca"—I think you will like them. I was very much perplexed about the doll's house; I would have gone gladly to draw it, and I should be so *very* sorry if Mrs. Warne or you thought me uncivil. I did not think I could manage to go to Surbiton without staying to lunch; I hardly ever go out, and my mother is so exacting I had not enough spirit to say anything about it. I have felt vexed with myself since, but I did not know what to do. It does wear a person out. I will manage to make a nice book somehow. Hunca Munca is very ready to play the game. I stopped her in the act of carrying a doll as large as herself up to the nest, she cannot resist anything with lace or ribbon; (she despises the dishes). I have had so very much pleasure with that box, I am never tired of watching them run up and down. As far as the book is concerned I think I can do it from the photographs and my box, but it is very hard to have seemed uncivil.'

By February 18th the dolls arrived from Norman Warne, and Beatrix Potter wrote, 'Thank you so very much for the queer little dollies; they are just exactly what I wanted and a curiosity—coming from Seven Dials . . . I will provide a print dress and a smile for Jane; her little stumpy feet are so funny. I think I shall make a dear little book of it. I shall be glad to get done with the rabbits . . . I shall be very glad of the little stove and the ham; the work is always a very great pleasure anyhow.'

The doll's food arrived a week later, and Beatrix Potter informed Norman

Warne, 'I received the parcel from Hamley's this morning; the things will all do beautifully; the ham's appearance is enough to cause indigestion. I am getting almost more treasures than I can squeeze into one small book.'

In another letter written shortly after, we hear that 'The little dishes are so pretty I am wondering if I have made enough of them? Shall I squeeze in another dish? I regret the roast duck being left out! . . . I have bought a gilt book case for 8½d. I wonder what is the colour of the Enc. Britannica, the advertisements don't say; it might be one of the things that would not go into the mousehole. *I* don't much like the mouse drawings at present but they are more like the originals of Peter; I am afraid I am getting into the way of making my work too soft and fine, forgetting that the process blocks will soften it. These are rather hard, but stronger.'

During the Easter holidays at Lyme Regis, Beatrix Potter put her mouse drawings on one side and did some sketching. In a letter to Norman Warne she confessed, 'I have been doing some pen-and-ink sketches in the town; but I will work hard at those mice when I get back.'

The photographs of the doll's house were sent to her on April 20th, and in one of them, Winifred was seen standing beside it. Beatrix Potter thanked Norman Warne and said, 'They are very good; and I have got an idea from the staircase and top floor. The inside view is amusing—the kind of house where one cannot sit down without upsetting something, I know the sort. I prefer a more severe style; but I do not see why you should be so depressed about the front door! I was going to make mine white and I will alter the top a little.'

By the end of May she wrote again, 'I have done eighteen of the mouse drawings. I was wondering whether you are wanting them if you have come back? I have begun the remainder; if I could go over them with you I should be rather glad as they may need altering . . . I think some of the new mouse drawings are rather good, the dolls are still difficult . . . I got the drawings mounted to save time, but can gladly make any alterations. I hope you will like them. I have been using the photographs.' And a week later—'I think that the banisters make the staircase drawing more intelligible—though they are not quite in the right position.'

By the middle of June some of the proofs of the text had arrived. At the beginning of the book, which was dedicated to Winifred Warne, it said, 'For the little girl who had the doll's house'. Beatrix Potter wrote, 'would you not put her initials to show more clearly that it belonged to a real child'; and so the initials W.M.L.W. (Winifred Mary Langrish Warne), were added to the dedication page. She also asked for some small amendments to the text:

> p. 21.   I wish the printer could set Hunca Munca
> in one line—at all events on this page
> where first mentioned. If line is too long—
> 'later' would be shorter than 'afterwards'.

p. 64. 'Leant against' instead of 'stood'?

p. 85. delete the first H.M. I think it did not
balance properly the first way suggested.

By June 29th Beatrix Potter had finished checking the proofs of the text, and wrote, 'I think the proof reads all right now and I am quite satisfied with the alterations—I am posting it to-night to save time.'

The proofs of the pictures were now beginning to come through, and she wrote to express her approval: 'I think that the blocks are good on the whole; I like the two pages of upright ones much better than the two sideways pages. The latter both seem over dark. I think the *bright colours*—especially the blue—will come out better in Mr. Evans' inks. At all events I sincerely hope so, for I was hoping that the blue frock—on the mouse and dolls—would brighten up the book. I think the blocks are all right; they have got such a variety of green, yellow and red mice on one sheet, I think it must be caused by the printing. I think it would be well to draw Hentschel's attention to the uneven printing—though I don't think it is the fault of the blocks. Compare the plate of taking the bird cage into the mouse hole with my original.'

Warnes were not entirely satisfied with the next set of block proofs, which arrived some four weeks later, but Beatrix Potter reassured them by saying, 'The proofs don't strike *me* as so very bad, perhaps because *I* did not care much for those four drawings. I always expected the red house would print up; I will keep it lighter on the Catalogue cover' (referring to the cover of Warne's 1904–1905 trade leaflet, which she had designed for them for the modest fee of two guineas), continuing, 'I should get them to print it again, making the green carpet a little darker and then the red would be less staring. The hearthrug has come out nicely. If you were really going to get another block of the mouse at the door (lower left block) I should like to have improved the drawing, but I suppose it would be awkward to do anything to it otherwise *I* should be inclined to let it pass.' She added, 'I think the little dummy book looks very fair all through upon the whole. There will always be some worse and better in the printing.'

There were two styles of binding—one with paper boards and one in decorated cloth with gold lettering. With regard to the latter, it is interesting to note that Beatrix Potter had contributed to the cover design, for some weeks earlier, when staying at Melford Hall, she had said in one of her letters to Warnes: 'I will do some sketches of designs for the cover while I am at Melford.'

When Warnes sent Beatrix Potter a pasted-up copy of *The Tale of Two Bad Mice*, together with samples of reds for the cover of the ordinary edition, she informed them, 'It is pasted up quite right. If you think it would be suitable I liked the stronger red for one cover, and I would be quite contented with any other colour you like to choose for the second colour; if there is one colour *I* like, it is surely enough.'

Unfortunately in the summer of 1905 Hunca Munca met with an accident. In a letter to Norman Warne on July 21st Beatrix Potter told him, 'I have made a little doll of poor Hunca Munca. I cannot forgive myself for letting her tumble. I do so miss her. She fell off the chandelier; she managed to stagger up the staircase into your little house, but she died in my hand about ten minutes after. I think if I had broken my own neck it would have saved a deal of trouble.'

It was during the preparation of *The Tale of Two Bad Mice* that Beatrix Potter and Norman Warne came to know each other well. They co-operated in a way that had not been possible during the writing of earlier books.

One of Norman Warne's photographs of the doll's
house which he made for his niece Winifred—she is
seen standing beside it. This photograph was used by
Beatrix Potter when planning her pictures for
The Tale of Two Bad Mice

The setting of Lucie's cottage in *The Tale of Mrs. Tiggy-Winkle*, at Skelgill, Cumberland

Enid Linder

The Tale of Mrs. Tiggy-Winkle
1905

The idea of Mrs. Tiggy-Winkle the washerwoman almost certainly had its origin in old Kitty MacDonald the washerwoman at Dalguise, Scotland, where Beatrix Potter spent the summer months of her childhood for eleven consecutive years from the age of five. Dalguise House where the Potters stayed was a seat on the river Tay, situated amongst beautiful Highland scenery.

In 1892 at the age of twenty-six, when staying at Heath Park, Birnam, near Dalguise, she visited old Kitty MacDonald, and described her in her Journal: 'Went out with the pony . . . to see Kitty MacDonald, our old washerwoman . . . Kitty is eighty-three but waken, and delightfully merry . . . She is a comical, round little old woman, as brown as a berry and wears a multitude of petticoats and a white mutch. Her memory goes back for seventy years and I really believe she is prepared to enumerate the articles of her first wash in the year '71.'

Although *The Tale of Mrs. Tiggy-Winkle* was the sixth of Beatrix Potter's books to be published, the story had been carefully planned as far back as 1901, although it was not actually written down until the following year. In a small exercise book found at Hill Top, believed to be the earliest manuscript of *The Tale of Mrs. Tiggy-Winkle*, Beatrix Potter had written on the title page, 'Made at Lingholm, Sept. 01 told to cousin Stephanie at Melford, Nov. 01—written down Nov. 02. There are no pictures, it is a good one to tell.'

It was while staying at Lingholm, near Keswick, that the Potters became friendly with the Vicar of Newlands and his wife, and their two children, Lucie and Kathleen.

As a Christmas present in 1901, Beatrix Potter gave Lucie a copy of her privately printed *Peter Rabbit*, inscribing it, 'For Lucie with love from H.B.P., Christmas 1901—I should like to put Lucie into a little book'. This she did some four years later in *The Tale of Mrs. Tiggy-Winkle*, and no doubt it was during the long summer holidays which Beatrix Potter spent at Lingholm, that Lucie saw much of her, and often played with her pet hedgehog Mrs. Tiggy-Winkle.

Curiously enough, when Beatrix Potter wrote down the story in 1902, it was apparently to be dedicated to Stephanie Hyde-Parker, of Melford Hall, Suffolk, her cousin Ethel's little girl, for the opening paragraph reads, 'Now Stephanie, this is the story about a little girl called Lucie; she was smaller than you and she could not speak quite plain . . .' In the end, however, *The Tale of Mrs. Tiggy-Winkle was* dedicated to Lucie, and Stephanie's name appeared on the dedication page of *The Tale of Mr. Jeremy Fisher* the following year.

Early in 1904 when work on *The Tale of Benjamin Bunny* and *The Tale of Two*

Bad Mice was nearing completion, Beatrix Potter was giving serious thought to her story about Mrs. Tiggy-Winkle and little Lucie Carr of Newlands. She had already been working on some backgrounds and had been carrying Mrs. Tiggy-Winkle around on some of her travels.

On March 15th she informed Norman Warne, 'I have been drawing the stump of a hollow tree for another hedgehog drawing; there is not much sign of spring yet but the moss is very pretty in the woods . . . Hunca Munca is very discontented in the small old box; I am accompanied by Mrs. Tiggy—carefully concealed —my aunt cannot endure animals!'

The summer of 1904 was spent at Lingholm, where Beatrix Potter went around sketching many backgrounds for *The Tale of Mrs. Tiggy-Winkle*. Unlike the backgrounds for *The Tale of Benjamin Bunny*, which were water-colours, they were nearly all pen-and-ink sketches in sepia. There were, however, some half a dozen attractive paintings of mountain and forest scenery in the small sketch-book already referred to, which was labelled 'Benjamin Bunny—Tiggy Winkle'; also a few rough water-colours of interiors of kitchens.

The little door in the back of the hill, which is mentioned in a note at the very end of the story, appears to have had its origin in some paintings made of a hillside path at Kelbarrow, Grasmere, in August 1899.

Just before returning to London, Beatrix Potter told Norman Warne, 'I think Mrs. Tiggy would be all right. It is a *girl's* book; so is the Hunca Munca, but there must be a large audience of little girls. I think they would like the different clothes.'

Back at Bolton Gardens, she was well stocked with backgrounds, but did not start work immediately, confessing, 'I have not begun on the hedgehog book yet I am ashamed to say; but I think it is not a bad thing to take a holiday; I have been working very industriously drawing fossils at the Museum upon the theory that a change of work is the best sort of rest! but I shall be quite keen to get to work on the books again.'

It was not long before Beatrix Potter again became absorbed in the preparation of her book, using Mrs. Tiggy-Winkle as a model when preparing the drawings. Writing to Norman Warne on November 12th she told him, 'Mrs. Tiggy Winkle as a model is comical; so long as she can go to sleep on my knee she is delighted, but if she is propped up on end for half an hour, she first begins to yawn pathetically, and then she *does* bite! Nevertheless she is a dear person; just like a very fat rather stupid little dog. I think the book will go all right when once started.'

Three weeks later we learn that 'The hedgehog drawings are turning out very comical. I have dressed up a cottonwool dummy figure for convenience of drawing the clothes. It is such a little figure of fun; it terrifies my rabbit; but Hunca Munca is always pulling out the stuffing. I think it should make a good book, when I have learnt to draw the child.'

By February 1905 some of the drawings were ready for the block maker, and Beatrix Potter asked Norman Warne if she might bring them along. 'Would Thursday afternoon be convenient to you to look over the hedgehog drawings, if I can arrange to bring them? I have finished a good many and should like to have them processed because I have used a different white. I expect it will photograph well, but I should be glad to be sure of it. I have re-drawn the birds and mice, it looks much better.'

Apparently Warnes wished to make these drawings up into 'sets' to reduce the cost of the blocks, for a week later Beatrix Potter wrote, 'I have not the least objection to the mounts being cut, and the drawings can be trimmed too. I mounted them while I was painting them because it was thinner paper, which cockled. I will do the next on thicker paper, in the old way; (only gummed at the edges).'

By the beginning of June the proofs of the text arrived. 'I have been correcting the text of Mrs. Tiggy-Winkle,' she wrote. 'I thought I would bring it on Thursday afternoon if convenient', and two days later, 'I do not think that rhyme is right grammar; it is the "no" that throws it out. If it were

> "Smooth and hot—red rusty spot
> never here be seen—oh!"

that would be all right. She is supposed to be exorcising spots and iron stains, same as Lady Macbeth (!). The verb is imperative, and apparently it is not reasonable to use "no" with a vocative noun. It is a contradiction to address "no spot!" I am afraid this is rather muddled; I used to know my Latin grammar but it has faded . . . I wish another book could be planned out before the summer, if we are going on with them, I always feel very much lost when they are finished.'

In some of the earlier drawings of Lucie, Beatrix Potter had painted her cloak red, but in a more recent drawing the cloak was blue. Norman Warne had noticed this slight discrepancy and pointed it out. She replied, 'I have been rather sorry about the little blue cloak. Shall I cut it out and make it red? I don't think it would take long. I would not have made it blue if I had remembered, but she just happened to have it and looked pretty; but I know I have no taste in colour and would gladly alter it. Your other corrections were right.'

In the end, however, both the blue and the red cloaks were changed to nut-brown, and on Sunday, June 18th Beatrix Potter wrote, 'I will bring the drawings again tomorrow unless prevented, *still* in doubt! I am at present strongly inclined to think a warm nut-brown cloak would do best, taking them all round; I'm sorry to say the red looks very hot in some of them, though in others it does better than the blue. I am pasting on white paper so I can colour it any shade when we have decided', adding, 'I had not time to stop and ask about another book on Friday, and you were busy the time before. I should like to have some other work in prospect when these are finished'; and in a postscript a week later: 'I do so *hate* finishing books. I would like to go on with them for years.'

The blocks for *The Tale of Mrs. Tiggy-Winkle* were made by Hentschel, and in some cases the proofs did not appear to do the pictures justice. This did not trouble Beatrix Potter unduly, as Mr. Evans was doing the final printing. 'The proofs are startling in colour,' she wrote, 'but I think it will make all the difference when they are printed with Mr. Evans' blue, especially the plants.'

Her work on the book was at last finished, and in writing to Norman Warne on July 2nd she said, 'I enclose the remainder of Tiggy regretfully'—for they had both enjoyed the planning of this book. Sad to relate, Norman Warne did not live to see the finished book.

The dedication page reads, 'For the real little Lucie of Newlands', and her copy was inscribed, 'For little Lucie with much love from Beatrix Potter and from dear "Mrs. Tiggy Winkle" Sept. 24th. 05.'

Perhaps the drawings of Lucie did not quite do Beatrix Potter justice when compared with those of Mrs. Tiggy-Winkle—but as she herself admitted when writing to a friend some years later, 'I am not good—or trained—in drawing human figures (they are a terrible bother to me when I have perforce to bring them into the pictures for my own little stories).'

Her pet hedgehog, Mrs. Tiggy-Winkle, was by no means young, and soon after the book was published she began to show signs of failing health. On February 1st 1906, in a letter to Millie Warne, Norman Warne's sister, Beatrix Potter wrote, 'I am sorry to say I am upset about poor Mrs. Tiggy. She hasn't seemed well the last fortnight, and has begun to be sick, and she is so thin. I am going to try some physic but I am a little afraid that the long course of unnatural diet and indoor life is beginning to tell on her. It is a wonder she has lasted so long. One gets very fond of a little animal. I hope she will either get well or go quickly.'

A few weeks later Mrs. Tiggy-Winkle was put to sleep and laid to rest in the back garden of Number Two, Bolton Gardens.

In 1913 Beatrix Potter redrew the picture of the 'spring bubbling out from the hill side', omitting the words 'How Keld' which appeared on the picture. At that time Warnes were planning the translation of some of her books into French, and it was considered advisable to remove any English wording from her pictures— also, as Beatrix Potter had said in one of her letters, ' "How Keld" is Norse for Hill Well, and brings inquiries occasionally.'

The impression old Kitty MacDonald made on Beatrix Potter remained with her to the end of her life, and a year before she died, when recovering from an illness, her thoughts again turned to the old washerwoman, whom she referred to now as old *Katie* Macdonald. Propped up in bed, scribbling on the back of a news-paper wrapper belonging to a copy of the *Yorkshire Post, Leeds Mercury*, she wrote:

Here am I—a cheerful old woman sitting up in bed—staring at the china-cupboard opposite. Cornflower and gold Crown Derby, Whieldon glaze, Staffordshire greyhound, old Bristol punch bowl—'Fill every man his glafs', and lustre amongst them holding its own, a willow pattern mustard pot—a little mug shaped pot with lid and handle—Seventy eighty years ago it belonged to another old woman, old Katie Macdonald, the Highland washer woman. She was a tiny body, brown as a berry, beady black eyes and much wrinkled, against an incongruously white frilled mutch. She wore a small plaid crossed over shawl pinned with a silver brooch, a bed jacket and a full kilted petticoat—She dropped bob curt-sies, but she was outspoken and very independent, proud and proper.

The younger lasses trod the washing with their large white feet. I remember two dancing together in our big wooden tub. Katie rubbed and scrubbed with her hands wrinkled like a monkey's, but like her neighbours along the burn—she batted the clothes with a flat thivel, in the burn that flowed at the foot of her garden steps. A pretty garden above the singing water, sweet briar and hollyhocks . . . The cottage was just butt and ben—a hearth fire redo-lent of peats, like Katie herself—a low stooping doorway; and green thatch garlanded with live long orpin and houseleek.

The joy of converse with old Katie was to draw her out to talk of the days when she was a wee bit lassie—herding the kine. The days when 'Boney' was a terror . . . the old woman wouldn't dwell upon hard weather and storms; she spoke of the sunshine and clouds, and shadows, the heather bells, the . . . 'the broom of the Cowden Knowes', the sun and wind on the hills where she played, and knitted, and herded cattle and sheep. A bonny life it was, but it can never come back . . .

BEATRIX POTTER'S 1902 MANUSCRIPT OF THE TALE OF MRS. TIGGY-WINKLE

The Tale of Mrs. Tiggy-Winkle

Made at Lingholm, Sept. 01, told to cousin Stephanie at
Melford Nov. 01—written down Nov. 02. There are no pictures,
it is a good one to tell—

'a very picturesque place'

Now Stephanie, this is the story about a little girl called Lucie; she was smaller than you and she could not speak quite plain. She had yellow white hair and pink cheeks and a blue frock, just like a wax dolly. She lived at a place called Little-town in Newlands. She was a nice little girl, but she had one fault—she was always losing her pocket handkerchiefs!

Now one day little Lucie came down the lane below Little-town crying and sobbing, oh she did cry!—

'I've lost my pocket-hand-ker-sniff! I don't like to go home! two pocket-hand-kersniffs—3 pocket handkersniffs—oh-oh-oh! and a *pinny*!—boo-hoo-ooo—Cock Robin have you seen my handkersniffs?'

Cock Robin sat upon a twig in the hedge. He looked sideways down at Lucie, with his little bright black eye. But he did not answer. He turned his head and looked up at the hill.

Then Lucie went a little further down the lane crying, and met a speckled hen and asked if she had found a pocket handkerchief? But the speckled hen ran under a gate and stood on one leg looking up at the hill and clucking—'I go barefoot! barefoot! barefoot!'

And Lucie squeezed under the gate too, and spoke to a big red cow that lay in the sun chewing the cud—

'Oh dear Mrs. Mooly cow, are you eating my pocket handkersniff?' But Mrs. Cow lay in the sun and looked across the grass—And then she asked the geese and the sheep and the pony, and the rabbits under the hedge but they all shook their heads and looked up the hill. And then she asked a white pussy cat sitting on a wall but it had not seen the pocket handkerchiefs.

And then Lucie scrambled up the wall herself and sat on the broad stone steps and looked up at the hill.

The hill goes right up, up, up! at the back of Little-town and all along the side of Newlands; and the clouds came down, down, down! so that it is like a wall shutting in the valley; a wall that has no top and is covered with fern.

But half way up there is a line—a sheep walk through the fern, a little ledge along the steep side of the hill.

And here and there there is a little open space in the fern, and the grass and wimberry leaves are very green—and surely there is a little black speck running along that path—and some little white specks on one of the patches of grass, like clothes spread out to bleach—Can they be the pocket handkerchiefs? and the pinafore?

Lucie scrambled off the stile and climbed up the hill as fast as her short legs would carry her, up, up, up, till she came to the path; there it was nice smooth walking, for the path ran sideways like a shelf; and Little-town was right away down below; you could have dropped a pebble down the chimney.

Lucie came along the path and found a little well with a stone trough. The water came sparkling and dancing from under the moss of the hill-side, and ran down a wooden spout and tumbled into the stone basin. The spring is called 'How-Keld'.

And where the water overflowed on to the path, and where the pebbles and sand were wet—there were foot marks of a tiny tiny person; and the person had left a little tin pail under the spout to fill with water.

It was running over already, for the pail was no bigger than an egg-cup!

Then Lucie started running to overtake the little person, but it ran away faster than Lucie. And when Lucie came to the patch of green grass—both the little black person and the white handkerchiefs that she had seen from down below—were gone!

But there were clothes props cut from bracken stems, and clothes lines of twisted cobbler's web—and there was a door!

Now I think that little door into the side of the hill called Catbells is the funniest thing I ever saw, and I have looked at it often! I have seen plenty of doors into houses, but this was straight into the side of a *hill* and so *very* small. When I saw it last, someone had gone in with a wheel barrow, but it must have been a very small one!

Lucie stared at the door; it was shut. Lucie came a little nearer; it was quite shut and fast; someone inside was singing—

My father left me three acres of land,
  Sing ivy, sing ivy—
I ploughed it with a ram's horn
And sowed it all over with one pepper corn,
  Sing nolly, go whistle and ivy!

I harrowed it with a bramble bush,
  Sing ivy, sing ivy,
And reaped it with my little pen-knife,
  Sing holly, go whistle and ivy!

I got the mice to carry it to the mill,
  Sing ivy, sing ivy,
And thrashed it with a goose's quill,
  Sing holly, go whistle and ivy!

Lucie did not wait to hear any more; she knocked rat-tat-tat-! The singing stopped suddenly.

The person inside was quite quiet. Lucie knocked again.

Then the person in a small frightened voice said 'come in!' and Lucie opened the door and went into the inside of the hill.

It was a very nice clean kitchen with a grey flagged floor and whitewashed walls and a wide fireplace and shining copper pans—just like any other Lakes Kitchen, only the ceiling was *very* low and the pans were as little as you have in a doll's house. There were two little pails of water on the floor in a corner, as small as the one Lucie had seen beside the spring—

'shorten this'

'leave out some'

Opposite the door was a wooden table with an ironing blanket spread upon it, and a nice singeing smell of hot clothes; and at the other side of the table—with a flat iron in her hand—and an anxious expression—stood the little person who had been singing.

She stared at Lucie and Lucie stared at her, across the table—She had on a print gown tucked up over a red striped petticoat, and a grey shawl fastened with a big brooch, and she was as broad as she was long, but that was not much. And she had little *black* wrinkly pinkly hands all puckered with the soap-suds, and a little *black* shiny *wet* nose that went sniffle snuffle, and little brown twinkly eyes, that looked very much surprised; and a white muslin cap very beautifully goffered, and underneath the frill of her cap where you have yellow curls—she had *prickles*!!!! '(in a mysterious whisper)'

'Are you a washerwoman? I've lost my pocket handkersniff?' said Lucie.

'Oh yes, if-you-please-'m, and an excellent clear-starcher, oh yes—if you please mum; my name is Mrs. Tiggy-Winkle.'

'I *thought* this was a gold mine?' said Lucie after a pause.

'Oh *yes*, if you please'm, look at my fine gold ring!'

'I *thought* this was a silver mine?' said the persistent child—

'Oh yes, if you please'm, look at my silver pin!'

'And a copper mine?' 'Oh yes! look at my copper pans!' 'And a lead mine and a tin mine?' 'Oh look at my little tin cans! Oh yes, if you please'm!' said Mrs. Tiggy-Winkle.

She took another hot iron off the fire and began another song—

> 'Gay go up with a gay gold ring,
> The parliament soldiers are gone to the king.
> Oh some they did laugh,
> And some they did cry,
> To see the parliament soldiers go by!'

'Oh yes, if-you-please-mum, I'm an excellent clear-starcher,' said Mrs. Tiggy-Winkle, taking damp clothes out of a buck basket and spreading them upon the ironing blanket.

'What is that?' said Lucie, 'that's not my pocket handkersniff?'

'Oh *no*, if you please'm,' said Mrs. Tiggy-Winkle, 'that's a little scarlet waistcoat belonging to Cock Robin.' And she ironed it and folded it and laid it on one side, and took something else out of the basket to iron.

'What is that?' said Lucie, 'that isn't my pinny?'

'Oh no, if-you-please'm, that's a damask table cloth belonging to Jenny Wren; look how it's stained with currant wine! It's very ill to wash,' said Mrs. Tiggy-Winkle.

'(The mines at the Lakes are not of much working value but contain such a variety of precious metals it is rather a joke.)'

Shorten this page.

'shorten'

'Goldscope mine has not been worked since civil-wars.'

'These clothes would amuse children, the chief difficulty would be to get enough variation in the *pictures* of the washer woman'

162

'She took another hot iron off the fire'

Sketches of ducks

'What's that?' said Lucie.

'Oh that's a pair of yellow stockings belonging to Chucky hen; look how she's worn the heels out with scratching in the ash pit! She'll very soon go bare foot!' said Mrs. Tiggy-Winkle.

'What's that?' said Lucie.

'Oh that's a pair of white mittens belonging to your pussy-cat! See how they are clean already! She licks them every morning.'

'What's that? Why that's one of my handkersniffs!' said Lucie; but Mrs. Tiggy-Winkle's nose went sniffle, sniffle, snuffle, and she dived into the clothes basket with her skinny brown hands and brought out a little woolly coat, 'What's that?' said Lucie.

'Oh that's a little flannel jacket belonging to one of the little woolly lambs of Keskadale.' 'Will their jackets take off?' asked Lucie. 'Oh yes—if-you-please-mum; look at the sheep mark on the jacket,' said Mrs. Tiggy-Winkle, 'and here's another with the sheep mark from Stair, and another from Ullock, and another from Manisty,' said Mrs. Tiggy-Winkle.

'Why, there's another handkersniff,' said Lucie, 'and what's that funny big thing?' 'Oh that's a flannel wrapper belonging to Mrs. Mooly cow; and here's a pair of ear-caps belonging to Bob-pony.'

'Why there's my last pocket handkersniff!' But Mrs. Tiggy-Winkle sprinkled and smoothed and ironed and drew more and more clothes out of the basket.

There was a pair of white woollen gloves belonging to a collie-dog, and five white cotton night caps belonging to the geese, and one grey brown night cap belonging to the Gander; and then came Lucie's pinafore. And there were some little little dicky shirt fronts belonging to an ox-eye; and some little brown coats of woodmice, and one velvety black moleskin. And there were some very starchy collars belonging to a little dog Tipkins, and a very large white waist coat belonging to poor Pig Robinson; and a very dirty blue jacket that had belonged to Peter Rabbit, and a red tail-coat (with no tail) belonging to Squirrel Nutkin; and some pillow cases, not marked, that had gone lost in the washing, and some sheets with large round holes in them, belonging to dear Sammy Rat—and then the basket was empty!

And when Mrs. Tiggy-Winkle had done up the clothes in bundles, she made tea—a cup for herself and a cup for Lucie.

They sat down side by side on a low bench before the fire, and looked sideways at one another. And Mrs. Tiggy-Winkle's nose went sniffle, snuffle, snuffle, and her eyes went twinkle, twinkle; and all over her clothes and through her shawl there were hair-pins sticking wrong end out; so that Lucie did not like to sit too near her.

'as many articles as the audience has patience for, there were several others I have forgotten.'

('Hedgehogs have very wet shiny little snouts')

163

They drank their tea, and banked up the fire with turf, and took up the clothes in bundles, and locked the door behind them.

And away down the hill through the fern trotted Lucie and Mrs. Tiggy-Winkle, and the bundles.

And all the way down the hill, little people came out of the fern, and took their bundles of clothes from Mrs. Tiggy-Winkle; rabbits and mice and birds, and Jenny Wren and Cock Robin—and the big yellow collie from Keskadale came through a gap in the wall and he put on his big white gloves, and carried away the little lamb-coats in a bundle in his mouth.

And then they had less to carry and went down hill faster and faster, and when they got to the gate into the lane there was nothing left at all except Lucie's handkerchiefs folded up inside the clean pinafore, and fastened with a safety pin!

And Lucie scrambled through the bars of the gate with the clean things in her hands, and turned round to say good night and to thank the washerwoman.

But what a *very* odd thing! Mrs. Tiggy-Winkle had not waited either for thanks, or for the washing bill!

She had turned back up the field, and she was running up hill through the grass, faster and faster and faster!

And where was her grey woollen shawl?

And where was her red striped petticoat?

And her white plaited cap?

And *how* small she had grown! and *how* round, and how *brown*! and covered with *prickles*!!!

Why! Mrs. Tiggy-Winkle was nothing but

a Hedgehog!

('Until this point of the story, Lucie and the washer woman are about of a size')

THE WANDERINGS OF A SMALL BLACK CAT

This set of verses describes an incident which happened to Lucie's father, the Vicar of Newlands. Many years later Beatrix Potter sent these verses to Betty Harris,[*] a friend who had visited her at Sawrey: 'in remembrance of a perfect day—August 5th 1930.' At one point Beatrix Potter interrupts the poem to explain that one of the verses is missing.

> The wanderings of a small black cat
> inspire my simple tale,
> It met a worthy clergyman
> at dusk near Portinscale.
>
> On serious thoughts his mind was bent,
> of cats he took small heed,
> So when that pussy followed him
> he walked with greater speed.
>
> 'Shuk! shuk!' said he—'go home! go home!'
> but faster still it ran;
> And still—as faster ran the cat—
> so ran the clergyman.
>
> It followed him, it followed him,
> through ditches, gates and stiles;
> And when the parson ran—it ran.
> It ran three weary miles!
>
> Now, persecution vexeth saints,
> (a thing I blush to own)
> —That most humane kind clergyman
> did throw a little stone.
>
> Yea, several stones. And all in vain;
> the cat nor turned, nor shrank,
> But followed perseveringly,
> until they reached Ghyll Bank.
>
> There, in the lane, a fox hound pup
> did hold the cat at bay,
> 'It's turned at last,' the parson said,
> 'I trust it knows its way.'

* By courtesy of Mrs. Richard Stevens (Betty Harris), Philadelphia.

(At this point a verse appears to be missing; if it ever existed I have forgotten it. It should describe Mrs. Carr waiting tea for the Rev. Mr. Carr. She was a large lackadaisical rather handsome lady with a quantity of yellow hair, in a 'bun' which was always coming down. When I first recollect her she was still sufficiently a bride to go out to dinner in her wedding gown, with a long train, shedding hair pins as she went. She was something both pleasing and comical.)

The vicarage lights and cheerful fire
   shone twinkling down the lane,
Scarce had he reached his friendly door
   when pelting came the rain.

Against the rattling window panes
   the storm beat—pit a pat—
'My dear,' said he, and stirred his tea,
   'I'm sorry for that cat!'

'I wish I had not thrown that stone,
   I trust it was not struck!'
'T'was thoughtless too,' his wife replied
   ''tis said black cats bring luck.'

'Hark to the rain!' 'Both luck and use,
   We're troubled here with rats.'
They went to bed remorsefully,
   and dreamt about black cats.

Next morning dawned. The mist rolled up;
   a day serene and fair,
No cat was seen. The parson said—
   'Perhaps its gone to Stair!'

Now Saturday is market day;
   and sermon day at that;
A busy day. The clergyman
   forgot the little cat.

On Sunday to the little church,
   tree shadowed like a nest,
Parson and people wend their way—
   abode of peace thrice blest

The pathway up which Lucie scrambled 'as fast as
her short legs would carry her'

Enid Linder

Newlands church where Lucie's father was vicar, and where the little
black cat was found curled up asleep on the reading desk

The Wanderings of a Small Black Cat

A little white washed village church
   hid in a valley deep—
—and, curled upon the reading desk,
   a small black cat asleep!

Demure it sat the sermon through,
   attentive, silent, sage,
And now, a most contented cat
   dwells in the parsonage.

H.B.H.

what awful 'poetry'?

The Pie and the Patty-pan
1905

In the summer of 1896 Mr. Potter rented Lakefield, a country house in the village of Sawrey. At the foot of the garden which looked over Esthwaite Water, meadows sloped down gently to the edge of the lake. The Potters also spent the summers of 1900 and 1902 at Lakefield which had then been renamed Ees Wyke.

It is of one of these visits that an old inhabitant of Sawrey wrote, 'They came with their servants, their carriage and pair, and Miss Potter with her pony and phaeton. Their coachman, Mr. Beckett, and his wife and two boys, always had rooms at Hill Top, and we played and went to school with the Beckett boys. Miss Potter was about the village sketching everywhere and often came to our house.'

Quite close to Lakefield was a group of three cottages, approached by a sloping path leading off at right angles from the road. They were known as Lakefield Cottages and were well below the level of the road, sharing a small enclosure with its mosses and spring, and a pump in one corner which provided water for the cottages. James Rogerson, the gardener and caretaker at Lakefield, lived in one of these cottages.

In the summer of 1902 Beatrix Potter made some drawings of the interior of the third cottage, at that time the home of a Mrs. Lord, and in recent years the home of the late Mrs. J. E. Brockbank, Mr. Rogerson's married daughter.

The drawings included a water-colour and pen-and-ink sketches of the living-room; also pen-and-ink sketches of the pots of geraniums on the living-room window-sill, of the entrance passage, the pantry, the stairs, and of some of the up-stairs rooms, including details of carved oak furniture. In some of these sketches Beatrix Potter had roughly drawn the outline of a cat. She also sketched Sawrey village, including the entrance to the sloping path which led down to Lakefield Cottages, and the attractive design on the door of the post office, which stands beside the grassy lane that runs alongside the post office meadow.

These became the background drawings for the 'cat' story she had been planning in 1903, but when *The Tale of Two Bad Mice* was chosen for the next book, nothing more came of the 'cat' story until the beginning of 1905, when it was decided that it should be published at the end of that year.

This story was about a cat called Ribby and a dog called Duchess. Ribby, or to be more precise, Mrs. Ribstone Pippin, was the cousin of Mrs. Tabitha Twitchit. To illustrate the story there were nineteen rough pencil sketches and an unfinished painting of Ribby sitting in front of the fire, which was marked 'frontispiece'.

The question of a larger format had already been discussed when planning

The Tale of Two Bad Mice, but no definite action had been taken. Now, however, it was decided to adopt the larger format and to increase the size of the book pictures.

As had already been hinted in a letter to Norman Warne, Beatrix Potter felt that the original 1903 story of Ribby and Duchess was too thin, so she altered the plot and rewrote the whole story, but kept the same setting and characters.

Margaret Lane tells how '*The Pie and the Patty-Pan* roams about the village of Sawrey, lingering over the tiger-lilies and snapdragons in cottage gardens, glancing into parlours and kitchens, pausing to admire a white-washed slate-roofed porch covered with purple clematis, and to consider the plants in cottage windows and the pumps in backyards. One or two of the street scenes were drawn in Hawkshead, but the book is Beatrix Potter's praise of Sawrey, and contains many village details that she loved.'

As well as the village of Sawrey, we get a glimpse in the frontispiece of Hill Top as it first appeared before the new rooms were added in 1906, where Ribby is seen walking across the post office meadow after fetching butter and milk from the farm.

Duchess in real life lived at Lakefield Cottage. In the story, however, she lived in another cottage, and when reading Ribby's invitation to come to tea, she is shown in the garden of Buckle Yeat, opposite Ginger and Pickles' shop. When 'Duchess came out of *her* house, at the other end of the village', the setting is the entrance to Ginger and Pickles' shop with its beautiful tiger lilies, combined with the picturesque post office doorway.

Duchess was a valuable Pomeranian dog, and Mrs. Brockbank wrote, 'Duchess was my mother's dog (Mrs. Rogerson's). She was a pedigree dog, and my mother bred some good show specimens from her.' Mrs. Rogerson also had another Pomeranian dog called Darkie, who was better looking than Duchess, so Beatrix Potter used Darkie as a model when painting the pictures, but it was the character and intelligence of Duchess which she had in mind when writing the story. Thus when Ribby said to Duchess, 'how beautifully you beg! Oh, how sweetly pretty!' Beatrix Potter was describing what she had actually seen—Duchess begging with the sugar on her nose, waiting until nine had been counted before she touched it, as she had been taught.

'When *The Pie and Patty-pan* went to Warnes', wrote Mrs. Brockbank, 'they did not think a Pom. could have such a mane, so she took the photo to show them. Of course Poms were not known so much then.'

'I enclose a photograph of the original Duchess (on a chair) in very bad coat,' wrote Beatrix Potter to Warnes. 'She was never much to look at herself, though a most valuable little dog.' The handsome Darkie was included in the photograph to show the fine mane which a Pomeranian could have.

Beatrix Potter now began work on her book drawings, using the background sketches she had previously made. Faithful to the smallest detail, she painted a pair of pattens by the entrance porch to Lakefield Cottage. 'Those were used by my mother,' explained Mrs. Brockbank, 'when she went outside to fetch water from the pump—she always kept a pair of pattens by the porch.'

'Cousin Stephanie' as a child remembers the picture of Duchess standing on a red cushion being painted when Beatrix Potter was staying with them at Melford Hall, and how as a great treat she was allowed to put some red paint on the cushion! 'I wonder if she took it off again,' said Stephanie.

When it came to the picture of Dr. Maggotty, who was putting rusty nails into a bottle of ink, Beatrix Potter decided to go to the Zoological Gardens to study magpies. In a letter to Norman Warne she informed him, 'Perhaps I can get to-morrow to draw a magpie at the Zoological Gardens.'

In a small sketch-book we find sketches of magpies, together with some notes on the colouring of their feathers—parts are 'very blue' and parts 'green'; there is also a brief note which reads, 'Brown black eye, nose a little hookier than jackdaw, less feathered'. She also observed that the tail of the magpie was 'more than half' of the bird's overall length.

Towards the end of May *The Pie and the Patty-pan* drawings were nearly finished, and Beatrix Potter wrote to Warnes saying, 'I think I had better bring the drawings on Wednesday afternoon on the chance that Mr. Norman Warne could look over them', adding, 'I think it promises to make a pretty book.'

Apparently Norman Warne criticized one of the drawings of Ribby, for Beatrix Potter wrote, 'If you are still doubtful about the little cat—will you post it back to me at once C/o F. Burton Esq., Gwaynynog, Denbigh. I remember they have a cat! I don't feel perfectly satisfied with the eyes of the large head, but I think I can get it right, by taking out the lights carefully, if you will ask Hentschel not to do it before we have proofs. The drawing is getting too much rubbed. I daresay I may post the other two on Sunday; it depends on the weather; it is difficult to sit at work on a fine spring day in the country.'

Both Norman Warne and Beatrix Potter were now working hard on the preparation of the book, and their letters were going to and fro—often crossing one another. On May 25th we find Norman Warne writing, 'I think you have two dummy books of *The Pie and Patty-pan,* could you spare me one of these for a time? as I want to be quite clear about the size of the plates before going on with the blocks. I have been looking again this morning at the six plates you left, but I am still not quite happy about two plates of the Duchess—There seems to me to be too much bend about her nose and the division between the legs should be made clearer; my brothers find the same fault, so I think I will keep these two plates back and get you to look at them once more before making the blocks.'

The following day, in reply to another letter from Beatrix Potter, he wrote:

Facsimile of a letter from Norman Warne to Beatrix Potter about her drawings for *The Pie and the Patty-pan*, dated May 26th 1905

Beatrix Potter standing in the porch at Hill Top,
about 1907

A winter scene showing the approach to
Hill Top by night

Lakefield, Sawrey, where Beatrix Potter stayed in the summer of 1896, and first became acquainted with Hill Top

The Pie and the Patty-pan: 1905

May 26th 1905

Dear Miss Potter,

I have to acknowledge with thanks the receipt of yours enclosing two more originals and the little kitten's head for the cover. I find the picture of the two sitting at tea still looks a little unfinished. I take it however that you want to keep the background light and shall therefore put in hand.

I like your brown pen-and-ink sketches very much, and I think if you carry out the outline pictures for the Pie and the Patty-pan in this spirit, there will be no difficulty in reproducing them in the brown ink. I am still keeping back the two dog plates about which I wrote yesterday and we can go over them again together when we see how those I am printing in hand come out. With kind regards and trusting you will have a pleasant holiday in Wales.

> Believe me,
> Yours sincerely,
> Norman D. Warne.

The dummy to which Norman Warne referred was made up from *Peter Rabbit* sheets folded to twice their normal size, on which cut-up proofs of the text were pasted. On the cover of Beatrix Potter's copy, she had written, 'Pie and Patty-pan dummy paste-up', and in it were various small changes to the text.

A complication now arose, when one of the pictures did not quite fit in with what she had written, and Beatrix Potter, always willing to help, offered to alter the drawing. When this was done, she wrote to Norman Warne saying, 'I have altered the oven as it will save a good many corrections. I did a good deal to the cat but she still is looking at the top one. I don't think it signifies as she talks about both ovens . . . I don't think I have ever seriously considered the state of the *pie*, but the *book* runs some risk of being over cooked if it goes on much longer! I am sorry about the little dog's nose. I saw it was too sharp. I think I have got it right. I was intending to explain the ovens by saying the middle handle is very stiff so that Duchess concludes it is a sham;—like the lowest. I think only two pages want changing; I think it will come right.'

The drawings for *The Pie and the Patty-pan* were at last finished, and early in June Norman Warne wrote to express his approval. In her reply Beatrix Potter said, 'I am very glad you liked the remaining drawings; if the book prints well it will be my next favourite to the "Tailor".'

The Potter family were now off to Wales for their summer holiday, and before she left, Beatrix Potter wrote to Norman Warne saying, 'I should like to get some new work fixed before going away to Wales. I am feeling all right for work.'

Not very long after her arrival at Merioneth in Wales, Norman Warne sent a written proposal of marriage, which she accepted. Then quite suddenly and unexpectedly, on August 25th 1905, he died of leukaemia at the age of thirty-seven—

thus ended four happy years of close co-operation, during which period they had together planned and produced the first seven of Beatrix Potter's books. Although Norman Warne did not live to see the published book, he had seen it in its final stages.

Not long before the book was due to be published, Beatrix Potter remembered that there was no end-paper design, and wrote to Warnes saying, 'I conclude there is no time to get an end-paper design done—unless Mr. Stokoe has already designed one—I do not mind one way or another; I had begun to scribble something but it looks a bit stiff. So *The Pie and the Patty-pan* was published with plain mottled lavender end-papers, and it was not until it was bound in a slightly different cover some years later that end-paper designs were used, featuring a pie and a patty-pan.

From 1930 onwards, to bring the book into line with the others in the series, it was printed in the ordinary small format, and the title changed to *The Tale of the Pie and the Patty-pan*.

It was dedicated to Joan and Beatrix Moore: 'For Joan, to read to Baby'.

FIRST VERSION OF THE STORY OF DUCHESS AND RIBBY

'Hastings, Nov. 26–Dec. 3 '03'

Something very very NICE

Once upon a time there was a Pussy-cat, called 'Ribby', and she wrote a letter inviting a little dog, called 'Duchess', to tea.

'Come in good time, my dear Duchess,' said the letter, 'and we will have something so very, very, nice for tea.'

Duchess read her letter and sent an answer by the postman—

'I will come with much pleasure at a quarter past four. But I hope it isn't fish? my dear Ribby?' said Duchess.

Then pussy-cat began to prepare for her tea-party.

First she went to the well for water to fill her kettle, and when Timothy Baker's cart came round, she bought a beautiful sponge cake.

Then she unlocked the cupboard where she kept her silver spoons, and she took them out and rubbed them bright with a bit of wash-leather.

And then she opened a wall-cupboard where she kept her china—tea cups and saucers and plates—and she took out a blue dish, and went to Buckle Yeat, and begged a comb of honey—and then she took a jug and a basket and she went to the farm for milk and butter.

And then she went to the village shop to buy half a pound of tea, and two pounds of lump sugar, and a pot of strawberry jam—but none of these things were the 'something very nice!' It was cooked and ready, covered up with a clean white cloth, upon the larder shelf!

Then Pussy-cat went upstairs, to her bedroom to dress.

She pulled out a drawer, and took out a black silk apron; and she put on her best black net cap trimmed with beads. And then she came down stairs and stood upon a sofa at the window watching for the little dog.

Duchess also had been very busy getting ready for the tea-party; but she did not put on any fine clothes, because she had such a beautiful black silky coat of her own.

She gathered a bunch of flowers in her garden as a present for Ribby, and she packed up something very precious in a basket with a lid—

'I don't believe that Ribby can have anything for tea that is half so nice as this!' said Duchess to herself—

It was rather too early when Duchess came trotting down the lane—it was only five minutes past four.

She came round the corner of Pussy-cat's house and looked in at the window as she passed.

She stood in the porch and knocked. 'Come in!' and 'How do you do, my dear Duchess?' said Ribby. 'How do you do, my dear Ribby' said Duchess, 'I've brought you some flowers; but I hope it isn't fish or mice?'

'Do not talk about food, my dear Duchess,' said Ribby, 'it is something much superior to either mice or fish! What beautiful flowers! and what a neat little basket,' said Ribby.

—'I wonder what is inside it! can it be anything to eat?'

'It is something delicious, my dear Ribby,' replied Duchess.

'Let us sit before the fire and put the kettle on,' said Ribby—'and tell each other news. Have you heard the dreadful story about James's hens?'

'Oh dreadful! dreadful! dreadful! my dear Ribby' said Duchess. 'One killed on Monday and two more on Tuesday—oh that wicked Fox! I shall be afraid to go home by myself after dark!'

'No, it was not a fox I believe, my dear Duchess; it was a rat. It was certainly a rat because he stole 4 white eggs.'

'No, my dear Ribby; there were only 3 in the hen-house and they were all brown ones. No; it was certainly a fox!'

'Were they all brown? how very interesting!' said Ribby.

'It was certainly a fox; he took a black chicken and two white hens!' said Duchess.

'No, my dear Duchess; the hen was the black one, and the two chickens were white!'

'Were they white with yellow feet? my dear Ribby?' asked Duchess, 'and what is the something very nice?'

'I'm going to the larder to fetch it,' said Ribby.

'If you please, my dear Duchess, will you pull down the blind? James goes past to his tea at a quarter to five!'

'What is it? oh what is it? my dear Ribby?' asked Duchess.

'It's a chicken pie, my dear Duchess!' said Ribby.

'Then it was not a fox after all? my dear Ribby?' said Duchess—

'No, I don't think it was. The plates are very hot, take care!'

'Do you like a good deal of pie-crust, my dear Duchess?' said Ribby.

'It smells very very nice, my dear Ribby!' said Duchess—'are there any pieces of hard boiled egg in the pie?'

'I couldn't find any at all, there were none in the hen-house,' said Ribby—'the rat—or the fox—had stolen them all—But why have you hidden your basket under the table? and what are you taking out of it, my dear Duchess?' said Ribby—

'Three beautiful brown eggs!'

The End

Ribby's porch as it is today (Lakefield Cottage)

Leslie Linder

Duchess's garden as it is today (at Buckle Yeat)

Enid Linder

The Sawrey Post Office of earlier times

This doorway was copied in the picture of Duchess carrying a basket with the veal and ham pie

Enid Linder

Rushes at the edge of Esthwaite Water, the home of Mr. Jeremy Fisher

Enid Linder

The Tale of Mr. Jeremy Fisher
1906

The story about Mr. Jeremy Fisher first took definite form in a picture letter written to Eric Moore, from Eastwood, Dunkeld, on September 5th 1893, the day after the Peter Rabbit letter was sent to Noel. This six-page letter, with pictures on every page, began:

'My dear Eric,

'Once upon a time there was a frog called Mr. Jeremy Fisher, and he lived in a little house on the bank of a river . . .'

Eastwood was situated on the bank of the river Tay, just below Dunkeld Bridge, and the grounds stretched for some distance on either side of the house alongside the river; so in 1893 Mr. Jeremy Fisher's home was on the bank of the Tay, and he sailed in a *boat*, like the fishing boats Mr. Potter and his friends used during their Scottish holidays.

Beatrix Potter was familiar with all the characteristics of frogs, and in her Journal we find how at the age of seventeen she studied and played with frogs. A year later we hear of the death of her pet frog *Punch*: 'Poor little *Punch* died on the 11th., green frog, had him five or six years. He has been extensive journeys.' She knew how important it was for her stories to be true to nature, and realized that only by careful study and observation could a writer fulfil this objective.

Many years later when commenting on one of Kenneth Grahame's books, Beatrix Potter wrote, 'Yes—Kenneth Grahame ought to have been an artist—at least all writers for children ought to have a sufficient recognition of what things look like—did he not describe "Toad" as combing his *hair*? A mistake to fly in the face of nature—A frog may wear goloshes; but I don't hold with toads having beards or wigs! so I prefer Badger.' Therefore in all aspects of Mr. Jeremy Fisher's appearance and activities, he remains true to nature.

In 1892 Beatrix Potter had sold a few of her drawings to a firm called Ernest Nister—a German firm of Fine Art Colour Printers who had a London office at 24, St. Bride Street, E.C. In July of that year, when staying at Heath Park, Birnam, near Dunkeld, she had referred to one of these drawings for Nister: 'I was busy in the morning finishing a drawing of a Jackdaw for Nister & Co. for which, by the way, they have not paid.' The jackdaw in question was carrying a set of long-handled brushes and impersonating a sweep.

She now wished to offer Nister something more ambitious, and wondered whether her story of Mr. Jeremy Fisher could be made into a booklet. The correspondence which followed is of particular interest as it shows the business-like way in which Beatrix Potter handled a situation in which the firm of Ernest Nister were endeavouring to get the most favourable terms they possibly could!

To Miss Beatrix Potter

May 25th 1894   24, St. Bride Street, E.C.

Dear Madam,

Many thanks for sending us these designs.

Will you kindly let me know how much you would want for the little booklet of the frogs fishing? I am a little doubtful whether we can take it, we certainly cannot make a booklet of it as people do not want frogs now. The only way in which we could use it would be as a double page in our 'Annual' and as you can imagine we cannot afford much for this. The days of these booklets are quite gone out, they do not pay to produce, people are so utterly tired of them and want some novelty.

I fear we cannot keep more than three of the other designs—the cat with the tea set, the mouse knitting, and the rabbit with the umbrella and basket. For these we should be pleased to pay you 7/6 a piece if you can see your way to take it. We could not afford more than this, as in order to fit them for our purpose we should have to do a little bit more to them.

I wish we could have used more of the other drawings, but—though most of them are very nice—the way in which they are painted unfits them unfortunately for the only method of reproduction by which we could make use of them.

Yours faithfully,
Robt. E. Mack.

Four days later Beatrix Potter accepted their offer of 7/6 each for the three miscellaneous drawings, and asked for twenty-five shillings for the set of frog drawings. Nister replied by return of post:

To Miss B. Potter

May 30th 1894   24, St. Bride Street, E.C.

Dear Madam,

In answer to yours of yesterday, I am afraid I cannot afford to give more than a guinea for the 'Pen & Ink' drawings, there are two or three of them that I shall not be able to use.

With regard to the coloured drawings, I have accepted two of them and am returning the other with this.

Yours faithfully,
Robt. E. Mac.

Beatrix Potter remained firm, and wrote to them as follows:

To Ernest Nister

2, Bolton Gardens, S.W.

Sir,

I have received your letter of 30th. inst. in which you accept two coloured drawings at 7/6 each, and shall be much obliged if you will remit the amount at your convenience.

I am not disposed to accept less than 25/- for the 10 pen & inks, but if you will return the two drawings of the series, which you find you cannot make use of, I will accept 20/– for the remaining 8. If you do not care to buy so many as 8, I am afraid I must trouble you to return all the ten.

> I remain Sir,
> yrs. sincerely,
> Beatrix Potter.

To which they replied:

To Miss B. Potter

June 2nd 1894   24, St. Bride Street, E.C.

Dear Madam,

Many thanks for your letter. I think the best way will be to make a compromise and return you one of the sketches and keep the rest for a guinea ($£1.1.0$). We cannot quite see how to take another picture away, for if we do, it breake [sic] up the story and spoils the whole thing.

A cheque for these designs and the two color ones we have kept will be sent to you on our next pay day.

If at any future time you have anything that you think would suit us we should be very pleased to see it.

> Yours faithfully,
> Robt. E. Mack.

The letter must have arrived the same day, for Beatrix Potter's reply is also dated June 2nd.

To Mr. E. Nister

June 2nd 1894   2, Bolton Gardens, S.W.

Sir,

I have received your letter of 2nd. inst. with reference to the pen & ink drawings, but regret to inform you that I am not willing to accept 21/– for 9, and I am of opinion that you had better return them without further discussion.

> I remain Sir, yours sincerely,
> Beatrix Potter.

Realizing that she was standing firm, they replied:

To Miss Potter

June 4th 1894   24, St. Bride Street, E.C.

Dear Madam,

We are sorry that you cannot see your way clear to accept a guinea for the sketches, as we pointed out to you that it was not that we wanted the whole series, that did not matter much to us, but the fact was that the omission of two of them rendered the story rather incomplete.

We are sending you with this a cheque for 22/6⎫
& 7/6 for 2 col. drawings 15/–⎭ $£1.17.6$

> Yours faithfully,
> Robt. E. Mack.

So Beatrix Potter stood her ground and they paid the price she asked. Of no great importance in terms of money, but a moral victory for Miss Potter!

In due course this set of nine drawings bearing the title 'A Frog he would a fishing go' appeared in one of Nister's Children's Annuals, under the imprint 'London: Ernest Nister, and New York: E. P. Dutton & Co.' The book was printed in Bavaria and was called *Comical Customers*.

The nine frog drawings occupied three full pages and illustrated a very indifferent set of verses which were signed C.B. Nisters had prepared the tenth drawing themselves, and it replaced the one they would not pay for. It was a drawing of a frog holding a fishing-rod, and the fishing-line was spread across the top of the page, shaped to form the letters of the title. Each of Beatrix Potter's drawings bore the initials H.B.P. (Helen Beatrix Potter).

For several years the story of Mr. Jeremy Fisher remained untouched, though not forgotten, for on November 6th 1902, a few weeks after Warne's edition of *The Tale of Peter Rabbit* was published, we find Beatrix Potter telling Norman Warne, 'I should like to do Mr. Jeremy Fisher too some day, and I think I could make something of him.'

The question now arose—who owned the copyright? The answer is to be found in a letter which Beatrix Potter wrote to Fruing Warne on June 16th 1926, telling him, 'I bought back Jeremy Fisher; both all the pen and ink drawings and zinc blocks for £6 directly after Peter Rabbit was printed. They professed to have destroyed them until I bid them up to £6, when they were promptly "found". They evidently thought me very eccentric to make a fuss about getting them back.'

Towards the end of her life, Beatrix Potter wrote on the back of one of Nister's letters, 'Nister was an unattractive German (?) Firm—but it was my first start at anything published. H.B.H.' After her death the nine zinc blocks of these frog drawings were found, and on the brown paper wrapping were the words 'Zinc blocks of Jeremy Fisher—bought back, with copyright from E. Nister . . .'

Little is known of the final planning of the story or of the preparation of the drawings, except that Beatrix Potter painted some beautiful studies of water lilies.

The Tale of Mr. Jeremy Fisher was dedicated to Stephanie Hyde-Parker, and the dedication page reads, 'For Stephanie from Cousin B'.

In 1940 when writing to Mrs. Miller, Beatrix Potter told her, '"Jemima Puddle-Duck", "Jeremy Fisher" and others lived at Sawrey in the southern part of the English Lake District.' This was the part of England she loved so much, and of Esthwaite Water, which was now Mr. Jeremy Fisher's home, she wrote in her Journal, 'I have often been laughed at for thinking Esthwaite Water the most beautiful of the Lakes. It really strikes me that some scenery is almost theatrical, or ultra-romantic.' So *now* instead of rowing in a boat on the river Tay, Mr. Jeremy Fisher sailed on Esthwaite Water sitting on a picturesque water lily.

Enid Linder

Cows knee-deep in Esthwaite Water, at the foot of the meadow
below Lakefield

View of Near Sawrey from Hill Top, showing Stoney Lane winding up the hillside

Sketches of frogs

Rough sketch for a picture sold to Ernest Nister,
Publisher and Fine Art Colour Printer, for one of
their children's annuals of the mid-90s

A set of nine drawings bearing the title 'A Frog he would a-fishing go' sold to Ernest Nister, Publisher and Fine Art Colour Printer, for one of their children's annuals of the mid-90s

The frog goes fishing

He jumps into his fishing boat

He waits for a bite

He tries again to catch a fish

He succeeds, but the fish nips his fingers

He decides that he has had enough of fishing

He goes home empty handed, and the fish laugh at him

He contents himself with a meal of grasshopper

The fish are still laughing at him

The Wallet containing the M.S. of *The Sly old Cat*

This is a sly old Cat,
who gave a tea party
to a rat.

This is the rat in his best
clothes coming down the
area steps. (They had
their tea in the kitchen

"How do you do? Mr Rat!
Will you sit on this chair?"
said the Cat.

"I will eat my bread and butter
first," said the Cat, "and then
you shall eat the crumbs
that are left, Mr Rat!"

"This is a very rude way
of treating visitors!" said
Mr Rat to himself —

Now I will pour out my tea said the cat, "and you shall lick up the drops that are left in the milk jug, Mr Rat; and then I will have some dessert!" said the Cat.

"I believe she is going to eat
me for dessert; I wish I'd
never come!" said poor Mr.
Rat.

She tipped up the milk jug
—That greedy old Cat! She
did'nt want to leave one
single drop for the rat.

But the rat jumped on
the table and gave the jug
a pat, and it slipped
down quite tight over the
head of the cat!

Then the cat banged about
the kitchen with its head
fast in the jug,

And the rat sat on the table drinking tea out of a mug!

Then he put a muffin in
a paper bag and went
away.

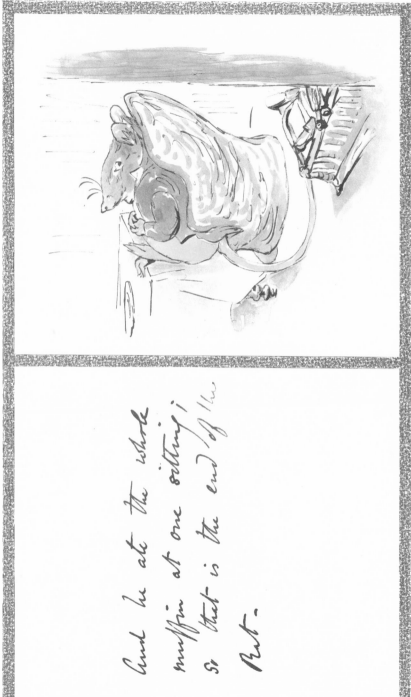

And he ate the whole
muffin at one sitting;
so that is the end of the
Rat.

and the Cat broke the jug
against the leg of the kitchen
table; so that is the end
of the Cat.

A photograph of Beatrix Potter with two of the Moore family, Joan (left) and Norah (right). Taken in 1912, when they were staying with her at Broad Ley's, Windermere

The Story of a Fierce Bad Rabbit; The Story of Miss Moppet; and The Sly Old Cat

1906

At the beginning of 1906 when working on *The Tale of Mr. Jeremy Fisher*, Beatrix Potter was also planning some stories for very young children.

Each story contained fourteen pictures and fourteen pages of simple text. The pictures and text were arranged in pairs and were in panoramic form, mounted on a long strip of linen, and folded concertina-wise into a wallet with a tuck-in flap.

Three stories were written in this form—*The Story of a Fierce Bad Rabbit, The Story of Miss Moppet*, and *The Sly Old Cat*; but only the first two were published.

The Story of a Fierce Bad Rabbit was written specially for Harold Warne's little girl, Louie, who had told Aunt Beatrix that Peter was much too good a rabbit, and *she* wanted a story about a really naughty one! The manuscript, which is dated 'Feb. 23rd. 06', was given to Louie, and her father had it specially bound in wallet form, just like the published copies.

Some years later, after her marriage to William Heelis, she wrote to Warnes saying, 'My husband undertakes to hold a gun properly, which was a defect in the Bad Rabbit pictures.' A new picture of the gun was prepared and sent to them, but apparently it was never used.

The manuscript of *The Sly Old Cat*, which is dated 'March 21st. 06', was given to Louie's sister Nellie, and this was also specially bound into a wallet. *The Sly Old Cat* would most probably have been published early in 1907 had not it been for an unexpected complication—the reluctance of the shops to stock copies of these panoramic books.

Towards the end of her life Beatrix Potter referred to this fact, saying, 'Bad Rabbit and Moppet were originally printed on long strips—The shops sensibly refused to stock them because they got unrolled and so bad to fold up again.'

In 1916 *The Story of a Fierce Bad Rabbit* and *The Story of Miss Moppet* were printed in book form, in a similar but slightly smaller format than the other books in the series.

Having changed these from panoramic to book form, Warnes were now considering the possibility of publishing *The Sly Old Cat* as an additional title in the series, and Mr. Fruing Warne wrote to Beatrix Potter asking if she would be willing to prepare the necessary drawings.

Beatrix Potter thought the story was quite amusing and had no objection to its being published, but she did not feel inclined to prepare a set of new drawings:

'I should have to re-draw the pictures and probably part trace them, to save the expression', she wrote.

She thought things over and then sent the following letter to Mr. Warne:

To Mr. Fruing Warne

August 12th 1916   Sawrey, Ambleside

Dear Mr. Warne,

After a week's reflection I see daylight. You had better engage Mr. E. A. Aris to illustrate *The Sly Old Cat*. His plagiarisms are unblushing, and his drawing excellent. If you showed him Nellie's little booklet I have little doubt that he would be sufficiently modest to copy the designs exactly, and do them really well. His mice have too large ears, he should be advised that rats have still smaller ears. He can draw cats much better than I can, and he would do the rat's clothing excellently . . .

I should be glad to hear what you think about it. I should think he would accept a sum down for a set of designs, certainly I would do the same—and a modest one rather than the cumbersome royalty, for the use of my name and the letterpress.

I have wished for a long time that you could find some second string—this man to my thinking is just what we want if he would draw to order and take suggestions—

You will have to get used to the idea that my eyes are giving way, whether you like it or not—and if I manage to do yet another book it would not be that cat story—(though I think it really amusing), but I do not draw cats well, and am away from that sort of background.

I am registering letter as the original is enclosed.

Let me know what you do, as I shall write to him if you don't, about a design I should like done and which I never could have drawn myself.

yrs. sincerely,
Beatrix Heelis.

The last paragraph of her letter is believed to refer to the story of *The Oakmen*. Nothing more came of this proposal, however, and the manuscript of *The Sly Old Cat* was eventually returned to Nellie Warne.

The Tale of Tom Kitten
1907

It was when staying at Lakefield, Sawrey, in the summer of 1896 that Beatrix Potter first became acquainted with Hill Top. About 1905 she said to one of the domestic servants there, 'If ever you hear of a small farm in Sawrey for sale, I think I could afford to buy one, and would very much like to own one.'

Not long after came the news of the forthcoming sale of Hill Top Farm, which was duly passed on to Beatrix Potter. And when the time came for the sale, she purchased it, with the royalties from her books and a small legacy from an aunt.

The farmhouse is situated just behind the Tower Bank Arms and is approached from the road through a wicket gate, from which a path leads up the garden to the house. It faces away from the village with a view across gently rising pasture land. From the hill above, there is a magnificent view beyond the farmhouse across Esthwaite Water, with the Coniston Fells in the far distance. There is also a carriage drive, with its entrance further down the road.

John Cannon, who was running the farm at the time of the sale, was kept on by Beatrix Potter to manage it for her. She hoped eventually to make it her Lakeland home, but in the meantime she would visit it whenever she could.

It was the garden at Hill Top which Beatrix Potter used as the setting for *The Tale of Tom Kitten*, and the pictures in the book give us delightful glimpses of this garden. In his Monograph on Beatrix Potter, Marcus Crouch says, 'The garden scenes give enduring delight . . . there are countless details for the small child to find for himself, of flower and tree and butterfly.'

We also see pictures of the interior of the farmhouse where Tom Kitten lived with his mother Mrs. Tabitha Twitchit and his two sisters Mittens and Moppet. In other pictures we see the wicket gate and path leading to the entrance porch, with its six-foot slabs of Brathay slate on either side; the gate at the far end of Smithy Lane where Stoney Lane winds up the hillside towards Bank Wood and High Wray; also some of the Puddle-Ducks—including Jemima, whose story is told in Beatrix Potter's next book.

Beatrix Potter appears to have started work on *The Tale of Tom Kitten* in the summer of 1906, and it is interesting to note that during the preparation of this book she was busily engaged in planning the garden at Hill Top. In her letters to Norman Warne's sister, Millie, we hear about the book pictures and also details of the garden.

On July 18th 1906, she wrote, 'Miss Woodward has had to go back to London today, but I am expecting someone else either Saturday or Monday. In the meantime

I have borrowed a kitten and I am rather glad of the opportunity of working at the drawings. It is very young and pretty and a most fearful pickle. One of the masons brought it from Windermere.' And a week later, to Harold Warne: 'I have not quite finished the Kitten, it is an exasperating model; and I always find it difficult to settle to indoor work in the country. I hope I have not been inconveniently long about it.'

Three weeks later, from Lingholm, where Beatrix Potter was on holiday with her parents, she wrote, 'I am wishing most heartily that I was back at Sawrey, but I suppose I shall scramble along here for a bit; at all events I must get some drawing done, that kitten book has been sadly neglected. I am up aloft with my drawing etc. in one of the attics. I thought there might be more air, but there is such a wind I think I shall be blown out. It is a curious (and unpleasant) place for atmosphere, very stuffy and at the same time very windy; draughts of wind between the mountains and a draughty house. I miss the sheltered open air and the gardening.'

On October 12th Beatrix Potter informed Millie Warne, 'My news is all gardening at present, and supplies. I went to see an old lady at Windermere and impudently took a large basket and trowel with me. She had the most untidy overgrown garden I ever saw. I got nice things in handfuls without any shame, amongst others a bundle of lavender slips, if they "strike" they will be enough for a lavender hedge; and another bundle of violet suckers—I am going to set some of them in the orchard . . . Mrs. Satterthwaite says stolen plants always grow. I stole some "honesty" yesterday, it was put to be burnt in a heap of garden refuse! I have had something out of nearly every garden in the village.'

The story of Tom Kitten is written out in a 'penny' exercise book, the text being divided into short paragraphs, and twenty-four pencil sketches are pasted in by their corners.

Some of the pictures of ducks were painted when Beatrix Potter was in London. It seems that she used the ducks belonging to a distant cousin, who lived at Putney Park, as models, for she wrote of these pictures to Warnes: 'I hope to bring the remaining four in a few days, if I get to Putney again tomorrow. I hope you will like them. I think myself that they will lighten up the book. It is a refreshment to do some outdoor sketching again.'

Of interest is a pencil sketch of three Puddle-Ducks which illustrated the sentence, 'They stopped and stood in a row, and stared up at the kittens'. In this rough sketch, the Puddle-Duck on the right is looking in the direction of the wall on which the three kittens are sitting, but the remaining two Puddle-Ducks are facing the *other* way—apparently in conversation with the first. In copying this sketch when painting her book picture, Beatrix Potter, apparently without realizing it, turned the head of the first duck in the same direction as that of the other two—so that all three now have their backs to the wall on which the kittens are sitting!

Sketches of kittens

MITTENS laughed so that she fell off the wall Moppet and Tom descended after her; the pinafores and all the rest of Tom's clothes came off on the way down.

"Come! Mr. Drake Puddle-Duck," said Moppet—"Come

"Come and help us to dress him! Come and button up Tom!"

QUITE the contrary; they were not in bed; *not* in the least.

There were very extra-ordinary noises during the whole of the tea-party some-how.

Somehow there were very extraordinary noises overhead; which disturbed the dignity and repose of the tea-party.

Galley proofs of *The Tale of Tom Kitten*

This small oversight would only be apparent to those familiar with the village of Sawrey, as the kittens themselves are not actually shown in the picture.

Beatrix Potter made various amendments to the text of her manuscript, individual words being changed and some of the sentences rewritten. The amendments were made by pasting over strips of paper on which the revised text was written.

Warnes criticized the line 'all the rest of Tom's clothes came off' and suggested that the word 'all' should be replaced by 'nearly all'. In answer, Beatrix Potter wrote, '"*Nearly* all" won't do! because I have drawn Thomas already with nothing! —That would not signify; I could give something over but there are not many garments for Mr. Drake to dress himself in; and it would give the story a new and criminal aspect if he forcibly took off and *stole* Tom's trousers!'

In due course the galley proofs arrived, bearing the date February 21st 1907, and Beatrix Potter looked through these very carefully, attending to any typographical errors and still further improving the text. Some of her last-minute improvements are of interest:

page* Text on Galley Proof	Text as revised
52 'Come! Mr. Drake Puddle-Duck,' said Moppet—'Come and button up Tom!'	'Come! Mr. Drake Puddle-Duck,' said Moppet—'Come and help us to dress him! Come and button up Tom!'
69 She called them to come down, smacked them and took them back to the house.	She pulled them off the wall, smacked them, and took them back to the house.
75 There were very extraordinary noises during the whole of the tea-party somehow.	Somehow there were very extraordinary noises over-head; which disturbed the dignity and repose of the tea-party.

When Beatrix Potter received her copy of the finished book, she told Mr. Warne, 'I am much pleased with "Tom Kitten". Some of the pictures are very bad, but the book as a whole is passable, and the ducks help it out.'

On the dedication page it reads, 'Dedicated to all Pickles,—especially to those that get upon my garden wall'—no doubt with the little 'Pickle' from Windermere in mind, as well as her Hill Top cats!

* For equivalent page numbers in the current edition see Appendix 2.

The Tale of Jemima Puddle-Duck
1908

Jemima was a real duck who lived at Hill Top Farm, and in *The Tale of Jemima Puddle-Duck* Beatrix Potter has shown her love of the farm by taking it as the setting for her story. Hill Top Farm at that time was still being managed by John Cannon, and it is interesting to find that in addition to the pictures of Jemima and the other animal characters, we can also catch a glimpse of Mrs. Cannon and her two children Ralph and Betsy.

Margaret Lane writes, '*Jemima Puddle-Duck* is her poem about the farm itself, and anyone who is curious to reconstruct its exact appearance in those days can do so from the pictures in that book. Mrs. Cannon appears at the back door, feeding the poultry; Ralph her little boy, discovers Jemima's nest under the rhubarb leaves, while Betsy Cannon passes beyond the gate. Miss Potter's cousin, Caroline Hutton, who was now Mrs. Clark and had a little boy of her own, remembered that she "was with her at Hill Top Farm when *Jemima Puddle-Duck* was being written, and went round about with her to find a suitable spot for the nest . . . Kep was a real dog, and his son whom she gave me was the dearest and cleverest dog I ever had." The idyllic landscape in which Jemima, wearing a shawl and a poke bonnet, is setting out to look for a secret nesting place, is precisely what one sees, even to-day, after passing through the gate at the bottom of the farmyard. If you turn round, on the very spot where Jemima is standing, you look straight up the farmyard to the house, as in the last picture in the book. In more than sixty years it has hardly changed.'

The ornamental ironwork gate leading into a small vegetable garden opposite the porch of the farmhouse can also still be seen. At the crown of the hill, by Jemima's wood, is the view across Esthwaite Water, with the Coniston Fells in the distance, and below to one's right, the farmhouse and the little village of Near Sawrey. Far Sawrey is a short distance along the road as it winds down towards Lake Windermere some two-and-a-half miles away.

There is a manuscript of *The Tale of Jemima Puddle-Duck* at Hill Top—a paper-covered exercise book with the text divided into short paragraphs, and spaces left for her rough sketches of the pictures. All but four of these rough sketches, which had been pasted in by their corners, have been taken out and in their place Beatrix Potter made notes of her progress to date: eleven pictures 'done'; three pictures 'to alter'; seven pictures 'begun'; two pictures 'to do' and one 'to finish'. At the end of this exercise book, slipped loosely in, is a photograph of the real Jemima, taken by Beatrix Potter on the farm. Throughout the manuscript there are paragraphs which have been rewritten on loose sheets and pasted over the original text, while in one instance a whole new page has been pasted in.

Beatrix Potter wrote two versions of the *opening* paragraph, the first: 'What a funny sight it is to see a brood of ducklings with a hen!' and the second, with its hint of a moral: 'What a gratifying thing it is in these days to meet with a female devoted to family life!' The first was the one she chose for her story. In the *second* paragraph one suspects that Warnes had intervened, for in the printed edition it reads, 'Listen to the story of Jemima Puddle-Duck, who was annoyed because the farmer's wife would not let her hatch her own eggs.' In the original text Beatrix Potter had written, 'was aggrieved', which she then altered to 'was provoked', adding 'aggrieved is a better word, but do children understand it?'

The Tale of Jemima Puddle-Duck was a much loved book. The late Mrs. M. E. Wight, wife of the forester for the Graythwaite Estate wrote, 'My daughter Mollie loved all the Beatrix Potter books, especially *Jemima Puddle-Duck*. A copy of this book was given her on her second birthday. It was quite worn out before another birthday came round and another copy had to be supplied. "Pudding" Duck became Mollie's familiar, her imaginary playmate and companion. When the time came for her to begin school I was told I should try to break her off from her imaginary friends or she would be a laughing stock among the school children. So I made the attempt and Mollie obediently tried to banish Pudding Duck, but she was very sad and when one day she came in from the garden and said "Mother, Pudding Duck is dead", I comforted her as best I could and told her of the joys awaiting her at school. It was useless. She lost interest in everything and became quite ill. Then one day when I was upstairs about my chores, I heard the rattle of china and sounds of a feast being prepared. I went to see what was happening and found the best china and silver and flowers set out and Mollie met me with a beaming face saying, "Pudding Duck is coming to tea". I said I thought she was dead and Mollie said, she was, but I had to "live" her again, I can't do without her. So Pudding Duck came to stay. I told Mrs. Heelis about this and she came to see Mollie and they had long talks about Mollie's woodland friends and habitations. They were perfectly happy together, Mrs. Heelis so thoroughly understood and identified herself with a child. Her books were just the right size and weight for their little hands.'

On another occasion, when Beatrix Potter was walking in the village of Sawrey, she came upon a group of children playing the story of Jemima—a little girl called Florence Dawson was acting the part of Jemima. She was very touched and gave the child an inscribed copy of the story, in which she wrote, 'For "Jemima", at Sawrey Camp from Beatrix Potter July 28th, '43'. It was given on her last birthday, when she was seventy-seven years of age.

The Tale of Jemima Puddle-Duck was dedicated to the Cannon children: 'A

Farmyard Tale for Ralph and Betsy'. Many years later Beatrix Potter gave a copy to the daughter of John Mackereth, one of her shepherds, and it bears the inscription 'Love to Isabel from Mrs. Heelis, in remembrance of Hill Top Farm, Sawrey.'

When Beatrix Potter died her ashes were scattered close to Jemima's wood—so the peaceful farmland of Hill Top became her last resting place.

A spinney of spruce trees close to Jemima's Wood

Enid Linder

Where Jemima stood when she 'reached the top of the hill'

Enid Linder

When Jemima 'reached the top of the hill, she saw a
wood in the distance'
When comparing this book picture with the photograph,
note the 'V'-shaped wall in the foreground

The dresser at Hill Top, past which Anna Maria ran with her plate of dough

The stairs up which 'Ribby and Tabitha rushed'

Enid Linder

The landing at Hill Top along which Mr. Samuel
Whiskers pushed the rolling pin

Enid Linder

'Mrs. Tabitha Twitchit searching for her son Thomas'
Duplicate book picture for *The Roly-Poly Pudding*, with its
setting at Hill Top

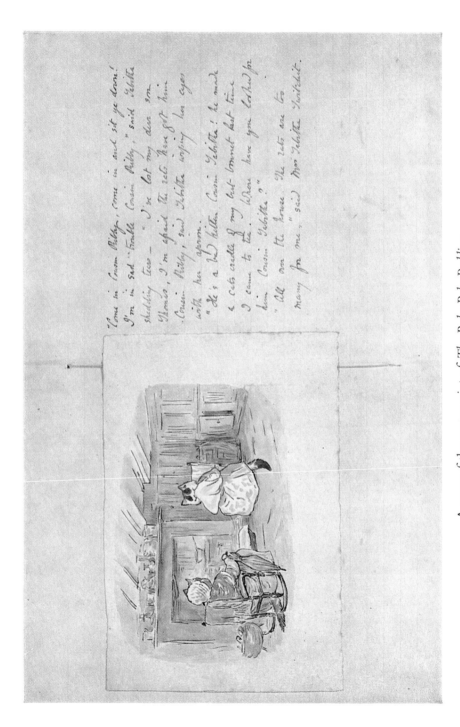

A page of the manuscript of *The Roly-Poly Pudding*
This manuscript was given to Winifred Warne, Christmas, 1906

The Roly-Poly Pudding
1908

In *The Roly-Poly Pudding* Beatrix Potter expresses her love of the quaint old farm-house at Hill Top, Sawrey, which she has taken as the setting for the story. The plot is evidently inspired by the numerous rats which were over-running the house at that time, and although the book was not published until the autumn of 1908, the story was actually written in 1906.

During its preparation Beatrix Potter was paying frequent visits to Sawrey so that she might keep an eye on the work being carried out at Hill Top, including repairs to the old farmhouse and an extension at the far end to accommodate Mr. and Mrs. Cannon. In due course she hoped to make Hill Top her Lakeland home, but for the time being she was lodging in the village.

In some of her letters to Millie Warne, Beatrix Potter told her about these visits, mentioning the rats and describing the old farmhouse. In a letter dated April 5th 1906, from Sawrey, she informed her: 'I had quite a hot dusty journey. I arrived at five and did some shopping at Windermere, and was out walking about till nearly bed time. It keeps light longer up here . . . I thought my property was looking extremely ugly when I arrived. I was quite glad you weren't there! The new works though doubtless an improvement are painfully *new* . . . I have had an amusing afternoon thoroughly exploring the house. It really is delightful—if the rats could be stopped out! There is one wall four foot thick with a staircase inside it. I never saw such a place for hide and seek and funny cupboards and closets.'

On these visits Beatrix Potter stayed at Belle Green with Mrs. Satterthwaite, wife of the village blacksmith, and followed with keen interest the work which was going on at Hill Top. On October 4th we hear more of the rats: 'The rats have come back in great force; two big ones were trapped in the shed here, besides turn-ing out a nest of eight baby rats in the cucumber frame opposite the door. They are getting at the corn at the farm. Mrs. Cannon calmly announced that she should get four or five cats! Imagine my feelings; but I daresay they will live in the out build-ings'; and a week later, 'The cats have not arrived yet, but Mrs. Cannon has seen a rat sitting up eating its dinner under the kitchen table in the middle of the after-noon. We are putting zinc on the bottoms of the doors—that and cement skirtings will puzzle them.'

Two days later in a letter to Millie Warne, Beatrix Potter described the entrance hall, which was now furnished and which appears in several of the pictures in the book. 'I came here last Tuesday', she wrote, 'and have been exceedingly busy . . . It was a perfect day on Friday, the little lake was like a looking glass, I think a still autumn day is almost the most beautiful time of year, but when there are such heavy hoar frosts at night it is always a chance whether the sun conquers the mist, or whether it turns to rain . . . I have done some gardening but no sketching or photographing yet! I don't know how I shall tear myself away in a fortnight. Another room has been got straight, the front kitchen—or hall—as I call it. I have not meddled with the fireplace, I don't dislike it, and besides it is wanted for the next book. I have got a pretty dresser with plates on it and some old fashioned chairs; and a warming pan that belonged to my grandmother; and Mrs. Warne's bellows which look well.'

The story of the Roly-Poly Pudding tells of the adventures of Tom Kitten and of Mr. Samuel Whiskers and his wife Anna Maria. When Tom Kitten was lost and Ribby and Tabitha were searching for him, Beatrix Potter told how they 'heard a door bang and somebody scuttered downstairs'. Warnes must have criticized the word 'scuttered', for Beatrix Potter wrote, 'I have been looking for "scutter" in Halliwell Phillip's Archaic words and I cannot find it, rather to my surprise. I think it is common Lancashire and probably good Anglo Saxon. There is another form of it "scat" or "scatter", and "scut" is a common name for *"tail"* of small animals. Rabbits or Hare's tails are generally called scuts.

'If you really want to change it I would have *scurried* rather than scuttle. "Scuttered" appears on p. 69[*] of the immortal Peter Rabbit which is a classic!' Warnes evidently withdrew their criticism, for the word remained unchanged.

The story was finished at the end of 1906, and at Christmas the manuscript was given to Fruing Warne's little girl, Winifred. Her father showed it to her saying, 'This is *your* manuscript, but it is very precious and *I* will look after it for you.'

The story was written in a stiff-covered exercise book, which contained in addition to the thirty-four pages of text, two water-colours and thirty-two pen-and-ink drawings in sepia. On the title page were the words 'The Roly-Poly Pudding, Christmas 1906', and just inside the front cover was the child's name and address, and the words 'From B.P.'

At the beginning of 1908 Beatrix Potter was working on the final book drawings, and on January 2nd in a letter to Millie Warne, she told her, 'I have got a lot of drawing done'. Warnes had agreed to publish the book in a large format, thus giving her scope for the fine detail work she liked to put into her drawings.

The kitchen range, which appears in the book pictures, was later replaced by an open grate, but apart from this, all the other details in the house are very much the same today as when the story was written, and there are many pictures in *The Roly-Poly Pudding* which show the interior of the old farmhouse.

In these pictures we see Ribby standing by the fine entrance door; Mrs. Tabitha Twitchit and Ribby sitting by the kitchen range; the dresser past which Anna Maria ran with her plate of dough; also a picture of Mrs. Tabitha Twitchit bathing

[*] Page 49 of the current edition.

her son Tom in the kitchen, while Ribby is in conversation with the dog John Joiner, named after old John Taylor's son from Ginger and Pickles' shop.

Another picture is of the stairs with their graceful balustrades, and halfway up, on the landing with the long window and claret-coloured curtains, Mrs. Tabitha Twitchit is seen searching for her son Thomas. In this picture, and also in a duplicate of it, Beatrix Potter has pasted on the head of the cat. Was this done because she was dissatisfied with the first face, or to obtain greater *relief* when viewing the picture, in which case there would never have been a first face?

Of one of the pictures Beatrix Potter wrote, 'The outside view of the old chimney with landscape is pretty . . . I remember I put it in because there was such a string of sooty inside pictures'.

At the very end of the story we get a glimpse of Miss Potter herself, standing at the end of Smithy Lane by Ginger and Pickles' shop, looking towards Farmer Potatoes' barn. Close to the barn we see Mr. Samuel Whiskers and his wife Anna Maria, who are on the run with big bundles on a little wheel-barrow. The picture of Farmer Potatoes in his barn was copied from a photograph which Beatrix Potter took of Farmer Postlethwaite, who lived nearby.

Although written about the rats at Hill Top, *The Roly-Poly Pudding* was dedicated to Beatrix Potter's tame white rat 'Sammy'. The dedication reads, 'In remembrance of "SAMMY" The intelligent pink-eyed Representative of a Persecuted (but Irrepressible) Race! An affectionate little Friend, and most accomplished Thief!' There must have been some criticism of the adjective 'pink-eyed', for Beatrix Potter wrote, 'I should like "pink-eyed" to stand, as "SAMMY" was an albino. I think it is sufficiently clear that the dedication is to an actual pet rat and "Mr. Samuel Whiskers" is never called "Sammy" in the book.'

Many years earlier Beatrix Potter had painted a picture of this tame rat, about whom she wrote, 'I have memory of him waddling along the floor, waiting to be picked up by my Aunt—a stout elderly lady who did not altogether appreciate his friendly advances. Poor Sammy. White rats are not very long lived; and he was always wanting to be petted in his declining months—But not everybody liked him—One of his scrapes was to cut a neat round piece, size of our half crowns, out of the middle of a sheet. He carried a curious collection of stolen articles to his box. I remember the Aunt providing a hard boiled egg, and watching the rolling of the egg along a passage; but she requested that his neat box might be kept firmly fastened.'

On the back of the half-title of *The Roly-Poly Pudding* is a mock book plate bearing Samuel Whiskers' coat of arms. The word 'Resurgam!!!' appears on the coat of arms, and underneath are the words 'Samuel Whiskers—His Book'.

For this book Beatrix Potter designed a special title page, introducing colour. At the top of the page there is a small painting of Mr. Samuel Whiskers sitting on his rolling-pin. At the sides of the title Moppet and Mittens are shown, and at the bottom there are some rats, with a central picture of Tom Kitten wrapped in dough, with his head and tail protruding at either end. The lettering and scroll designs linking the drawings together are all in blue.

Above and below the frontispiece there are some more scroll designs, and it is interesting to note that in 1902 Beatrix Potter experimented with similar scroll designs above and below her pictures in the privately printed *Tailor of Gloucester*, but they were only faintly pencilled in and never used.

In March 1918 there was a cheaper edition of *The Roly-Poly Pudding*, still in the large format, bound in paper boards in place of cloth.

In 1926 to bring it into line with the other books in the series, it was printed in the ordinary small format, which pleased Beatrix Potter, and the title was changed to *The Tale of Samuel Whiskers*. The mock book plate was omitted. (The title was not changed in the American copies.)

Beatrix Potter always regarded this story as her tribute to the old farmhouse at Hill Top, and in a copy which she inscribed for her shepherd's little girl, Isabel Mackereth, she wrote, 'To Isabel from Mrs. Heelis, in remembrance of the old farm house'.

Before she died, Beatrix Potter arranged that Hill Top Farm should eventually become the property of The National Trust, and in her will there is the request that 'the rooms and furnishings used by me at Hilltop Farm may be kept in their present condition'. She also left detailed instructions as to where many of her treasured possessions should be placed in the various rooms.

Her wishes were respected, and today, anyone visiting Hill Top may go over the house and see it just as it was during her lifetime. In particular, children will find delight in seeing the actual rooms and staircase pictured in *The Roly-Poly Pudding*, and they will be able to recognize the old farmhouse from the many beautiful pictures in the book—and to quote Beatrix Potter's own words, 'It is a funny old house, it would amuse children very much.'

The 'front kitchen—or hall' at Hill Top. The old kitchen range which
was used as a model for some of the pictures in *The Roly-Poly Pudding*
was later replaced by an open grate

Beatrix Potter

And when I was going to the post, late in the afternoon — I looked up the lane from the corner, and I saw Samuel Whiskers and his wife on the run, with large bundles on a little wheel-barrow.

They were just turning in under the gate, to Farmer Potatoes's barn.

A page of the manuscript of *The Roly-Poly Pudding*
This is one of the two occasions when Beatrix Potter put
herself into a book picture—the other occasion occurs in
The Tale of Pigling Bland

The Tale of the Flopsy Bunnies
1909

Beatrix Potter frequently visited her uncle and aunt at Gwaynynog, a fine old house in Denbigh, North Wales. She was staying with them in March 1909 when working on the illustrations for *The Tale of the Flopsy Bunnies*, so it was natural that she should choose their garden as the setting for the story.

Describing it in her Journal, she wrote, 'The garden is very large, two-thirds surrounded by a red-brick wall with many apricots, and an inner circle of old grey apple trees on wooden espaliers. It is very productive but not tidy, the prettiest kind of garden, where bright old fashioned flowers grow amongst the currant bushes.'

In her fairy-tale *Llewellyn's Well*, written partly at Gwaynynog, Beatrix Potter gives a further description of this garden.

The Tale of the Flopsy Bunnies is a sequel to *The Tale of Peter Rabbit* and *The Tale of Benjamin Bunny*. On the dedication page we read, 'For all little friends of Mr. McGregor and Peter and Benjamin'.

Benjamin was now grown up and married to Peter's sister Flopsy, and they had a family of six—which according to some of the miniature letters, consisted of two boy-rabbits, followed by three girl-rabbits, and finally another boy-rabbit!

Beatrix Potter prepared a number of water-colours of the garden at Gwaynynog —which she described as 'Sketches for backgrounds'. On one of these we find notes as to colouring to guide her when making the book drawings.

On March 10th 1909 she told Mr. Warne, 'I have done lots of sketches—not at all to the purpose—and will now endeavour to finish up the F. Bunnies without further delay.'

At the beginning of the story the word 'soporific' is introduced. Beatrix Potter loved unusual words and realized that children appreciated them also, although sometimes she used them against the advice of her publishers. The word 'soporific' was carefully explained on the opening page of the story, so that when used later on, the child would know its meaning.

In the picture of the market garden belonging to Peter's mother, there was a notice board which read, 'Peter Rabbit & Mother—Florists—Gardens neatly razed. Borders devastated by the night or year'. This picture was shortly replaced by one *without* the notice board, because of the question of foreign translations.

In 1942 when an admirer of Beatrix Potter wrote an article on Gwaynynog called 'Mr. McGregor's Garden' and assumed it to be Peter Rabbit's garden as well as that of the Flopsy Bunnies, Beatrix Potter's comments on the article were both sympathetic and tolerant: 'Peter Rabbit's potting shed and the actual geraniums were in Hertfordshire', she wrote, 'but what does it matter? I called Gwaynynog garden Mr. McGregor's garden in the Flopsy Bunnies, and it makes a good name for a charming little essay, stet! I suppose she thinks B.B. was also at Gwaynynog? it was the garden at Fawe Park, Keswick—Let her print it. *I* won't contradict!'

Although not directly associated with the story, a description of the fine old house at *Gwaynynog* is not without interest, and we find it in an unfinished story about two bats called *Flittermouse and Fluttermouse,* which Beatrix Potter referred to as 'A Tale without a Story, for myself':

Once upon a time there was an old house—an old old very old house, with panelled rooms, and a coat of arms over the great open hall fireplace, and beams across the low ceilings —The staircase was wide with broad low oak steps and carved balustrades—It led up to a long gallery and branching passages and many bedrooms with doorways in and out of each other and up-and-down uneven oaken floors and steps, and closets in the wall. And one side of the passage between the doors there are carved oak cupboards, chairs and pictures; on the other side of the passage, the wainscoting is mostly doors. When you open these doors, sometimes it is into a bedroom on the same level, and sometimes it is head first down two or three steps, and one door—I never can remember which—it is nearly pitch darkness. And when one's eyes become accustomed to the shadows it is a steep attic staircase of black oak blocks with a corkscrew twist, a slippery rail, a slanting beam of light across the shadows overhead. When I climb the stairs I find a smell of yellow soap and a twilight labyrinth of beams, joists, passages and slanting roofs, and little leaded window panes, and there amongst the dusty rafters live Flittermouse and Fluttermouse, the bats . . . It is never very light in the attics at Gwaynynog, but Flittermouse and Fluttermouse love twilight and have little blinking winking eyes like small black beads. They sleep all day in the darkest attic hanging from a rafter over the middle of the floor . . . The attics are silent and deserted now.

Ginger and Pickles
1909

The story of *Ginger and Pickles* has its setting in the village of Sawrey, and describes the little village shop in Smithy Lane, situated close to Hill Top.

Margaret Lane tells how this book 'celebrates the actual little village shop, and with such appreciative feeling that its pages almost smell of candles and tea.' The shop is run by a yellow Tom-cat called Ginger and a terrier called Pickles. The only other shop in the village is kept by Mrs. Tabitha Twitchit, but *she* does not give credit.

In this story Beatrix Potter explains the meaning of credit: 'Now the meaning of "credit" is this—when a customer buys a bar of soap, instead of the customer pulling out a purse and paying for it—she says she will pay another time. And Pickles makes a low bow and says, "With pleasure, madam," and it is written down in a book.'

One of the attractions of the story is that so many of Beatrix Potter's animal characters are introduced—sometimes in the text and sometimes in the pictures. Peter Rabbit is there, wearing his little blue jacket; Squirrel Nutkin and his brother Twinkleberry are after the nuts in a bag by the entrance door to the shop; Lucinda and Jane from *The Tale of Two Bad Mice* also appear; and Mrs. Tiggy-Winkle is seen putting goods into a bag while Pickles solemnly writes out her credit account. Other customers who may be seen are Mr. Jeremy Fisher trying on galoshes, Mr. Samuel Whiskers, Anna Maria, Jemima Puddle-Duck; and in the frontispiece, Tom Kitten, Moppet and Mittens are visible from the inside, peering through the shop window.

Although it is now a private house, there are still traces of the original shop. The old meat hooks in the ceiling of the back room, where Ginger and Pickles made up their accounts, were still there in 1951, and the arch in the passage leading to this room can clearly be identified.

The original manuscript of *Ginger and Pickles* was given to Harold Warne's little girl, Louie, as a Christmas present. The story is written in a stiff-covered exercise book; in it there are twenty-one pages of text, seventeen pen-and-ink drawings in sepia, and three water-colours. The inscription reads, 'Ginger and Pickles. With love to Louie from Aunt Beatrix, Christmas, 1908.'

Beatrix Potter rewrote the story in a similar exercise book, making some alterations to the text and extending the story to introduce Old John Taylor who owned the shop.

She was always realistic with regard to details, of which there is an interesting example in Louie's manuscript. It is indicated that there was a seasonal price for butter—thus, at Ginger and Pickles' shop, it was sold for 10d lb. in July, and

1/1½d lb. in November. It would appear that Ginger and Pickles made up their accounts twice a year. In the final version of the story, one price only is given—1/3d lb. With regard to another small detail, Beatrix Potter pointed out to Mr. Warne, '*My* rates and taxes don't come in one envelope, does it matter?' Apparently it did not matter!

Beatrix Potter sometimes felt that when she copied a picture from the sketch in her manuscript, she could not always recapture the charm of the original, and in one or two instances suggested that the earlier sketch should be used for the printed book.

At least one of the sketches in Louie's manuscript was used in this way; 'I think the drawing of "Lucinda and Jane" had better be used,' she said, 'as I don't believe I can hit it off again—It is rather spotty, but could be scraped out in the block. Also the sketch of the till might do. They are easily slipped off with a knife.'

The removal of the former from the manuscript shows that it was used, but the latter is still there.

Beatrix Potter considered using still another picture from the manuscript, and when sending a picture of Ginger, she wrote, 'With regard to Ginger reading the letter, there was a pretty good sketch in the original book. I do not know whether this is better or worse?' The sketch in the manuscript was, in fact, a better drawing, but nothing was done about it, and it is still there.

Although not in the printed book, in Louie's picture of Sally Henny Penny serving Mr. Samuel Whiskers after the shop has changed hands, Beatrix Potter has added the following wording under the picture:

S. Whiskers:	Put the snuff down to my account.
S. Henny Penny:	Cash please.

and she has also labelled the little parcel which is being handed to Mr. Samuel Whiskers 'snuff'.

There are a few interesting sidelights on the story, in the letters Beatrix Potter sent to Warnes: 'I should like "little small" to stand, I have several times used piled up adjectives', she wrote. 'The contradiction of Ginger eating a haddock instead of a biscuit was intentional', and again 'I suppose Mr. Leadbeater will edit the American text; he will no doubt change the coinage—"halfpenny" etc.' Mr. Leadbeater *did* change the coinage, and dollars and cents appeared in the American edition of *Ginger and Pickles*. She also added, 'I don't know whether they require dog licences in America.'

Later, from Bolton Gardens, she wrote, 'I have left the kittens rather light because they are seen through the glass.'

When the proofs arrived Beatrix Potter was pleased with them, although she had one or two small criticisms to make: 'The green drawing of Pickles with the gun is spotty, but it will be all right with Mr. Evans' blue. Same applies to the dormouse green subject. The only two *I* think over heavy are the hedgehog buying soap, and the kittens looking in at window. Possibly the cover inset is dark, but an excellent colour.'

There are also letters which tell us something of the background history of this story.

On November 17th 1909 Beatrix Potter wrote to Millie Warne, 'The "Ginger and Pickles" book has been causing amusement, it has got a good many views which can be recognized in the village which is what they like, they are all quite jealous of each other's houses and cats getting into a book. I have been entreated to draw a cat aged twenty "with no teeth"; its owner seemed to think the "no teeth" was a curiosity and attraction! I should think the poor old thing must be rather worn out.'

Towards the end of her life, when writing to Mrs. Miller, Beatrix Potter recalled some memories of Ginger and Pickles' shop: 'Old John Taylor was the Sawrey joiner and wheelwright; his wife, and later his stout elderly daughter "Agnes Anne" kept the little general shop for years and years. After their deaths a daughter-in-law took it on. In turn she became old and invalidish and made it over to a niece-in-law —who has closed the long chapter; Ginger and Pickles is no more . . . Agnes Anne was a big fat woman with a loud voice, very genuine in her likes and dislikes; a good sort. Old John was a sweet gentle old man, failed in his legs, so he kept to his bed, but was the head of the family, and owned several cottages. He professed to be jealous because I had put his son John in a book as John Joiner. When I saw old John, who was very humorous and jokey, I asked him how I could put him—old John—in a book if he insisted on living in bed? So a week afterwards, enclosed with an account, there came a scrap of paper "John Taylor's compliments and thinks he might pass for a dormouse".'

On the dedication page of *Ginger and Pickles* is written, 'DEDICATED With very kind regards to old Mr. John Taylor, who "Thinks he might pass as a Dormouse" (Three years in bed and never a grumble!)'.

'I do not know what you will say to this dedication', wrote Beatrix Potter to Harold Warne. 'In a way—it ought to be Louie's book, but she can look forward; I sometimes think poor old John Taylor is keeping alive to see this one printed. I should rather like to put his name in if you don't object?' And later, on September 11th, 'Old "John Dormouse" was given up last Wednesday, but is now extremely lively smoking his pipe in bed. Let me have a copy for him as soon as there is one to spare and ready'. Sad to say he did not live to see the book in print.

This was the third of Beatrix Potter's books to be printed in a large format, but from 1930 onwards it was printed in the ordinary small format, and the title changed to *The Tale of Ginger and Pickles*.

It is of interest to compare Louie's manuscript with the extended story in Beatrix Potter's second version, both of which are given here. Her desire to please old John Taylor by introducing him into the story as the dormouse seems to have slightly thrown it off balance. Her original version is thought to be the better of the two.

Louie's Manuscript	*Second version*
Once upon a time there was a village shop. The name over the window was—	Once upon a time there was a village shop. The name over the window was Ginger and Pickles.
'Ginger and Pickles'	
It was a very small shop, but it sold everything—except a few things that you want in a hurry, like boot laces and hair pins and mutton chops.	It was a little small shop just the right size for dolls—Lucinda and Jane Doll-cook always bought their groceries at Ginger & Pickles.
The door was small and low, and the window was low and little. It was just about the right size for rabbits—and for dolls—Lucinda and Jane Doll-cook used to buy their groceries at Ginger and Pickles!	The counter was a convenient height for rabbits to peep over. Ginger and Pickles sold red spotty pocket handkerchiefs at a penny three farthings; also snuff and galoshes. In fact although it was such a small shop it sold nearly everything—except a few things that you want in a hurry—like boot laces and mutton chops.
And it was also patronized by mice— only the mice were always rather afraid of Ginger.	
Ginger and Pickles were the people who kept the shop.	Ginger and Pickles were the people who kept the shop. Ginger was a yellow Tom-cat, and Pickles was a terrier.
Ginger was a yellow Tom-cat, and Pickles was a terrier.	
The rabbits were afraid of Pickles.	The rabbits were always a little bit afraid of Pickles.
But still—in spite of being afraid—they nearly all bought everything at that shop, because there was only one other shop in the village.	The shop was also patronized by mice— only the mice were always rather afraid of Ginger.
The other shop was kept by Mrs. Tabitha Twitchit, and she did not give credit.	Ginger usually requested Pickles to serve them, because he said it made his mouth water—'I cannot bear,' said he, 'to see them going out at the door with their little parcels.'
Ginger and Pickles gave unlimited credit. Now the meaning of 'credit' is this —When a customer buys a bar of soap, instead of the customer pulling out a purse and paying for the soap—she says she will pay another time.	'I have the same feeling about rats,' replied Pickles, 'but it would never do to eat our customers; they would leave us and go to Tabitha Twitchit's.' 'On the contrary they would go nowhere,' replied Ginger gloomily.
And Pickles makes a low bow and says 'With pleasure, madam,' and it is written down in a book.	(Tabitha Twitchit kept the only **other** shop in the village. She did not give credit.)

And there is no money in what is called the 'till'.

And the customers come in crowds and buy quantities in spite of being afraid of Ginger and Pickles.

Ginger always requested Pickles to serve the mice, because he said it made his mouth water—'I cannot bear', said he, 'to see them going out at the door with their little parcels.'

'I have the same feeling about rats,' replied Pickles, 'but it would never do to eat our customers; they would leave us and go to Tabitha Twitchit's.'

'On the contrary they would go no-where,' replied Ginger gloomily.

So the customers came again and again, and bought quantities. But there was always no money. They never paid for as much as a pennyworth of peppermints!

And when it came to Jan 1st. there was still no money; and Pickles was unable to buy a dog licence.

'It is extremely unpleasant. I am afraid of the police,' said Pickles.

'It is your own fault for being a terrier. *I* do not require a licence, and neither does Kep the collie dog.'

'It is very embarrassing. I am afraid I shall be summoned,' said Pickles.

Ginger and Pickles retired into the parlour behind the shop, which had a window in the door.

They did accounts. They added up sums and sums and sums.

'Samuel Whiskers has run up a bill as long as his tail, he owes 22/9 for bacon. What is 18 lbs of butter at 10½ in July and 1/1½ in November, Ginger?'

'I do not believe he intends to pay at all, and I feel sure that Anna Maria pockets things.'

Ginger and Pickles gave unlimited credit.

Now the meaning of 'credit' is this—when a customer buys a bar of soap, instead of the customer pulling out a purse and paying for it—she says she will pay another time. And Pickles makes a low bow and says 'with pleasure madam', and it is written down in a book.

And the customers come again and again and buy quantities, in spite of being afraid of Ginger & Pickles.

But there is no money in what is called the 'till'.

The customers came in crowds and bought quantities; but there was always no money. They never paid for as much as a pennyworth of peppermints.

But the sales were enormous, ten times as large as Tabitha Twitchit's!

But there was always no money, and Ginger and Pickles had to eat their own biscuits.

Pickles ate biscuits and Ginger ate a dried haddock. They ate them by candle light after the shop was closed.

When it came to Jan 1st. there was still no money, and Pickles was unable to buy a dog licence.

'It is very unpleasant, I am afraid of the police,' said Pickles. 'It is your own fault for being a terrier. *I* do not require a licence, and neither does Kep the collie dog.'

'It is very uncomfortable, I am afraid I shall be summoned; I have tried in vain to obtain a licence upon credit. The place is full of policemen. I met one as I returned from the post office. Send in the bill again to Samuel Whiskers, Ginger; he owes 22/9 for bacon alone.'

'I do not believe that he intends to pay at all,' replied Ginger. 'And I feel sure that Anna Maria pockets things. Where are all

'Send in the account again "with comp^{ts}", Ginger, he has had an ounce and ¾ of snuff.'

Presently there was a slight noise in the shop. Ginger and Pickles looked through the window in the parlour door.

There was an envelope lying on the counter, and there was a stuffed policeman writing in a note book.

Pickles nearly had a fit. He barked and he barked and he barked, and made little rushes out of the back parlour.

The policeman took no notice but went on writing, writing in the note book, twice he put his pencil in his mouth and once he dipped it in the treacle.

'Bite him, Pickles! bite him!' sputtered Ginger from behind a sugar barrel—'He's only a German doll!'

The policeman still took no notice, he had bead eyes and a vacant expression. The Metropolitan police are sometimes most affable, especially when they come inside and take off their helmets. But this creature's helmet was sewed on with stitches.

Pickles barked till he was hoarse, and made little rushes out of the back parlour. On the last of his little rushes he discovered that the shop was empty.

The policeman had disappeared! But the envelope remained upon the counter.

'Do you think that he has gone to fetch a real live policeman? I am afraid it is a summons,' said Pickles.

'No,' replied Ginger, who had opened the envelope, 'it is the rates and taxes; two pounds nineteen shillings and eleven pence three farthings.'

'This is the last straw,' said Pickles. 'Let us close the shop.'

They put up the shutters hurriedly and left.

the cream crackers?' 'You have eaten some yourself,' replied Ginger.

Ginger and Pickles retired into the back parlour which has a little window in the door looking into the shop. They did accounts. They added up sums and sums.

'Samuel Whiskers has run up a bill as long as his tail, he has had an ounce and ¾ of snuff since October. What is four pounds of butter at 1/3, and a stick of sealing wax and matches?'

'Send in all the bills again to everybody "with comp^{ts}",' replied Ginger.

After a time there was a slight noise in the shop. They looked through the window in the door. They saw an envelope lying on the counter and a stuffed policeman writing in a notebook.

Pickles nearly had a fit, he barked and he barked and made little rushes out of the back parlour.

'Bite him Pickles! bite him!' sputtered Ginger behind a sugar barrel, 'he's only a German doll!'

The policeman went on writing, writing in his note book; twice he put his pencil in his mouth and once he dipped it in the treacle. Pickles barked till he was hoarse.

But still the policeman took no notice. He had bead eyes and his helmet was sewed on with stitches.

At length on the last little rush—Pickles found the shop was empty—The policeman was gone. But the envelope remained.

'Do you think that he has gone to fetch a real live policeman? I am afraid it is a summons,' said Pickles. 'No' replied Ginger who had opened the envelope, 'it is the rates & taxes—£3 19 11¾.'

'This is the last straw,' said Pickles, 'let us close the shop.' They put up the shutters, and left.

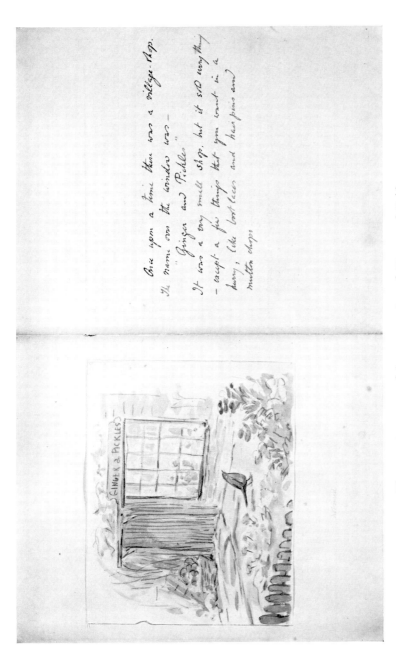

Once upon a time there was a village shop.

The name over the window was —

"Ginger and Pickles"

It was a tiny small shop, but it sold everything — except a few things that you want in a hurry, like boot laces and hairpins and mutton chops.

The opening page of the manuscript of *Ginger and Pickles*
This manuscript was given to Louie Warne, Christmas, 1908. The water-colour facing page 1, does *not* appear in the finished book

A sketch from the manuscript of *Ginger and Pickles* which shows Ginger reading a letter. Beatrix Potter considered this 'a pretty good sketch', but it was not used for the book

But they have not removed from the neighbourhood.

Ginger is living in the warren. I do not know what occupation he pursues, but he looks stout and comfortable.

Pickles is at present a game keeper.

The shop has been re-opened by Sally Henny Penny. She gets very flustered when she counts out change; and she insists on being paid ready money. But she is quite harmless.

The End.

But they have not removed from the neighbourhood. In fact some people wish they had gone further.

Ginger is living in the warren. I do not know what occupation he pursues. He looks stout and comfortable.

Pickles is at present a gamekeeper.

The closing of the shop caused great inconvenience. Tabitha Twitchit immediately raised the price of everything a halfpenny; and she continued to refuse to give credit.

Of course there are the tradesmen's carts—the butcher, the fish man—and Timothy Baker. But a person cannot live on 'seed-wiggs' and sponge cake and 'butter buns'—not even when the sponge cake is as good as Timothy's!

After a time Mr. John Dormouse and his daughter started to sell peppermints and candles. But they did not keep self fitting, and it takes 5 mice to carry one. Moreover, the candles which they sell behave very strangely in warm weather.

And Miss Dormouse refused to take back the ends when they were brought back to her with complaints.

And when Mr. John Dormouse was complained to, he stopped in bed, and would say nothing but 'very snug!' which is *not* the proper way to carry on a retail business.

Therefore there was universal satisfaction when Sally Henny Penny sent round bills announcing that she was about to re-open the shop—

Henny's grand co-operative opening Jumble

Penny's prices too insignificant to [unfinished]

Come buy, Come try, Come buy

—the handbills really were most 'ticing.

Second version (continued)

There was a rush upon the opening day. The shop was crammed and there were crowds of mice upon the biscuit canisters.

Sally Henny Penny gets rather flustered when she tries to count out change, and she insists on being paid ready money.

But she is perfectly harmless.

And she has laid in a remarkable assortment of bargains.

The Tale of Mrs. Tittlemouse
1910

This story is about a wood-mouse called Mrs. Thomasina Tittlemouse, and tells of her numerous visitors—*friends* as they were called in the manuscript—but in the book they are more appropriately referred to as *visitors*!

Beatrix Potter found delight in drawing the various intruders in Mrs. Tittlemouse's house—bees, a beetle, lady-bird, butterfly, and spider, not to mention Mr. Jackson, the toad. Long ago she had studied the habits and characteristics of these small creatures, and had painted many pictures of them—including microscopic studies showing the beautiful coloured scales of butterflies' wings, and the highly magnified anatomy of spiders and beetles. At the age of seventeen, we find her commenting in detail in her Journal, on the behaviour of land-newts, frogs and toads.

Mrs. Susan Ludbrook tells of Beatrix Potter's superb knowledge of Natural History: 'The two books I have chosen to illustrate my point', she writes, 'have characters which on the surface may seem alike, but in their essence are so very different as to bear out my contention, that Beatrix Potter came to her work with a full and complete understanding of every phase of natural history, and brings this to bear on all her characters in the various situations in which she places them. Jeremy Fisher though he is indeed an amphibian, cannot stay long under water and must hide under a lily leaf and come to the surface from time to time to take in air. In addition, his limbs are so arranged that he must hop and leap.

'Mr. Jackson on the other hand can and does walk crab-wise along a dry ditch, and does not need to go near the water except in spring-time to spawn. He carries his wife on his back to make this annual journey, and they can be seen on any spring-time evening wending their way in this original fashion along the dusty main roads. Moreover Mr. Jackson's limbs are so arranged, that he would easily be able to sit upright in a chair in Mrs. Tittlemouse's kitchen and puff and blow the thistle seeds in the air and say "Tiddly, Widdly, Pouff, Pouff". Beatrix Potter moreover knew quite well about the toad's inordinate love of honey, and his power to smell it out, where the wild bees had made their nest in the pantry-window, and his ability to wait outside, still saying "Tiddly, Widdly, Pouff, Pouff".'

In her manuscript Beatrix Potter introduced 'wood-lice' into the story: 'There were three wood-lice hiding in the plate-rack', she wrote; but Warnes objected. They did not consider it was a suitable creature to mention in a children's book! Beatrix Potter was amused, for such distinctions mattered nothing to her but, always accommodating when she could make alterations without detriment to her story, she changed 'wood-lice' to 'three creepy crawly people'. 'I can alter the text, when I get the proofs', she wrote, and 'will erase the offensive word "wood-lice"!'

Margaret Lane writes, 'Mrs. Tittlemouse, the "woodmouse with a long tail", is exquisitely domesticated, a "most terribly tidy particular little mouse, always sweeping and dusting the soft sandy floors" of her burrow, and though mops and brushes are not seriously to be looked for in the holes of woodmice, Mrs. Tittlemouse, inveterate nest-maker, typifies the beautifully observed fastidiousness of her mouse nature.'

The original manuscript of *The Tale of Mrs. Tittlemouse* was given to Harold Warne's little girl, Nellie, as a New Year's present. The story is neatly written in a small leather notebook measuring 150 mm. × 85 mm.; in it there are twenty-one pages of text and eight paintings. The inscription reads, 'For Nellie with love and best wishes for A Happy New Year. Jan. 1st. 1910'. The family called it 'Nellie's little book', and these are the words which appear on the dedication page of the printed book.

A later manuscript of *The Tale of Mrs. Tittlemouse* is at Hill Top—a small paper-covered exercise book consisting of twenty-six pages of text and seven rough pencil sketches. It is divided into short paragraphs and the sketches are pasted in.

When comparing the text of this Hill Top manuscript with that of the finished book, the changes though slight, indicate the care with which Beatrix Potter selected her words. She was always particular about her opening paragraphs, and the following comparisons show how they have been re-arranged and clarified:

Text in Manuscript	*Published Text*
Once upon a time there was a wood-mouse and her name was Mrs. Tittle-mouse. Her house was in a bank under a hedge.	Once upon a time there was a wood-mouse, and her name was Mrs. Tittlemouse. She lived in a bank under a hedge.
Inside the house was a kitchen and a parlour, and a pantry and a larder.	Such a funny house! There were yards and yards of sandy passages, leading to storerooms and nut-cellars and seed-cellars, all amongst the roots of the hedge.
And there were yards and yards of sandy passages leading to store rooms and nut-cellars and seed-cellars, all amongst the roots of the hedge.	There was a kitchen, a parlour, a pantry, and a larder.
And there was Mrs. Tittlemouse's bedroom, where she slept in a little box bed.	Also, there was Mrs. Tittlemouse's bedroom, where she slept in a little box bed!

A small alteration near the beginning of the story is also of interest, for Beatrix Potter changed her text from 'sometimes an earwig lost its way' to 'sometimes a beetle lost its way'. Was it because Warnes thought that small children would be more at home with a beetle than with an earwig? So the painting of Mrs.

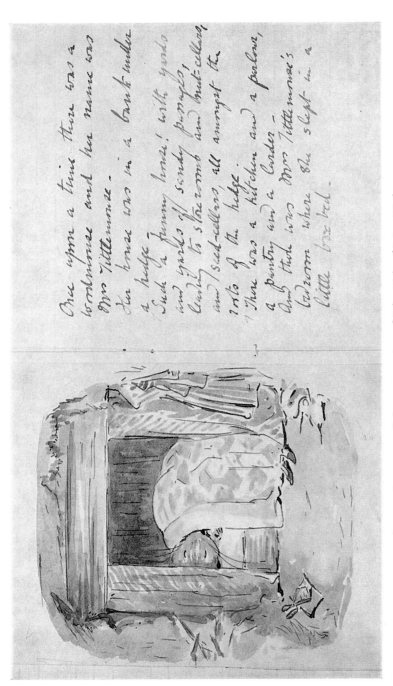

Once upon a time there was a
wood-mouse and her name was
Mrs Tittlemouse.

She lived in a bank under
a hedge.

Such a funny house! with yards
and yards of scurvy passages.
And it had so many rooms and nut cellars
and seed-cellars, all amongst the
roots of the hedge.

There was a kitchen and a parlour,
a pantry and a larder;
And there was Mrs Tittlemouse's
bedroom where she slept in a
little box-bed.

The opening page of the manuscript of *The Tale of Mrs. Tittlemouse*
This manuscript was given to Nellie Warne as a New Year gift in 1910

'There were yards and yards of sandy passages'
A book picture for *The Tale of Mrs. Tittlemouse*

Studies of Mice

An unused book picture for *The Tale of Mrs. Tittlemouse*

This drawing was discarded when Beatrix Potter decided to change the centipede to a butterfly. The text was altered accordingly

Tittlemouse clattering her dust-pan and looking askance at the earwig was put on one side and a new painting prepared in which a beetle appeared in place of the earwig!

Another painting which she discarded was that of a centipede hiding behind a soup tureen—Beatrix Potter decided to change this creature to a butterfly, and the corresponding paragraphs, which refer to Mr. Jackson the toad, read as follows:

Text in Manuscript	*Published Text*
Then he squeezed himself into the larder. Miss Maggie Manylegs the centipede was hiding in a soup tureen, but she rushed away under a door.	Then he squeezed into the larder. Miss Butterfly was tasting the sugar; but she flew away out of the window.

Two further examples show how carefully Beatrix Potter considered her text:

Text in Manuscript	*Published Text*
'Mother Ladybird, fly away home to your children!' said Mrs. Tittlemouse.	'Your house is on fire, Mother Ladybird! Fly away home to your children!'

and towards the end of the story:

Next morning she got up very very early and commenced a spring cleaning that lasted a fortnight.	Next morning she got up very early and began a spring cleaning which lasted a fortnight.

When the bound copies of *The Tale of Mrs. Tittlemouse* arrived, Beatrix Potter expressed her delight with them: 'The buff copy is the prettiest colour, though it may not keep so clean', she wrote to Warnes. 'I think it should prove popular with little girls.'

The Tale of Timmy Tiptoes
1911

Until 1910 Beatrix Potter had produced an average of about two books a year, but from this year onwards she found that this was not possible. Her parents were getting on in years and needed more care and attention than in the past. She also had her work at Hill Top Farm to occupy her.

'I did not succeed in finishing more than one book last year', she wrote to a friend on January 1st. 'I find it very difficult lately to get the drawings done. I do not seem to be able to go into the country for a long enough time to do a sufficient amount of sketching and when I was at Bowness last summer I spent most of my time upon the road going backwards and forwards to the farm—which was amusing but not satisfactory for work. It is awkward with old people, especially in winter, it is not very fit to leave them.'

Beatrix Potter's books were now becoming widely known, and she frequently received letters of appreciation from children in all parts of the world. 'I think I have little friends all over the world,' she wrote, and in a letter to Millie Warne in 1909, she told her that she was devoting her Christmas to answering an accumulation of letters from unknown children. In some of these replies she told them more about her animal characters.

Beatrix Potter had by now many American friends and admirers, some of whom were children's librarians. It is believed that *The Tale of Timmy Tiptoes* was written primarily for American children because they would be familiar with both chipmunks and bears. They would also be familiar with grey squirrels like Timmy Tiptoes and his wife Goody, who stored nuts for the winter months and met with various adventures while so doing.

In a note in her manuscript, Beatrix Potter described chipmunks: 'According to "American animals" the chipmunks dig out the sand from a back entrance, and then open a clean small hole from their burrow on to smooth grass scarcely noticeable.' There is also a note referring to the bear: 'Intended to represent the American black bear, it has a smooth coat, like a sealskin coat'.

It is said that the grey squirrels are much fatter and bigger than the slim little chipmunks. This throws an interesting light on the paragraph in *The Tale of Timmy Tiptoes* which tells how 'a fat squirrel voice and a thin squirrel voice were singing together'.

By the end of June 1911 Beatrix Potter had completed most of the drawings for the book. 'I am sending 12 drawings,' she wrote to Harold Warne. 'I have kept back some of the earlier finished as patterns for the *squirrel colour*. I have all the plates sketched except two or three. I think I can do some good ones for the finish.

I have compressed the words in the earlier pages; but it seems unavoidable to have a good deal of *nuts*. The songs of the little birds will be easier to judge as to spelling when one sees it in type.'

The dedication page of the book reads, 'For many unknown little friends, including Monica'. 'I do not know the child', she wrote, 'she is the school friend of a little cousin, who asked for it as a favour, and the name took my fancy.'

The Tale of Mr. Tod
1912

The hills around Sawrey are the setting for this story, and we are told that in winter and early spring Mr. Tod 'might generally be found in an earth amongst the rocks at the top of Bull Banks, under Oatmeal Crag.'

'I think this story is amusing', wrote Beatrix Potter when sending the manuscript to Mr. Warne on November 18th 1911, 'its principal defect is imitation of "Uncle Remus". It is no drawback for children, because they cannot read the negro dialect—I hardly think the publishers could object to it? I wrote it some time ago. I have copied it out lately. It would make pretty pictures; the situation of Mr. Tod's house is fine, and the moonlight would be weird.'

Two days later she arranged to call and discuss the story. 'I will come *Tuesday* morning. It is no good saying "weather permitting". I have got a new waterproof —Mr. Tod is surely a very common name for fox? It is probably Saxon; it was the word in ordinary use in Scotland a few years ago, possibly is still amongst the country people—The same way "brock" or "gray" is the country name for badger —I should call them "brocks"—both names are used in Westmorland; "Brock holes" "Graythwaite" are examples of place names; also Broxbourne and Brockhampton . . .

> ' "Hey quoth the Tod
> it's a braw bright night!
> The wind's in the west
> and the moon shines bright—"

mean to say you never heard that?'

Unlike Beatrix Potter's earlier books, the principal characters are villains! and in the opening paragraph we are given a hint of this fact. When sending Warnes some of the book drawings, Beatrix Potter referred to the one about the fight between Mr. Tod and Tommy Brock—which she found difficult to draw: 'You will see a very confused one of the combat. I could hardly shirk one picture of it; but it was difficult to work out in detail so I made it dark.'

It is of interest to compare the opening paragraph of the manuscript with that of the published book—no doubt modified at the galley proof stage:

Opening paragraph in manuscript	*Opening paragraph in book*
I am quite tired of making goody goody books about nice people. I will make a story about two disagreeable people, called Tommy Brock and Mr. Tod.	I have made many books about well-behaved people. Now, for a change, I am going to make a story about two disagreeable people, called Tommy Brock and Mr. Tod.

I am quite tired of making goody goody books about nice people. I will make a story about two disagreeable people, called Tommy Brock and Mr Tod.

Nobody could call Mr Tod "nice." The rabbits could not bear him; they could smell him half a mile off. He was of a wandering habit and he had foxey whiskers; they never knew where he would be next.

One day he might be smelt living in a stick house in the coppice, causing terror to the family of old Mr Benjamin Bouncer.

Next day he would move into a pollard willow near the lake, frightening the wild ducks and the water rats.

In winter and early spring he might generally be found in the wood at the top of Bull Banks, living in an earth amongst the rocks.

He had half a dozen houses, but he was seldom

Facsimile of the opening page of the manuscript of
The Tale of Mr. Tod

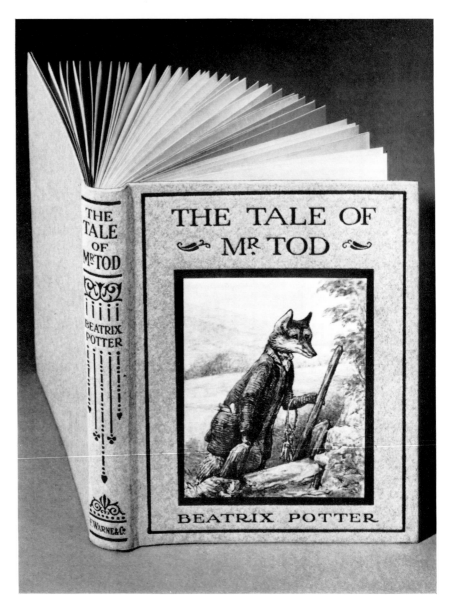

The Series II new style of binding, first used for *The Tale of Mr. Tod*

Warnes for some reason or other did not like this opening paragraph, and sent one or two suggestions of their own to Beatrix Potter. 'I cannot say I like the samples', she wrote, 'they are too conversational. I don't like "young readers". . . I cannot think what you are driving at, "this time" is no improvement on "now". Can it be that you think the making of many books is too Biblical—but I had so "many" before.

'If it were not impertinent to lecture one's publishers—you are a great deal too much afraid of the public; for whom I have never cared one tuppenny-button. I am *sure* that it is that attitude of mind which has enabled me to keep up the series. Most people, after one success, are so cringingly afraid of doing less well that they rub all the edge off their subsequent work.

'I have always thought the opening paragraph distinctly *good*, because it gets away from "once upon a time".'

Tommy Brock was a badger and Mr. Tod a fox, and *they* are the villains in this fourth book about the adventures of Beatrix Potter's rabbit characters. We hear more of old Mr. Bouncer, who was now living with his son and daughter-in-law, Benjamin and Flopsy; of Peter, and his sister Cottontail, who had married a black rabbit and lived up on the hill; and of the Flopsy Bunnies who were kidnapped by Tommy Brock.

The text is not divided up into short paragraphs as in Beatrix Potter's earlier books. While there are fewer coloured pictures, there are many small pen-and-ink drawings, each enclosed within a border line. These line-drawings are inserted in the text, and include both landscape and interiors.

This format was adopted because Beatrix Potter had no longer the inclination to produce the number of coloured pictures used in her other books; and she had told Warnes that she was finding it 'so difficult to continue to make "fresh" short stories'.

Warnes suggested advertising an entirely new series, but Beatrix Potter did not agree with them: 'Do you really think the advantage of an entirely fresh series will make up for the loss of the "Peter Rabbit book" name?' she wrote. 'I feel convinced that children would prefer the same familiar size, and as little change as may be'.

So in the end *The Tale of Mr. Tod* and her following book *The Tale of Pigling Bland* were advertised as 'The Peter Rabbit Books, Series II, New Style' and they had a slightly more elaborate binding with a rounded back, but were the same format. In a few years' time Warnes reverted to the ordinary binding.

The Tale of Mr. Tod was published in 1912, the year that her cousin Caroline's little boy was born. She had married the Laird of Ulva, and was now Caroline Clark, and it was to her baby boy that *The Tale of Mr. Tod* was dedicated: 'For

Francis William of Ulva—someday!'—the 'someday' meaning the time when he would be old enough to enjoy the story.

When the dedication was first printed a mistake was made, for the child's name appeared as William Francis of Ulva—this was corrected in later editions. He was, in fact, Francis William, like his father, and it was a tragedy for 'Ulva's isle' that this quiet steadfast young man, a fine oarsman and swimmer at Shrewsbury, should have died of wounds in Italy in 1944 as a major in the Argyll and Sutherland Highlanders.

The Tale of Pigling Bland
1913

The Tale of Pigling Bland was most probably in Beatrix Potter's mind as early as 1910 when she was working on *The Tale of Mrs. Tittlemouse,* for about that time she mentioned in one of the miniature letters from Peter Rabbit to Master Drew Fayle that he (Peter) was to be put into one picture at the end of the pig book.

Sure enough, on the last page of *The Tale of Pigling Bland,* there is a picture of Peter and two other rabbits, watching Pigling Bland and Pig-wig as they dance together 'over the hills and far away'.

The Tale of Pigling Bland tells about two of Beatrix Potter's pigs at Hill Top, whom she called Alexander and Pigling Bland, who were sold because food was getting short and they had such big appetites—it is also about a little black girl-pig called Pig-wig. The Lancashire farmers referred to pigs in that way, for an old advice-note from Farmer Scales, which Beatrix Potter had kept, reads:

> 'Stott Park, Lake Side.
> to Mrs. Heelis
> Your pigs are ready
> but there is no Girl
> pigs.
> Yours truly
> J. Scales.'

This story about Pigling Bland has an element of truth in it, for on November 17th 1909, in one of Beatrix Potter's letters to Millie Warne, sent from Hill Top, she wrote, 'The two biggest little pigs have been sold, which takes away from the completeness of the family group. But they have fetched a good price, and their appetites were fearful—five meals a day and not satisfied.'

Beatrix Potter frequently made sketches of her Hill Top animals and sometimes referred to these in her letters: 'I have done a little sketching when it does not rain, and I spent a very wet hour *inside* the pig sty drawing the pig. It tries to nibble my boots, which is interrupting'; and again, 'Have spent some hours inside the pig sty to-day, drawing the little pigs before they cease to be interesting.' Her reference to 'inside' would most probably mean the *yard* surrounding the sleeping quarters.

In *The Tale of Pigling Bland* there are many pen-and-ink drawings which depict Hill Top Farm, and in one of these Beatrix Potter herself appears, handing over some papers to Alexander. The story concludes with Pigling Bland's rescue of Pig-wig from Mr. Piperson's house, after which they both escape over Colwith Bridge and live in Little Langdale—'over the hills and far away'.

The origin of Pig-wig is a story in itself, and is told by Mrs. Ludbrook, who had it from Farmer Townley's daughter-in-law. It was to Farmer Townley's two children that the story was dedicated: 'For Cecily and Charlie. A Tale of the Christmas Pig'.

Mrs. Ludbrook writes, 'Cannon who ran the farm for Beatrix Potter, often bought baby pigs for breeding from another farmer at some distance, nearly always ordering them before they were born, because their mother had a pedigree, and all her children would have one too, and pass it on right down the line. Cannon was very particular about this, because pigs who had a pedigree always sold for more money.

'One day Cannon had ordered some new baby pigs from Townley who had another farm, and as he had not time to go to get them, Beatrix Potter said she would like to go over and get them and see Townley and his farm and the pigs. When she got there and saw the pigs, there was one, a very tiny baby pig, a little girl-pig, which was jet black. "Please, I will buy that one too." "Oh no, I couldn't let you have that," Townley said. "Cannon would never forgive me if I let you go home with that." I suppose it was the wrong colour, and perhaps had no pedigree and would spoil Cannon's herd. Still Beatrix Potter pleaded: "I must and will have it. It is not for Cannon, I want it for myself. I shall take it." So with much misgiving, Townley let her take the wee black lady-pig, saying, "You must tell him I refused you, but you took it and I couldn't stop you." '

'Sure enough when Beatrix Potter arrived with her load of baby pigs, Cannon was shocked to see the black girl-pig, and refused to have it anywhere near the others. Then she was really cross, found a basket, put the little black pig in it in a blanket, got a feeding-bottle and put it beside her bed and fed it herself night and day, until in the end it became her pet, and followed her everywhere indoors and out. Of course we know she had seen a story in it, and the little black pig as a wife for Pigling Bland. Oh dear, Cannon would have been more shocked than ever.'

The story is written out in a paper-covered exercise book as a continuous narrative without the usual sub-divisions into short paragraphs. In the margin of one page Beatrix Potter has scribbled a little pencil note, commenting on that part of the story where Mr. Piperson entered the wooden hut to catch six fowls, and his eye fell upon Pigling Bland who was sheltering there for the night. In the story Mr. Piperson said 'Hallo, here's another!' but in the note she wrote, 'What he would really say "By gum, hires anothur!" or, had he been Irish—"Praise the pigs! hires anothur!" '

The story was finished by the beginning of April 1913, and in her letter of April 7th to Warnes she wrote, 'I enclose the pig story. I think it is rather pretty; but cannot say how it may strike other people. I think it is about the same length as Mr. Tod. I should keep it as short as I can as I should prefer to have a less tall block of

A duplicate of the frontispiece in *The Tale of Pigling Bland*. On the back Beatrix Potter has written 'This is much better than the one used in book'. The setting of this picture can be seen in the colour photograph of the Cross-roads

The Cross-roads, Sawrey

Setting for the frontispiece in *The Tale of Pigling Bland*

letterpress opposite the colour plates. Probably I shall not have time to do quite so many *pairs* of line blocks; so I think it will go in. It should be printed on a strip and I will cut it up. I have a dummy book. *The sooner I have it* the better so as to see where the plates come.'

She then started work on the drawings, but found it unwise to do very much until the galley proofs were cut up and mounted in her dummy. The reason for this was to ensure that both colour plates and line drawings appeared in appropriate positions against the adjacent text. The fact was, that to comply with Warne's new printing arrangement, the colour plates could only be placed at required positions throughout the book.

By April 19th she informed them, 'I have been drawing pigs, but cannot do much till I see where the plates fall in the letterpress'; and again, on April 25th, 'I do hope I shall get the pig text soon; I am almost completely at a standstill till I know where the plates come.'

Beatrix Potter had another reason for wanting the galley proofs as soon as possible, for when pasting up, she wished to shorten the text. 'I was anxious to get it shorter than Tod,' she said, 'because I consider it is for smaller children . . . I will see how it cuts up'; adding, 'I do not think the plates for the pig [book] would take me long, if I am able to stay here and do them on the spot.' She was then at Hill Top.

There was much work to be done in planning out the text and in cutting up and pasting the galley proofs into her dummy. Apparently Beatrix Potter was not yet satisfied with her efforts, for on May 3rd she wrote to Warnes saying, 'I think it would be as well if you would send me another dummy book *and* a third proof if you have one. It will take a good deal of cutting about, and it would be an advantage to me to have a second pasted up copy, as I remember I was in difficulty last year when my only dummy was at the printers. I should of course send one dummy to you before doing very much drawing, for your opinion . . . If I can only get the pen and inks down here on the spot, I should do them scribbly—and I believe better.'

The dummy and proof sheets were duly received, and on May 7th Beatrix Potter wrote, 'I will send a pasted up copy of Pigs and a sample of the illustrations, directly after Whitsuntide. Much obliged for dummy and proofs.'

After a fortnight's work, she was able to send Warnes a revised pasted-up dummy, and in her letter of May 17th she told them, 'I enclose paste-up of Pigling; it cuts up nicely, but has been a long job. I should be rather glad to have the coloured drawings back, as a standard.'

Evidently Beatrix Potter had sent a few drawings in advance, including the one of the two pigs used for the frontispiece, which she referred to as 'the front'. Other details of the book were also discussed in this letter: 'Pig-wig's song "A funny old mother pig" this is in some primer that is used by board-school children in London;

it sounds like an old fashioned song—I suppose quoting only that much—it *isn't infringing copyright*? . . . I shall keep the line blocks mostly to two sizes, but when there are only six lines of type instead of seven—or four instead of five—I should make the line block a little deeper. I do not intend to put lines round them as they are mostly light subjects. The enclosed colour drawings are on the same paper as Tod; it looks rough, but photographed well last time. I have kept a second dummy. I have been over it so often and carefully, I think the printer might revise it from this. There are some inverted commas wrong, but I *cannot* put my finger on them a second time.'

On June 10th Beatrix Potter, still 'behind hand' summed up the position in a letter to Mr. Wilfred Evans, the printer of her books, who had asked if she would care to invest some money in his business. In reply (in the negative, for at that time she was saving money towards the cost of adding some rooms to Castle Cottage), she referred to her Pigling Bland book: 'I must not talk of "behind hand",' she wrote, 'though I can't think how I am to get this book done in time. I took so very long to get over my illness. I had my heart bad for weeks and could do nothing. I am all right now but it might have been wiser to give up the book, before they took orders for it.'

On July 17th, however, she was still persevering with the book, and in a letter to Warnes asked, 'Is it desirable to put in lettering on this signpost? (French etc.) I think it might be put in, and engraved out in the rather unlikely event of these larger books being translated.'

The last we hear of the drawings is on July 25th when Beatrix Potter wrote to Warnes from Lindeth Howe, Windermere, where she was staying with her parents, who had taken the house for two months: 'I enclose eight—probably some of them will want touching up. It is awkward working under difficulties. I fear the drawings may be worse for it. The grocer and *horse* are carefully copied from a photograph—to the red-nosed party's great pride! I took the horse standing up hill; its head seemed big, I reduced it a little.'

Other local backgrounds for the pictures in *The Tale of Pigling Bland* were the fireplace in the house of Mr. Piperson, which was drawn from the fireplace in Spout House, Far Sawrey, and the cross-roads by the signpost, which appear in the frontispiece, and are situated just behind Hill Top. There is also a number of line drawings of Hill Top Farm which can still be recognized.

As in Beatrix Potter's other books, she made last-minute additions to her galley proofs. For example, after the sentence 'I whipped them myself and led them out by the ears', she added, 'Cross-patch tried to bite me'; and by way of emphasizing the fact that Aunt Pettitoes' family of eight needed so much food, we find an additional sentence pencilled in the margin: 'And they drink bucketfuls of milk; I shall have to get another cow!'

Beatrix Potter also rearranged the wording of some of her text, and the following is a typical example:

Text in Galley Proof	*Rearranged Text*
Slowly jogging up the road below them came a tradesman's cart. The reins flapped on the horse's back, the grocer was reading a newspaper.	Suddenly Pigling stopped; he heard wheels.
Suddenly Pigling exclaimed: 'Take that peppermint out of your mouth, we may have to run.	Slowly jogging up the road below them came a tradesman's cart. The reins flapped on the horse's back, the grocer was reading a newspaper.
	'Take that peppermint out of your mouth, Pig-wig, we may have to run.

The Tale of Pigling Bland was at last finished—somewhat wearily, for on September 24th in the postscript of a letter to her friend, Miss Woodward of the Natural History Museum, Beatrix Potter wrote, 'I only got rid of the revised proofs last week; it is disgracefully late. It has been such a nuisance all summer.'

It must be realized, however, that the year 1913 had not been an easy one for her. During part of the year she had been unwell, there had been the arrangements to make for her forthcoming marriage, and the supervision of alterations and improvements to Castle Cottage, which was to become her new home.

On October 14th 1913 Beatrix Potter became Mrs. William Heelis and shortly after moved into Castle Cottage which is close to Hill Top. From then onwards her whole life was devoted to running her new home and to farming.

On November 4th 1913, when sending a presentation copy of *The Tale of Pigling Bland* to a friend, Beatrix Potter wrote, 'As I am in London now for a few days, and not likely to be in London for Christmas—I am taking the opportunity of posting off some copies of the new book which has just come out. I hope you will like it. I'm afraid it was done in an awful hurry and scramble. The portrait of two pigs arm in arm—looking at the sunrise—is not a portrait of me and Mr. Heelis, though it is a view of where we used to walk on Sunday afternoons! When I want to put William into a book—it will have to be some very tall thin animal.'

The Tale of Kitty-in-Boots
1914

After her marriage, and with her increasing interest in farming, Beatrix Potter found less and less time for the writing and illustrating of her books.

During the previous twelve years at least one story had been published each year, and generally two—but from this time onwards only a few more were to follow.

There was no book published in 1914, but there *had been* a story planned for this year, called *The Tale of Kitty-in-Boots*. In her letter of February 23rd to Harold Warne, Beatrix Potter told him, 'It is about a well-behaved prime black Kitty cat, who leads rather a double life, and goes out hunting with a little gun on moonlight nights, dressed up like puss in boots. As the gun is only a pop gun (which continually goes off), the bag is neither large nor painful. Miss Kitty ends in a trap, loses one of her boots and a claw, which cures her of poaching.' Mr. Tod and Mrs. Tiggy-Winkle appear in the story, and Ribby and Tabitha Twitchit are also mentioned.

On March 21st Beatrix Potter wrote to Harold Warne about the pictures for this story, saying, 'I have several drawings begun—perhaps rashly!—for this cat story. I'm afraid it's all I can offer this spring—so make the best of it! It will illustrate very well, plenty of variety, and I could do them quickly if I had the proof to cut and *place*.' And of the story she writes, 'The earlier part wants compressing, the later part goes better. Of course there is a question of the sentimental dislike of traps . . . still I don't think this story is extra harassing.'

By the summer of 1914 the drawings were still unfinished because Beatrix Potter had suffered so many interruptions. She had been 'unwell for six weeks with continuous colds and sore throat'. Her father had died on May 9th, and since then her mother had taken up much of her time for while she was without a companion she could not be left alone. After staying with Beatrix Potter in Sawrey, where it appears 'she found it rather dull', she then went to Lindeth Howe, Windermere, and Beatrix Potter spent three weeks with her there—going 'backwards and forwards'.

From Lindeth Howe Beatrix Potter told Harold Warne, 'I have tried to get on with the book but there are no plates finished yet . . . I am interested in the drawings again—in the sense of getting my mind on it, and feeling I could make something of it—if only I had time and opportunity. I do wish I had got more done last winter before interruptions began, but I was a good deal damped by neither you nor Fruing seeming to care much for the story, and then it was

Frontispiece for *The Tale of Kitty-in-Boots*
The story was not published, and this is the only picture
which Beatrix Potter finished

Now most cats love the moonlight and staying out at nights; it
was curious how willingly Miss
Kitty went to bed. And although
the wash-house where she slept—
locked in—was always very clean,
upon some mornings Kitty was let
out with *her fur all draggled and wet.*

, And on
those mornings her tail seemed
rather thicker, and she scratched.

It puzzled me; but it was a long
time before I guessed that there
were really *two* black cats!

Galley proof of *The Tale of Kitty-in-Boots*, cut up and
pasted into a dummy copy, with Beatrix Potter's
pencil corrections

too late to think about another. It is very difficult to keep to a fixed level of success.'

The story was set up in type and galley proofs printed, but only one picture, the frontispiece, was finished, so the book remained unpublished. The full text is given here.

KITTY-IN-BOOTS

Once upon a time there was a serious, well behaved young black cat. It belonged to a kind old lady who assured me that no other cat could compare with Kitty. She lived in constant fear that Kitty might be stolen—'I hear there is a shocking fashion for black catskin muffs; wherever is Kitty gone to? Kitty! Kitty!'

She called it 'Kitty', but Kitty called herself 'Miss Catherine St. Quintin'.

Cheesebox called her 'Q', and Winkiepeeps called her 'Squintums'. They were very common cats. The old lady would have been shocked had she known of the acquaintance. And she would have been painfully surprised had she ever seen Miss Kitty in a gentleman's Norfolk jacket, and little fur-lined boots.

Now most cats love the moonlight and staying out at nights; it was curious how willingly Miss Kitty went to bed. And although the wash-house where she slept— locked in—was always very clean, upon some mornings Kitty was let out with her fur all draggled and wet. And on other mornings her tail seemed thicker, and she scratched.

It puzzled me; but it was a long time before I guessed that there were really *two* black cats!

If we had been outside the wash-house one summer night by moonlight, we might have seen one black cat cross the yard and jump upon the window sill— 'You are late, Winkiepeeps,' said another black cat inside.

'Sorry, Squintums,' answered the first black cat, unfastening the outside shutter.

'I object to being called names,' said Miss Catherine, jumping gracefully out of the window.

219

For this was naughty Kitty's plan, when she wanted to go a-hunting—*Winkiepeeps* opened the window and came in, to wait till Kitty came home.

Tonight he stopped outside. Kitty had put on her coat and little boots, 'Get in through the window, Winkiepeeps.'

'Shan't', said Winkiepeeps defiantly.

'What?' said Miss Catherine, preparing to scratch him.

Winkiepeeps changed his tone, and began to purr and coax.

'Please, Miss Kitty, let me go a-hunting too; Slimmy Jimmy is doing rabbit holes; with his cousin John Stoat Ferret.'

'Where? where?' asked Kitty. Her cat's eyes flashed; she had once seen a rabbit in the garden.

'In the wood behind Cheesebox's house, they want to borrow your gun, Miss Squintums,' purred Winkiepeeps. 'Cheesebox wouldn't give it to them.'

'Certainly not,' said Miss Catherine. Nevertheless, she and Winkiepeeps hurried away up the lane, towards Cheesebox's house where Kitty kept her gun.

Cheesebox was a stout tortoise-shell cat who washed and baked, and lived at the edge of the wood. I do not think Cheesebox herself ever went rabbiting; she had more sense while there were rats and mice in plenty. But she collected odds and ends for Mr. Worry Ragman, a little knowing terrier who drove about the country in a little rattling cart.

He bought rabbit skins and mole skins, rags and bones, and (oh shocking) feathers and eggs from Cheesebox and from Winkiepeeps, and from Tommy Brock the badger and Mr. Tod the fox.

'There's your gun, Miss Q; much good it may do you! *I* don't hold with poaching along with dirty ferrets. Mr. Worry Ragman buys other sorts besides mole skins; he says Mr. Tod has been setting steel traps.'

'Is that for rabbits?' asked Miss Kitty eagerly.

'I guess it's for whatever he can catch. Mind that—' At this moment the gun which Miss Kitty was loading went off; Winkiepeeps fled from the house with a squall, and Cheesebox cuffed Kitty.

When Kitty came out, Winkiepeeps was nowhere to be seen. 'I am sorry; I think Cheesebox may be right about ferrets.' Miss Kitty shut the gun with a snap, and it went off again. She carried it unloaded for some distance. She sat down under a tree, and took another bullet out of a 3d. mustard tin. The gun was an air gun, so Miss Kitty ran no risks with gunpowder. 'I will mouse,' said she, snapping it shut; it went off sideways.

'Was that meant for me? if you please, Sir; it's gone through the washing!' inquired a chuckling voice under a bush. Miss Kitty was rather flattered to be mistaken for a sportsman; she apologized to the person who came out with a bundle, curtseyed and trotted down the field. 'I wonder what sort of people it would be proper to shoot? Certainly not washerwomen who are hedgehogs,' said Miss Kitty, watching Mrs. Tiggy-Winkle; 'No; I suppose I must mouse.'

Miss Kitty stalked behind trees. She saw a mouse, took a long aim and pulled the trigger; but the gun was not loaded at all, and the mouse jumped away from Miss Kitty. Another mouse she missed, another she durst not fire at because it was carrying a basket; and twice she shot at sticks and stones that were not mice at all. Except for the pride of carrying a gun, it was only poor sport.

'Perhaps I could shoot birds—are those crows?' She came through a gate into a field, and found both crows and a flock of mountain sheep. 'Mutton?' said Kitty doubtfully, presenting her gun. The sheep stamped their feet and began to walk up to the odd little cat, while the crows swooped over her head—Miss Kitty took to her heels. 'I cannot waste bullets on rocketing birds!' She hid at the back of a wall.

Presently there was a scuffling noise of falling stones; Kitty was all attention. The noise moved further on. Something poked out at a hole and whisked in again. After several false starts, Kitty's gun went off and there was a squeak. She ran forward and met—not a mouse—but a large white ferret, rubbing his head, while another brown ferret in gaiters dropped off the top of the wall and wrenched the precious gun out of Miss Kitty's hands, exclaiming, 'Give us that there gun! *You* ain't fit to carry a gun! What do you mean by shooting my cousin Slimmy Jimmy?' Here Slimmy left off rubbing his head, and seemed much inclined to drag the gun away from John Stoat-Ferret—'Give us your bullets this minute!'

Miss Kitty replied by a very painful scratch across both their faces. She also spat at them. I once saw a copy-book heading to the effect that 'Evil communications corrupt good manners'; Miss Catherine's manners were not improved by associating with poaching ferrets. And at home that kind old lady was giving *Winkiepeeps* breakfast, and wondering why 'dear Kitty's' chin was black!

Up in the wood the real Kitty, sulky and spitting, followed the ferrets; she would not give them the bullets and they would not give up the gun.

We will not go into details; they took it in turn to go underground, and I believe they did bag a few young rabbits. But at last they met their match. Slimmy Jimmy suddenly came out of a burrow, pursued by a stout buck rabbit in a blue coat, who was prodding him violently and painfully with an umbrella. They upset John Stoat-Ferret who was waiting outside with the net; and before he could pick himself up, Miss Kitty had seized the gun.

The rabbit after several violent pokes went off, walking fast and brandishing the umbrella; the ferrets followed him; Miss Catherine also followed at a distance. The rabbit made no attempt to get right away, from time to time he stopped and waved the umbrella defiantly. They saw him go over a mossy tumble-down wall and disappear.

John Stoat-Ferret and his cousin Slimmy, being short-legged and in gaiters, went through a conveniently arranged tunnel under the wall. But they did not come out at the other side; they had walked into one of Mr. Tod's traps! There we will leave them, as the rabbit did, after he had come near enough to make sure that they were fast.

Miss Catherine, rather out of breath, sat on the top of the wall and eyed the rabbit. He was very fat. He winked at Miss Catherine, pointed at the ferrets, made a bow, and turned to go home.

Now why could not Kitty have the sense to go home too? It is true that Winkiepeeps would have been there, so that there would have been *two* black cats; but she might have stayed quietly at Cheesebox's until dark. No; I fear Miss Catherine was a born poacher; nothing would serve her but she must follow that rabbit. She did not like to shoot, because he was wearing such an elegant jacket. But she followed him.

The rabbit at first took no notice. Then he became uneasy, and hid behind trees. Miss Kitty could see the tips of his ears; whenever he stopped she lifted her gun. The rabbit opened his umbrella and set off again; it bobbitted along under the bushes like a live mushroom.

Miss Kitty followed and followed. The rabbit led her round and round the wood, till at length they came back to another part of the same wall. He shut his umbrella, waved it defiantly, took a long jump off the top of the wall and disappeared.

Miss Kitty—avoiding all risks of drains and tunnels—took a jump too, but not quite so long a jump as the rabbit's. She came down flop in another of Mr. Tod's traps, caught by both toes across her lovely fur boots. She gave a loud caterwaul and then sat still. After a few minutes she noticed ears peeping round a tree. Miss Kitty with pardonable temper shot at the ears, and missed them. While she reloaded, the rabbit came out and went home.

Miss Kitty sat on the trap. She sat and she sat. She ate one mouse (raw) which was all the game in her bag. Her toes were not really hurt, but so very very fast. Her feet went to sleep and she had pins and needles.

She sat there all night; her green cat's eyes peered into the dark. Once there was a noise like a cat in the distance; could it be Winkiepeeps? Kitty mewed, but there was no answer. It was very sad; but Miss Kitty ought not to have gone out on the sly, poaching. It served her right. It seemed plain she would have to remain in the trap till the person who had set it, let her out.

And when he arrived—it was Mr. Tod the fox. Miss Kitty's fur bristled; she gripped her gun.

'Oho,' said Mr. Tod, getting over the wall, and throwing down a rather bulging bag; 'Oho? Is this the rest of the black catskin muff?' Miss Kitty shivered! 'It seems to match,' said Mr. Tod, opening the bag. It contained mole and fur—and furs of various sorts, and he drew out half of a fine thick black cat tail! 'A complete set of furs,' said Mr. Tod, edging up towards Miss Kitty, who immediately pointed the gun at him.

'Gently, gently, Madam!' cried Mr. Tod, skipping over the wall, 'I was only going to release you from your uncomfortable position. Allow me to push forward the catch of the—oh! oh! that went through my coat sleeve!' Mr. Tod's nerves were thoroughly upset, 'Madam, I beg you to put down that most unsafe fire-arm. Allow me to unfasten the trap and pick up my bag.'

'The bag?' thought Miss Kitty, 'he dare not come for it; I have only five bullets left; but he does not know that.'

Mr. Tod and Miss Kitty argued all day. In the evening Mr. Tod went off. 'Perhaps you may have come to your senses before morning, madam!'

Kitty sat disconsolately in the trap and eyed the bag. When we stare at anything for a long long time—at last we begin to think it moves. Kitty had doubts, but at last it was unmistakable—The bag wobbled, turned over and rolled within reach of Kitty. 'Winkiepeeps?' inquired Kitty in a horrified whisper. The bag lay perfectly still—'Is that the rest of Winkiepeeps?' asked Kitty; she had recognized the tail!

'Oh sir, if you please, it's only me; oh please let me out, I'm nearly smothered!'

Kitty unstrapped the bag, which contained five mole skins, a brown and white fur of good quality but unpleasant smell, half a cat's tail, two young rabbits partly eaten, and a hedgehog.

'Oh, Sir, I'm that grateful—'

'M'am; Miss Catherine St. Quintin; you do my washing.'

'Why, M'm, Miss Squintums, is it you? Whatever is the matter?'

'I'm fast by the feet; and I'm awfully hungry.'

Mrs. Tiggy jerked up her prickles. 'You wouldn't go to eat me, M'm? not to mention the washing?'

'Indeed I wouldn't and couldn't, Mrs. Tiggy; do pray help me to get loose.'

'And a knave he is, M'm, that Tod; do you know what he did to my Uncle Pricklepin? Took him in a bag, which it might be that bag, and tumbled him into a pond. And when my Uncle Pricklepin was forced to uncurl himself, for to swim, M'm, Mr. Tod grabbed him under the waistcoat where he hadn't no prickles! Now let me put a little stone in the hinge of the trap, and we'll try to unlace your boots.'

It was a painful struggle, but at length Miss Kitty with the loss of one toe wriggled out, leaving her boots in the trap. It was of less consequence, as she immediately threw away her coat and gun—'Never again will I poach,' said Miss Kitty.

She limped home, and into the drawing-room. There upon the hearth rug sat *Winkiepeeps*, wrapped in a shawl, with sticking plaster on his tail. Kitty chose to look upon Winkiepeeps as the cause of her misfortunes; she rushed upon him and they fought all over the drawing-room.

For the rest of her days Kitty was a little lame; but it was an elegant limp; and she found quite enough occupation about the yard catching mice and rats; varied by tea-parties with respectable cats in the village, such as Ribby and Tabitha Twitchit.

But Winkiepeeps lived in the woods.

Appley Dapply's Nursery Rhymes
1917

As far back as 1893 Beatrix Potter illustrated the rhyme 'You know the old woman who lived in a shoe?' which appears in the 1917 *Appley Dapply Nursery Rhymes*. It was in the form of a booklet.

Also, some time in the '90s she prepared a booklet with paintings, illustrating the verse 'Three little Mice Sat down to Spin'—one picture for each line of the verse. It was all ready for printing, but apparently no publisher could be found. Some years later one of the pictures was redrawn and used in *The Tailor of Gloucester*.

Beatrix Potter had always been interested in traditional rhymes, and many of these were used in the privately printed *Tailor of Gloucester*, but the majority of the *Appley Dapply* rhymes were of her own composition.

As a child she had possessed books by Randolph Caldecott, which undoubtedly influenced her work when planning the 1905 *Appley Dapply* book of rhymes; furthermore, her father Rupert Potter was a keen collector of Caldecott's original drawings, and apparently possessed about thirty.

At one time Beatrix Potter belonged to a small drawing society. The drawings by the members were circulated for comment, bearing a 'pen name'—Beatrix Potter used the name 'Bunny'! Some of the drawings she submitted were inspired by Caldecott's work, but it appears they were not received with enthusiasm—for she wrote, 'I notice that those with a bit of landscape are the favourites. Nobody cares for the cocks and hens, and it comes rather near Caldecott's Cat & Fiddle, and comparisons are undesirable.'

In 1902, when the drawings for *The Tale of Peter Rabbit* were nearing completion and Beatrix Potter was wondering what to do next, she gave serious thought to this book of rhymes. On July 15th 1902, in a letter to Warnes, written just before the Potter family left for three months' holiday at Ees Wyke, Sawrey, she told them, 'I will try to bring one of the frames of Caldecott's to Bedford Street in the autumn. I have been looking at them a good deal. They seem to have been drawn with brown ink and a very fine pen—I wonder if it is the habit of Evans' line blocks to come out thicker? The one from Hentschel was rather the other way, inclined to be wiry and thin. It makes a good deal of difference; and I have been doing my larger drawings with a quill pen. It may sound odd to talk about mine and Caldecott's at the same time; but I think I could at least try to do better than *Peter Rabbit*, and if you did not care to risk another book I could pay for it. I have some-times thought of trying some of the other nursery rhymes about animals, which he did not do.'

Not being quite clear as to the most appropriate printing process for this larger book, she added, 'Do you think everything has to be coloured now,* or can one still have part in pen and ink? I should not fancy three-colour process for larger blocks, and I don't know anything about the other printing, which is my excuse for troubling you about it, and I very much enjoyed doing the rabbit book. I would go on with it in any event because I want something to do, but I thought you might know about the printers. I did not mean to ask you to say you would take another book. All our Caldecott's—about 30—are the *same size* as in the books, and quite curiously fine. I wonder that they could be photographed at all.'

A week later, from Ees Wyke, Beatrix Potter wrote to Warnes about the nursery-rhyme drawings which she had already prepared, as they had expressed some interest in them: 'I am very much obliged to you for being willing to consider some more drawings. I am rather sorry that I did not bring them before leaving London. The old drawings which I have done at different times are coloured, and various sizes—I mean to say, they would have to be drawn again and it would take some time—but I am rather inclined to send them to you to look at as they are, to see what you suggest about the size of the plates, and how much illustrations to each rhyme. I would understand clearly that if I made them up into shape for a book—the book would still be only on approval. I could make a rough plan of some of the pages and send them next week, or any other time. This is a convenient place for subjects to draw, and it seems a pity to miss the chance of going on with them.'

At that time she was giving serious thought to the preparation of *The Tailor of Gloucester*, which was to be privately printed at the end of the year—but still had every intention of her *Appley Dapply* book being printed one day. In the meantime she would continue *thinking* about it.

She was wondering how many rhymes it ought to contain, and Warnes were consulted on this point. 'If eighteen were a reasonable number of full-page plates', wrote Beatrix Potter, 'I am inclined to think seven rhymes would be enough; I should like to spin out the illustrations a little more. I don't know whether it would be better to do the small ones in pen and ink, or in colour? The coloured sample page looks rather nice, and I think would make a prettier book . . . I had thought the book might be in a style between Caldecott's and the Baby's Opera; I cannot design pattern borders, but I like drawing flowers. I will go on with it on approval if you are undecided, or for myself if you decline it; I should not intend sending it to another publisher; but I hope very much you may like the drawings.'

During the next three years the planning of the book became a spare-time occupation, for at that time she was actively engaged on the preparation of several other books.

* Warnes had accepted her *Peter Rabbit* book only on condition that the original black-and-white drawings were coloured.

Appley.dapply, a little brown mouse,
Goes to the cupboard in Somebody's house.

In Somebody's cupboard, there's everything nice;
Cake, cheese, jam, candles— delightful for mice!

Preliminary sketches for the 1917 *Appley Dapply's*
Nursery Rhymes

Preliminary lay-out of a page for the 1905 *Appley Dapply* book of rhymes

On January 1st 1904 Beatrix Potter wrote to Norman Warne and told him, 'If neither the cat nor the mice would do, one *might* fall back on the rhymes—*Appley Dapply.*' She was referring to the three stories she had sent him to choose from— *The Tale of Tuppenny, Something very very Nice,* and *The Tale of Hunca Munca.*

However, the story of the mice was finally chosen—so once again her *Appley Dapply* book took second place. Still with the rhyme book in mind, and half apologizing for not getting on with her mouse story, she wrote, 'I shall be ashamed to show you how little I have done of the mice; but I did several rough sketches for backgrounds of the larger (Ap. Dap.) book in case we should be doing it next winter.' And at the end of May, referring to the mouse story, 'When this book is finished I should like to get a rough idea of the *Appley Dapply* book before we go away in July; I am very much inclined for working.'

During 1904 a good deal of thought was given to the planning of *Appley Dapply*, and from time to time we hear of its progress. On August 6th Beatrix Potter wrote, 'I have made some more rhymes for the new book but I have not done much drawing yet; it would be a great pleasure to get settled to work again.' And on September 14th, 'Thank you very much for your letter and for making out a plan of the larger book; the plan of it which you suggest is just *exactly* what I should like. If my rhymes are good enough, I don't think I should have much difficulty in filling that number of pages! and I would rather try to make it a real pretty book than try to have more royalty. I shall have to learn to do pen and ink better, but I daresay I shall get into it.'

In a letter to Norman Warne on October 20th 1904 she told him, 'We return to Bolton Gardens on October 28th . . . I have thought of ever so many more rhymes—most extremely odd ones some of them! but of course if they strike you as too fanciful they can easily go. I think it ought to make a nice book. I have been scribbling a great deal of pen and ink not exactly useful subjects—but to get my hand into the way. I find it interesting to do, and I think pretty good results.'

On November 2nd Beatrix Potter received from Warnes a ninety-four page 'dummy' for the rhyme book. It was a large format, bound in boards having bevelled edges, and measuring 200 mm × 150 mm. When acknowledging this dummy she wrote, 'I am much obliged for the dummy book, it is a very nice size —I only hope I shall do it justice.'

A stiff-covered exercise book in which Beatrix Potter had written out her proposed rhymes for *Appley Dapply* had already been sent to Norman Warne for his comments. In due course the book was returned, and his initials NDW appeared against twenty-one of the thirty rhymes, indicating his approval of these.

Peter Opie, who is an authority on Nursery Rhymes, was asked if he thought the rhymes were composed by Beatrix Potter. In his reply he wrote, 'When saying that the *Appley Dapply* rhymes are Beatrix Potter's, I must quickly add that I am not widely familiar with minor composed children's verses, and I could not swear that every specimen was original; but these pieces appear to be all by the same hand, and are certainly not traditional, although a few have been "set a jogging" by familiar metres. One or two of them are delicious.'

On July 21st 1905, in one of the last letters Beatrix Potter wrote to Norman Warne, she spoke of these rhymes, and asked if she could call at Bedford Street the following morning to discuss her *Appley Dapply* book, as there seemed little chance of her coming to town in August.

Shortly after, Norman Warne died, and in these sad circumstances, the 1905 *Appley Dapply* book of rhymes was put on one side and left untouched for many years.

In June 1917 Fruing Warne asked her for another story, but she was not prepared to undertake this work—however, she said, 'According to the proverb, half a loaf is better than no bread (and *such* bread too). Would it be too shabby to put Appley Dapply into a booklet the size of Miss Moppet? I find I could scrape together sufficient old drawings to fill one; they would require some "linking up". A few are in square edges, but in a mixed book, I think it would not signify?

'The original idea was a large one with borders, but it would mean large expensive plates, and more time and eyesight than I see my way to at present. If you think this worth doing—you might send me either a blank book—or a copy of "Moppet" with papers pasted over the pictures and I would scribble in outlines that would do for the travellers. I have just remembered with a shock that they used to start about July 1st. Why not type the rhymes and paste in? I could do several pencil outlines if you will supply pasted up blank books. I'm afraid this sounds very lazy, but you don't know what a scramble I live in; and the old drawings are some of them better than any I could do now. I suppose the larger ones would reduce all right.'

In October 1917 an abridged edition of the book was published—called *Appley Dapply's Nursery Rhymes*. It contained six of the original rhymes together with one new one; and the verses were printed without their framed borders.

When Beatrix Potter received her first copies of the book from Warnes, she was delighted with them and wrote, 'I am much pleased with Appley Dapply, it makes a pretty little book.'

Towards the end of her life she came across the original 'Dummy' for her 1905 *Appley Dapply*, and wrote in it, 'Dummy for a book of rhymes, never used. Some were used without framed borders, for Appley Dapply. It would have been a pretty book, nid, nid, noddy!'—adding—

> 'Nid nid noddy
> We stand in a ring,
> All day long,
> And never do a thing.'

The title she gave to this rhyme was 'The Mushrooms', and Beatrix Potter was evidently recalling the years from 1887 to 1901, during which she made an intensive study of fungi, and painted several hundred different varieties.

After her death this *Appley Dapply* dummy was found in a drawer at Hill Top. In it were inserted many loose sheets on which were verses with their framed borders, and rough sketches illustrating these verses. On the title page were the words 'Appley Dapply', and inside the front cover Warnes had pencilled:

Title	want a different one
Edition	10,000 or more
Price	2/6 net.

Beatrix Potter's rhymes for the 1905 *Appley Dapply* are given in the order in which they were entered in the exercise book she sent to Norman Warne.

BEATRIX POTTER'S RHYMES FOR HER 1905 APPLEY DAPPLY

NDW   1

> Appley Dapply, a little brown mouse,
> Goes to the cupboard in Somebody's house;
> In Somebody's cupboard, there's everything nice—
> Cake, jam and candles—delightful to mice!
> Appley Dapply has little sharp eyes,
> And Appley Dapply is *so* fond of pies!

This rhyme is about one of Beatrix Potter's pet mice. In various drafts there are small changes in the wording—thus, 'very sharp eyes' has been changed to 'little sharp eyes'; and the line which first read, 'Cake, cheese, jam, candles—delightful for mice!' has been twice altered—first to 'Cake, jam and candles—delightful to mice!', and then, as in the book, to 'Cake, cheese, jam, biscuits—All charming for mice!'

NDW   2

> Old Mr. Prickly Pin,
> With never a cushion to stick the pins in!
> His nose is black, and his beard is grey,
> And he lives in the ash-stump over the way.

Old Mr. Prickly Pin is a hedgehog—sometimes referred to as Old *Mister* Prickly Pin. We are told in *The Tale of Kitty-in-Boots* that he was Mrs. Tiggy-Winkle's uncle.

NDW   3

> You know the old woman who lived in a shoe,
> And had so many children she didn't know what to do?
> I'm sure if she lived in a little shoe house,
> That little old woman was surely a mouse!

In her earlier version of this rhyme, the last two lines read:

> She gave them some broth without any bread,
> She whipped them all round and put them to bed.

NDW   4

> If acorn-cups were tea-cups, what should we have to drink?
> Why! honey-dew for sugar, in a cuckoo-pint of milk;
> With pats of witches' butter and a tansey cake, I think,
> Laid out upon a toad-stool on a cloth of cob-web silk!

The title Beatrix Potter gave to this rhyme is 'Toad's Tea-Party', and in her finished painting there is a group of toads with very expressive faces, sitting on toad-stools having tea. In a later version the last two lines are transposed.

Of this rhyme, Mr. Opie writes, 'Inspired by "If all the world were paper"' ODNR No. 548.*

5

> Knitting, knitting, 8, 9, 10, I knit socks for gentlemen;
> I love muffin and I love tea; knitting, knitting, 1, 2, 3!

Of this rhyme Mr. Opie writes, 'Original, but with traditional undertones in the phraseology.' Under this verse is written the word 'mouse'.

NDW   6

> Kadiddle, kadiddle, kadiddle!
> Come dance to my dear little fiddle?
> (Kadiddle, kadiddle, kadiddle,
> Come dancing along down the middle . . .
> Oh silly Kadiddle, Kadiddle!)

On June 28th 1904, in a letter to Norman Warne from Melford Hall, Beatrix Potter said, 'I should think your editor will be distracted when he has to correct

* Oxford Dictionary of Nursery Rhymes, by Iona and Peter Opie. Oxford University Press, 1951.

'Toad's tea-party'

An unfinished page for the 1905 *Appley Dapply* book of rhymes, illustrating the verses about Tommy Tittle-mouse

"Appley Dapply". I wonder if he knows how to spell the Suffolk way of calling ducks. It is very comical to hear the children—"Kadiddle C'diddle K'diddle".'

In a later draft, Beatrix Potter amended the second line to read 'Come dance to my little brown fiddle?'

7

> Fishes come bite! Fishes come bite!
> I have fished all day; I will fish all night.
> I sit in the rain on my lily-leaf boat,
> But never a minnow will bob my float.
> Fishes come bite!

Under the rhyme Beatrix Potter referred to the picture she was going to paint, and wrote 'Frog on lily-leaf'. In the picture there is a quotation from Shakespeare's *Twelfth Night*: 'The rain it raineth every day'.

NDW   8

> I've heard that Tommy Tittle-mouse
>   Lived in a tiny little house,
> Thatched with a roof of rushes brown
>   And lined with hay and thistle-down.
>
> Walled with woven grass and moss,
>   Pegged down with willow twigs across.
> Now wasn't that a charming house
>   For little Tommy Tittle-mouse?

Beatrix Potter intended to write three verses for this rhyme, but the middle verse was only partly finished, and reads:

> .   .   .   .   . green
> .   .   .   .   . between
> A fluffy bed, so warm and nice
> For little Tommy Tittle-mice.

NDW   9

> Diggory, Diggory, Delvet, a little old man in black velvet!
> He digs and he delves like the mowdwarps themselves,
> Diggory, Diggory, Delvet.

This rhyme is called 'The Mole', and against her rough sketch of a mole, Beatrix

Potter has written, 'digging in sand bank—I have some good sketches for this—brown border, daisies and columbine'. She then added a note: 'mowdwarp = mole, north country word.'

> NDW   10

> Two little mice were playing a game—
> —Thingummy-jig and Whatzisname—
> 'You're too little and I'm too big,'
> Said Whatzisname to Thingummy-jig.

> 'You're too tiny but *I* am too tall!'
> '*I*'m enormous but *you* are too small!'
> Up and down—'Why we're just the same!'
> Said Thingummy-jig to Whatzisname.

This rhyme, written about 1904, is about Thingummy-jig and Whatzisname—two of Beatrix Potter's pet mice, who lived in a cage with Appley Dapply and some other mice. There is no drawing, but in a pencil note Beatrix Potter has written, 'Piebald mice on sea-saw'.

> NDW   11

> There once was an amiable guinea-pig
> Who brushed back his hair like a peri-wig,
> He wore a sweet tie, as blue as the sky,
> And his hat and coat buttons were very big.

> 12

> To Market! To Market! Now isn't this funny?
> You've got a basket, and I've got some money!
> —We went to market and I spent my money,
> Home again! home again! Little Miss Bunny!

> 13

> Pretty Lambkin went to play,
> Through the fern and lost his way;
> Climbed on a rock and called his dam.
> —Cried and shouted—pretty Lamb!

Norman Warne has underlined the word *dam* and put a question mark in the margin!

14

Pea-straw and parsnips! Pussy's in the well!
The doggie's gone to Guildford—gone to buy a bell;
   Dingle dingle dousy! Ding dong bell!
   Laugh little mousey! Pussy's in the well!

Underneath this rhyme Beatrix Potter has written 'adapted from a German rhyme'.

NDW   15

Babbity Bouster Bumble Bee!
  Fill up your honey bags, bring them to me!
Humming and sighing—with lazy wing
  Where are you flying—what song do you sing?

'Who'll buy my honey-pots? Buy them? Who'll buy?'
  Sweet heather honey—come weigh them and try!
— Honey-bag, honey-pot, home came she!
  Nobody buys from a big Bumble Bee!

Of this rhyme, Mr. Opie writes, 'The name Babbity Bouster is that of a singing game'.

NDW   16

  Galeny, galeny, galene!
  —Now what *is* that waving between
  The nettles and docks on the green?

  Potracket, potrack, potrack!
    The thing wavered forward and back—
  Potrack! potrack! potrack!

  Then the cowman crossed over the green,
  And explained to Galeny, galene!

Beatrix Potter has added the following note:

     'galeny (galeeny?) = guinea hen
      Fox's Tail—a true story.'

The incident which inspired this rhyme is described in a picture letter which Beatrix Potter wrote to Freda Moore in 1897 when staying at Harescombe Grange (facing page 134).

NDW   17

Big Box, little Box, Band-Box, Bundle!
You hold tight, and don't you tumble
When the train comes in, with a rush and a rumble.

The train came in, the barrow gave a trundle—
Off jumped Band-Box, little Box, Bundle!

Of this rhyme, Mr. Opie writes, 'First and last lines from fortune-telling chant'. For the illustration Beatrix Potter has drawn a sketch of a barrow holding three boxes on each of which is a little face. Below, a train has just arrived, and alongside, a man is pulling an empty barrow, with the three little boxes on legs, running after it!

NDW   18

When the dew falls silently
   And stars begin to twinkle,
Underneath the hollow tree
   Peeps poor Tiggy-Winkle.

Where the whispering waters pass—
   Her little cans twinkle,
Up and down the dewy grass
   Trots poor Tiggy-Winkle.

Below this rhyme is the word 'Hedgehog'. The middle verse is unfinished and reads:

.   .   .   .   .   .

Her little eyes twinkle,
A glow-worm for a candle
Lights poor Mrs. Tiggy-Winkle.

NDW   19

Tabitha Twitchit is grown so fine
She lies in bed until half past nine.
She breakfasts on muffins, and eggs and ham,
And dines on red-herrings and rasp-berry jam!!

Of this rhyme, Mr. Opie writes, 'Inspired by Elsie Marley who grew so fine (ODNR No. 152).' The picture which illustrated the verse was later redrawn, and

One of the drawings for the 1905 *Appley Dapply*
book of rhymes, illustrating the verse 'Tabitha,
Twitchit is grown so fine'. Redrawn and coloured,
it was used in 1929 as a frontispiece for *The Fairy
Caravan*, with the title 'Louisa Pussy-cat sleeps late'

The
Rain
It
Raineth
Every Day

'Fishes come bite'
(See rhyme 7 in the 1905 *Appley Dapply*)

used as the frontispiece for *The Fairy Caravan*; it was called 'Louisa Pussy-cat Sleeps Late'.

NDW   20

> Old Mother Goose and her flat-footed daughter
> Live on the hill, near a fine spring of water;
> Their grey-slated cottage is seen from the road,
> Bench, tubs, doorway, chimney—a cheerful abode!
>
> The peat smoke puffs up from their fire as we pass;
> See, the blankets and sheets spread to bleach on the grass—
> And when the sun shines, and the west wind blows high,
> They'll wring out their washing, and hang it to dry.

Below the rhyme Beatrix Potter has briefly described the picture she was going to draw: 'Old mother goose washing clothes in a stream, her daughter hanging them on a line, cottage and birch trees in background'.

NDW   21

> Now what is that tapping at Cotton-tail's door?
> —Tap tappit! tap tappit! we've heard it before?
> But when she peeps out—there is nobody there—
> —And a present of carrots is found on the stair!
> Hark, I hear it again; tap tap tappit! tap tappit!
> Why I really believe it's a little black Rabbit!

                         22

> I'm a little 'Pussy Butcher' with a natty little cart,
> My manners are superior, and my apron's clean and smart,
> My billy-goat can trot a race with any tradesman's van—
> —Then kindly do not call me common 'Cat's-meat Man'!

In a later draft, Beatrix Potter changed the words 'a natty little cart', to 'a tidy little cart'.

NDW   23

> I found a tiny pair of gloves
>   When Lucie'd been to tea,
> They were the dearest little loves—
>   I thought they'd do for me—

I tried them—(quite inside them!)
　They were *much* too big for me!
I wear gloves with *one* button-hole
　When *I* go out to tea.

I'll put them in an envelope
　With sealing wax above,
I'll send them back to Lucie—
　I'll send them with my love.

This rhyme was originally given to Lucie Carr of Newlands. Written at the top of the rhyme are the words, 'Piebald mouse', and on Lucie's copy there are pictures of the little mouse with the gloves.

24

Nid, nid, noddy, we stand in a ring,
　All day long, and never do a thing!
But nid nid noddy! we wake up at night,
　We hop and we dance, in the merry moon-light!

On July 2nd 1905, in a letter to Norman Warne, Beatrix Potter wrote, 'There was one of the Ap. Dap. rhymes that would want little faces; you did not mark it, but I think it might be pretty—"nid nid noddy, we stand in a ring". I meant it for mushrooms dancing in the moonlight with little faces peeping underneath their caps.' Two days later, in a letter from Bolton Gardens, Beatrix Potter wrote, 'I met a small child yesterday who smiled at me under an immense mushroom hat!'

Beneath a painting of three mushrooms with little faces, which illustrated the first two lines of this rhyme, Beatrix Potter wrote, 'border, clover, grass and button mushrooms, all brown.' The picture which illustrated the last two lines was a scene with a full moon and a field of mushrooms below.

25

'Oh who will come open this great heavy gate?
The hill fox yaps loud, and the moon rises late;
There's snow on the fell, and the flock's at the farm!'
'Little black Hoggie, we'll keep thee from harm!'

26

Billy brown shrew with the velvet clothes,
No eyes whatever and very long nose,
Call up your children as fast as you can!
—He whistled and twistled, that little brown man!

In a later draft, the last line reads, 'He twistled and whistled, and up they ran.'

236

NDW   27

> There came a lady from Fairy-land,
>   Who carried a primrose in her hand;
> The green grass leapt after, wherever she trod,
>   And daisies and butter-cups danced on the sod.
>
> Her locks were pale may-flowers, a sunbeam her nose;
>   Her breath was the cowslip's, she'd bells on her toes;
> Her eyes were blue violets, her lips were red flame,
>   Her voice was the throstle's—and S p r i n g was her name!

Beatrix Potter has marked the first line of verse 2 'alter'.

NDW   28

> Shepherdess of fields on high,
>   Drive in your thousand sheep!
> Flocks that stray across the sky,
>   And clouds that sail the deep!

Above this rhyme are the words, 'Moon and Clouds'. In line 2 Beatrix Potter has given three alternatives for the first word—Drive, Fold, or Call. She also gives an alternative version:

> Shepherdess of fields on high
>   That hold ten thousand sheep!
> Drive your flocks across the sky,
>   The clouds that sail the deep.

NDW   29

> Rushes grow green! rushes burn red!
> We'll sup on rush candle, the little mice said.

NDW   30

> There once was a large spotted weevil,
> Whose looks were peculiarly evil.
> But his looks were to blame—
> He was perfectly tame,
> Herbiverous, harmless and civil!

The title Beatrix Potter had given to this rhyme was 'The Monster'.

Although not in the exercise book sent to Norman Warne, the four rhymes which follow belong to this period:

31

There was an old snail with a nest—
    Who very great terror expressed,
Lest the wood-lice all round
    In the cracks under-ground
Should eat up her eggs in that nest!

Her days and her nights were oppressed,
    —But soon all her fears were at rest;
For eleven young snails
    With extremely short tails,
Hatched out of the eggs in that nest.

32

'Either *Over the Hills and Far Away* or *Buttercup Land*'

When swift cloud shadows race over the hills—
    Where tinkling water leaps down the steep ghylls
On wide brown sands at the edge of the sea—
    Little odd people come whisper to me!

Under the bracken and wood moss they peep,
    And play in the moonlight when other folks sleep,
They hide in the sweet-smelling hay in the barn,
    And under the wainscots and tubs at the farm.

Land of kind dreams, where the mountains are blue,
    Where brownies are friendly and wishing comes true!
Through your green meadows they dance hand in hand—
    —Little odd people of Buttercup Land.

A set of verses which Beatrix Potter gave to Marjorie Moore. She may have originally intended to use these verses for her 1905 *Appley Dapply* book of rhymes

I saw a ship a-sailing
A-sailing on the sea;
And Oh! it was all laden
With pretty things for thee!

There were comfits in the cabin
And apples in the hold;
The sails were made of silk
And the masts were made of gold.

And 4 and 20 sailors
That stood upon the decks
Were four and twenty white mice
With chains about their necks

The captain was a guinea-pig —
The pilot was a rat —

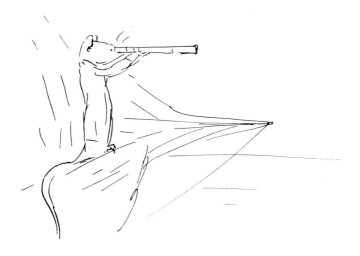

the Captain

The Ship

the passengers embarking

And the passengers were rabbits
Who ran about, pit pat!

All of which will have to be carefully drawn,
but I think the words are lovely. Just imagine
the white mice letting down the bags of confits
into the hold!

33

The Tom-tit's Song

I made my nest in a hollow pear-tree,
Nobody lived there but Titmouse and me!

I lined that nest with feathers black and grey,
—There came a wicked sparrow and stole them half away!

Ten very tiny eggs, speckled white and red!
Soft fluffy feathers hid them over-head.

Ten speckled white eggs and three speckled grey,
Quite of different sizes in that nest soon lay.

I'm not good at counting—ten and one two three!
It was very puzzling to Titmouse and me!

Thirteen little naked birds with yellow mouths gaped wide,
—And three of them *such* big ones—we looked at them with pride.

Calling for their breakfast—ten and one two three!
Hard work providing for Titmouse and me—

But when their feathers came—what a shocking sight!
Three of them were brown birds, mine are blue and white;

Three horrid sparrows, as greedy as could be!
Crowding and imposing on Titmouse and me!

Greedier and noisier they grew every day—
Just when we were desperate, the monsters flew away!

—Ten little tom tits, as merry as can be!
Chasing one another round a Perry pear-tree!

'Perhaps this might be too complicated Natural History? but the cuckoo's similar habits are well known to children—

The above incident happened in a wooden nest box; we opened the lid—found three big young sparrows sitting on the top of an incredible family of little tom tits, the whole brood having been hatched and reared by poor Mrs. Titmouse.'

The Oakmen
1918

William Heelis had a sister with a family of five children, and it was not long after their marriage that Beatrix Potter met her new niece Nancy Nicholson, who was about six years old at the time. Seven years separated her from the brother who came next to her in age.

She and Beatrix Potter were friends at once, for they had much in common. Both were full of imagination and loved fairy-tales. Nancy tells how she used to play with imaginary people called Oakmen who lived in trees. 'I remember my amazement on my first visit to Sawrey,' she wrote, 'when this new aunt left the grown-ups and came to me to imagine windows and doors in the trees with people peeping out.'

In 1916 Beatrix Potter wrote a story about the Oakmen, a reminder of their first meeting, which she gave to Nancy as a Christmas present that year. It was written in a loose-leaved book in which were six pages of text, each page illustrated by a water-colour sketch.

At the end of 1917 when Beatrix Potter sent Nancy a copy of her *Appley Dapply's Nursery Rhymes*, she asked, 'Will you let me borrow the story about the Owl and the Oakmen for a short time? I have no copy, and there is a plan of printing some other story, as these rhymes have sold so well—either the Oakmen or the story I told you of Johnny Town-Mouse . . . I don't want to lose the story. I cannot remember the words.'

The Oakmen story was sent to her, but before Beatrix Potter had finished working it out in detail, she found that the idea about Oakmen had come from some story book which had been read to Nancy as a small child, therefore the use of the name 'Oakmen' might possibly be an infringement of copyright—so the story was put on one side, and *The Tale of Johnny Town-Mouse* took its place.

It is of interest to know that Beatrix Potter had already commissioned another artist to prepare the finished drawings for *The Oakmen*. He was to work from her rough pencil sketches on which were written instructions as to composition and colouring. The artist was Mr. Ernest A. Aris, with whom she had been in touch on several previous occasions to try out the quality and scope of his work. 'My feeling was that my eyes were failing and my hands getting stiff,' she wrote, 'but I had still brains and ideas which I might get carried out by an assistant.' *She* would, of course, design and plan the drawings to the very last detail.

Beatrix Potter had always loved to put in much fine detail into her pictures, but this was no longer easy. 'I remember her telling me', wrote Nancy, 'that someone had suggested that she should try to enlarge her drawings, but Beatrix Potter said "however large a space I start with, I keep on putting in more and more detail, so it's no use".' An assistant with technical ability was needed, but not necessarily with creative power.

The set of six drawings which Mr. Aris had prepared were bought by Beatrix Potter together with copyright—and her comments were—'His little men which I bought are uncommonly good'.

The Oakmen were often mentioned in Beatrix Potter's correspondence with her niece. In one letter she told Nancy:

I am very sleepy. I have been cross-cutting firewood from a large broken oak tree with Ethel Green. A little robin has been watching us all day, hopping on the logs. He was so tame he nearly touched us—He had very bright beady eyes, and a very red cap—no, not a cap, a red waistcoat. I did not feel quite sure whether he was a real robin, till he found a worm in some rotten bark—I do not feel quite sure. He kept flying round behind the tree, to speak to someone, and coming back. He came back dozens of times and I had nothing for him—except a bit of apple. He went home before we did on account of chilblains on his toes. I believe he lives with the Oakmen. At all events he had supper with them. He sat on a chair with his feet in hot water and ate pickled caterpillars out of a pie dish!

Some years later, in February 1924, in a letter to Mr. Fruing Warne, Beatrix Potter told him, 'I should have liked to have made a book of some of my "letters to Nancy"; they were more fairy-tales; and I see the little men peeping round the mossy stumps and stones whenever I go up the wood—but I cannot draw them.'

THE OAKMEN

Christmas 1916

My dear Nancy,

I have given Prickle-pin to the Oakmen, to have for a little dog. I hope they will be very kind to him; he was a nice animal—such a soft little waistcoat under his prickles! I gave him to an Oakman who lives under a tree. I put Prickle-pin in, through his front door, and covered it up with dead leaves.

Now I will tell you about the Oakmen who lived in the larch wood. There were lots and lots of them, each living inside a tree. Oakman Number 2 invited Oakman Number One and Number 3 to a Tea party. He set out his tea cups on a toad-table, and the toad stools were chairs.

He heard a noise, thump! thump! He thought it was his friends knocking—But when he opened the door he saw Oakman Number 3 and 1 hiding behind trees—and two wood fallers were cutting down larch trees with axes!

And one of the trees they were cutting down was the top story and attics of Oakman Number 7.

And when I went up the hill a week later—I *was* surprised. That big black wood was nearly all gone—nothing but stumps, and chips, and trunks of trees. I could see nothing of the Oakmen, and there was nobody to ask—not even a rabbit. I felt sad.

On my way home, I met our white owl, flying up to the intake. Said I—'Jimmy Howlet! Jimmy Howlet! Stop!' He lit on a tree, and answered me.

'Too whit, hoo, hoo, hoo!'

'Jimmy Howlet,' said I, 'tell me, have you seen the Oakmen? What *has* happened, up here?'

'Indeed, it is most serious,' replied Jimmy Howlet—'These wood fallers are cutting down every house.' 'And where are the Oakmen?' 'They keep moving up; they are all squeezed into those few trees that are left at the top of the wood. Oakman Number 11 has 16 neighbours sleeping on his kitchen table, and 3 in the dolly tub.'

'It must be very uncomfortable.'

'It is worse than uncomfortable; Oakman Number 8 did not get out in time; and was buried in chips. I held the lantern while they dug him out. And Oakman Number 14 has had 6 chairs broken, and a grandfather clock which he valued extremely much—'

'Why deary me, Jimmy Howlet, this is quite intolerable! It is worse than Zeppelins. These Oakmen are most particular friends of my niece, Miss Nancy Nicholson. It is really shocking that they should be buried in chips, and their houses pulled down on top of them.' 'Indeed half their pots and pans are broken,' replied Jimmy Howlet.

'Go to them at once, with a message, Jimmy Howlet—Tell them I have been planting a new little wood all of my own—Tell them to harness the rabbit waggon and pack up their bags, and move over the moor. My trees—I fear, are rather small, there are 1700 little larches and 500 little spruces, like little Christmas trees. But there is a nice dry humpy hillock in the bog overlooking the tarn—we have already dug lots of little holes in it. These I will give to the Oakmen, for lovely snug dugouts. And I have an idea; I will send up a hen house, to be used for storing a kettle, and cups and saucers, for the convenience of my niece, Miss Nancy Nicholson, when she goes picnicking. This we will lend to the Oakmen, for tea-parties in wet weather. Perhaps in return—they will gather us some dry sticks and bale the punt!'

When I next went up the hill, the wood was deserted—the punt was baled out —and I think—I think I saw some little red caps peeping out of the hillock. When Nancy goes up to the tarn, she will know where to look for the Oakmen.

A page from the manuscript of *The Oakmen*
This manuscript was given to Beatrix Potter's niece, Nancy Nicholson,
Christmas, 1916

Studies of mice dancing

The Tale of Johnny Town-Mouse
1918

The theme of this story was taken from Aesop's Fable, 'The Town Mouse and the Country Mouse'. Beatrix Potter called her version *The Tale of Johnny Town-Mouse* and for its setting she chose the Lakeland villages of Hawkshead and Sawrey. Timmy Willy the country mouse lived in a garden in Sawrey, and Johnny Town-Mouse lived under the floor boards of a house in Hawkshead some two-and-a-half miles distant at the far end of Esthwaite Water. Mrs. Susan Ludbrook writes, 'The house with the tall staircase where the town mice lived belonged to a Mrs. Bolton, who received vegetables from Sawrey each week, and sent back laundry. I was told by a lady who visited Hill Top, that in this story Dr. Parsons was the Town-mouse. She said "the long bag Johnny Town-Mouse carrried contained golf clubs, and Dr. Parsons and Mr. Heelis used to play together".'

'When anyone wanted the doctor in the village, the villagers would say, you must find Mr. Heelis, they have gone out together with bags of sticks, and where one is you will find the other. Golf was very new then, and few knew anything of the game, but Dr. Parsons and Mr. Heelis had a private golf course constructed for their own use at Sawrey and played together there.' When asked if she would recognize Dr. Parsons in *The Tale of Johnny Town-Mouse*, she said at once 'Of course, the identical figure.'

In the book pictures, the house-maid with the hamper was Mrs. Rogerson as seen in her younger days, who worked for the Potter family when they stayed at Ees Wyke.

The arch in one of the pictures is at Hawkshead, and can be recognized today—also, the carrier's cart and horse were drawn from life, and Beatrix Potter tells us it was a grand old horse called Old Diamond. Towards the end of the story, when Timmy Willie returned to his garden home in Sawrey, we see the carrier's cart proceeding down the road, and catch a glimpse of the fine old weather-vane on the roof of Ginger and Pickles' shop.

Of her illustrations Beatrix Potter wrote, 'Do you think this mouse story would do? It makes pretty pictures, but not an indefinite number as there is not a great deal of variety . . . I am doing them on card as I thought perhaps the life and expression (which I can still get in a sketch) might make up for sketchiness in direct work; rather than work up repeated copies as used to be my habit. The text comes out well.'

The story was sent to Warnes to be typed, and a simple method of preparing the text for the printer was adopted. One of Beatrix Potter's previous books, which happened to be a copy of *The Tale of Mrs. Tittlemouse*, was used as a dummy, and the typed paragraphs were pasted in. Beatrix Potter then inserted rough thumb-nail sketches of the pictures she was drawing, and placed them in their correct positions throughout the book. A plain sheet of paper was pasted over the title page and the appropriate wording written on it. Inside the front cover Warnes had pencilled, 'Mrs. Tittlemouse contains 1135 words'—comparing favourably with their count of 1133 words in Beatrix Potter's manuscript.

Beatrix Potter altered the title from 'The Tale of Timmy Willie' to 'A Tale of a Country Mouse'; then after further consideration she changed it to 'The Tale of Johnny Town-Mouse'.

This called for a new opening paragraph, which was pencilled in the dummy. The respective paragraphs read:

Original Text	*Revised Text*
Timmy Willie went to town by mistake in a hamper. Timmy Willie was a little country mouse, born in a garden.	Johnny Town-mouse was born in a cupboard. Timmy Willie was born in a garden. He was a little country mouse; he went to town by mistake in a hamper.

The Tale of Johnny Town-Mouse was finished by the beginning of November, 1918, and the dedication page reads, 'To Aesop in the shadows'. On November 8th 1918 Warnes wrote to say, 'We are sending you herewith six advanced copies of "Johnny Town-Mouse" from actual stock, which we think look much nicer than the earlier specimen we forwarded to you. In the next binder's delivery we shall have the backs flatter; at present they are not quite pleasing to us in this respect.'

The books were on sale in the shops in time for Christmas, but not without effort on Beatrix Potter's part. 'I had an awful scramble to do this little book,' she wrote, when sending a presentation copy to Mrs. Moore.

The book was well received, as can be seen from the following review in *The Bookman*, which Fruing Warne sent to Beatrix Potter on December 31st 1918: 'Another volume for the Peter Rabbit bookshelf. Oh, such charming pictures and exciting letterpress! We like Timmy Willie, who was born in a garden, better than Johnny. Poor Timmy Willie who had such simple country tastes, and who fell asleep by mistake in a hamper of vegetables which went up to town! The pictures are among the very best Miss Potter has done, that of the dinner of eight courses held by Johnny Town-Mouse and his friends under the floor is utterly delicious, also Johnny's questioning of Timmy—"A garden sounds rather a dull place. What do you do when it rains?" The whole secret of Miss Potter's success lies in the fact that there are plenty of pictures for her impatient audience, and that the pictures can be readily understood, and that the story is just modulated at the right tone to please a child's ear. Miss Potter need not worry about rivals. She has none. "Johnny Town-Mouse" does even so accomplished an artist and writer as herself much credit.'

The Tale of the Birds and Mr. Tod
1919

Beatrix Potter had always been interested in Aesop's Fables and amongst her un-published work are several which she retold in her own individual style and with her own settings.

She decided to use this material for her 1919 book, and to work up a story about Miss Jenny Crow.

Her first draft was sent to Warnes. 'I hope very much this may find favour?' she wrote, 'as I have (perhaps rashly!) started some of the pictures—also crow shooting starts on Saturday so I have hopes of both models and pies.' The draft did not find favour. Mr. Fruing Warne was disappointed. He wrote, 'The criticism I personally have to make of the story is as follows: you call it "The Tale of Jenny Crow"—I should rather say the proper title of the book was "Tales of Mr. Tod" 2nd. Series, or perhaps "Aesop Fables applied to Mr. Tod"—The "Jenny Crow" part of the story is exceedingly interesting and entertaining, but unfortunately it is short. If the whole book could have been made out of the Jenny Crow incident, it might have been a different thing, but you introduce grapes, and then frogs, and then King Stork and then finally the fox and the stork. Practically you have adopted the idea of putting together five of Aesop's tales into modern language for children—with the result that your Publisher is disappointed; it is not Miss Potter, it is Aesop.' Why, he added could not they have her pigeon story (The Faithful Dove), which was brilliant?

But Beatrix Potter found the pigeons 'namby-pamby' and reminded them of the problem of preparing twenty-eight illustrations, as for her other books—how-ever, though thoroughly discouraged by their criticism, she would try and improve her story of Miss Jenny Crow. She suggested that the title of the book should be *The Tale of the Birds and Mr. Tod*.

As the weeks and months passed by Beatrix Potter grew more and more frustrated. Her eyes were not as keen as they used to be, and themes for stories, particularly in the *Peter Rabbit* series, came less easily to her—her mother was getting old and needed more attention, and anyway, there were quite a lot of other things that she would sooner do.

The little books were a gold mine to the travellers in the firm, so naturally they clamoured for at least one new Beatrix Potter story each year. *They* worried Warnes, and *Warnes* worried her. It was all most unfair especially as Warnes did not seem to be particularly interested in *The Tale of the Birds and Mr. Tod* which she was offering to them, and trying very hard to finish.

Finally her wrath over-ran all bounds and she wrote: 'I am glad you are having a good season—apart from my misdeeds—which you will have to put up with sooner or later—for you don't suppose I shall be able to continue these d . . . d little books when I am dead and buried!! . . . I will try to do you one or two more for the good of the old firm . . .' She did send them her kind regards, but could not refrain from a final fling—'and very moderate apologies'.

Beatrix Potter struggled on but found it impossible to finish the book that year. 'I will try and get one finished by next spring,' she wrote, 'but I rather doubt the policy of going on with this one . . . I think you had better send me back the three or four drawings which I forwarded in July, and when I see them together I can consider what it looks like.'

So the drawings were returned, and that was the last that was heard of *The Tale of the Birds and Mr. Tod.*

Three of these fables are given: the story of Jenny Crow (The Fox and the Crow) which Beatrix Potter called *The Folly of Vanity*; *The Fox and the Stork*, the only one she fully illustrated, with its setting at Melford Hall where the stork lived at the top of one of the fine old red-brick towers; and *Grasshopper Belle and Susan Emmet* (The Ant and the Grasshopper).

This last fable, which Aesop gives us in a few short paragraphs, was developed by Beatrix Potter into quite a long story. As always, her animal characters are true to type. Susan Emmet is reminiscent of Mrs. Tittlemouse who went about with a dustpan and broom in an attempt to keep her house tidy—but the kindly little mouse would never have treated her marauders as the waspish ant treated Grasshopper Belle. Mr. Jackson, though denied access to Mrs. Tittlemouse's house, is given acorn-cupfuls of honey and drinks her very good health outside in the sun; but Grasshopper Belle is left outside to die in a storm.

Twenty-three years later, when approaching seventy-six, Beatrix Potter began to rewrite this fable, but unfortunately her revised version was never finished. The original version is given in this book.

THE FOLLY OF VANITY

Mr. Fox walked along the edge of the turnip field. He slashed at the heads of the docks and nettles in the ditch with his walking stick. Presently two or three wood pigeons rose from the turnips; Mr. Fox cocked his ears.

He got upon a stile, and looked over into the wheat. A rustle in an oak tree overhead caught his attention. He got down again off the stile, and walked backwards, craning up at the tree—something blue black and shiny twinkled amongst the oak leaves. It was Miss Jenny Crow upon a bough half way up, holding in her big coarse bill a large white chunk of cheese. She had stolen it from the farm boy's dinner basket, hidden in the hedge while he singled turnips.

The cheese was an awkward mouthful even for Miss Crow's big beak. She fumbled and sidled on the bough as if she would put it down and hold her foot upon it, but she feared to drop it.

Mr. Fox backed further out amongst the turnips; Miss Crow caught sight of him. She started, clutched the cheese more securely, and gave a choking sort of croak.

'Exquisite bird! Oh adorable smutty Venus!' cried Mr. Fox, throwing himself into an attitude—'Do my eyes deceive me? or is this a black peacock up a tree?'

Miss Jenny Crow held her head on one side; perhaps she may have blushed under her feathers; but she did not let go the cheese.

Mr. Fox moved closer under the tree and continued to talk—

'Beautiful black lady bird, elegant as a newly tarred railing'—(Miss Crow held her foolish head on the other side and did not know how to look at all.)—'the dusky swans of Tasmania are not equal to your gliding gracefulness'—(Miss Crow sidled along the branch, turning her toes in; but she did not let go the cheese.)

'Your tail is as bushy feathered as a turkey-cock's or an eagle's'—(Miss Crow spread her tail, made a bob curtsey, and grabbed the cheese just as it began to slip.)—'Coal is less funereal than your wings,—expansive as a vulture's! Your voice—your voice is doubtless as sweet as a nightingale's—' (Miss Crow gave a chuckling croak.)

'Ah! ah!' cried Mr. Fox, 'she sings, she sings! louder! louder, sweet sky lark!' Miss Jenny Crow fluttered her black wings, threw up her vain head, opened her great ugly bill, and uttered a hoarse 'Caw-aw-w-w!'

Down dropped the cheese into the very mouth of Mr. Fox!

Mr. Fox laughed until he cried; he took no further notice of poor silly Miss Crow. He had got what he wanted. He sat upon the stile, and ate the cheese.

GRASSHOPPER BELLE AND SUSAN EMMET

Once upon a time there was a frugal ant, and her name was Susan Emmet.* Her house was under a dock leaf, where she lived all by herself.

She never cut the string that tied up any parcel; she never passed a pin without picking it up, she used the latter end of candles. Her motto was 'waste not, want not'; her store rooms were always fully furnished, and her pantry was never empty.

A rusty black gown with tight black sleeves, a black net cap with two long bows like horns, a sharp set nose, a wide crooked mouth and a nut cracker chin, and near sighted eyes had Miss Susan Emmet. Her head with the black ribbon bows went waggily bobbit, as she stooped to pick up gleanings this way and that way, never tired and ever eager.

She gathered in her apron and emptied it into a sack. She ran this way and that through the hot prickly stubble till her sack was full. Then she swung it on her shoulder and tore away to her dwelling, wig way waggity, bending under her sack, with little quickly steps, treading on her heels.

Along the passages bumpety squeeze, rushing and running came Susan Emmet. Her store room was underground through long passages in the sand. It was full of sacks and bags from floor to ceiling. And her cupboards were full of spotless linen; her china cupboard was full of china with never a crack or snip, her blankets were put away with lavender, her cutlery was sharp and keen, her fender and steel fire irons without a speck of rust, her spotless floors were never trodden by a stranger— a notable good housekeeper that kept herself to herself was industrious Miss Susan Emmet.

Of another sort of nature were the grasshoppers, idle, sun-loving and merry, and the merriest and idlest was Grasshopper Belle; no sun was too hot, the hotter the sun the louder they sang, chirp chirp chirruppy, from the clover where the grass-hoppers danced and played—Green grasshoppers and brown grasshoppers and little red and gold grasshoppers in uniform, and Grasshopper Belle in green satin with pink silk sleeves and gauzy wings. Her large gold eyes gleamed in the sunshine, her horns swayed in the breeze; her comb whirred the loudest of any, her foot was the lightest, and bounded over the meadow—a very fair creature was Grasshopper Belle.

Chirr, whirr, whirr, fiddled the gentlemen grasshoppers in the clover. 'Whirr, whirr, whirr, and who goes there?' sang one of them. 'Oh chirr, whirr, whirr, while the day is fair, and have a race in the sun. Sing leader, neadle, treaddle, wheedle, whadle, sudle, chirr, whirr, whirr, oh, who is so fine, in silver gossamer as Grasshopper Belle?' Fiddle, fiddle, went the gentlemen grasshoppers on a corn

* Emmet is a dialect word for ant; both words are derived from the Old English æmete, emete.

stork; chirr, whirr, whirr, Grasshopper Belle danced this way and that way, her silver gauze wings spread gleaming and gleaming—chirr, whirr, whirr, endle, windle, chodle. 'Vanity of vanity, disgusting idleness,' snapped Miss Susan Emmet hurrying past the clover foot with another empty sack.

Chirr, whirr, whirr; 'Dance a turn, Susan Emmet, come lille black ant, come dance to our piping.' 'Get you out, you idle good for nothing!' 'Come dance to our music.' 'Let her a-bee,' laughed Grasshopper Belle. 'Poor silly fool,' said Susan Emmet. She ran scurrying under the clover stalks backwards and forwards with her sacks.

The sun dipped, a thin haze quivered over the clover, angry sulphurous clouds piled up against the sun. The grasshoppers' fiddles droned drowsily and stopped play; only Grasshopper Belle slept amongst the clover, only Grasshopper Belle sang drowsily—chirr, whirr, whirr.

Again Susan Emmet passed, running nimbly with her full sack, another, yet another. 'Stay to rest, Susan Emmet, I will sing you to sleep.' 'The rain will come full soon, hie you home.' 'Home, my home is in the barley grass, no cellars for me, come upon the grass stalk and watch the sun slip behind a cloud.' 'I must run, it will rain,' said Susan Emmet.

Grasshopper Belle folded her gauze wings and laid her golden horns back; she lay silent along a grass stork, her great gold eye fixed on the fiery edge of the cloud. The cloud slid higher; the rain pattered in big big drops; the clover bells hung their heads. Grasshopper Belle folded her gossamer wings closer, and shivered. Deep low peals of distant thunder rolled up over the land.

Susan Emmet ran twiggly, wriggle, wriggly, trotting on her heels, bending under her last sack of corn, and ran into her door as the storm broke. She shut it and barred it, and drew the curtain and lighted the fire to shut out the lightning.

All night the thunder rolled, nearer or further; now the rain came in a torrent, now it slackened in great single drops. Often Susan Emmet rose from her narrow bed and went round with a candle to see that her shutters were fast and to lay the mat closer against the door. The lightning flashed through the cracks.

At daylight the wind rose and the storm blew away, but the rain beat piteously; out in the meadow the clover was battered down, driving sheets of rain swept over the meadow.

Snug in her house Susan Emmet dusted and mended, and sorted seeds from little sacks to large sacks and counted her gleanings. Towards evening the rain turned to sleet, the wind rose higher and whistled shrill in the chimney. 'It blows from the north,' said Susan Emmet, darning black stockings, with her feet on the fender.

The wind whistled and roared, a gust shook the shutters. 'It blows from the north east, it will cut too,' said Susan Emmet, and she drew a wrinkled brown hand out of her darning, to throw on another log. The wind came in gusts and rattled the latch. Susan Emmet, snuffing her candle, drew her chair closer to the fire, with her toes on the fender. The kettle sizzled on the hob. The north wind blew in gusts, and shook the latch; the east wind bent the dock leaf.

The wind moaned and moaned and sighed, 'Susan Emmet! Susan Emmet!' Susan Emmet stayed her needle. The latch rattled. The wind sighed—was it the wind?—The ball of wool rolled on the floor. Susan Emmet turned her head and looked at the bar across her door. The east wind shook the shuttering, the door latch moved and fell again—'Who is that at my door? Is there anyone there?' Only the wind sighed louder—Susan Emmet drew nearer the hearth and plied her needle.

The gust of wind came up with loud pattering rain, and shook the shuttering. The wind whistled, and amongst the moaning and sighing came a sobbing voice, 'Susan Emmet, Susan Emmet, let me in!' Susan Emmet sat up and listened, her needle suspended—'Let me in, let me in, I am dying, Susan Emmet'—Susan Emmet listened a-while, and went and listened close to the door—nothing, only the wind. Susan Emmet went down to the granary with a candle, and tried all the shutters. She came back and listened inside the door.

The wind sighed and whistled—Susan Emmet sighed too, and set the table for a frugal supper. The wind had dropped. Susan Emmet ate. The wind rose again, the latch rattled—Susan Emmet stayed her hand with the fork suspended. The wind shivered—'Susan Emmet, Susan Emmet—let me in Susan Emmet—oh the wind— the wind!'

Susan Emmet took a very large mouthful to finish her supper. She rose and cleared the table, collecting the broken bread and victuals in a basin. 'She has had her lesson, I suppose I must let her in; she can sleep on the door mat'—She set the basin of broken meat on the dresser and moved the candle out of the wind.

She opened her door and stood gazing out into the dark—Grasshopper Belle lay dead on the doorstep.

Mr. Tod got up and stretched himself—'You caught them well, old Daddy-longlegs.' King Stork looked severely down his bill in silence.

'Sir,' said Mr. Tod; 'no offence; will you honour me by taking tea with me?' King Stork bowed; he walked home with Mr. Fox, he took long strides and Mr. Tod trotted.

Mr. Tod is a stingy person. He regretted the invitation as soon as he had given it, when he considered the size of Mr. Stork. So he made a plan. Said he to Mr. Stork —'When I have visitors I use Great Grandmother Vixen's Crown Derby tea set.' He poured the tea into two flat saucers.

King Stork dipped the point of his bill into the saucer, but he could scarcely scoop up a drop. Presently he made a bow and took leave. Mr. Tod lapped up the remaining tea himself.

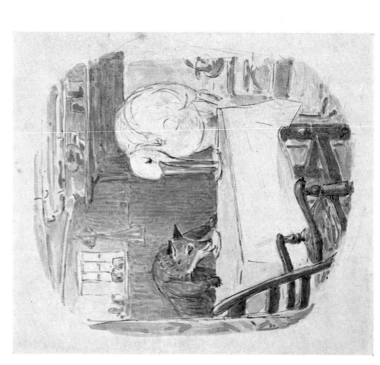

As he had a conscience which told him that he had behaved shabbily—Mr. Tod was surprised to receive an invitation to lunch with King Stork.

The note was brought by a very nervous lapwing.

King Stork's home was upon the top of a high chimney-stack over the roof of a tall old house.

As Mr. Tod has no wings for flying up aloft on to roofs—King Stork came down and met him in the courtyard of the house, and led him inside and up a corkscrew staircase.

There was a pleasing smell of broth when they reached the attic —The broth was served in two narrow-necked pitchers.

King Stork plunged his long bill into one pitcher and sucked up the broth. Mr. Tod could only lick his lips and sniff.

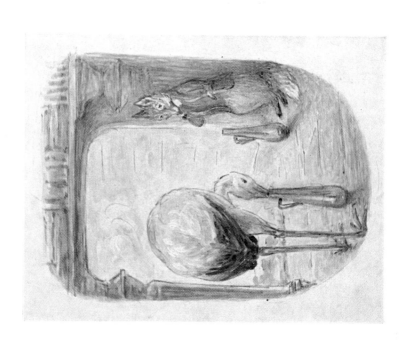

Presently he got up and said
Good Day!

King Stork drew his bill out
of his empty pitcher. He was a
silent old bird. All he said was
'Tit for tat!'

Melford Hall, Suffolk

Enid Linder

There once was an amiable guinea-pig,
Who brushed back his hair like a periwig;
He wore a sweet tie, as blue as the sky,
And his Hat and his buttons were very big.

'There once was an amiable guinea-pig'
One of the book drawings for the 1917 *Appley Dapply's*
Nursery Rhymes, which was not used because there was no
room for it

Cecily Parsley brewing cider

'Gentlemen came every day'

A 1902 painting for the Cecily Parsley rhyme (given to Noel Moore)

Cecily Parsley lived
in a Pen,
And brewed good ale
for
Gentlemen.

Cecily Parsley brewed good ale for gentlemen
The first page of a small booklet illustrating the Cecily
Parsley rhyme, dated January 1897

Cecily Parsley's Nursery Rhymes
1922

Cecily Parsley's Nursery Rhymes is a sequel to *Appley Dapply's Nursery Rhymes*, but the rhymes and pictures used for this book have even earlier associations than those for *Appley Dapply*.

In her Journal Beatrix Potter recalled her childhood memories of Camfield Place, Hertfordshire, where she frequently stayed with her Grandmother Potter. She wrote, 'I remember when I was a child lying in a crib in the nursery bedroom under the tyranny of a cross old nurse—I used to be awakened at four in the morning by the song of the birds.'

It would appear that as a child, Beatrix Potter and her small cousins called the old nurse *Nanny Nettycoat*—'that little old lady with white woollen stockings, black velvet slippers and a mob-cap, who must have been just like my grandmother.' Sometimes the children who stayed at Camfield Place would have their tea by candlelight. In describing these teas Beatrix Potter wrote, '*Nanny Nettycoat* presided in the middle of the table, guttering, homely, lop-sided with fascinating snuffers in a tin dish.' Perhaps it was the nanny's white woollen stockings, and possibly a red nose, which prompted this analogy? The verse beginning 'Ninny Nanny Netticoat' at the end of *Cecily Parsley's Nursery Rhymes* is based on an old traditional rhyme. Two early manuscripts of this rhyme have survived—one is dated, 'Aug. 4th. '97', and the other is undated. As we turn to the last page of the latter, we read, 'The Answer—A Candle'.

Another of the rhymes in this book dates back to 1893, when Beatrix Potter borrowed some guinea-pigs from a friend and neighbour to paint. The rhyme, sometimes referred to as 'Guinea-pigs' Garden', begins with the words, 'We have a little garden, a garden of our own', and one of these early paintings is inscribed, 'H.B.P. Jan. '93'. Many years later the paintings were redone for the book.

On February 5th 1893, in her Journal, Beatrix Potter wrote, 'I went to the Pagets somewhat guilty. This comes of borrowing other people's pets. Miss Paget has an infinite number of guinea-pigs. First I borrowed and drew *Mr. Chopps*. I returned him safely. Then in an evil hour I borrowed a very particular guinea-pig with a long white ruff, known as *Queen Elizabeth*. This PIG—offspring of *Titwillow the Second*, descendant of the *Sultan of Zanzibar*, and distantly related to a still more illustrious animal named the *Light of Asia*—this wretched pig took to eating blotting paper, pasteboard, string and other curious substances, and expired in the night.

'I suspected something was wrong and intended to take it back. My feelings may be imagined when I found it extended a damp—very damp disagreeable body. Miss Paget proved peaceable, I gave her the drawing.'

In 1897 Beatrix Potter illustrated the Cecily Parsley rhyme, and made it into a small booklet. One of the pictures is of a rabbit, wearing an apron and carrying a tray on which are two glasses of ale; below is a close-up view of the barrel of ale. Another picture is of two rabbits sitting on a bench smoking their pipes and drinking ale; there is also an outside view of the Pen Inn, with its sign, a bottle of ink and a quill pen, and the notice-board 'To Let' attached to the door of the inn. Finally there is a picture of Cecily Parsley running away with a wheel-barrow containing her belongings. On the wrapper of this little booklet are the words 'Nursery Rhymes—"Cecily Parsley" drawings original, Beatrix Potter, Jan. '97.' 'I never met Cecily in print,' she wrote; 'it is an old rhyme; there is another version in *Halliwell's Nursery Rhymes.*'

In 1900 we find Beatrix Potter at the British Museum studying a book of old nursery rhymes. In a picture letter to Marjorie Moore which is dated March 15th of that year, she wrote, 'I went to the Reading Room at the British Museum this morning to see a delightful old book of rhymes, I shall draw pictures of some of them whether they are printed or not. The Reading Room is an *enormous* big room, quite round, with galleries round the sides, the walls covered with books and hundreds of chairs and desks on the floor. There were not many people, but some of them were very funny to look at!'

Following the success of *Appley Dapply's Nursery Rhymes* in 1917, Warnes asked for a sequel. 'People worry me for just one or two more books,' Beatrix Potter wrote to a friend, 'but my eyes are getting weak and I am tired of doing them . . . and since the war there is so much to do . . . I have a big farm as well as my housekeeping; so I seldom sit down except to meals and necessary letters.'

In her portfolios were the two paintings of 1893 illustrating the verse about 'Guinea-pigs' Garden'; the Cecily Parsley booklet of 1897; and two versions of her 'Nanny Netticoat' rhyme.

These, and some of her other early drawings, were recopied and used for the book. In a letter dated November 12th 1922, we are told, 'I found time, somehow, to collect some old drawings and piece them together with some additions for a little book of nursery rhymes.'

In a letter to Warnes we find Beatrix Potter discussing the cover picture, which at that time was to have been the previously mentioned picture of a rabbit carrying a tray: 'I forgot to send the drawing for the cover,' she wrote, 'and upon reflection I think it would be better to use it in outline on the title page, instead, as it is too much like Ap. Dap. cover figure. The wheel-barrow subject might be vignetted for cover as you suggest.' So this rabbit picture was used as an outline drawing for the title page, and the painting of Cecily Parsley running away with her wheel-barrow and belongings became the cover picture.

In the same letter Beatrix Potter also discussed her pictures of rabbits outside the

Pen Inn—drawn in a natural setting: 'I don't know why, but I have never been able to imagine dressed up rabbits coming to the inn door; it comes to my mind's eye deserted!' The letter concludes with a reference to drawings which are still unfinished: 'I would have got these done this week but I am plagued with visitors and poultry, and a bad drought!'

This was the second and last of Beatrix Potter's books of rhymes, and the dedication page reads 'For little Peter of New Zealand', now Dr. R. P. Tuckey, a family doctor in Wellington. She was much pleased with the book, for she had 'always wanted *Cecily Parsley's Nursery Rhymes* as a companion volume to Appley Dapply.'

Peter Rabbit's Almanac for 1929

During 1926 Beatrix Potter was planning a Peter Rabbit Almanac, for in December of that year she wrote to Warnes, 'The dummy Almanac seems a nice sized little book . . . I should have to make new drawings for the spring-summer months because the chief part of the old ones which I have by me are snow scenes, suitable for winter months . . . I don't think it would be difficult to supply sufficient drawings. The borders would be quite all right if they were little more than a line, like the treatment in Miss Greenaway's; the book should be kept rather light.'

On January 13th 1927, in a letter to Fruing Warne, she told him, 'I am making a start with the calendar; I wish there were more light. I think I can make a good job of it, but I will not put in too many miscellaneous animals, in case there might be another later.'

Two months later, when referring to the pictures for this Almanac, she told Mr. Warne, 'I am sending four of the remainder = ten out of thirteen. Other two are partly done; the border I am still puzzled with. If I cannot finish them next week we shall have to make out with old drawings, but I partly thought to make them all *rabbits* and keep the odds and ends for another calendar. I shall not be able to do much more; these are good but they try my eyes very much. I cannot see to do them on dark days, and the lambing time is beginning, when it is not possible to neglect out of door affairs.'

The border to which Beatrix Potter referred was a pen-and-ink decoration which appeared around each page of text. At the sides there were outlines of branches of a tree, and along the bottom of the page, five little rabbits—one standing and the others sitting.

In the frontispiece, Peter, spade over shoulder and basket in hand, is seen setting out to do some gardening, and in the foreground there are yellow pansies. The setting of each of the twelve pictures which follow, is characteristic of one month of the year:

JANUARY   A rabbit is seen digging away the snow from his garden path.

FEBRUARY   A rabbit is posting a letter, no doubt a valentine, in an old-fashioned post-box attached to a wall. Two other rabbits peeping round the corner seem to be wondering if it is addressed to one of them.

MARCH   Two rabbits are caught in a shower on a windy day. One is tugging at an umbrella that has blown inside-out.

APRIL   A rabbit is seen walking in his garden amongst the daffodils.

MAY   A rabbit with two daffodils in its paws is surprised by a cat appearing round a bend in a garden border.

JUNE   A goose standing on a plank across a stream looks down as her goslings swim by. Two rabbits watch from the bank.

JULY   In the centre of the picture a rabbit sits on a high stool playing the flute, while six other rabbits frisk and play in a circle around.

AUGUST   The setting is of sheaves of corn, with a rabbit peering from behind a sheaf, watching some field mice playing in the foreground.

SEPTEMBER   Mrs. Rabbit opens her front door to greet a robin standing on a sandy path outside.

OCTOBER   Two rabbits are busily gathering apples from a tree.

NOVEMBER   A rabbit, sheltering under a large green umbrella and carrying a laden basket, arrives at his door in a snow storm.

DECEMBER   There is snow on the ground and two rabbits are carrying bundles of faggots into their house in preparation for the Christmas festivities.

The coloured end-papers have a border of little rabbits, and in the centre there is a spray of cabbage leaves.

On the cover is a coloured picture of Peter in his little blue jacket. He is facing us, with a post-bag over his shoulder and a letter in his hand. On the back the full title again appears, and Peter is seen walking away, his white fluffy tail in full view, and still with the post-bag over his shoulder.

Peter Rabbit's Almanac for 1929 was Beatrix Potter's first and only Almanac.

The Tale of Little Pig Robinson
1930

Although *The Tale of Little Pig Robinson* was the last of Beatrix Potter's stories to be published in the *Peter Rabbit* series, it was one of the first she ever wrote. The earliest association with the story is found in a letter written to her father from Ilfracombe in April 1883 when she was seventeen years of age; in this letter there is a description of a scene at Ilfracombe.

Years later Beatrix Potter came across the letter and pencilled on the envelope, 'Worth keeping, an early impression leading to Pig Robinson'. She had written, 'They were unloading coal in Watermouth Harbour. The tide was coming in very fast. One old lady who seemed very anxious to get her coal drove her horse and cart at full speed into the water making such a splashing.' This particular scene is illustrated on page seven of the current edition. Again, on one of her background sketches we find a pencil note which reads, 'The harbour in Pig Robinson was a description of Ilfracombe.'

When writing to Mrs. Miller in November 1941, Beatrix Potter told her, 'Ilfracombe gave me the idea of the long flight of steps down to the harbour. Sidmouth harbour and Teignmouth harbour are not much below the level of the towns. The shipping—including a pig aboard ship, was sketched at Teignmouth, S. Devon. "Stymouth" was Sidmouth on the south coast of Devonshire—Other pictures were sketched at Lyme Regis; the steep street looking down hill into the sea, and some of the thatched cottages were near Lyme. The tall wooden shed for drying nets is (or was?) a feature of Hastings, Sussex—so the illustrations are a comprehensive sample of our much battered coasts.'

Six weeks before she died Beatrix Potter wrote, 'I was turning out a drawer, sorting waste paper, setting aside, and I found an old draft of Pig Robinson's first chapters dated 1893—! I remember that story stuck on board the Pound of Candles.'

This draft is one of three paper-covered exercise books containing early versions of the story, which are now at Hill Top. Inside one is the following note:

'Written first at Falmouth 189—
Sidmouth April 1901
Copied again April 1902'

At that time the title was *The Tale of Poor Pig Robinson*, and the story finished at the end of Part 1, with the words 'Then Robinson fainted, and fell flat upon the deck of "The Pound of Candles".'

Another note tells us it is 'a long story; there is only about half written; all the Part I and bits of II and III . . . most of it written at Sidmouth.' There is also a faint pencil note, initialled, 'H.B.P. Oct. '43' which says, 'The Tale of Pig Robinson was invented very long ago. I have some recollections of writing down this first part of the book in 1901. I do not think that Robinson's subsequent adventures were committed to paper until the story was wanted (?) for publication—note the different handwriting.'

This story was influenced by Edward Lear's rhyme *The Owl and the Pussy Cat*, which Beatrix Potter illustrated for her own amusement some time in the '90s. Thus, in the published story we read, 'You remember the song about the Owl and the Pussy Cat and their beautiful pea-green boat . . . Now I am going to tell you the story of that pig, and why he went to live in the land of the Bong tree.'

Parts II and III of the story are summarized by Beatrix Potter—'(R. is so extremely sea-sick that he becomes *thin* and so they keep him alive and treat him with great kindness, to make him fat again; descript. of voyage, and friendship with cat. Cat has quarrel with cook, and in revenge it assists R. to escape. After an exciting chase he gets away in a boat and lands on an island where he lives happily and is visited by the owl and the Pussy Cat. It is most dreadful rubbish)'.

Soon after the publication of *The Fairy Caravan* in 1929, Alexander McKay, Beatrix Potter's American publisher, asked her for another book. Realizing that Warnes had been very disappointed when *The Fairy Caravan* was published in America only, she offered *The Tale of Little Pig Robinson* to both Alexander McKay and to Frederick Warne & Co.—at a time, wrote Beatrix Potter, 'when I had left off writing and was scraping together something to appease my publishers.'

In February 1930 Beatrix Potter told Mr. McKay, 'I have at last got the type-written "Pig". I think I shall spread the last two or three chapters a little; they are abrupt.' Apparently this idea was dropped, for in June she wrote, 'I am so much "at sea" on land, upon the subject of boats and desert islands, that I find it prudent to concentrate upon Robinson's Devonshire adventures; and I am sure every one will be tired of him before the last chapter. Minor corrections and alterations I could make on the galley—if I had it. I am putting in a sentence after passing Styford Mill, to bring in the big dog called Gypsy who barks, "but the big dog Gypsy only smiled and wagged his tail at Robinson."* And please put your children's names on the dedication page if it would please them.' This was done, and the *American* edition of *The Tale of Little Pig Robinson* is dedicated to Margery, Jean and David McKay.

In her letter of July 8th 1930, Beatrix Potter told Mr. McKay that Frederick Warne & Co's scheme 'is going to leave out a number of illustrations which I con-sider the best,' adding, 'but I hope you may care to include them in the U.S.A. edition . . . It is a good book to illustrate, I should quite enjoy doing a few more!

* Gypsy was Margery McKay's airedale, and she sent a photograph of the dog to Beatrix Potter. The picture with Gypsy in it, appears on page 47 of the large-format American edition.

If you want any to fill up—just tell me the number of the (type written) page, as I have kept the duplicates.'

Mr. McKay was willing to produce a book with more black and white drawings than Warnes, and the American edition contains twelve more drawings, plus thirteen 'heads and tails' to the chapters. Referring to these latter as 'chapter ends', Beatrix Potter told Mr. McKay, 'I think myself that some of the"chapter ends" are the best drawings of any.' She sent him sixteen for the eight chapters, but owing to lack of space, only thirteen were used. Of the other drawings she said, 'I think Pig Robinson looking into a shop window is the best black-and-white.' The colour plates were the same in both English and American editions.

At the very end of the story Beatrix Potter used a word which was not in the dictionary, and this was challenged by Mr. McKay. In her reply she wrote, 'I agree with all your corrections, except possibly "fatterer"! Of course there is no such word; but it is expressive! If you don't like it, say "fatter and fatter and more fat". It requires three repeats to make a balanced ending.' But Mr. McKay withdrew his objections, and the story ended, 'He grew fatter and fatter and more fatterer; and the ship's cook never found him.'

Pig Robinson bathed by Aunt Dorcas

A drawing from the American edition of *The Tale of
Little Pig Robinson*

'The big dog Gypsy wagged his tail'

A drawing from the American edition of *The Tale of Little Pig Robinson*. Margery McKay sent Beatrix Potter a photograph of her dog Gypsy so that he might be put into this picture

Pig Robinson 'looking wistfully into another window
in Fore Street'

A drawing from the American edition of *The Tale of Little
Pig Robinson.* Of this picture Beatrix Potter wrote, 'I think
Pig Robinson looking into a shop window is the best
black and white'

The interior of the tea and coffee tavern belonging to
the two Miss Goldfinches. It was here that they gave
Pig Robinson a cup of tea. From the American
edition of *The Tale of Little Pig Robinson*

70   Rémi descend de la brouette. Il court à toutes jambes derrière les groseilliers. Il faut passer tout près de Mr MacGregor ; mais cela ne fait rien ; voici la porte. Rémi s'empresse de glisser par dessous ; il arrive sain et sauf dans le bois.

75   Mr MacGregor enlève l'habit et les souliers. Il en fait un épouvantail. Mais les oiseaux s'en moquent.

76   Rémi rentre chez lui. Il se laisse tomber sur le bon sable ; il s'étend ; il ferme les yeux. La mère Lapin fait la cuisine, "Hein ? dit elle _ "où est ton habit, mon fils ? et les souliers ?" Rémi ne répond rien ; il est endormi. Il rêve ; il pousse de pied, comme s'il courre encore ; les oreilles se dressent. Rémi ne se porte pas bien. La mère est mécontente. Il n'y a qu'un mois, il a perdu encore un habit et des souliers.

80   Rémi se trouve malade ce soir. La mère Lapin le fait coucher. Elle infuse une tisane de camomille, très amère ; elle en donne une grande cuillerée à Rémi. Décidément il a trop mangé ; il ne se porte pas bien.

85   Mais voici Flopsaut, Trotsaut, et Queue-de-Coton qui partagent le joli souper ! du pain, du lait, et de bonnes mûres.

La fin.

The last page of a revised draft of the French translation of *The Tale of Peter Rabbit*, in which the ideas of Beatrix Potter and Mlle Ballon have been combined.

Beatrix Potter preferred to keep to the name Mr. Mac Gregor, rather than change it to M. l'Ogre as Mlle Ballon had suggested. The story was at that time called *Le Récit de Rémi Lapereau*, but the title was later changed to *Histoire de Pierre Lapin*

One of a pair of end-papers drawn for the foreign
translations. The English titles of the books which
the various animals are holding have been purposely
omitted

The other end-paper of the pair drawn for the
foreign translations. As compared with her English
end-papers, the colouring is more brilliant and the
style bolder

Criticism and comparison la phrase bien *comme* des oreilles françaises
9f I do not like this sentence "Ils habitaient avec/leur mère
dans un terrier sablonneux —
It sounds like a rhyme—which has not quite arrived'
And "sapin 'partly rhymes with "lapins".
10 In parts I prefer yours. I like the "accident affreux" etc, better.

15 ? I. like the sauvez vous etc.
11 I prefer yours; except Madame Lapin
20 I like a mixture.
22 Prefer yours.
27-28.35. I prefer the English-french (provided it were correct.)
39-40 prefer a mixture of the two
45 I think the English is more spirited?
46 Prefer yours, but I think it is an advantage to mention les
morceaux.
51 mixture
52 prefer English version.
57 mixture
58 prefer yours, excellent.
63 mixture
54 mixture
69 mixture, I like the légumes.
70 prefer yours
75 prefer English   76. 80.95 English

Beatrix Potter's 'criticism and comparison' of Mlle
Ballon's translation of *Peter Rabbit* and her own. It
was submitted to Mlle Ballon together with her
revised draft

4

Foreign Translations
of the Peter Rabbit Books

Foreign Translations of the Peter Rabbit Books

As early as 1907 Warnes were considering the possibility of translating some of Beatrix Potter's books into French and German. Apparently a French translation was made by an English person, but Beatrix Potter did not think very highly of it, for in September 1907 she wrote to Warnes saying, 'That French is choke full of mistakes both in spelling and grammar. I dare say it is the English type-writer's slip-shod reading of the M.S.S.; but we shall have to have the proof sheets read very carefully. I don't think it is nearly such a good rendering as the German; it is too English and rather *flat* for French. I should think a French person would tell the story in the present tense with many exclamation marks. I will ask my cousin to read it over.'

Nothing more appears to have developed in regard to foreign translations until the 1912 season, when the first two of Beatrix Potter's foreign translations were actually published. They were in Dutch, and were *The Tale of Peter Rabbit* and *The Tale of Jemima Puddle-Duck*—published under licence by Nijgh & Van Ditmar's Uitgevers-Maatschappij of Rotterdam, in November, 1912.

Also about that time at least three different French translators were approached by Frederick Warne & Co., one of which was Mlle Victorine Ballon of Rue de la République, Honfleur.

In a letter dated May 15th 1912 Beatrix Potter told Harold Warne, 'Mlle Ballon's translations are infinitely better than the others. I think you had better make excuses to the poor professor. I am ashamed to have given him so much trouble in re-writing. Don't forget him. I still don't like the Peter completely; the other two are most ridiculous. I have written direct to Mlle B. to thank her for the amusement she has given me—and I have told her I like another "Peter" better; by "*une Anglaise*", and requiring French correction—if she guesses it is my own, very likely she might offer to look it over—Something between mine and hers would be excellent. I said of course I had nothing to do with business arrangements; but I would tell you *I* am pleased with her French. It is just right—colloquial without being slangy . . . I am keeping the French for the present—there may be a question of altering one or two names.' In a postscript, she added, 'You had better find out if her charge is reasonable, and then she and I could settle the text between us.'

At that time Mlle Victorine Ballon was a teacher in one of the French schools, but the following year she received an appointment which according to Beatrix Potter was a general Inspectorship of French Infants' Schools. The various translations, including the one by *une Anglaise* were worked on by Mlle Ballon and Jullienne Profichet, another teacher who had assisted her, and in due course they were returned to Beatrix Potter for her approval.

On November 11th 1912 Beatrix Potter wrote to Mr. Warne and told him,

'The improved translation of Peter is very good and spirited. I think Mrs. Tiggy is perfectly charming in French. I hope you may decide to print *Peter*, *Jemima* and *Tiggy*. The Famille Flopsaut is still my favourite of the rabbit series; but it is useless for a start as it is a sequel to Benjamin Bunny . . . I hope you may decide to go ahead with setting up the French.'

This work was now put in hand, and at the beginning of 1913 Beatrix Potter was sent some of the printer's proofs. 'I have gone through the French proofs, she wrote on March 3rd, 'and will send one copy to the schoolmistress and suggest she might correct it in the Easter holidays—The *printers* have made very few mistakes.'

By April 7th she was getting concerned. 'Have you heard from Mlle Ballon? I wrote again to her. We really mustn't miss yet another season for French if it can be managed.'

Later in April Mlle Ballon sent back the proofs, and various discussions took place; in particular about the names of the characters. 'Could the translator suggest French names instead of Flopsy, Mopsy and Mr. McGregor?' wrote Beatrix Potter. 'Madame Lapin and Queue-de-Coton sound all right.' So the names of the four little rabbits became, 'Flopsaut, Trotsaut, Queue-de-Coton et Pierre'; but Mr. 'Mac Grégor' hardly changed at all.

The corrected proofs were duly returned to Mr. Warne, and Beatrix Potter then discussed future procedure: 'The question of how many books to start with is rather for *you*', she wrote. 'Personally I should like to see the five launched at the same time—because myself I thought 'Sophie Canétang' and 'Poupette-à-l'Epingle' are more pleasing than the rabbits; and I should think it might be an advantage for your traveller to be able to offer an assortment of these little books *as they are said to be something new* in France. There may not be a stock of similar sized books for them to be added to as in England.' (The five titles to which Beatrix Potter was referring were *Peter Rabbit*, *Benjamin Bunny*, *Mrs. Tiggy-Winkle*, *Jemima Puddle-Duck* and *The Flopsy Bunnies*.)

The question of suitable end-papers and of amendments to certain pictures in which writing occurred had also to be discussed: 'Decidedly a new block for the Flopsy market garden scene—and no reading on any end-paper or pictures', wrote Beatrix Potter.

The market-garden scene *was* redrawn, omitting the notice-board, and some wording on two of the Benjamin Bunny pictures was removed. Also, the words 'How Keld' were omitted from the picture of the 'spring bubbling out from the hill side' in *The Tale of Mrs. Tiggy-Winkle*. In the case of the end-papers, however, apart from using plain end-papers for some of the early printings, the existing ones with English titles on the little volumes were used. Beatrix Potter did, however, prepare a pair of end-paper designs without any lettering on them, but they were apparently never used.

In May 1913 an advance copy of *The Tale of Peter Rabbit* in French was ready. 'The French Peter looks well,' said Beatrix Potter, 'and is very amusing.' But for some time after this nothing more was done, even though Beatrix Potter, in a letter to Mr. Warne, dated August 13th 1913, had asked what had become of the French editions.

On October 16th 1918 a French kindergarten teacher in Paris, Alice Robert Hertz, sent a postcard to Beatrix Potter via Frederick Warne & Co. It read, 'I wrote to you years ago (1912) about a translation of your "Peter Rabbit" *as near as possible* of the English text. I do not think that any of the French imitations or adaptatiory are quite as nice as your excellent little book. We French kindergarten teachers, would very much like to have a French edition of your books, as we use them constantly in our schools . . . Perhaps you will be astonished to hear of me after such a long time. But we feel more than ever the necessity to work and have some *results* in our work.'

The effect of this postcard was to focus attention upon the French editions, and when Mr. Fruing Warne sent it on to Beatrix Potter, he wrote her a long letter reviewing the situation as it then stood. 'It raises the whole question once more of French editions. As you know, the difficulty in the past has always been the finding of a French Publisher who would risk a fair edition, without wanting all the margin of profit for himself, and also that they had an idea that French people could afford less money than English people, and if we published the edition here at 1/-, they would want it sold for 1 franc there. I did not have the conversations with you, but I gathered at various times that these were two of the difficulties; another thing was to find a satisfactory translation . . . I am not aware of any arrangement having been come to that finally brought the matter to a definite result.

'The object of this letter is to say that we feel here we are quite prepared to risk a French edition on our own . . . We seem to have by us proofs of *Benjamin Bunny, Flopsy Bunnies,* and *Tiggy-Winkle* and *Peter Rabbit.* We are sending you proofs of these . . . We also appear to have got up binding cases for these four and also for *Jemima Puddle-Duck,* although we cannot trace that any text of the latter was set up.' Also, a few weeks later, Mr. Warne informed Beatrix Potter, 'We find we have by us a bound copy of Peter in French, as well as a duplicate proof of the text.'

So once again work was started on the French editions, but it was another three years before the first two books were published: *The Tale of Peter Rabbit* and *The Tale of Benjamin Bunny*; to be followed a year later by *The Tale of Mrs. Tiggy-Winkle* and *The Tale of Jemima Puddle-Duck. The Tale of the Flopsy Bunnies* did not appear until 1931.

In the years that followed there were many more translations of the books, and apart from those in French and Dutch, there were translations into Afrikaans, Danish, German, Italian, Norwegian, Spanish, Swedish, Welsh and Japanese, and even into Latin, for teaching purposes.

5

The Painting Books

The Painting Books

AN UNPUBLISHED PAINTING BOOK

In an early unpublished manuscript of a painting book, Beatrix Potter described some of her farm animals at Hill Top. Small sketches indicated that the pages were to be in pairs—one picture 'plain' and the other in 'colour'—and under each picture there were to be a few words of simple text.

The manuscript is undated, but because the animals described in it are in many cases the same as those described in a letter to Louie Warne, which Beatrix Potter sent to the child in July 1907, it is probable that both the manuscript and this letter were written about the same time.

'I have got two lovely pigs,' she wrote; 'one is a little bigger than the other. She is very fat and black with a very turned up nose and the fattest cheeks I ever saw; she likes being tickled under the chin; she is a very friendly pig. I call her Aunt Susan. I call the smaller pig Dorcas; she is not so tame; she runs round and round the pig-sty and if I catch her by the ear she squeals. But Aunt Susan is so tame I have to kick her when she wants to nibble my galoshes. They have both got rings in their noses to prevent them from digging holes in the field, but at present they are shut up in their little houses because the field is so wet . . . There are six cows, they have got very funny names, the best cow is called "Kitchen". I watched her being milked tonight, such a big bucketful. There is another cow called "White stockings" because she has white legs, and another called "Garnett"; and calves called Rose, and Norah and Blossom.'

According to the manuscript there were to have been pictures of White Stockings the cow, Rose the calf, and Aunt Dorcas the pig; also pictures of other Hill Top characters such as Smutty the farmyard cat, Kep the collie, Jemima Puddle-Duck who lived on the farm, and Betsy the milk-maid, who no doubt was Betsy Cannon to whom, with her brother Ralph, *The Tale of Jemima Puddle-Duck* was dedicated.

The text of the manuscript reads as follows:

This is my farmyard.
Her calf is just like her.

This is Betsy with the milking pail.

Mrs. Ribby would like some milk.
And Mrs. Tiggywinkle would like some too!

This is White Stockings the cow.
It has a curly coat and little white stockings.

She sits on a little stool and milks the cow called Rose.

She has brought a jug.
She brings a little tinkling can.

This is Prince, the horse who
brings the hay.

When we ask him to pull the cart to the
next hay cock, he always says 'Humph!'

This is my sow called
Aunt Susan.

She has [eight] little black and
white pigs.

These are my sheep, they are glad
to eat chopped turnip in the snow.

They run to Willie for their
breakfast.

But they love green grass in
summer.

The little lambs dance amongst
the buttercups

The rabbits come out of the wood.

They nibble the grass.

I wonder if Peter Rabbit and Benjamin Bunny

will ever get into my garden!

The hens scratch in the farm yard.

They do not wear a fine bonnet like
Jemima Puddle-Duck.

This is Kep the collie dog.

He fetches the cows, and he guards
the house.

The farmyard cat is called Smutty.

She catches very big rats.

I hope she will not catch Samuel
Whiskers!

I am rather fond of Sammy.

And I am fond of mice—

Nice mice like Hunca Munca.

The farmyard mice are bad, they
steal the corn.

A white owl flits over the barn
and catches them.

Sometimes the swallows fly in at
the window while I am at dinner.

Their nest is under the Eaves.

And sometimes an old hen with her chickens

comes into the kitchen.

And I should never be surprised if
Aunt Susan dropped in to dinner!

But I should be shocked, because
she would eat all the broth and
leave none for me!

And that is all the animals
at my farm.

It is a funny place!

PETER RABBIT'S PAINTING BOOK

This was the first of the three painting books, and it was published in October 1911. It contained twelve pairs of pictures. The pictures were of Peter Rabbit, Benjamin Bunny, Squirrel Nutkin, Mrs. Tiggy-Winkle, Tom Kitten and Jemima Puddle-Duck; and there were also some of the characters from *Ginger and Pickles* and *The Tale of Two Bad Mice*.

Apart from providing amusement for the child, Beatrix Potter also wished to impart some useful information. Just inside the front cover on the end-paper is written, 'You will want a brush and 5 paints—Antwerp Blue, Crimson Lake, Gamboge, Sap Green and Burnt Sienna', beneath which is a drawing of Peter standing with a paint-box in his hands and a painting book on the ground, with four little rabbits looking at it. Below she added, 'You can mix Blue with Sienna to make dark Brown. Don't put the brush in your mouth. If you do, you will be ill, like Peter.'

Beatrix Potter sent some proofs of the plain pictures to the Moore family to see how the children would manage when colouring them. A few of these have survived, some coloured by nine-year-old Hilda and some by her sister Beatrix, who was eighteen months younger. Their mother had put the children's initials, H.M. and B.M. on the pictures so that Beatrix Potter would know which picture each child had painted.

As the painting book in its original form is now out of print, it is of interest to give Beatrix Potter's original text which appeared under each pair of pictures:

1	This is Mr. McGregor chasing naughty Peter Rabbit round the garden.	He waves a rake and shouts 'Stop Thief!'
2	Peter jumps into a can, to hide from Mr. McGregor.	There is water in the can; it will be damp for Peter.
3	Peter feels ill afterwards. His mother gives him camomile tea;	because he has eaten too much, in Mr. McGregor's garden.
4	Peter is still feeling ill, next day. His cousin	little Benjamin Bunny is sorry for Peter.
5	Little Benjamin and Peter have got into the garden again!	They see a cat. They hide, just like boy-scouts.
6	The cat is called Tabitha Twitchit. She has three kittens,	called Moppet and Mittens and Tom. She dresses them very fine.
7	Tom Kitten looks over a wall, and sees Jemima Puddleduck.	She is a vain and foolish bird.
8	Jemima Puddleduck takes a walk; she meets a foxy-whiskered gentleman.	I am surprised that Jemima ever came home!

9　But here she is—quite safe and sound,—buying sugar at Ginger and Pickles'.

Mrs. Tiggywinkle is going to buy soap.

10　Mrs. Tiggywinkle is a washerwoman; she washes clothes for funny people. The pinafore is Moppet's,

the blue coat is Peter's, the little frock belongs to a mouse, and the red coat is Squirrel Nutkin's.

11　Squirrel Nutkin lives up a tree; he lost his tail

because he was rude to old Mr. Brown the owl.

12　The little baby mice live down a hole; their mother rocks them in a cradle.

The pictures are all finished now; the visitors shall come and see them!

On the cover is a coloured picture of Peter dressed in his little blue jacket, sitting on the ground, with a paint-brush in his hand and the painting book propped up at his feet.

On the back of the cover is a circular picture of a notice-board on which are the titles of all the 'Peter Rabbit' books up to date. Various animal characters are gazing at the board and Squirrel Nutkin is sitting on the top of the wall on which the board is placed, looking down at them.

In the summer of 1911, Beatrix Potter wrote to Warnes and told them, 'I find there would be a large demand for the black and white sheets of the painting book loose and extra in an envelope', suggesting that they should print sets for the children:

'(1)　They want to *pin up* their productions, the Manager of "Boots" was right.

(2)　Several children want to paint at once.

(3)　Some particular children, as well as the parents, do not like to spoil the book.

'The only difficulty is the words, if they are stereotyped—either they must come out, or else all go on the page to which they belong. Children would like to have them on the pinned up thing. If you think it is competing with the bound book, *you* might prefer to leave them out.

'People don't buy two or three copies of the book for one family, but I quite think they would nearly all buy extra prints, and children might come again for more from their own pocket money if it were done for 3d or 4d. I should think it would cost very little—don't have an elaborate or good envelope. I should certainly like some for myself as soon as you have any.'

Warnes accepted her suggestion, and single sheets were printed of the 'outlines' with the full text on each sheet. These sets of 12 sheets were enclosed in an envelope and sold for 4d.

TOM KITTEN'S PAINTING BOOK

In June 1917 *Peter Rabbit's Painting Book* was divided into two. The first five pairs of pictures together with three new pairs, became the second edition of *Peter Rabbit's Painting Book*, and the last seven pairs of pictures together with one new pair, became *Tom Kitten's Painting Book*. In each book there were *eight* pairs of pictures.

The text under the new pictures read as follows:

(a) 'My dears,' said old Mrs. Rabbit to her children—'Do not go to Mr. McGregor's garden.'

But Peter was naughty; he ran to that garden, and he ate lettuces and radishes.

(b) Round the end of a cucumber frame

whom should he meet but Mr. McGregor!

(c) When Peter and little Benjamin get home they are whipped.

They will not go to Mr. McGregor's garden again.

(d) Mrs. Tiggywinkle hangs up the clothes to dry in her kitchen.

Squirrel Nutkin's coat has no tail; and Peter Rabbit's coat has shrunk.

The new arrangement of the pictures was as follows:
Peter Rabbit's Painting Book (2nd. edition) a, b, 1, 2, 3, 4, 5, and c making eight in all. *Tom Kitten's Painting Book* 6, 7, 8, 9, 10, d, 11 and 12, making eight in all.

In *Tom Kitten's Painting Book* the instructions in regard to painting were slightly amended, the lower paragraph now reading, 'Or you can colour these pictures quite nicely with Crayons.' The accompanying drawing is of three kittens playing around a painting book and some crayons which are lying on the ground.

On a hand-coloured proof of the picture of Mrs. Tiggy-Winkle hanging up the clothes to dry, Beatrix Potter had written, 'Please compare and be guided by the colour of the old plate of Mrs. Tig. This paper will not wash out I find after colouring it.' She criticized her colouring, and against a little red coat is a pencil note which reads 'rather strong', while alongside the chair on which Mrs. Tiggy-Winkle is standing, we read 'top of chair too red'.

Tom Kitten's Painting Book was published in June 1917. On the cover is a coloured picture of Tom Kitten with a paint-brush in his hand, standing in front of an easel. On the notice-board in the picture on the back of the cover, the book titles have been brought up to date.

JEMIMA PUDDLE-DUCK'S PAINTING BOOK

This was the last of the three painting books, and it was published in August 1925. It contains eight pairs of pictures, all of which include Jemima, and are largely based on the pictures in *The Tale of Jemima Puddle-Duck*.

In a letter dated December 30th 1924 Beatrix Potter told how the book had been delayed. 'No new book; should have been a painting book, re-drawn from Jemima, but the engravers were slow.'

The instructions in regard to painting are the same as in *Tom Kitten's Painting Book*, except that in place of the drawing of kittens, there is a drawing of six little chicks—one is in a jug of paint-water, two are paddling in the palette, beside which are two paint brushes, and the other three are looking on.

On the cover is a coloured picture of Jemima painting one of the pictures in her book—the book is lying on the ground and Jemima has a paint brush in her beak. In the notice-board picture on the back of the cover, the book titles have again been brought up to date, with the exception of the *Appley Dapply* and *Cecily Parsley* titles.

The text under the pictures reads as follows:

'Quack,' said Jemima Puddleduck, 'I am provoked.'

'I want to hatch my eggs myself; I will make a nest in the wood.'

Jemima Puddleduck flew over the tree-tops,

She saw a foxy-whiskered gentleman reading a newspaper. 'Madam, have you lost your way?' said he.

'Indeed! My woodshed is both dry and snug.' He opened the door and showed Jemima in.

Then the foxy-whiskered gentleman said to Jemima

But Kep and two foxhound friends had been watching.

Jemima Puddleduck made another nest under a hollybush.

'Why do they always give my eggs to a tiresome hen?'

'Jemima, you are a silly bird,' said the collie.

till she came to the middle of the wood and alighted.

'Oh, no, kind sir, I am only looking for a nice dry nest.'

She came every day for a fortnight, and laid a nice nestful of eggs.

'Bring me some sage and onions and we will have a feast.'

They took Jemima home, and nothing more was ever seen of that foxy-whiskered gentleman.

The lambs know where it is, but they will not tell.

6
The Plays

The Plays

In October 1923 Beatrix Potter received from Mr. E. Harcourt Williams, husband of Jean Sterling Mackinlay, a rough draft of a play. It was an adaptation for the stage of her book *The Tailor of Gloucester*, and he asked permission to publish it and use it in the children's performances which his wife gave for several weeks each Christmas.

Beatrix Potter was charmed with the little play, but some alterations in the text would have to be made before she would agree to publication. She criticized the names given to the mice and in particular to one called Lady Golightly: 'My live tame mice were Tom Thumb, Pippin, Hunca Munca and Cobweb', she wrote. 'There is nothing new under the sun—I agree it is better *not* to use the name of Cobweb—But the mice working for humans, by night, *were* an honest unashamed imitation of Puck, Robin Goodfellow and the Scottish Brownie.' She also criticized some of the wording. 'I care far more for the Tailor than for Peter', she told Warnes. 'If they print a book of words I must be allowed to revise it.'

Mr. Harcourt Williams accepted most of her suggestions—all but two were adopted: Beatrix Potter thought, 'the Tailor should have heard little twittering voices *before* he actually talked to the mice, instead of "having an idea" afterwards'; and she did 'not like sending back Gammon and Spinach to wash their hands and tidy their hair—children; not *animals*. I said "send them back for thimbles; the Tailor's were too big". Besides mice have *fur*, not hair.'

When Mr. Harcourt Williams asked if she would mind the names of two of the mice being changed to Master and Mistress Hickory-Dickory, Beatrix Potter told Warnes, 'I think the Hickory Dickory are an excellent idea, a great improvement.'

Later Warnes asked Beatrix Potter to prepare a 'drawing-room version' of the story, but she replied, 'Between ourselves the present version is so far mine (by quotation and corrections) that I could not write a different version if I tried.'

The Tailor of Gloucester play was published in 1930, and the following year a dramatized version of *Ginger and Pickles* was also published, adapted by E. Harcourt Williams; and in 1933, there was a dramatized version of *Mr. Samuel Whiskers* (*The Roly-Poly Pudding*), adapted by Theron H. Butterworth.

At some unknown period Beatrix Potter began to write a *Peter Rabbit* play, but it was never finished. She also wrote a *Squirrel Nutkin* play.

Christopher Le Fleming, who had composed the music for *The Peter Rabbit Music Books*, was given a copy of the *Squirrel Nutkin* play and was told by Beatrix Potter that if at some future date he cared to write some music for this play, he had her permission to have it published. In 1967 this was done and the play appeared under the title *Squirrel Nutkin, A Children's Play Adapted by Beatrix Potter from her original story, Music adapted from traditional tunes by Christopher Le Fleming.*

PETER RABBIT PLAY
(*Unfinished*)

One of these here Hopperattas—

Scene: a barn, a gate stuck up against one of the wings (left wing a side door, right wing a hay mow.) A placard 'This is Mr. McGregor's garden'. *Tune* Ropley Village*—Enter Mrs. Rabbit—(a grown-up—scene director, general superintendent)—She has a print dress, large apron, close fitting cap with two large ears on it, and whiskers, edging of rabbit fur round face—a large fluffy tail on her back— Her back should be stuffed out and humped with a pillow and the tail fastened on to her waistband over her clothes.

Enter Mrs. Rabbit, walks round the floor to see all is right, and goes out, exhibiting her absurd back view. Ropley Village continues—

Enter dance of vegetables etc.—two and two—dancing on. The little girls have green paper leaves over their short skirts. The little boys are pears and beans and parsley (one parsley), etc. Each child has a wand or stick with the real vegetable, or can swing a little bunch in their hand if preferred.

They do a country dance, in and out, singing to the tune of Ropley Village (song).

Rather suddenly they stop and fall aside standing quietly (I do not think they need disappear out of sight, but they must stand completely aside). Music stops—

Enter Mrs. Rabbit; she carries a large basket and umbrella—She calls out 'Cottontail, Flopsy, Mopsy, Peter?' Nobody comes—

She calls again and thumps her umbrella on the floor—(like a rabbit stamping to summon its family).

Cottontail, Flopsy and Mopsy run in and stand before her.

Mrs. Rabbit calls 'Peter, Peter, Peter,' and stamps.

Peter comes in very leisurely—puts his hands in his pockets and turns his back on the others.

Old Mrs. Rabbit—Now my dears—(setting their cloaks, ties ribbons straight)— Now my dears, I am going out, now be good children—You may go to the hill and up Stoney Lane and gather blackberries—But you must not go into Mr. McGregor's garden. (Cuffs Peter who is not attending.)

Your father had an accident there and (solemnly) he was put in a pie by Mrs. McGregor.

Now run away and don't get into mischief, I am going to the Bakers, to buy a loaf of brown bread and 5 currant buns.

Exit Mrs. Rabbit.

Music Song.

* The song 'Ropley Village' has not been identified.

Peter stands in the middle, he looks round after his mother—then I fear he pulls faces. Flopsy, Mopsy and Cottontail dance round him.

Finally they dance out—Peter following.

Placard   Mr. McGregor's garden.

Dance of vegetables.

Enter Peter, squeezing under gate—he goes up to each child in turn or in and out pretending to nibble, towards the end of the rows he begins to press his hands on his tummy.

He says (if he can be persuaded to say his part)—I think I am going to be sick. Where's the parsley? . . . (The parsley hastily hides behind a cabbage. Peter and the parsley play hide and seek in and out round the cabbage children. In the end the parsley disappears behind a cucumber frame.)

i.e. the end of the hay mow. Peter is following: when who should he meet but Mr. McGregor. They stare at one another for a moment, then Peter tears back and is pursued by Mr. McGregor holding a rake and crying [stop thief].

[The manuscript ends here.]

THE TAILOR OF GLOUCESTER PLAY

(*From Beatrix Potter's manuscript*)

The Tailor. Dame Simpkin, his housekeeper, a cat. The Mayor of Gloucester. Andrew, Pippin, Gammon, Spinach, Mice.

Scene: The Tailor's house in College Court. *Time:* Christmas Eve. *Period:* 18th Century.

'Good King Wenceslas' is being sung by carol singers in the street.
The Tailor is discovered working on his table.

Tailor. This is the finest coat that ever I made and the waistcoat is bravely cut out. There is naught now to finish except the button holes, with cherry coloured twisted silk. But I have no more twist (looking towards window)—How it snows! Alas my poor rheumatic bones! (rubs his knees) Dame Simpkin must fetch it for me from the silk mercer's. See there is no stuff cut to waste (holding up little pieces). No more than will make waistcoats for mice! Ribbons for mob caps for mice! (Calls) Simpkin, Dame Simpkin!
Enter Dame Simpkin. 'Miaw, miaw.'
Yis, I know it snows. But we are going to make our fortunes. His worship the mayor of Gloucester is to be married on Christmas day in the morning and he hath ordered a coat and an embroidered waistcoat.

Simpkin. Miaw, miaw.

Tailor. This is Christmas Eve and I must hurry, Dame Simpkin, I must hurry. I wish I had more time for the work even though there are only the button holes. How the snow keeps falling! It is very cold to-night Simpkin. Don't you think we might have a dish of tay to cheer our hearts?

Simpkin. G r r r Miaw (puts kettle on hob).

Tailor. Dame Simpkin don't be cross. I do so want a dish of tay, my rheumatics are bad, very bad. I have four pennies left; you will find them in the tea pot on the dresser. Simpkin, do be kind and good; and brew the tay before you go.

Simpkin. (less cross) Miaw, miaw.

Tailor. Aye, Simpkin, good Simpkin; you would talk if you could. Well, well, who knows? Old men talking to themselves—old men, old times, old tales. What said the old story?—that all animals can talk in the night between Christmas Eve, and Christmas day in the morning. But only the kind hearts can hear them, and know what it is that they say.

Simpkin.   (showing empty trencher) Miaw, miaw!

Tailor.   What? Have the little mice eaten our last crumb of bread?

Simpkin.   (looking about) Miaw, miaw!

Tailor.   No, no, Dame Simpkin. The little things must eat. They mean no harm. And how clever and nimble; never cross or rheumatic. Why, behind the walls of this old house there are little mouse staircases—little secret trap doors and the mice scamper through long narrow passages from house to house. They can run all over the town without going out into the streets.

Simpkin.   Miaw.

Tailor.   Don't be a cruel cross-patch, Dame Simpkin. You mustn't sniff at mouse holes and whisk your wicked tail. Now take the china pipkin and buy a penn'orth of bread, a penn'orth of milk—and a penn'orth of sausage. And oh, Simpkin, with the last penny of our fourpence buy me one penn'orth of cherry coloured silk. But do not lose the last penny of my fourpence or I shall be undone and worn to a ravelling for I have no more twist.

Simpkin.   (Taking money and pipkin.) Miaw!

Tailor.   Poor Simpkin, I know you hate the snow, but I must have that twisted silk.
(There is a knock at outer door. Dame Simpkin opens and the Mayor enters. With a last plaintive miaw Dame Simpkin goes out closing the door behind her).

Mayor.   (pompously) Now, Master Tailor, is my cherry coloured coat and embroidered waistcoat ready?

Tailor.   Oh, your worship must give me until tomorrow. There's a deal of work in a cherry coloured corded silk coat embroidered with pansies and roses—not to mention a cream coloured satin waistcoat trimmed with gauze and green worsted chenille.

Mayor.   Come, come, my man. This is Christmas Eve and my wedding is on Christmas day in the morning. If it is yet unfinished, I see not how you can compass the work in the time.

Tailor.   It shall be ready, your worship. It shall be ready. I give you my word.

Mayor.   The word of a tailor, indeed! If you fail me (at the door) you shall eat your plum pudding in the stocks tomorrow, Christmas day or no Christmas day.
(The Mayor goes out. The Carol singers pass again, a clock strikes twelve.)

Tailor.   Alack I am undone. I am worn to a ravelling. I have no more strength and no time—where is Simpkin with that twist—(sinks into chair)— Oh dear, oh dear,—the waistcoat to be lined with taffeta—and the taffeta sufficeth—there is no more left over in snippets than will serve to make tippets for mice—(there is a tapping noise) now what can that be? This is very peculiar. Ah naughty Simpkin, has she set the mouse trap —Poor little frightened thing, I'll let you out.
(Pippin steps out and curtsies.)

Pippin.   Mistress Pippin at your service.

Tailor.   (bowing) I wish you a merry Christmas, Ma'am (goes back to chair). Queer. I must be dreaming—I have an idea that mouse said something —the waistcoat is cut from peach coloured satin—tambour stitch and rosebuds in beautiful floss silk—was I wise to entrust my last fourpence to Simpkin—but we shall be rich if all is ready for his worship in the morning—I must go on working . . . one and twenty button-holes of cherry coloured twist.
(Tapping noise again)
This is passing extraordinary—there must have been two mice in the trap (opens it—Andrew steps out and bows).

Andrew.   Master Andrew at your service.

Tailor.   (bowing) Your humble servant, Sir, and I wish you the compliments of the season (back to chair). Odd, very odd. One and twenty button-holes of cherry coloured silk—to be finished by Christmas morning— and it is after midnight already—was I right to let out those mice? Undoubtedly they belonged to Dame Simpkin. Alack I am undone for I have no more twist—no more twist—(he falls asleep).

Andrew.   Where are Gammon and Spinach?

Pippin.   Here they are. I had to send them back for thimbles; the Tailor's were too big.

Gammon. Oh, poor old tailor!

281

Andrew.   I fear he is very ill.

Pippin.   La! how pale he looks.

Andrew.   Let us finish the coat and waistcoat for him, then the joyful surprise will make him well again.

Spinach.   (looking at the clothes) Are they not truly elegant?

Gammon.   Delicious!

Andrew.   Come now, to work, to work, and meanwhile do you, Master Spinach, give us a tune on your fiddle.

Pippin.   First let us bar the door in case naughty Simpkin comes back.

Andrew.   Well said, Mistress Pippin (he bars the door).

Gammon.   These needles are very large, though easy to thread. (They have mounted the table and begin business of threading needles and stitching. They sing)

> Four-and-twenty tailors
> [Went to catch a snail,
> The best man amongst them
> Durst not touch her tail;
> She put out her horns
> Like a little kyloe cow,
> Run, tailors, run! or she'll have you all
> e'en now!]

(Dame Simpkin opens the grill in the door and pushes her face through.)

Simpkin.   Miaw!

Gammon.   (laughing) No, no the door is barred; you can't get in.

Spinach.   (laughing) Hey diddle diddle, the cat and the fiddle!

Simpkin.   What a charming sight. Please unfasten the door.

Pippin.   No thank you, Dame Simpkin, we don't want to be baked in your Christmas mince pies.

Spinach.   Three little mice sat down to spin.

Gammon.   Pussy passed by and she peeped in.

Simpkin.   What are you at, my fine little men?

Gammon.   Making coats for gentlemen.

Simpkin.   Shall I come in and cut off your threads?

Spinach.   Oh no, Miss Pussy, you'll bite off our heads.

Simpkin.   Once upon a time a cat and mouse kept house together—

Andrew.   Thank you, we have heard that story—May I trouble you for the scissors, M'am?

Pippin.   More twist please—

Gammon.   Why there is no more twist.

Pippin.   No more twist?

All.   No more twist!

Simpkin.   Ah Ha, I have the twist. I have been out to buy it—So now you must let me in.

Pippin.   No, no, you will gobble us up, Dame Simpkin.

Simpkin.   No, I give you my word.

Pippin.   Your word?

Simpkin.   Indeed I won't eat you.

Spinach.   I don't think a cat('s word is sufficient) is to be trusted.

Simpkin.   But I promise.

Andrew.   Promise. Oh very well then. But you must sit at the other end of the kitchen.

Pippin.   And not to wave your tail. (you mustn't)
(They open door.)

Simpkin.   (purring) Oh I am glad to come in. It is very cold outside and my coat is quite wet with snow, and you know how cats hate that (puts milk and bread down). I have been thinking—this is Christmas day, so I won't be a cruel old cat any more—and you kind little mice have been helping my poor tired old master! So here is the cherry coloured twist—

Andrew.   Quick, quick! to work, to work! Time is flying (a rapid song 'Nick-nack paddywack'). During the singing the lights fade out leaving only the one candle by which they work. The voices become very soft. The Tailor snores. Then in the distance is heard the cry of the watchman. 'Eight o'clock and a fine frosty morning!'

Andrew. Away, away!
(They scamper about clearing up. The Christmas bells ring out. A loud knocking at the door.)

Simpkin. Who can that be?

Gammon. Ready?

Spinach. All ready.

All. Away! (The mice vanish. Dame Simpkin opens door. Enter the Mayor.)
Now then, Madam, where is your Master?
(Dame Simpkin gently paws the tailor.)

Tailor. (waking up) Eh? eh? One and twenty button holes, I am undone.

Mayor. How now, Master Tailor, are my coat and waistcoat finished?

Tailor. Oh, forgive me, your Worship. Alas, I fell asleep.

Mayor. Fell asleep, you villain—you breaker of words?
Do you mean to tell me they are not completed?

Tailor. Oh, I shall be ruined. Oh, Simpkin, Simpkin, if only you had brought me that cherry coloured silk twist.

Mayor. Twist, indeed. I'll twist you!
(Dame Simpkin jumps on table and makes violent signs.)

Mayor. Ho there! I will call the watch.

Tailor. What is it, Simpkin? (seeing finished clothes) Oh, how can it be—look they are finished, and what beautiful work, every button hole.

Mayor. Neat, very neat, I wonder how they could be stitched by an old man in spectacles with old crooked fingers and a tailor's thimble.

Tailor. (peering at work) Yes, your Worship, the stitches are uncommon small, so small, one might almost think that they had been worked by little mice.

Simpkin. (dancing on trap) Miaw!

Mayor. But that's preposterous!

Tailor. Simpkin, was it really the mice? How very very kind of them. We won't set traps again, will we, good Simpkin?

Simpkin. (repentant) Miaw!

Mayor. I think you have both gone crazy.

Tailor. Here, your Worship, is your suit and may it bring you great happiness in your married life.

Mayor. I thank you, Master Tailor. It is indeed well done. I shall recommend you to my friends, and here is the gold I promised you with a little more besides because it is Christmas morning.

Tailor. I thank you, Sir, for your graciousness. Dame Simpkin, will you please open the door for his Worshipfulness?

Tailor. Simpkin, we have made our fortune. The Mayor will recommend us to his friends. Come give me my hat and my cloak. I feel a new man. Do you put on your bonnet. We'll go shopping. You shall have cream for breakfast. The little children next door shall have some toys. We'll have a Christmas goose and plum pudding for dinner, and the mice shall have some toasted cheese!
(they open the door, a carol greets their ears)

Curtain.

7
The Music Books

The Peter Rabbit Music Books

In December 1935 two Peter Rabbit Music Books were published under the combined imprint of J. & W. Chester Ltd., and Frederick Warne & Co. Ltd. Book I contained six easy pieces for the piano, and Book II six easy duets; they were intended for children between the ages of ten and twelve.

The titles of the pieces were as follows:

Book I Six Easy Pieces	*Book II Six Easy Duets*
1 Peter Rabbit pays a visit to Mr. McGregor's Garden	1 The Flopsy Bunnies
2 At Mrs. Tiggy-Winkle's	2 Mr. Jeremy Fisher
3 Squirrel Nutkin	3 Two Bad Mice
4 Jemima Puddle-Duck	4 The Puddle-Ducks take a walk
5 Tom Kitten	5 Mr. Jackson calls on Mrs. Tittlemouse
6 At Ginger and Pickles'	6 Samuel Whiskers and Anna Maria

The music was composed by Christopher Le Fleming, and at the beginning of each piece of music there was a drawing to illustrate the characters mentioned in the title. A short foreword by Beatrix Potter appeared in each book, and read:

> The rippling melody of this pretty music calls back many little friends.
>
> Again the Puddle-Ducks pass: pit pat paddle pat; while kittens, squirrels, rabbits, frisk and gambol. Tiddly widdly widdly! Mrs. Tittlemouse with a mop follows the big dirty footprints of Mr. Jackson. And Lucie sips her tea, while dear Mrs. Tiggy heats her smoothing iron.
>
> Good luck to the merry company of Christopher Le Fleming's tuneful numbers, and to those lucky little People who will learn to play them some day!

In a letter to Mr. Le Fleming dated September 13th 1935, Beatrix Potter referred to her drawings, and told him, 'I have been very long over them—doing them at odd times in a busy season of the year. Some are better or worse than others. The frog and the nut-cracking squirrel are my own favourites, and Jemima with Mr. Tod . . . The ducks are least satisfactory—I am having another try at Pit Pat Puddle. The tune still hums.'

Unlike the rest of her work, the drawings were finished off by someone else. In a letter to Mrs. Josephine Banner, Beatrix Potter described what actually happened: 'I made preliminary designs in pencil; and rather to my surprise Messrs Chesters said they could get *pencil* drawings reproduced quite well. I don't understand who did the deed but someone took a vast amount of pains to overlay my pencil with a vast crowd of little fly-like scratches in *ink*! which could be reproduced. The result was better than might have been expected; though they need not have taken the trouble to make a double set of foot marks where I had tried to rub out. I do not think Messrs Warne would do that. A few years ago the real way would have been for you yourself to lithograph the designs on stone.' The result is that much of the delicacy and charm of Beatrix Potter's work has been lost in the process of inking over.

There were eighteen designs in all—six for Book I and twelve for Book II, because it contained duets. Beatrix Potter liked the music but considered it difficult. 'I am sending you Christopher Le Fleming's music', she wrote to a friend; 'it was very charming when he played it, but I think it is difficult for children.'

The music books were supplied either in paper covers or in boards, price 2/6 and 3/6 for Volume 1, and 3/- and 4/- for Volume 2, respectively. The size was 305 mm × 240 mm.

8

The Fairy Caravan

The Fairy Caravan
1929

With the exception of *The Tale of Little Pig Robinson*, which was published in 1930, Beatrix Potter had now finished her *Peter Rabbit* series of stories. On the other hand, she loved writing for her own amusement, particularly about her farm animals, and sometimes referred to these writings as 'scribbles'.

She had no intention of producing another book until Alexander McKay came over from Philadelphia and persuaded her to do so. It was intended that this book should be printed *only* in America, and would contain some of the writings about her farm animals in a fairy caravan setting, pieced together with fragments of her miscellaneous unpublished work.

Beatrix Potter did not wish for an English edition of *The Fairy Caravan*, because she felt that the stories were 'too personal—too autobiographical' to publish in this country.

It is about a travelling circus known as Alexander and William's Circus, which was invisible to humans. 'The little dog in this story I have called "Sandy",' she wrote, 'after the first dog I possessed as a child. But he is really drawn from a much better behaved little dog called "Kiltie" who belonged to my next door neighbour.' His partner was Pony William, generally known as Pony Billy. Another character in the story was 'Charles', Beatrix Potter's favourite cock, who had a magnificent tail and a big red comb, and lived at Hill Top Farm. She explained how he came by his name:

'Charles' was not named by me. He was named by old James Walker the mason, who was helping to build another room to our cottage. At that time, 8½ years ago, Charles was an impertinent young chicken.

The workmen used to sit in the sun eating their dinner. As soon as old Walker opened his dinner-box, Charles hopped on to his knee, his shoulder, or his head! He never failed to receive a bit of pasty or cake: in fact it seemed to me that he took more than his share. Old Walker encouraged the bird and christened him 'Charles'—why, I know not.

When he died Beatrix Potter mounted some of his feathers on sheets of notepaper, adding a few appropriate words. One of these sheets reads:

This is a feather of poor old
—'Charles'—
who died lamented and respected
on November 17th 1929.
He was 8½ years old, and had
never been beaten in battle.

The Fairy Caravan: 1929

A year before she died Beatrix Potter described how she first became aware of the Fairy Caravan:

All by myself alone, I watched a weird dance, to the music of Piper Wind. It was far away in the lonely wilderness that stretches to Dale head, behind the table-land of Troutbeck Tongue. In the midst of that waste of yellow bent grass and stones there is a patch of green grass and a stunted thorn. Round the tree, round and round in measured canter went four of the wild fell ponies. Round and round then checked and turned, round and round reversed; dainty hoofs, arched necks, manes tossing and tails streaming.

I watched a while, crouched behind a boulder. I stood up. They stopped, stared and snorted; then galloped out of sight. Who had taught them? Who had learned them 'dance the heys' in that wilderness? Often times I have seen managed horses cantering round a sawdust ring under a circus tent; but these half wild youngsters had never been handled by man. Had they too seen Pony Billy? Even while I watched them I remembered how I had been puzzled once before.

In a soft muddy spot on the old drove road I had found a multitude of un-shod footprints, much too small for horses' footmarks, much too round for deer or sheep. I wondered were they foot marks of a troupe of fairy riders, riding down old King Gait into Hird Wood and Hallilands—away into Fairyland and the blue distance of the hills. I did not know at that time that there were ponies on the Troutbeck fells, though I knew they were at Matterdale, and Mardale, beyond the Nan Bield pass. The finding of those little fairy foot steps on the old drove road first made me aware of the Fairy Caravan.

Although the wild ponies on Troutbeck Tongue gave Beatrix Potter the idea of a *fairy* caravan, it was in 1903 that the idea of a *caravan* was first introduced into one of her stories. This was in *The Tale of Tuppenny*.

The Tale of Tuppenny was never published in its original form. It was one of three stories written at Hastings in December 1903, when Beatrix Potter was in her prime as a writer. The first two were published in 1904 and 1905, but before the third had been accepted as one of the stories in the series, Beatrix Potter had bought Hill Top Farm; her heart and soul was in the Lake District, where for the next few years she drew inspiration for many of her books, using Hill Top and Sawrey as their setting. However, in 1929 *The Tale of Tuppenny* was rewritten as Chapter 1 of *The Fairy Caravan*.

Not long before *The Fairy Caravan* was written, an American boy from Boston, Henry P. Coolidge, visited Beatrix Potter with his mother, and greatly admired her work. They were shown over Hill Top, and then taken to Castle Cottage to see some of the beautiful drawings and paintings in Beatrix Potter's portfolios. Henry was also impressed by her numerous background drawings—but Beatrix Potter's comments on the latter were: 'my studies made for backgrounds, whose quantities impressed Henry P, are very scribblesome.' It was this Henry P. to whom *The Fairy Caravan* was dedicated.

Apart from the numerous pen-and-ink drawings for *The Fairy Caravan*, there were to be a number of coloured illustrations, and it was the latter which Beatrix Potter felt would be somewhat of a strain. In a letter to Mr. McKay she told him, 'I have found no assistant yet. I wrote to an Art School which did not even reply, and lost time . . . should you get two or three designed in America?—*How long have I?*' But in the end she painted them all herself.

Her next concern was to obtain English copyright. After making inquiries, she told Mr. McKay, 'It is evident that the English copyright must be secured by me. I told you—in our back yard—that I am shy about publishing that stuff in London— my real wish and present intention is to have one hundred copies semi-privately printed by the Ambleside printer—a small local publisher—just a paper backed thing—A few would have to be sold over the counter, and there are certain formalities about depositing copies for registration purposes.' So she asked for one hundred sets of sheets to be sent over in order to have them bound privately. This was done by George Middleton, printers and publishers, Ambleside, Westmorland.

In the privately bound copies of *The Fairy Caravan*, the first eighteen pages of the American edition, including the preface and dedication page, were discarded, and a new set of pages printed at Ambleside. An additional page was added on which were sketches of dogs she knew, with their names written underneath. On the title page, Beatrix Potter used her married name, Beatrix Heelis.

The preface was omitted from the private edition because it had been written specially for American readers. In it she explained that the tales 'in the homely idiom of the old north country speech' were not originally intended for printing, and were sent on the insistence of friends beyond the seas.

A copy of her privately printed edition was deposited at the British Museum. It bears the date October 25th 1929.

Copies of the American edition arrived at Castle Cottage on October 10th, and the following day Beatrix Potter wrote to Mr. McKay, 'I think it is beautifully printed—I like type, paper and all . . . There might have been more line blocks, there are big slabs of print not illustrated—but then I never would have finished it if I had not been rushed, and the rushed drawings are the best. My favourites are Tomasine staring at the fire (a 17th family arrived next day), and Dolly trotting over the shadows.' (Tomasine was Beatrix Potter's cat, and Dolly was Pony Billy. These two drawings appear on pages 169 and 165 respectively of the current edition of *The Fairy Caravan*.)

She then thanked Mr. McKay for turning out such a handsome book, continuing, 'and I hope it will give satisfaction to both of us—and I may add—to my most exacting critics—my own shepherds and the blacksmith. I do not care tuppence about anybody else's opinion . . . Take out a few feeble pages—the book is none so bad.'

Nine years later when writing to a friend she said, 'If all the chapters had been as charming as "Bird's Place"—it would have been a fine book! As a whole I think it is too rambling; and the pig is tiresome.'

Apart from Mr. McKay's ordinary edition, he also produced one hundred copies which were signed and numbered. Some of these, at Beatrix Potter's request, were given to her American friends, and the rest were distributed as gifts at the discretion of Mr. McKay. The relevant sheets had previously been sent to England for signature.

By the last week in October Beatrix Potter was giving copies of her *privately bound* edition of *The Fairy Caravan* to relations and friends, and to some of her shepherds and farmhands. Her Lakeland friends were quick to recognize many of the pictures with their local settings, and the descriptions of the animals from her farms and those belonging to neighbours. In referring to this privately printed edition, Beatrix Potter wrote, 'It has been received with acclamation by the men— only they are all claiming bits, and disputing who's who.'

Each of these presentation copies was numbered and inscribed, and one or two typographical errors were corrected. A typical inscription, from Copy No. 4, which was given to one of her shepherds, reads, 'To John Mackereth in remembrance of Hill Top and the sheep, with kind regards to all at Sawrey ground, from Beatrix Heelis, October 29th 1929'.

Apparently an offer was received for the original paintings of *The Fairy Caravan*. Beatrix Potter's reply, however, indicated that she still had the interest of her English publishers at heart—for she wrote, 'It would not be wise for me to sell the coloured drawings; in case an English edition were required at some future time', adding, 'it makes my eyes so sore trying to paint colours, I would not like to have to do a set of new ones for it.'

Some years later, permission was given for an American edition of *The Fairy Caravan* in Braille. In a letter to Mr. McKay, Beatrix Potter wrote, 'I am pleased to hear that you have given leave for the transcription into Braille of *The Fairy Caravan*—rather a bulky volume in embossed form. I have an old interest in Braille; years and years ago when it was all to do—i.e. duplicate—by hand, my mother transcribed many volumes for a Blind Association in London. A process of stereotyping was invented later.'

By this time Beatrix Potter had come to know the McKay family personally, and felt that it would add to their interest in the book if she told them more about the places and characters mentioned therein. So in the privately bound copy of *The Fairy Caravan* presented to Mr. McKay and his family, there are copious notes neatly pencilled in the margins, and written on the end-paper are the words, 'Your children may like some "explains" about the pictures.'

These 'explains' are reproduced by courtesy of Mrs. Cridland (*née* Margery McKay).

BEATRIX POTTER'S EXPLANATORY NOTES
ABOUT THE PICTURES

(Unless otherwise stated page numbers apply to all editions)

Frontispiece   The bed with green damask curtains was my grandmother's best bed when she set up housekeeping 90 years ago. When I was a little girl it was a 'second best' bed, in the green room. How often I have sat up in that bed listening to the nightingales! When her furniture was dispersed and divided after her death, aged 90—I asked for the bed, to keep it, because the green curtains were full of pretty dreams. The browny red table cloth is a paisley shawl that belonged to my other grandmother—we used it for a table cloth. The cat was drawn from our Tomasine. The old frame is also in our dining room, only it is a picture of birds.

Page of dog drawings in privately bound edition   *Scotch Fly* is an extremely good sheep dog, only very nervous. She has run in 'Trials', but she loses her head. She was brought from Scotland when a pup, by my Scotch shepherd, E. Wood. She now belongs to me, as Ted has left. Anthony Benson's *Bess* is past work, but much valued, as she saved his life. *Nip* is a black and white bitch, a very good one. She was bred at Brothers' Water. *Lassie* is Scotch; I do not know whether she will ever work, she is too playful. I have trained several of Nip's pups myself, but Lassie is too lively for anything serious at present. (Lassie)—my puppy that I am bringing up. (Nip)—my favourite colley now growing old.

Page

9   No place. Fancy picture!

11   This is Keswick market place, done from memory.

17   This is Hawkshead—The Bank; slightly shortened.

21   Nowhere.

23   Worst picture in the book—I should have liked to draw this again.

31   Quarry at Hill Top Farm, Sawrey.

35   Stoney Lane, Sawrey—Barn is imaginary.

37   Lane at Sawrey, going down to Ees bridge.

44   The Pound, in Troutbeck. Troutbeck Tongue and High Street in distance. The farm house is Long Green Head.

45   Thimble Hall in Hawkshead, opposite Post Office.

49   Little window in Thimble Hall.

59   Bird's Place near Essenden, Hertfordshire. My grandfather Potter lived at Camfield Place near Hatfield in his old age; this was part of his land.

65   Sawrey.

68 (facing) Jack is one of Nip's puppies. 'Sandy' is drawn from a little dog called 'Kiltie' belonging to my neighbour Miss Hammond. I do not like the name 'Kiltie'; it's not a real name at all. The first dog I ever had was a Scotch terrier called Sandy. But he was brown, with longer hair.

73*   At Sawrey—Wilfin Beck, and a water gate. Wilfin Beck is a pretty stream that crosses the road between Far Sawrey and Near Sawrey. The County Council put a stone on the bridge with the name spelt all wrong 'Whinfill!', the old right name is 'Wilfin'.

76 (facing) Wilfin Beck, above the water gate. The portrait of our prize ewe Queenie is *not* approved. I am accused of having given her a lump under her jaws and a crick in her neck! The Herdwick lambs are born with black faces, they turn white at a year old.

81   Wilfin Beck, a bank in the little wood which I call 'Pringle Wood' in the story.

84   Fancy picture.

85   Skiddaw. Walla cragg.

94   This picture is copied from an etching by my brother, the late Walter B. Potter. I think he did it in Newlands near Keswick, but it is not unlike Broad How in Troutbeck.

97   The head of Troutbeck—from Troutbeck Tongue. From left to right—Troutbeck river, Sad Ghyll, Broad How, Threshthwaite mouth, Hartsop Fell, Thornthwaite Cragg, a ram belonging to W. Wilson, hired by me.

104   Wilfin Beck. In Pringle Wood, behind Redmayne's pasture.

105   Nowhere!

112   This is Low Lindeth Farm near Windermere. Charles is very old but still he fights on!†

* This picture does not appear in current editions. A hitherto unpublished one has been used in its place.
† Charles died on November 17th, three weeks after these notes were written.

117   Dogs—starting in foreground, clockwise: Matt—not so good. Boy, very like. Third dog, unnamed: a character—grins all over his face—rather bandy legged—gets sore feet in summer on the rocks—colour, yellow and white. Matt belonged to Tom Storey, one of my shepherds, the other two are mine. This picture is considered the best in the book. The background is at Troutbeck Park. Matt was recently dead —I drew this dog's head from Nip, it looks too black and white. Poor Matt was blackish tan and white—a quiet dog, much troubled with the mange which was his end.

119   Mettle belongs to F. Satterthwaite the Sawrey blacksmith. I am in trouble over this picture—two men claim the horse! To the best of my belief (and memory) it was J. Kirkbride's. If it had been white it would have been Ambrose Martindale's—but I do remember it was a *brown* horse that was waiting while I sketched. As for Maggret, she was only a pony, dead many years. W. Postlethwaite insists it is *his* horse, wrong colour!

122   Troutbeck Park farm house. The shelf is not really there, with bee hives.

123   Sawrey village. Clockwise from left: Hill Top farm house; Tower Bank Inn; Buckle Yeat, a cottage; Sawrey Post Office; Coniston 'Old Man' five miles away; our house; our meadow in snow.

135   Near Hill Top farm house.

136   Ing Bridge in Troutbeck.

148 (facing)★   The wood at top of Redmayne's pasture.

153   From lower left, clockwise: Fan; Bobs; the other terrier Nip; Twig, an awful fighter; Roy; Cheesebox; anybody's luckless dog; Mettle; Scotch Fly again; Lofty? Waggon horses: Dolly Pony Billy; Mag; Our Spot; Bess; Rags; Glen; Lassie; my Nip; Scotch Fly.

162   Tongue Ghyll, Troutbeck. Many a hunt I have seen there. As a matter of fact John Peel never hunted at Troutbeck, though sometimes put that way in the song. It should be 'Caldbeck'.

163   Near Ees bridge, Sawrey.

165   In the Graythwaite woods.

★ The coloured plate of the Wood faces page 148 in the privately bound edition. In the first American edition the corresponding page number is 108, and in current English and American editions it is page 142. (There are no variations in the page numbers of the other five coloured plates.)

Page
169 This is drawn from our cat Tomasine. There is a fine open fireplace at Mrs. Scale's—but it is wider than this, and a lower ceiling. This is at Sawrey.

173 In our orchard.

179 Thimble Hall, Hawkshead.

196 Rather a 'take off' of George Scott before he got a motor van.

211 Not a faithful picture—not like Cuckoo Brow Lane.

215 (facing) In Cuckoo Brow Lane, Sawrey.

225 The hawthorn bush up the lane.

BEATRIX POTTER'S EXPLANATORY NOTES ABOUT THE TEXT

(Page numbers apply to all editions)

Page
9 These words 'In the Land . . .' etc. were invented when I was a small child, I think the story was different. This Tuppenny story was written in 1903.*

83 Jack is a very fine 'merl' coloured colley belonging to John Mackereth my old shepherd, now retired to a cottage, but still 'going strong'.

84 This is an old song still sung at the clipping suppers.

86 *Blue Ewe*: She died spring 1921. She had lambs up to the last season when she was pensioned, into the orchard, a fine old sheep—pedigree bred.
Blindey: pee't = blind of one eye—she died winter 1927.
Lonscale ewe: A favourite of mine, and very old.

87 *Two Lonscales*: They were brought back several times. Once they were stopped by the Brathay river.
Isabel: A little scraggy ewe belonging to John Mackereth the shepherd —always the first to lamb.
Hill Top Queenie: Our best ewe at present.
Hoggie: Alas, I found him starved to the death! He belonged to my neighbour, Postlethwaite.

---

* Written at Hastings together with earliest versions of *Two Bad Mice* and the *Pie and the Patty-Pan*.

Belle Lingcropper in Falcon Crag: by Derwentwater—happened several years ago—Frequently happens. In fact it is worth while to send up a man on a rope to strip the sides of ledges, so the sheep may not be tempted to go along them.

89   '*A brave shepherd, truly*': Anthony Benson; [the accident] happened at Thirlspot, Thirlmere. 'Frank' was no worse. He is very fond of the old dog. She is bandy legged.

90   *Dale Head wall*: On Troutbeck Park farm.
'*A twinter*': A very inexperienced young sheep.
'*the heaviest falls*': All our snow storms come out of 'the low east'.★
The fells shelter us from the Scotch snow storms.
Blue Ghyll: On the High Street range. High Street got its name from the old Roman road that follows the tops from Troutbeck to Penrith and Carlisle.

91   '*the cams*': Rough top stones.
'*never heard the cuckoo again*': Expression used by shepherds about a weakly sheep that is not likely to live through the winter.

92   *Collie Allen*: Belonged to Val Allen of Hartsop Hall. I wrote and asked him about the dog's name, but got no reply. I think he got a bit laughed at. It was marvellous how the dog had got down alive.
Brill: Brill is a hound belonging to the Coniston Pack—she lives at Troutbeck Park when not at work.

93   *Nip*: She has killed one or two foxes.
Broad How: Troutbeck in west valley.
'*three little fox cubs*': This pretty description was given to me word for word by the shepherd Ted Wood.

95   *Pavey Ark*: Crags in the Langdale Valley.
'*Time and again I jumped*': I saw this incident some years ago.

112   *Codlin Croft*: Fancy name of farm—occurs several places in Lake District.

113   *Codlin Croft orchard*: I was thinking of an orchard at Fold Yeat near Hawkshead—but the farm house is not like. Codlin Croft Farm is a compound of various farms.

★ Bruce Thompson writes: 'A possible explanation of "the low east" is that *from Sawrey* the hills are *low* towards the east, but towards the north the hills are high and afford some shelter "from the Scotch snow storms"; it is not a usual expression.'

115   *Farmer Hodgson's orchard*: This description applies to our own orchard behind this house.

118   *Hodgson*: A common name pronounced Hodgin; no special person.

134   *Squire Browne's parrot*: Squire Browne of Tallentire. Old Miss Browne his daughter lived at Portinscale twenty years ago.

137   *Helsington*: A name just now for convenient sound. There is no show at Helsington.

138   *Daisey*: Daisey belonged to old Mr. George Dixon of How End, Sawrey. She was a wonderful pony—she never did die; she was drowned in the river Troutbeck★ in a flood when she was well over 40. I once asked Mr. Dixon her age and he said—'She's a lady, she does not tell!' By her history he knew she was over 40. I had her in her 'old age'. She could trot and cart hay. She was a Yorkshire cob, thickset, iron gray, very fat with a long back like a pig. In her youth at about 30 years, Daisey was bitten in the face by a viper, or 'hag worm' while grazing. She lost the sight of that eye, which made her apt to shy and probably caused her end. The meadow was flooded and she walked into the river.

139   *Cheesebox*: A cat that belonged to the Satterthwaite's long ago. She was a fat tortoise-shell cat. I think she was born in the box where they kept their cheese!!

141   '*a stony lane*': Stoney Lane, Sawrey.

149   *Mary Ellen*: Mrs. Scales really had a cat called Mary Ellen. Mrs. Scales was very knowledgeable about cows and pigs. I am not quite sure whether these rowan berries did any good; but they did not harm! They were to keep off witches, I believe. She lives at Stott Farm in the woods. She is very old now, a little old body.

152   *Ginger*: Willie Warriner's.
        Fanny: Georgie Scott's.
        Tommy: Timothy Askew's.†

154   *Hog-maned mare*: Milner's mare that had been through the war.
        Queeny Cross: George Cross.
        Will-Tom's team: Tom Nicholson an old driver of John Rigg's.

★ A small river that runs into the Eden in North Westmorland.
† Bruce Thompson writes of Timothy Askew: 'He is the baker in *Ginger and Pickles,* I remember his horse and cart well.'

BEATRIX POTTER'S GLOSSARY OF FAIRY CARAVAN TERMS

(Page numbers apply to all editions)

Page	Term	Meaning
24	Polecat	Animals of the stoat or sable tribe.
30	Thivel	A smooth wooden stick used for stirring a pot.
42	Taed-pipes	Water horse-tail—an undesirable plant.
48	Lug	Ear. As thin as a cat's lug—extremely thin.
74	Wilf	The old name for willow. Wilfin is the plural of Wilf.
74	Wagoners	Lumber-men
74	Snigging	To snig or snigging—to drag a tree along the ground with a horse and chain.
75	Beck	A stream.
84	Tarrie woo'	Fleeces of the hill sheep are water proofed with greasy preparation, on which is put a distinguishing Tar mark.
86	Herdwick	A distinct mountain-breed of sheep peculiar to the Lake District.
86	Peet	Signifies partially blind (i.e. one-eyed).
87	Langle	To tie a piece of sacking from a fore leg to the opposite hind leg in order to prevent sheep from jumping walls.★
87	Heaf	A tract of unfenced pasture where a sheep is accustomed to graze; as the high fells are not divided by fences it is important to have heafed flocks which will not stray from their own land.
88	Herb	Vegetation; grass is a word seldom used by shepherds.
90	Rush	A small avalanche, stones, snow or rock.
90	Plash	Fall of rain (i.e. splash).
90	Twinter	A young sheep once shorn, 16 months old.
90	Two-shear	A twice shorn sheep, 28 months old.

★ The practice is now illegal.

Page	Term	Meaning
91	Cams	Slaty top stones of a wall set on edge like a comb.
91	Lish	Active, supple, lively.
92	Cragged	Fallen over a crag.
93	Hunting	The Lake foot packs are supported by the sheep farmers in order to keep down the depredations of foxes amongst the lambs. The hound puppies on walk are reared on the farms, and returned to their homes when the hunting is over for the season. It frequently happens that a few hounds are benighted after a long chase. They take themselves to the nearest farm where they are hospitably received and cheerfully welcomed. Next morning they go on their way again.
95	Borran	A fox's hole under rocks.
95	Tailed and Marked	Lambs have their owner's mark put on with tar or red paint and their tails cut when they are about two weeks old.
95	Chimney	A rift or gully, up the perpendicular face of the crag.
95	Shelf	A ledge on the crag.
96	Keld	A spring of water.
96	Brackens	A fern with a running root that covers many hundred acres of land.
96	Fell	Mountain land.
96	Stone-men	The ancient inhabitants of the Lake District had sheep. A fragment of woollen material has been found in a stone barrow or burial place.
96	Early numbers	The old manner of sheep counting.
96	Grassings	Hill pastures which often retain their Scandinavian names to this day.
96	Ridged	Through countless generations the sheep have worn tracks along the hills, not unlike the lonely Roman Road along the summit of the mountain called High Street.
98	Webster	Hand loom weavers.
98	Bridewain	Wedding festivities and gifts.
98	Bedding chest	Panelled chests with heavy lids were in use before chests of drawers.

Beatrix Potter's Glossary of Fairy Caravan Terms

Page	Term	Meaning
101	Colludie Stone	A water-worn stone with a natural hole through it.
114	Hull	A farm building.
115	Middenstead	A place for storing farmyard manure.
116	Widdershins	Contrary way.
116	Uveco	A cattle food prepared from maize corn.
120	Rose Comb	A thick comb of many points.
121	Cairngorm	A Scotch crystal found in the Cairngorm mountains.
123	Demerara Sugar	A moist form of sugar, not refined to whiteness.
213	Intake	A mountain pasture taken in or enclosed from the open fell.
219	Wood-mongers	Merchants who buy woods and sell timber.
220	Hoppus	Hoppus & measurements—old Lake Country complicated tables for reckoning the quantity of timber in trees.
222	Thill-horse	Shaft horse.
225	Lonnin	A lane.

THE TALE OF TUPPENNY
1903

In the land of Green Ginger there is a town called Marmalade, which is exclusively inhabited by guinea-pigs.

They are of all colours, and of two sorts—the common ordinary smooth-haired guinea-pigs who run errands and keep green grocers shops—and the kind that call themselves Abyssinian Cavies—who wear ringlets and walk upon their toes.

And the short-haired guinea-pigs admire and envy the curls of the long-haired guinea-pigs.

Both kinds of guinea-pigs go to the Barber especially on Saturdays.

The Barber brushes and combs and curls the top-knots of the Abyssinian Cavies, and trims their whiskers, but he cannot do very much for the smooth-haired guinea-pigs—except apply pomatum—which has no effect, only making their smooth hair even flatter than it was before.

Now this Barber was an ingenious person, he invented a new hair-wash in the back shops. I do not know what it was made of (which is perhaps well).

He called it Quintessence of Abyssinian Artichokes, and drew up an untruthful advertisement, to the effect that it would cause asparagus to grow upon a door-knob—and bushy hair upon the tails of rats (which is said to be really the case amongst the Pyrenees!).

Then he put the advertisement, and 6 large bottles of the new essence, in the shop window.

There was immediately a crowd of short-haired guinea-pigs.

The barber's little guinea-pig son came out and distributed hand-bills which stated that the Quintessence of Abyssinia was an infallible cure for chicken-pox.

The Abyssinian Cavies were disgusted.

The smooth-haired guinea-pigs came daily and flattened their noses against the barber's window; but they hesitated to buy; because one bottle cost 8 pepper-corns —(or post-free for half a potato)—and also because the long-haired guinea-pigs had spread an insidious and libellous report that the hair-wash was made of slugs.

The short-haired guinea-pigs discussed the matter at street corners—but no one would try the first bottleful!

Now it happened that in that town there was a guinea-pig called Tuppenny, who was a miserable object, because most of his hair had been pulled out—

(I do not know what for, but I have no doubt that he deserved it.)

The friends of Tuppenny were sorry for him, and condoled with him; and told him that he was not fit to be seen, and they offered to subscribe for a bottle of the new Quintessence.

Tuppenny himself had become indifferent to appearances; but he was over-persuaded by the sympathetic affection of his friends, and permitted himself to be led away.

At the Barber's, the friends produced 8 peppercorns, and the Barber applied the hair-wash with a garden syringe, in order—(as he explained)—not to wet his own hands with it. He said that the prescription was very powerful.

It had a peculiar smell which immediately excited the attention of Mrs. Tuppenny, when her husband returned home. His friends accompanied him as far as his door.

Tuppenny passed a disturbed night, but looked much as usual in the morning. His hair had *not* grown.

His friends again conducted him to the Barber's and expostulated. The Barber was perplexed. After some argument he agreed to supply a second bottle at half-price. Tuppenny's head felt very hot during the night. But his hair was not any longer next morning!

All the short-haired guinea-pigs in Marmalade were indignant. They demanded a third bottle of hair-wash free—gratis—for nothing at all.

The Barber was seriously alarmed, and remonstrated; he said the stuff was so powerful that an over-dose might turn Tuppenny blue or even make him grow a tail.

But the friends carried their point.

There was quite a crowd of smooth-haired guinea-pigs in Tuppenny's front garden next morning—until Mrs. Tuppenny came out with a mop.

Tuppenny himself stayed late in bed. And when he did appear he looked very odd: his hair was certainly growing, especially on his nose.

His friends conducted him in triumph to the Barber's; his hair grew another inch while on the way; and when he reached the shop it was all over his ears, and he was surrounded by a twittering crowd of short-haired guinea-pigs.

The Barber received them with jubilation and raised the price per bottle to 20 peppercorns.

There was no immediate sale however. The other guinea-pigs decided to wait a few days, to see whether Tuppenny's hair might change colour—or fall off!

Tuppenny would have been thankful had it done so! The way that guinea-pig's hair grew, was perfectly frightful!

The family couldn't bear him! and when he went out the rude little guinea-pig boys ran after him shouting 'old whiskers!!'

He went to the Barber's every morning to have it cut; but it grew again before he got home.

When he had spent all his money upon shaving, his family cut it themselves with scissors, all crooked and jagged behind, and stuffed pincushions with the snippings.

As for the Barber—his shop was deserted, and after a time he put up his shutters and ran away.

Then the rats took possession.

They ate up all the pomade and drank up all the remaining bottles of the celebrated hair-wash; but it had no effect upon them (they being bailiffs).

—And what has become of Tuppenny?

He has sold himself to a travelling show-man; who goes about the country with a tent; and a brass band; and a menagerie of five Polecats and Weasels; and a troupe of performing fleas; and the Fat Dormouse of Salisbury; and

TUPPENNY the HAIRY GUINEA-pig

who lives in a caravan!

The End.

9

A Sequel to the Fairy Caravan

A Sequel to the Fairy Caravan

Soon after *The Fairy Caravan* was published, Mr. McKay wrote to Beatrix Potter asking for another book. 'I am glad to hear that the Caravan has done so well,' she replied. 'I will think things over. Only you must remember that I am *not* a prolific scribbler. I wrote myself out on the rabbit series. We must talk over the future of the Caravan and consider where its wheels can travel without upsetting—not "most haste worst speed".'

On November 5th 1930, Beatrix Potter wrote, 'There are a good many other stories of the Caravan in existence. I will think the matter over . . . I would like to do another volume some day; but I would not put so much crammed into it, as there was in the first one. And perhaps rather more pictures', adding with regret—'I am afraid I ought to do the Guide Book first.

'I have let myself in for a troublesome business, a book about the Lake District. Messrs Warne brought out a rather handsome volume about the next county, Yorkshire, illustrated by R. Smith; and Mr. Stephens asked me if I would care to do one. I have always had rather a fancy to do a Lakes guide-history-description. But now I am shying at the job—it is a task for one's declining years! not a job to do in a hurry; it would entail much "reading up". I tried to back out of it; but Mr. Reginald Smith turned up here with some very good pictures. I do wish they would get someone else to write it . . . It ought to be written by three or four people, agriculture, history, sport, scenery. I wish I had turned it down decidedly right off at first.' Finally, however, W. G. Collingwood revised his 1902 book and it was called *The Lake Counties*.

In the end there was no sequel to *The Fairy Caravan*, but some of the material which Beatrix Potter had in mind for this book is given here. It tells of the old farmhouse at Hill Top; of funguses growing in the woods near Cherry-tree Camp, where in the month of May 'the cherry blossom and hawthorn are in flower'. There is also the story of *The Solitary Mouse*, with its setting at High Buildings amongst the fells above Beatrix Potter's sheep farm at Troutbeck. The mouse was named Joseph, after her Scottish shepherd Joseph Moscrop: 'He is wonderful with lambs and dogs', she wrote, 'we all love Joseph. I do not think he would approve of me calling a mouse "Joseph Mouse-trap".'

Of her fairy-tales and Fairy Caravan stories, Beatrix Potter wrote—'It seemed to me they are just sufficiently curious that it would be a pity to let them float away out of existence.'

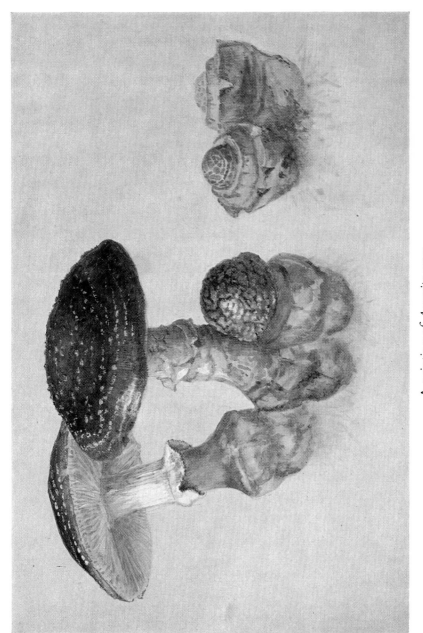

A painting of *Amanita asper*

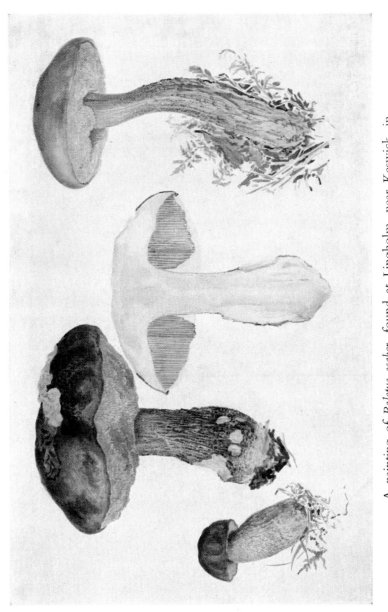

A painting of *Boletus scaber*, found at Lingholm, near Keswick, in October 1897

Enid Linder

Tom Storey and his son sheep-shearing at Hill Top

Leslie Linder

Farm buildings at Hill Top

THE OLD FARMHOUSE AT HILL TOP

'I suppose that it is out of the question,' said Xarifa wistfully. 'You cannot visit a house where there are cats,' said Sandy with decision. 'There are no cats in the unoccupied end of the house,' said Pippin. 'Nobody is living there just now except me and Cobweb and Dusty and Smut and Rufty Tufty.' 'There are always cats at farm houses,' said Sandy firmly, 'even when there is nobody there—Did not Mistress Heelis go to Windy Brow to buy a calf, and there was nobody except five cats, locked out, sitting on the door-sill while every one had gone to market?'

'The cat at our house sits in the kitchen end with Mrs. Mackereth.' 'That settles it,' said Sandy, 'there is a cat.' Pippin drew himself up to the magnificent height of three inches and looked along his whiskers at Sandy—'I and Cobweb and Dusty live in the panelled parlour end; not in the farm kitchen end of the house.—We do not keep a cat,' said Pippin. 'I am sorry if you are disappointed Xarifa'—but Xarifa had fallen fast asleep. She woke up hearing her name. 'Tell us about the old house, Pippin; then I will be able to see it in my dreams; to see it lazily and comfortably, untroubled by cats, or downspouts choked with that moss, running over in the summer rain, or skylights that rain down upon the floor and ceiling when there is thawing snow—or paint peeling off the window sashes, or gray slates, slipping, slipping, on the roofs'—'Nay, that is a chapter of dilapidations!'

'It is a good dry sound old house; it has stood a many hundred years and may stand as many more—barring accidents. Do you remember, Dusty, what our great grandparents told about the fire that nearly started when they were building the new wing, for the dairy and big room above? How the masons made a hole for a door in an old old wall, and it was like two walls with rubbish filled in between, and amongst the rubble stones in the middle of the four foot wall was chigged up chopped up straw and hay—hay nests that the rats had been carrying in for hundreds of years and they had made their nests behind the kitchen chimney? So that when the masons let in the wind and air a little thread of smoke and smouldering red crept along the rat hay inside the wall and along right away from the chimney?' 'It was put out safely.'

'Rats are a nuisance,' said Cobweb—'Did they find anything in the walls?' 'Nothing much; some clay marbles that a child had pushed into a hole long ago, an old broken pipe or two, a pewter ink pot. Xarifa, you should see the key of our door, *I* cannot lift it,' said Pippin—'You needn't laugh, Sandy! it weighs [   ]*
It turns wrong way, and the wards work in a wooden box. One time it wouldn't work at all, and when the box was unscrewed what do you think was jammed in the wards of the lock? A great big George III penny! Oh, that is only a new thing to the age of our house.

* Beatrix Potter did not fill in the weight.

'First there is the porch made of great slabs of Brathay slate, on either side a slate six foot high, with two smaller slates for the roof, and honeysuckle and cabbage roses hanging over. The flowers love the house, they try to come in! The golden-flowered great St. John's wort pushes up between the flags in the porch; it has peeped up between the skirting and the flags inside the porch place before now. And the old lilac bush that blew down had its roots under the parlour floor, when they lifted the boards. Houseleek grows on the window sills and ledges; wisteria climbs the wall, clematis chokes the spout's casings. Wall flowers and cabbage roses in season; rosemary and blue gentian, and earliest to flower the red pyrus japanese quince—But nothing more sweet than the old pink cabbage rose, that peeps in at the small paned windows.

'The hall place has low beams, and a broad window seat. The fireplace is wide, there is a brass turning spit, and a brass coal scuttle, and brass knockers on the doors, though the main of the doors are just cupboards—cupboards and cupboards. How many wall cupboards are there, Dusty?' 'Eleven in our part of the house,' said Dusty. 'Twelve if you count the dark closet under the staircase, Dusty,' corrected Cobweb.

'There is the big cupboard like a room on the left of the fireplace, with a little wall cupboard inside it, and shelves. And there is the long deep cupboard with one deep shelf on the right of the fireplace, and a hole under the door that we run through, and next it on the same wall, two more cupboards one above the other, funny shaped because underside of the old back staircase goes through them, so that the ceiling of cupboard is the back of steps.' 'It makes them an awkward shape, they are dusty,' said Dusty. 'Then there is a tall wall cupboard, a shallow cupboard with many shelves, where Mistress Heelis keeps the marmalade and jam; she comes for it with a basket—thirty to forty pounds of marmalade, at this time of year,' said Pippin, licking his fingers, 'and strawberry jam and plum and blackberry jelly, and rowan jelly to eat with herdwick mutton, and on the upper shelves china, and glass, and finger bowls and wine glasses and engraved decanters, frosted patterns on the glass that did belong to Mistress Heelis's grandmother, and there are little silver labels that hang with tiny chains on the decanters, with funny names, "Canary", "Madeira" and "Mountain".*

'Then there is the dresser with crooked legs, and great plates, of blue willow pattern, and then a funny little recess that might have been another cupboard, but it is not, only a bandy legged mahogany chair stands in it, a chair that was once painted green. Over the chair hangs a copper warming pan. It and the old steel candlesticks also belonged to Mistress Heelis's grandmother.

'Then there comes folding doors to the oak stairs. We will not describe through the folding doors yet. We will follow the left side of the house place; there is

---

* 'Mountain' is the old name for 'Malaga' wine.

another door that is a passage—In there is hanging the best black harness—And the door of that cupboard passage corresponds with the parlour door; and between the two doors there is a picture and a gate legged table, a picture of a sunset. But the little parlour is the room that is prettiest—Xarifa.

'The hall place is panelled with dark painted cupboards; but this parlour is panelled with some foreign pine wood, and in the panelling there is yet another cupboard, a buffet that has had a table shelf to let down.

'There are pillars in the panelling with groovings and cornices. In old days it has been a bettermer* sort of yeoman's house. How old is it? I know not; the front part that I am describing to you was built somewhere about 1602. But the old old wall that was opened to make a door, was part of an older house. Is that all the cupboards in the parlour? Nay there is another door that is a sort of square closet, and there is a bell wire in it, which seems funny in a cupboard, but old Mrs. Swainson that lived to be ninety said she was born in that cupboard; it used to contain a box bed.

'The walnut carved chairs are covered with satin damask; there are crimson damask window curtains and little old pictures in gilt frames and miniatures. The staircase is black oak, there are polished turned banisters, and there is a rail upon banisters across the tall window on the first landing, a window with old panes of glass mounted in the original lead. A tall clock stands half way up, and oil paintings hang on the walls; there are dark crimson curtains and a worn Brussels carpet, that has credit to be worn, for Mistress Heelis remembers it for sixty years.

'Then there is the big landing very slippery oak; and the book room over the porch with the pleasant dusty parchment smell, and two little cheerful bedrooms looking out on to the smiling roses and lilies, and the attic with the skylight in the sloping roof—and the dark closet that is full of books and has a door that is bad to open—and the biggest dark spot like a little room without a window that has a provoking history.'

A WALK AMONGST THE FUNGUSES

While the Fairy Caravan was on holiday at Cherry Tree Camp, Xarifa the dormouse, and Tuppenny the guinea-pig, took a walk hand in hand.

The dormouse was much smaller than the guinea-pig; but her presence of mind was superior (so long as she could keep awake). Her coat was short and glossy and she had a pretty tail. Tuppenny was twittersome and nervous, and he had such an inconveniently long mop of hair that he was obliged to wear it plaited and rolled up, except at circus performances.

* A Cumberland word meaning of the better sort.

Xarifa and Tuppenny stood under the shade of a bracken fern, cooling their bare toes pleasantly in the short wet grass. The grass twinkled in the bright sunshine. The field rose steeply in front of them like a green wall, with blue sky and white clouds above. Many ferns grew at the edge of the wood. Beyond the fringe of ferns there was a colony of yellow funguses spotted about on the turf.

Tuppenny was staring seriously at the funguses. 'Are they made of butter, Xarifa?' 'Certainly not. Why do you think so?' 'There are mooly cows in the field.' 'Cows do not leave butter lying about. It comes out of a churn. Those are funguses called Boletus.' 'Are they alive?' inquired Tuppenny, peeping round the fern. Xarifa did not reply; she was brushing dew drops off her chestnut coat. 'Can they walk about, Xarifa?' said Tuppenny, throwing a nut at the nearest Boletus.

The Boletus took no notice; it sat out in the sun, drying its sticky cap. 'Do not do that, Tuppenny,' said Xarifa, 'it is injudicious to throw nuts at things which we do not understand.' 'I beg your pardon, Boletus, sorry, I am not to do that, not to throw nuts again,' twittered Tuppenny—'Xarifa, let us go away! I am sure the smallest Boletus shook its head at me!' 'I can perceive no movement,' said Xarifa, 'but I should not like to express a positive opinion without consulting Petronella; you heard her fairy rhyme about the mushrooms—

> "Nid, nid, noddy, we stand in a ring
> All day long and never do a thing!
> But nid nid noddy, we wake up at night,
> We dance and we sing in the merry moon light!"

'Xarifa, do you think they are standing quite—quite in the same place? Look at that little button Boletus with some moss sticking to its shiny cap; and that big fat one, I am sure it has a yellow face under its cap.'

'The shadow of the fern moves in the wind.'

'I am going back into the wood,' said Tuppenny, scurrying down hill all of a twitter. He ducked under the railings; his nervous twitterings continued to be heard in the wood below.

Xarifa went on with her toilet under the fern, dry-cleaning her chestnut coat, her white front, her tail and whiskers. The colony of Boletus stood about in the wind and sunshine. Having finished her toilet, Xarifa made three separate curtseys to the three nearest Boletuses, and one elaborate curtsey to the rest.

The Boletuses did neither bow nor nod, they continued to sit in the sun. A rabbit feeding high up the bank, lifted its head, looked round, and went on feeding.

Nothing is ever lost by politeness. Xarifa smoothed her chestnut coat and went leisurely across the grass to the railings. She felt satisfied that she had shown proper politeness to the Boletuses, whether they were alive or not.

She slipped underneath the bottom rail of the fence, amongst brown leaves and moss. The wood below was dark compared with the sunny field, dark, sandy, dry, full of dead leaves and sandy rabbit holes.

Tuppenny waiting under the beech tree was still all of a twitter; he had come across more funguses. The first was like a very tall cream-coloured umbrella with brown spots on top, and a white fringe round its waist. And a few yards further on there were others amongst the leaves, apricot orange coloured and sweet almond smelling, crinkled like shells—'That is Cantharella, a friend of Petronella's; she plays about among the beech leaves in September.'

'Does she dance too, Xarifa?' 'I really cannot tell you, Tuppenny; I know Mixomycetes walks about; I have seen him go from one end of a log to another. With regard to the others, I only quote Petronella. She said that the mushrooms danced at night.' 'Do you think they are fairies? Xarifa?' 'Hush,' said Xarifa.

The sun went in and a few big drops of rain pattered down from leaf to leaf within the wood. 'Let us shelter under the root of this beech tree, it is but a shower. We might have sheltered under the umbrella fungus if we had been near him.' 'I will stay here, Xarifa; I think Cantharella is smiling at us; how sweet she smells.' 'I will cover up her toes with some more leaves. When the sunbeams dart down between the branches after the shower they might be too hot for her.' 'I am sure she smiled at you, Xarifa.'

'Let us go now, the shower is over, and Jenny Ferret will have dinner ready. I have thought of a tale to tell you, Tuppenny.' 'Oh, Xarifa, how lovely! What is it, what is it?' 'After dinner, if I can keep awake. Come along this bank and we will go out at the end of the railing, come along under the nut bushes—See, Tuppenny, here are more funguses—look at that very big one, solitary, under the birch tree, with chestnut cap and speckled white gray stem; he too is a Boletus, his name is Scaber. And here is another Boletus, cousin Edulis; and look, Tuppenny, lower down the bank, there is a beauty, but do not touch him, he is poisonous. Look at his velvet coat, all buff and crimson; but if a bit were broken off his edge it would turn verdigris blue.'

'I do not like them, Xarifa, let us go away.' 'I like Cantharella, she is sweet smelling and pretty,' said Xarifa, 'and I like the ring dancers. I cannot say that I am fond of the fierce red fly Agaric. It does not grow in this wood but we will see it under the scattered birch trees on the moor. In a few weeks there will be many many others.'

THE SOLITARY MOUSE

The enjoyment of travel by caravan depends upon the weather. One day rain and sleet drove in sheets down Hagg Ghyll although the time of year was April. Sandy and William's Circus—a draggled procession—struggled against the storm.

They had conquered the first climb behind Troutbeck Park farm-house and they were on the old road which runs like a shelf along the east side of the Tongue.

At the head of the valley the road loses itself in bogs. (Once after a water spout Roman paving stones were revealed, scattered a yard deep amongst peat and shingle.) The road emerges, east of the marsh and climbs in steep zig-zags up 'High Street' mountain. At 2,000 feet it follows the skyline northward, to join the Maiden Way; a green ribbon marching straight across brown moors toward the Scottish Border. For long years the road has been lonely and deserted except by shepherds and sheep.

The little Folk of the Circus Company battled with the wind. The shepherds themselves are sometimes beaten back by winter blizzards on the Roman road.

Sandy led the van, with his ears blown inside out. Pony William plodded between the shafts, with his head down and his ears back—Behind the caravan, striving to keep up, Paddy Pig pulled the go-cart, squealing—'Whoa! Way, Pony Billy, wait till I catch up! Way, way, I'm winded. Wee, wee, wee, stop, stop!' Pony Billy plodded on; he had made up his mind where to camp. Far up the valley through mist and rain he could see a tall slated barn, High Buildings in Hagg Ghyll.

The Big Folks used to sow and reap there in the days of 'Boney' and Waterloo. The mountain turf still shows traces of the plough rigs. Pony Billy paused at last, at a gate below the road. He took the caravan down a bank, through a ford. Tawny peat water swirled through the floor boards. Jenny Ferret inside the caravan drew up her feet. Pony Billy went back through the flood to fetch the go-cart.

High Buildings stands on the further bank of the beck, with its back towards the storm and a snug walled yard in front of it. 'What is this, a new gate? and no slates off?' 'There are frequent repairs when Mistress Heelis takes over another sheep farm. I trust the stable door is not locked? Hold that gate open,' said Pony William.

He swung the caravan round into a sheltered corner, unharnessed, shook the rain from his coat like a big dog, and clattered over the cobble stones into the stable, where he commenced to munch hay. 'Hinny ho, I knew where to come to.' Other people might unpack, and carry in hampers. Pony Billy had earned his supper.

Paddy Pig had not visited High Buildings before. 'A jolly snug sty and warm bedding.' He approved of the finely powdered old dry bracken upon the floor— the accumulation of many years. (In spite of its clean dryness it is a fact that an unlikely animal crop of tree mushrooms reappears in one corner. I have cooked and eaten them.)

One stall had been swept bare of bedding, and fenced off with a hurdle. It contained a varied assortment of articles. 'Hulloa? someone else has been camping here. But no one is likely to be astir in this weather. And we have fern seed.'*

---

* The Fairy Caravan animals always carried fern seed because it made them invisible to the Big Folk.

Behind the hurdle on the swept floor was an oil stove, a paraffin can, a camp stool, two large biscuit canisters, a smell of cheese, a galvanized pail, a lamb bottle not properly washed with sour milk in it, another bottle marked 'caster ile for lambs', a double pail, and some more bottles. Other things hung on nails on the rafters above. For instance a suit of brown clothes much patched, a tea kettle, an old macintosh, four enamel mugs and two biscuit bags. Sandy was interested in the bags until he discovered that they contained soap, and a pair of cork soles, and four tea spoons.

'This building has been used at lambing time. I have found two lamb jackets and I recognize that macintosh; it is the property of Joseph. But shepherds do not use cork soles. Some of these things belong to Mistress Heelis,' said Sandy. 'Do you think she would mind if I borrow the oil stove?' inquired Jenny Ferret, 'I'm only an old body and I'm wanting my tea very badly.' 'So am I,' said Sandy—'Mistress Heelis never minds anything, until she loses her temper. Did you remember to bring my dog biscuits, Jenny Ferret?' 'Here, take them! That milk bottle is a disgrace; I will do some cleaning in return for borrowing, before we leave.'

Jenny Ferret bustled around and unpacked her basket. 'Reach me down that kettle, it's smaller than ours. I will try if it will sing as quickly as Sally Benson's.'—'What is that Jenny Ferret? is it a story?' exclaimed Xarifa and Tuppenny together. 'I don't know stories, I'm only an old body. Spread the butter, Xarifa, while I cut the loaf.'

The biscuit canisters side by side made a table; they used their own doll cups and tea pot and borrowed three mugs. 'Here is strawberry jam—where is the cheese? Don't tell me it has been left in the caravan. It may be vulgar to eat cheese at tea time but I have a tooth for cheese. Is it raining?' 'Pouring,' said Sandy, 'there is a smell of cheese about that canister without getting soaked again.

'What are you two looking at, Xarifa and Tuppenny? You keep whispering and twittering?' 'Hush,' said Xarifa, holding up a small pink hand for silence. 'Hush, keep quiet. We think we see something.' 'Cheese. A smell of cheese,' said Xarifa slowly in a distinct voice.

A small brown nose and long whiskers peeped out between the stones of the wall and popped in again. 'Cheese,' repeated Xarifa encouragingly. The brown nose peeped out a little further and a pair of bright beady eyes observed the newcomers.

'Bread and butter?' said Xarifa, holding out a piece in her small pink hand. 'We will not harm you; we have only come in to shelter. Please accept a bit of our bread and butter, Mr. Mouse. (Take no notice of him, he will come out presently).' Which he did. He proved to be a very pretty house mouse with a long tail and fine whiskers. 'What are you doing here, so far away from dwelling houses?' asked Sandy. Instantly the mouse whisked into the wall. But he more and more came out and when Xarifa gave him a crumb of sponge cake, he sat down beside her.

'What is your name?' inquired Xarifa. 'Joseph,' replied the mouse bashfully. His voice was small and pleasant. 'You are a very shy mouse,' said Xarifa, after he had had another fright and whisked in and out again. 'Is that all your name?' 'Joseph Moscrop,' replied the mouse. 'Why "Moscrop"? It sounds like a sheep.' 'It is not my own name; it is only what I call myself. It was the name of one of the shepherds.' 'What is your own name, then?' 'I do not know. I am the last of my family. There is no one left to call me anything.' The mouse shed a tear, and washed his face with it. 'Why do you live here?' The mouse seemed to be at a loss to explain.

'It is a long and melancholy story,' said the mouse—'We love stories—me and Tuppenny—' But the mouse had taken fright when Jenny Ferret lifted the kettle off the stove. 'Have a doll-cup of tea?' said Xarifa kindly, when he peeped out again. 'It is pleasant to feel the warmth of the stove,' said the mouse spreading his little paws and blinking at the glow. 'It has not been lighted since Mistress Heelis and the shepherds went away.'

He warmed his paws and came a little closer. 'I know that there are matches and cheese in that canister; but it has not been opened since Mistress Heelis went away. I call myself Joseph after one of the shepherds. If I had been a she mouse I would have called myself Beatrix after Mistress Heelis. Do you know any she mice?' inquired Joseph Moscrop plaintively.

'It seems to me,' said Xarifa, who had been considering the earlier part of his statement—'it seems to me it would have been more appropriate if you had called yourself Mousecrop instead of Moscrop.'

'I thank you for the suggestion. Mouse crop. Yes, Mousecrop. A pleasing name is sometimes a recommendation. But there are no lady mice up here. I am the last mouse in the valley.' 'Field mice?' said Sandy. 'Surely there are swarms of field voles right up the fell sides?' 'I take no interest in voles; they have short tails. I am the last of my family.' He shed another tear, and washed his face and whiskers briskly.

'How did you come to live up here?' 'I did not come. I was born at High Buildings. Until the shepherds came and Mistress Heelis, I had never heard of cheese, much less tasted it. My parents and my great grandparents lived in this barn, eating hay seeds and wild fruits. Gradually we dwindled. I am the last mouse left.' (Never the less he seemed extremely sleek and cheerful.)

'But how did there come to be house mice in this far away building?'

'That I know, because my grandmother told me before the owl caught her,' said Joseph shivering slightly. 'Our fore elders lived at the Mill. Did you notice as you came up the valley a square of fallen walls, and grass more green where once had been a garden? and on the hill side above there is a patch of daffodillies? Those walls are where the Mill house stood when Hagg beck turned the water-wheel years and years ago. Nothing is left alive except nettles and the daffodillies, and me—a Solitary Mouse.

'When the Mill was burnt down and the roof fell in there was no more corn.

My ancestors left the mill and moved to High Buildings. True, it was still further up the valley; further from cheese and habitations of men. But it was a shorter journey from the Mill, much nearer than the nearest farm house which the swallows tell me is a mile away below the waterfall in the wood. Perhaps there may be other mice at the farm. But I dare not run there by daylight for fear of buzzard hawks, nor go so far by moonlight for fear of the horned owl who lives in the quarry. So here I live alone, a solitary mouse,' said Joseph, washing his face and whiskers briskly. 'Do you know any she mice?' he inquired again.

'There are always mice in villages,' said Xarifa. 'I am afraid villages are a great way off,' said Joseph. 'I should so like a taste of cheese. I feel sure Mistress Heelis would give me a taste if she were here. I cannot get the lid off the canister.' 'I think I can open it for you, Joseph. Perhaps you would lend us a bit of Mistress Heelis's soap to wash up with?' 'The soap is in one of the biscuit bags hanging up; it has a nasty taste,' said Joseph. Sandy opened the canister and took out a piece of cheese, half a pound wrapped in butter paper.

The mouse nibbled off a bit about the size of a thimble. 'Please put back the big lump of cheese and put the lid on. I might be tempted to eat more than I ought to do. I am an honourable mouse.' He divided the small piece of cheese equally into the size of two half thimbles. 'Mistress Dormouse, pray accept a piece of Mistress Heelis's cheese,' said Joseph. 'I thank you; but it was not I who said that I liked to eat cheese at tea time; it was Mrs. Jenny Ferret.'

'That is not just the same thing,' said Joseph eating the whole thimbleful himself. It seemed to encourage and cheer him, he washed his face and whiskers briskly. 'I wonder whether you know any lady mouse who would like to live up here?' 'It is a warm dry building, though remote,' said Xarifa, stirring the sugar in her doll-tea-cup with a tiny tea spoon, 'possibly some mouse might fancy the spot.' 'Do you really think so?' said Joseph much gratified. 'Will you marry me?' '*I* ??!' said Xarifa, '*I* ? "Mrs. Joseph Mouse-trap"! *I* marry you! I would as soon think of marrying a guinea-pig.'

All the company burst out laughing except Tuppenny. He twittered with embarrassment. As for Joseph Mouse—he was so much upset by Xarifa's contempt, by the general merriment and by the mention of mouse-trap—Joseph whisked into the wall, and he did not come out again until next day dinner-time.

The Circus had travelled on its way when I myself saw the Solitary Mouse. In those calm, spacious days that seem so long ago, I loved to wander on the Troutbeck fells. Sometimes I took with me an old sheepdog—Nip—or Fly; more often I was alone. But never lonely. There was company of gentle sheep, and wild flowers, and singing waters. Clouds slid over the crest of the Tongue. Sunbeams chased cloud shadows. I listened to the voices of the Little Folks.

Troutbeck Tongue is uncanny; a place of silences and whispering echoes. It is a mighty table land between two streams and valleys. North of the Tongue the streams rise in one maze of pools and bogs confusedly, hardly a water-parting. On either hand they flow; the Hagg Beck in the eastern valley, and on the west the Troutbeck river. They meet and re-unite below the southern crags, making the table land almost a mountain island; an island haunted by the sounds that creep on running waters which encompass it.

The Tongue is shaped like a great horseshoe, edged by silver streams, and guarded by an outer rampart of high fells. From the highest point of the Tongue I could survey the whole expanse. Woundale and the standing stones; Swaindale* and Hallilands named by the Norsemen; Sadghyll and the hut circles; the cairns built by the stone men; Broad How of the fox borrans, Threshwaite Mouth the pass over to Hartsop; the Roman road on High Street above Thornthwaite Cragg, Blue ghyll and the land slide on Froswick; Ill Bell; and the walls of the old Norman deer park stretching for miles—'Troutbeck Park'.

Far away in Dale Head I saw the black Galloway cattle, dark specks slowly moving as they grazed. Sometimes I came upon the herd on the lower slopes of the Tongue—a reason for not taking Nip. The little shaggy cows were quiet with me, but fierce in defence of their calves against dogs. Sometimes I timed my ramble to cross the track of the shepherds, driving down a thousand sheep from the high fell for dipping. More rarely I saw a hiker who had lost his way, mistaking the pass from Hartsop, descending over into Troutbeck, instead of over Nan Bield pass into Hawes Water. Once there were two ravenous boys who had been out all night on Caudale moor in a mist. Usually I saw nobody the long day round.

Myself, I think the mist is beautiful; though troublesome for sheep gathering. It takes strange shapes when it rises from the valleys at sunset. Once I saw a gigantic image of the Norse Freya Holda, with her distaff, a monstrous female form half a mountain high, her sheep about her knees. They glided up the Rake on Ill Bell to mingle with celestial flocks, a myriad fleecy clouds overhead.

During storms the mist rushes down the valleys like a black curtain bellying before the wind, while the Troutbeck river thunders over the cauldron.

Old unhappy far off things, and battles long ago; sorrows of yesterday, today, and tomorrow; the vastness of the fells covers all with a mantle of peace.

I used to come back by High Buildings. I sheltered from a passing shower, or ate my bread and cheese while I rested on the sunny door-sill. I was watching a pair of hawks soaring high above the Tongue on motionless wings. The level sun

---

* Bruce Thompson writes, 'I have never heard "Swaindale" used as a place-name, but there is a "Swine Crag" near Hallilands, and Mrs. Heelis may have thought this is a corruption of "Swain Crag", hence "Swaindale" below it.'

gilded the under side of their feathers, pale buff against the blue. (So do we watch the great golden Hurricane planes.)*

I heard a rustling in the stable behind me, and I saw a solitary mouse; a house-mouse, with a long tail. He did not look thin or hungry; but his eagerness for cheese equalled poor Ben Gunn's on Treasure Island. He all but took it from my fingers. He whisked into his hole in the wall with crumbs, coming out again for more and more. I gave him as much as was good for him.

Another day I brought him cheese, I could hear him in the wall. He would not come out while I was there; but the cheese disappeared. A third time I brought cheese to High Buildings, there was nobody to eat it except me—the Solitary Mouse had departed!

He had run away down to the farm, with all his belongings tied up in a red pocket handkerchief. How do I know? I know because I know, and I know, and I *know*! Because once I was whirled through Hagg Ghyll, blown along by a merry March wind which tossed the Lent lilies and hustled my petticoat—and Piper Wind whistled a tune, a song without reason or rhyme unless it concerned that same Mouse?

This was the song of Piper Wind, in Hagg Ghyll.

> 'A cat came fiddling out of a barn
> With a pair of bag pipes under his arm,
> He could play nothing but Feedle cum fee,
> The mouse shall marry the Humble Bee!
> Pipe Wind! dance Mouse
> We'll have a wedding
> In our good house!'

* Written during World War 2, when Hurricanes and Spitfires were to be seen in the skies.

10
Sister Anne

Sister Anne

1932

After *The Tale of Little Pig Robinson* had been published in America, Beatrix Potter promised Mr. McKay another story.

Her version of the story of Bluebeard had been intended originally for inclusion in *The Fairy Caravan*, but it was found to be too long, so she now decided to offer *Bluebeard* to Mr. McKay as a story on its own. She omitted references to her Fairy Caravan characters and called it *Sister Anne*.

Beatrix Potter had always been interested in the seventeenth-century fairy-tales of Charles Perrault, and although she had followed the outline of his story, her version was about seven times as long. She drew freely on her imagination when writing it. The setting is in Lancashire, but except for one or two glimpses of country life, the tale has little in common with the rest of her work. It is too long to quote, but a brief résumé is given here.

Baron Bluebeard had been married seven times and had acquired several fortunes but no heir, so for the eighth time he married Fatima, the favourite daughter of a wealthy widow, in the hope that she would give him a son—but first making sure of a rich dowry. Five days after the wedding Fatima sent a message via a pigeon to her sister Anne, begging her to stay with her in Bluebeard's castle.

Anne found her sister sadly changed. She seemed terrified of her husband, and was obsessed with the fear that the castle held some grisly secret—a fear which was emphasized by the gruesome hints in the macabre songs sung by the one-eyed porter Wolfram, such as:

> '*What did he do with her tongue so rough?*
> *Unto the violl it spake enough!*
> *What did he do with her nose ridge?*
> *Unto the violl he made it a bridge.*
> > *Down, down, hey down.*
> *What did he do with her fingers small?*
> *He made him pegs to his violl withal.*'

Bluebeard's uncertain temper grew worse when he heard of a spinster who had been left a vast fortune, for now he wished he had not been in such a hurry to marry Fatima. He decided that she stood between him and the spinster's riches and would have to be removed. Perhaps he meant to frighten her to death because he left her the keys of the castle so that she could roam through the dismal passages in search of the hideous secret. Sister Anne found her insensible upon the floor of a dark chamber in front of a closet. Beatrix Potter does not disclose to her readers what awful sight met the terrified eyes of poor Fatima, but in a few well-chosen words she effectively conveys the spine-chilling atmosphere: 'The guttered candle had gone out and fallen from her hand. Her eyes were glazed upon the nameless horror that its light had made visible.'

Fatima recovered consciousness but was near madness. When Bluebeard returned he accused her of prying and threatened to make her look at the ghastly thing again, but fortunately he was interrupted by a visitor. Anne took her sister to the safety of their bower, and she at last managed to send a dove with a message to her brothers, asking for help. The brothers came and rescued Fatima and Anne, and slew the wicked Baron and his men. The castle crumbled into ruins to become a legend to the village children, who called it 'Bluebeard's Cupboard.'

It seems strange that in the preface of such a story Beatrix Potter should introduce three mice, one of which relates the tale to his companions. Later, at a very critical part of the plot, the mice are mentioned again as having 'nerves and fur on end', but after this Beatrix Potter seems to have forgotten all about the storyteller and his audience in the horror of the narrative, for they do not appear again. Perhaps they are remnants from *The Fairy Caravan* version.

The manuscript of *Sister Anne* was sent to Mr. McKay early in 1932. It was prepared with great care, some of the chapters being written and rewritten several times.

There were comparatively few amendments to her galley proofs, and apart from slight rearrangements of some of the paragraphs and the correction of a few small errors, only one sentence was altered—the last few words being changed from 'bringing small rain' to 'bringing small rain from the sea.'

Anne Carroll Moore, a children's librarian in New York, criticized *Sister Anne* unfavourably; but Beatrix Potter said, 'I did not agree with her objection to *Sister Anne*——(which I re-read with enjoyment and detached interest, whereas I am sick of Peter Rabbit!!)'.

Beatrix Potter, who was approaching sixty-six years of age, regarded the preparation of illustrations to be too much of a strain. The illustrations for *Sister Anne* were therefore prepared in America.

In commenting on the pen-and-ink drawings by Katharine Sturges, she told Mr. McKay, 'The illustrations are fine; Katharine Sturges has conveyed the sense of giddy height so well in the out-door subjects; and the black backgrounds give an effective air of mystery. Brother John who 'rode light' could not possibly have scrambled up and down a dry ditch in heavy plate armour; but that is a mere detail. The women's figures are beautiful, especially Fatima on horseback behind the Baron, and Anne coming down the cellar steps. Do thank Katharine Sturges from me for interpreting just what I meant! She cannot draw dogs—but no more can I. I should have sent a photograph of a wolf hound; they have *not* flap ears.'

Sister Anne was never published in this country, and apparently only unbound sheets were submitted for registration purposes. 'I dare say I can copyright this type unbound, without the pictures in it', she wrote.

Sister Anne was the last of Beatrix Potter's stories to be published during her lifetime.

11
Wag-by-Wall

Wag-by-Wall

(Printed posthumously)

The story of *Wag-by-Wall* dates back to November 1909, and at that time it was called *The Little Black Kettle*. The middle part of this story is unfinished, and the songs sung by the little black kettle and others are only roughly sketched in, but at least they show Beatrix Potter's method of planning her verses. 'I remember', said Beatrix Potter many years later, 'Sally's story stuck because the kettle was obstinately dumb.'

The old woman was Sally Scales who lived at Stott Farm in the woods, about a mile from Graythwaite, from where many of the Hill Top pigs were bought. She was very knowledgeable about cows and pigs.

This unfinished story of 1909 was then put on one side and it was not touched again until 1929, when it was rewritten as a part of *The Fairy Caravan*—but it was eventually taken out of *The Fairy Caravan* manuscript and never published in that form.

In the 1929 version of the story, the title was altered to *Wag-by-the-Wa'*, and the name of the old woman changed to Sally Benson. The 'Wag' was the pendulum of the ancient wall-clock, and Wa' was an abbreviation for 'Wall'.

Another ten or more years passed, and then towards the end of 1940 Mrs. Miller asked if she might print the story in *The Horn Book Magazine*, suggesting that it could be made into a Christmas story with its setting on Christmas Eve. In response to her request Beatrix Potter again rewrote it, this time leaving out all references to her Fairy Caravan characters.

In November 1941 in a letter to Mrs. Miller, she referred to the story saying: 'I cannot judge my own work. Is not *Wag-by-the-Wa'* rather a pretty story if divested of the "Jenny Ferret" rubbish? I thought of it years ago as a pendant to *The Tailor of Gloucester*—the lonely old man and the lonely old woman; but I never could finish it all.'

A year later she told Mrs. Miller, 'I think "Wag" is a pretty little story; I should like to print it some day in book form.' But little more was done until the following year, and then in August 1943 Beatrix Potter wrote, 'I am posting (ordinary post) a write-out of *Wag-by-the-Wall*, with some pruning which I hope you will think is an advantage? The longer verses left out—John Bunyan's too good, and my own too bad, at the end!' In a previous letter she had already asked Mrs. Miller, 'Do you think it is good taste to put in the Shepherd Boy's song in a story book? *Pilgrim's Progress* is next to the Bible; one would not wish to make it common place.'

'The corrections in the text are small', she wrote, 'but I am always inclined to go polishing. It was a very good idea of making it Christmas Eve.'

Wag-by-Wall

Mrs. Miller decided that she would like to hold back the story for the twentieth anniversary number of *The Horn Book Magazine,* and on November 5th 1943, Beatrix Potter wrote again saying, 'I cordially agree with the delay until May for printing the story in the Horn Book. It leaves time to see proofs, and I would like to make it as nearly word-perfect as I know how, for the credit of your 20th. anniversary. The winter's snow will be over by then. Would you desire to drop "Christmas Eve?" I am inclined to leave it *in,* with perhaps an added sentiment about the return of spring—(How the sad world longs for it!) I liked your suggestion of Christmas Eve because I like to think some of your story tellers may read the story, turn about with the old *Tailor of Gloucester* at Christmas gatherings in the children's libraries.'

In the final version, which is given here, Beatrix Potter left out not only all reference to her Fairy Caravan characters, but also the Shepherd Boy's song, and the following three verses of her own:

> Spring comes to the uplands, the cuckoo is calling,
> Sweet gale and green withy unfolding their leaves.
> There's honey bees humming and swallows a-coming
> —Come back pretty wanderers! come nest 'neath the eaves!
>
> Now Summer is smiling mid roses beguiling.
> With hay cocks and harvest and 'taties to store,
> Brave autumn comes prancing with fiddles and dancing
> And leads the kern supper with jigs on the floor.
>
> Blow cold winds of winter, we'll shutter the window!
> Shine keen frosty starlight when tempests are stilled;
> Is there snow on the door stane? Heap peats on the hearth stone!
> Sing little black kettle—the year is fulfilled.

Beatrix Potter never saw the final proofs, for seven weeks later she died.

THE LITTLE BLACK KETTLE
(Nov. 25th '09)
—Unfinished—

Once upon a time there was a frosty night, eh but it was cold. The stars twinkled and the crisp herb crinkled, and the sheep fleeces froze to the ground.

All across the fields was spread a sea of blue and silver moonlight, and the shadows of the trees and walls were very long and black. White gable ends and chimney stacks, and black under the eaves, and a floating whiff a peat smoke above Sally Scale's chimney. A white owl sat on the rigging and coughed.

Then he flitted across to the roof of the inn where there is a row of pot chimneys with round smiling faces—at least there seem to be faces in them by moonlight—like five little old women in bonnets.

The white owl made a bow to each old woman chimney. Then he flitted off the roof and over the little meadow, skimming over the white rag grass, and back across the orchard to Sally Scale's roof.

There was ivy on the end of Sally Scale's house, shimmering in the moonlight, and she would not have it cut; and she would not board the broken window of the peat house where the owl goes out and in, and she would not fill up the holes on the broken hearth-stone where the crickets sing; and she would not sweep the chimney or mend the slated roof—perhaps she could not afford. And she would not sell the carved oak kist★ that had been her Granny's, or Wag-by-the-wall her clock. And she would not buy herself a new kettle instead of the lile one she took to be patched. 'Patch it and patch it again, Isaac Blacksmith, but dursnot you mell with the spout,' says she, going up by the bellows and the anvil in a whisper 'I tell you it can sing!'

'More patch than bottom,' says Isaac Blacksmith, 'it will cost you a new one.' 'Them that pays the piper calls the tune; you mun patch it, and then you mun patch it, and you mun patch it again; I tell you it can sing.' 'Oh aye,' says Isaac Blacksmith, 'like a toom barrel.'

Sally Scales had her patched kettle home that very cold night, and the last of the peat and the last of the tea. And the patch had cost the last penny; old Sally's money was spent.

'Lile black kettle, lile black kettle'—said old Sally, 'sing me one more tune.'

Old Sally Scales sat by the hearth on a rocker, with a Book on her knees and a dying end of candle; she gathered up the peats with the tongs—'Lile black kettle, lile black kettle, just one more tune,' said old Sally.

And straightway the little black kettle began a low droning tune, murmuring and mumbling, and twittering and mumbling; old Sally leant over the hearth and the white owl up above peered down into the chimney and coughed.

★ Kist—Cumberland word for Chest.

The kettle sang louder, and a little clearer and louder, and words and a song came out of the spout—

'Lile black kettle—oh, lile black kettle—turn me about and about!' And old Sally turned the kettle and gaddered the peats—

It began again in a different tone and much faster—

[Here follows Beatrix Potter's rough outline of the unfinished song.]

> Little and slow, gather and go . . . . before
>
> and the kist answered it . . . . more
>
> Then the kettle sang again . . .
>
> Golden and bright . . .
>
> and the plates answered in the dresser . . .
>
> . . . . winter storm
>
> and the crickets answered . . .
>
> . . . . warm
>
> . . . . afford
>
> and the Book upon Sally's knees answered .
>
> . . . . in the Fear of the Lord
>
> . . . . day
>
> and the clock answered Work while its day, . . arise work pray
>
> . . . . bright
>
> . . . . silver light
>
> and the white owl leant further down over the chimney
>
> . . . . gold
>
> . . . . told

and the peats fell together with a shower of sparks, and a whiff of peat smoke went up the chimney that made the white owl cough and sneeze so that he tumbled over and came down into the hearth in a shower of soot, rattling stones and mortar, and something shining upset the kettle.

And old Sally woke up with a start, nearly smothered with soot, and the white owl was standing on her clean deal kitchen table bobbing and bowing and covered with soot. And old Sally made a bob curtsey to him and set open the house door and he flew out. And she shirk the soot out of her apron and crept away to bed.

And when she got up the next morning, the spout was broken off the lile black kettle and lying amongst the soot. And there was something shiny amongst the soot, five golden guineas; and when old Sally had tied her apron over her head and fumbled in the chimney and the soot, there was a many more, full up in an old woollen stocking, with a hole in the toe where they were coming out.

And Sally Scales bought blankets, and a pig, and more tea, and peat, and she had the spout mended but she would not buy a new one, she lived to the end of her days with the little black kettle.

WAG-BY-WA'*
1943

Once upon a time there was an old woman called Sally Benson who lived alone in a little thatched cottage. She had a garden and two fields, and there was grazing for a cow on the bog in summer while the fields were shut off to grow hay grass.

While her husband was alive, and able to work, they had lived comfortably. He worked for a farmer, while Sally milked the cow and fed their pig at home. After Sally became a widow she had a hard struggle. Tom Benson's long illness had left debts.

The cottage had belonged to Sally's mother, and to her grandparents before her. Her grandfather had been a cattle dealer. He bought and sold cattle at fairs, and made a bit of money. Nobody knew what he had done with it. He did not seem to spend much; and he never gave away one farthing. The old furniture was poor and plain; the only handsome piece that had belonged to the old man was 'Wag-by-the-wall' the clock. 'Tic tock: gold toes: tic: tock: gold: toes;' it repeated over and over; till any body might have felt provoked to throw a shoe at it—'Tic: tock: gold: toes:'

Sally took no notice. The clock had been saying those words ever since she was born. Nobody knew what it meant. Sally thought the world of the clock; and she loved her old singing kettle. She boiled water in it to make balm tea. She made it in a jug, and she grew the lemon-scented balm in her own garden. The kettle had been cracked and mended more than once.

The last time Sally took it to the smithy, Isaac Blacksmith looked at it over his spectacles and said—'More patch than bottom. It will cost you more than a new kettle.' 'Nay, nay! thou mun patch it, Isaac Blacksmith! I tell thee, thou mun patch it, and thou mun patch it again!' Sally stood on tiptoes to whisper—'I tell thee—it can sing.' 'Aye, aye? like a toom barrel?' said Isaac Blacksmith, blowing the bellows.

So Sally went on using her old kettle, and it sang to her. The kettle sang on the hearth, and the bees sang in the garden, where she grew old-fashioned flowers as well as potatoes and cabbages. There were wall flowers, pansies and roses in their season; balm for her own herb tea; and thyme, hyssop and borage that the honey bees love.

When Sally sat knitting by the cottage door she listened to the bees—'Arise—work—pray: Night follows day: Sweet Summer's day.' The bees hummed drowsily amongst the flowers—'To bed with sun: day's work well done.' The bees went home into their hives at dusk.

* In her letter to Mrs. Bertha Mahony Miller of August 28th 1943, Beatrix Potter gives the title as *Wag-by-the-Wall*.

Presently, indoors, the kettle began to sing; at first it sang gently and slowly, then faster and faster and more loud, as it came to boiling and bubbling over. It sang words something like this—to the tune of Ash grove—

'With pomp power and glory the world beckons vainly,
    In chase of such vanities why should I roam?
While peace and content bless my little thatched cottage,
    And warm my own hearth with the treasures of home.'

Sally Benson sitting by her fire on a winter's evening listened to the song of the kettle and she was contented. The cottage was warm and dry; it was whitewashed within and without, and spotlessly clean. There was no upstairs; only the kitchen, with cupboards and a box bed in the wall; and behind the kitchen was another tiny room and a pantry. Sally thought it was a palace; she had no wish to live in a big house.

Above the kitchen hearth at the south end of the cottage, there was a tall stone chimney stack standing up above the roof. Dry thatch is dangerous for catching fire from sparks, but there was plenty of green moss and house leek growing beside Sally Benson's chimney. Under the same long low roof at the north end was a wood shed.

A pair of white owls lived in the shed. Every summer, year after year, they nested there—though it could scarcely be called a 'nest'. The hen owl just laid 4 eggs on a bare board under the rafters. The little owlets were like balls of fluff, with big dark eyes. The youngest owlet, that hatched out of the last laid egg, was always smaller than the other three. Sally called him Benjamin.

When the little owlets were old enough to come out, they climbed up the thatch and sat in a row on the ridge of the roof. They hissed and craned their necks, and twisted their heads to watch their parents, mousing over the bog. The old owls flitted noiselessly over the coarse grass and rushes; they looked like great white moths in the twilight.

As the young owlets grew older, they became more and more hungry—the mother owl used to come out hunting food by daylight in the afternoons. The pee-wits over the bog swooped at her, crying and wailing, although she only sought for mice. Little breezes stirred the cotton grass; and Nancy Cow, knee deep in sedge and meadow sweet, blew warm breath lazily. Her big feet squelched amongst moss and eyebright and sundew; she turned back to firm turf and lay down to wait until Sally's voice called her home for milking.

When the old owls brought back mice they fed each wide gaping mouth in turn. Amongst the jostling and hissing and snatching, Benjamin was often knocked over. Sometimes he rolled down the thatch and fell off the roof. Sally picked him up and put him back. If the night had been wet she dried him by the fire. One morning she found all four baby owlets on the door step hissing at the cat.

Sally was very fond of the owls. Indeed she was fond of all things; a smiling friendly old woman with cheeks like withered apples.

But 'good times and hard times—all times go over'. While the hard times lasted they hit poor Sally very hard. There came a year of famine. Rain spoilt the hay and harvest, blight ruined the potato crop. Sally's pig died, and she was forced to sell her cow to pay the debts. There seemed to be nothing for it but to sell the cottage also, and end her days in the Poor House. She had nobody that she could turn to, no one to ask for help.

She and Tom had lost their only child—a daughter. Such a dear pretty girl she had been, with yellow curls, rosy cheeks, and blue eyes always laughing, until she ran away to marry a wastrel. Sally had sent money when a baby girl was born—another little 'Goldie-locks'. Time and again they wrote for money. When Sally had no more to send them they faded out of sight.

On Christmas Eve Sally Benson sat by the fire reading a letter, which the postman had brought her. It was a sad letter, written by a stranger. It said that her daughter and her son-in-law were dead, and that a neighbour—the writer—had taken in their child into her home out of pity. 'A bonny child she is; a right little Goldie-locks; eight years old, and tidy and helpful. She will be a comfort to her Grannie. Please send money to pay her fare, and I will set her on her way. I have five mouths to feed so I cannot keep her long. Please send money soon, Mrs. Benson.' Poor Sally! with no money and no prospect but the Poor House.

That Christmas Eve in the moonlight, a white owl sat on the chimney stack. When a cloud came over the moon, the owl dozed. Perhaps a wisp of blue smoke floating upwards made him sleepy—He swayed forward and fell into the chimney.

Down below Sally Benson sat by the hearth, watching the dying fire. One hand crumpled the letter in the pocket of her old black skirt; the other thin trembling hand was twisted in her apron. Tears ran down her poor old nose; she mopped them with her apron. She was not crying for her daughter whose troubles were over. She was crying for little Goldie-locks. She sat on and on, into the night.

At length there was a noise high up in the chimney. There came a rush of soot and stones; small stones and mortar came first. Several large heavy stones tumbled after; and the white owl on the top.

'Save us! what a dirty mess!' said Sally, scrambling to her feet and forgetting her troubles. She picked up the owl gently, and blew the soot off him, and set him on a chair. The soft feather tip of one wing was scorched; otherwise he was unhurt. But the soot had got into his eyes and his gullet; he blinked and gasped and choked. Sally fetched a drop of milk and fed him with a spoon.

Then she turned to sweep up the mess on the hearth. There was a smell of charred wood and burning wool. Amongst the stones was a black thing which smoked. It was an old stocking tied round the ankle with a bit of string. The foot was full of something heavy. Gold showed through a hole in the toes. 'Tic: toc: gold: toes:' said Wag-by-the-wall the clock.

Something seemed to have happened to Wag-by-the-wall; he went whirrr, whirra, whirr! trying to strike. When he struck at last he struck 14 instead of 12; and he changed his tick. Instead of saying 'Tic: toc: gold: toes: tic: toc: gold: toes!' he said 'Tick:er: tocks: Goldie: locks: tick:er: tocks: Goldie locks,' and those were his words ever after.

Sally Benson fetched her little grand-daughter to live with her. She bought another cow, and a pig, and she grew potatoes and balm and sweet flowers in her garden for the honey bees. And every summer the white owls nested in the wood shed.

Sally enjoyed a cheerful contented old age, and little Goldie-locks grew up and married a young farmer. They lived happily ever after, and they always kept the singing kettle and Wag-by-Wall the clock.

12

The Tale of the Faithful Dove

The Tale of the Faithful Dove

(Printed posthumously)

The Tale of the Faithful Dove tells the story of a pigeon called Mr. Vidler. In escaping from a hawk, his wife Amabella becomes trapped in the chimney of an empty house. She is befriended by a mouse, and eventually rescued with her new-born son, Tobias.

There are two manuscripts of *The Tale of the Faithful Dove*. The first, a stiff-covered exercise book, is inscribed 'Hastings Feb. 4th—14th. 07'; and the second, a paper-covered exercise book, is inscribed 'Hastings Feb. 14th.' In the latter, the text has been slightly amended.

Many years later Beatrix Potter wrote inside the cover of the first manuscript, 'Founded upon fact, but the incident occurred at another seaside town. I think Folkstone or Dover.' In the second, she tells us 'I used Winchelsea and *Rye* as background. This story was written for the Warne children.'

Nothing further was done until the following year, when Beatrix Potter sent the manuscript to Harold Warne and wrote:

2, Bolton Gardens
November 18th 1908

Dear Mr. Warne,

I am sending this to Primrose Hill in case you care to try it on the children. It seems to me to be more like the Tailor—older and sentimental.

If it went into print, the name 'Vidler' or Viddler' would perhaps have to come out—It tickled my fancy—but *the* 'Mr. Vidler' in Rye is a respectable citizen and brewer, several times Mayor!

It could be changed to Tidler (Thomas of silver and gold).

I have plenty of sketches and photographs of Rye, and it is a lovely background, but there would be great repetition in a *large* number of illustrations—

It seems to me to run to 3 or 4 little pen and ink sketches of the old houses, with birds on a small scale; and perhaps one large coloured drawing.

You will notice it is about a chimney and laying eggs. It was made before Roly Poly and Jemima. It is an objective. The story has been lying about a long time, and so have several others—

I should like to get rid of some one of them—when a thing is once printed I dismiss it from my dreams! and don't care what becomes of the reviewers. But an accumulation of half-finished ideas is bothersome.

I remain, yrs. sincerely,
Beatrix Potter

Although it was not printed then, Beatrix Potter seems to have managed to

roof be main rotten "said the boy.
"Butter fingers!" said the plumber.

Mr Tidler taught his son to fly in the course of the afternoon And Amabella exceedingly enjoyed a bath under the town pump.

By the time she had preened and dried her feathers, Toby was down in the road, taking short flights and running after his father, who was beside himself with rediculous joy. He turned round and round in circles, cooing with his head wrong side up, and his bill on the ground.

They roosted at home in the Ypres Tower that night

And ever after Mr Tidler billed and bowed devotedly upon the battlements, in proud admiration of his wife Amabella —

The last page of the second manuscript of *The Tale of the Faithful Dove*, written at Hastings in February, 1907

Mermaid Street, Rye
Rye 'has steep cobbled streets that go up like the ribs of a
crown'

Enid Linder

f

dismiss the story from her mind, for nothing more is heard of it until December 1918, when Fruing Warne wrote:

'Turning over some old papers, I came across a little M.S. of yours, apparently sent to H. in 1908, "Tidler" (Thomas of silver and gold). I send it back for your perusal. It certainly is very charming, and now that so many animals have been done, perhaps it is time to introduce a pigeon to the family.'

But although Mr. Warne called it 'A brilliant little MS', Beatrix Potter was not to be persuaded. Her eyesight was not what it used to be and she felt the story did not lend itself to the number of illustrations she had always had in her other books. 'The backgrounds of Rye are attractive,' she wrote, 'but it is nothing but pigeons over and over as regards illustrations. I could not possibly "dress up" the pigeons; no birds look well in clothes.'

A suggestion that another artist, Thorburn, noted for his fine bird paintings, should provide 'about 4 pictures of doves in appropriate positions', while she supplied half a dozen more pictures, was turned down by Mr. Warne. 'Thorburn's public and your public are at opposite poles,' he wrote, 'and in my opinion, the one incorporated with the other would injure both. Quite apart from that, I do not think it possible to get Thorburn to entertain such a scheme . . . Mr. Thorburn himself is, I believe, actively engaged on an important work.'

In reply Beatrix Potter wrote, 'I am sorry to tell you I have jibbed at the pigeons. I have never been good at birds; and whatever you say—I cannot see them in clothes—the story is sentimental not comic. I did think at the time, that with the example of a good painter of birds, I might have done part—but probably you were right in saying Mr. Thorburn would be too busy and too big.'

So the pigeon was never introduced into the family, and it was not until 1956 that the story appeared in print posthumously. It was again published in 1970.

The *Tale of the Faithful Dove* as given here, is taken from the second of the two manuscripts referred to above. The name 'Tidler' is used instead of the original 'Vidler'. Beatrix Potter has lightly pencilled this alteration in both the manuscripts.

THE TALE OF THE FAITHFUL DOVE

There is a town—a little old red-roofed town, a city of gates and walls. It has steep cobbled streets that go up, like the ribs of a crown; and a grey flint church on the summit.

The gold weather-cock glitters in the sunshine, and the pigeons wheel round it in quick short flights. As they turn and tumble, their wings gleam white against the thunder clouds over the sea.

On hot harvest days they fly out to the cornfields; but always with an eye on safety and their nests high up in the Ypres Tower—and the other eye for the falcons across the marsh at Camber—

But more often they are pecking about in the grass-grown streets, amongst the cobble stones of the market place or in the dusty yard of the windmill by the river.

'Why should a pigeon risk his tail in Winchelsea Marsh, while there is corn in Rye?' said Mr. Tidler, bobbing and bowing and strutting around.

'*My* ancestors were Antwerps. *We* carried messages for the smugglers. My great great grandfather used to cross the Channel twice a fortnight in a fishing boat, Mr. Tidler!' replied Amabella, preening her wings.

'My love, your great great grandmother was a tumbler!' said Mr. Tidler.

But although Mr. Tidler had differences with his wife Amabella, they were a most devoted pair, after the habit of pigeons who marry for life. They made their nest of rubbishy twigs and straws in a hole on the Ypres tower, where the wall-flowers grow.

Amabella had laid an egg in the nest. She had left it and was sunning herself on a broad flat stone at the edge of the battlements.

Mr. Tidler was hurrying up and down and round and round, cooing excitedly, turning in his bright pink toes, and bobbing and bowing, regardless of the complete inattention of his wife.

A score of other doves slanted across the face of the cliff below—Amabella slid off the stone and followed them, with a sudden clapping of wings in the hot silent air.

It was Sunday; but indeed even on week days the little old town seems always asleep. The sea has slipped away across the marsh and left it stranded, and it dozes through the lazy summer days like the Castle of Sleeping Beauty.

But the doves are not 'asleep upon the house top'. They are down in the Miller's yard, outside West Gate on the Winchelsea Road.

There are a dozen red and particoloured tumblers, black and white nuns, ruffled jacobins, and dusky blue-rocks, trampling about and bobbing their heads as they gobble up the grain.

340

Mrs. Tidler is in the thick of it, very hungry and pick peck pecketting.

Mr. Tidler is on the outskirts, anxious and indignant, but still bobbing and bowing.

'When a person has laid an egg, a person should *not* leave the fortifications,' said Mr. Thomas Tidler.

He himself spent much of his time doing fancy steps on the long black muzzle of a rusty French gun.

'My great grand-uncle carried little screws of paper twisted round his leg between Rye and Sandwich,' said Amabella.

'Why should we stay within walls in times of peace?' asked a little white dove.

Mr. Tidler had just tripped over a straw, and before he had time to gather himself together, to reply in argument—something came round the sails of the windmill like a thunder bolt.

Down went the little white dove; and then up and away in the claws of a peregrine falcon.

The falcon's mate was following close behind; he only missed his mark because he hesitated whether to strike Mr. or Mrs. Tidler.

He swept between them undecided and wheeled up in circles over the mill, ready for a fresh stoop at the pigeons as they raced back into the town.

The short-winged doves threaded their way amongst the sheds with sudden twists and turns, flying low and dodging into the streets, where they hoped that the peregrine would not follow them.

One of them in its terror dashed in at an open window.

The cock pigeon with pathetic senseless courage flew behind his wife, to keep between her and the danger.

But alas, the tiercel was a judge of pigeon-pie, and he had taken a fancy for the plumpness of Amabella! He singled out his intended victim, and ignored the other pigeons.

Twice he missed his stroke, as she dodged frantically amongst the chimney stacks; most unaccountably missed the second time, when Amabella's fate seemed sealed!

But Mrs. Tidler reverted to the habit of her ancestral relations—she gave an unmistakable 'tumble' and mysteriously disappeared.

The peregrine, overshooting his mark, found himself above the church, where he was disconcerted by the sweet strains of the organ.

He soared upwards high over the town and away across the marsh.

Mr. Tidler, panting and scared almost to death, tumbled into a holly bush in the church yard.

The congregation were just coming out. 'There do have been a hawk after them pigeons,' remarked the sexton.

Mr. Tidler wished that the hawk had taken *him* instead of the little white dove, when he could not find Amabella. Pigeons are not very intelligent but they are unusually faithful.

He flew back to the Ypres Tower, in faint hope that she might have slipped home by Watch Bell Lane. But the nest was deserted and the egg was cold.

Mr. Tidler could not bear to look at it; he did not go near it again.

He wandered about the red tiled roofs, moping and disconsolate. At night he roosted on the ridge of the church, all out in the rain.

A white owl came and looked at him and seemed about to make a remark; but it changed its mind and went away.

Next day Mr. Tidler ate nothing and moped; his draggled appearance attracted the attention of a black tom cat. It climbed on the roof of a shed in the street called 'The Mint', with the intention of catching him.

Mr. Tidler flopped languidly across the road on to another roof, and mourned for Amabella.

Amabella's history was simple. In twisting and ducking amongst the chimney stacks to escape from the peregrine, she had—half by accident—half of purpose—dived down the mouth of a tall red chimney pot.

The chimney belonged to the garret of an empty house, and the fireplace was stuffed up with a sack.

Mrs. Tidler, breathless and terrified, fell down upon the sack, and lay there comfortably enough.

There was sufficient room for her to stand up and flap her wings when she recovered. But it was impossible for her to fly upwards and out at the chimney-pot three yards above her head—a little circle of blue sky and scudding clouds over a shaft of darkness.

It is one thing to dive down a narrow hole with the wings closed; and quite another matter to mount—as a pigeon does—with beating wings and in circles.

Amabella was trapped!

She had a good deal of corn in her crop, which sustained her during the first night.

And next morning she laid another egg.

She made a satisfactory warm nest for it in the sack, and commenced to sit.

'I shall have to sit here for 16 days,'[*] said Amabella with contented resignation.

But towards night she began to get hungry. And by the time that the stars came out and peeped down the chimney—Amabella was decidedly faint.

[*] In Beatrix Potter's first draft she wrote 'for   weeks', leaving a space to be filled in later. In her second draft she pencilled in 'for 16 days?' Warne's published edition states 'for seventeen days', having evidently verified the correct period for sitting on the eggs.

Once she woke up suddenly and saw a queer round face looking down upon her as she sat on her nest. Amabella thought that it was the moon; but it was a white owl.

And there were strange noises in the garret of the empty house, noises of a very very little squeaky fiddle, and noises of pattering and dancing, and the buzzing of blue-bottle flies in the middle of the night.

Amabella between dreaming and fainting cooed drowsily to the music.

Early in the morning while she dozed upon her nest, there came a scrambling amongst the bricks of the chimney place—

'Who was that cooing to my dancers? Who has been making music in my chimney?' asked a little old mouse.

'For the love of wheat and barley, send a message to Mr. Tidler! I cannot leave my egg, I cannot get out to feed! I am starving, Madam Mouse!' said Amabella.

The mouse, who was very small and old and dressed in antique fashion, in a silk gown with lace ruffles, examined Mrs. Tidler through a pair of tortoiseshell glasses—

'Indeed, Madam, I commiserate you. I have had no experience in laying eggs; but I comprehend the pangs of hunger. The Ypres Tower? I will despatch a messenger at Cockcrow. I fear that I have no refreshment to offer to you, Madam,' added the friendly mouse. 'This is an empty house, and we are church mice. We removed to our present abode on account of the owls. I am a mouse of genteel descent,' said she, smoothing her faded silk petticoat.

Amabella thanked her warmly. She was revived by friendship and described the exploits of her own ancestors, the Antwerp carriers—

'You do not say so, Madam? The lace of these ruffles was smuggled; my great great grandmother found it in the secret recess of an old bureau—'

'You interest me extremely, Madam; *my* great great great great grandfather was a cellar-mouse in the house of a Huguenot grocer.'

'You may command my services; I will despatch a dozen starlings. They shall scour the roofs of Rye for Mr. Tidler.'

So it happened that in the grey dawn of the second morning Mr. Tidler, moping and dozing upon the roof of Rye Town Hall, was aroused by a cock starling.

It pecked him, and directed him, half awake to the top of a tall red chimney-pot in Mermaid Street.

'Bless my tail and toes! Amabella, my love? Amabella?' exclaimed Mr. Tidler, strutting round the top of the chimney-pot, and craning over the abyss, at imminent risk of falling in head foremost.

'Leave off that ridiculous noise, and fetch me corn at once! I have laid an egg,' said Mrs. Tidler in smothered tones below.

So for more than two weeks, day by day industriously, Mr. Tidler picked up corn for two—for two? enough for half a dozen; it would have filled a sack!

He collected such quantities in his ardour, and with such boldness, that folks talked about him in the market. They threw him handfuls of grain, and wondered to see him fly away with it and return presently with an empty crop for more and more.

In and out between the horses' feet, under carts and barrows, or perching fearlessly on an open sack to sample the oats—bobbing and bowing his thanks—there seemed to be no limit to the appetite and industry of Mr. Tidler.

He flew backwards and forwards to the chimney pot and dropped in the grain.

All day long he either carried corn, or strutted round and round the top of the pot, cooing to the imprisoned Amabella.

At night he roosted on the pot with his tail inside, and cooed in his sleep.

The church mice grew quite fat in that empty house. And so did Mrs. Tidler, and so did her son who had hatched out of the egg.

'I have called him Tobias, Mr. Tidler,' cooed Mrs. Tidler down below.

'You have called him nothing of the sort, Amabella. He shall be named Toby. Your great *great* grandmother was a tumbler!' replied Mr. Tidler strutting round and round up above, and shutting out half the sky.

'How shall we ever get out? He will be ready to fly tomorrow,' said Mrs. Tidler.

'Do you see ere a blue-rock dove up thur? He do pick up corn by the bushel, and carries it up by yonder,' the sexton down in the road called up to a plumber and his boy, at work on a leaking roof.

'A cock blue-rock? He's been strutting and bobbing these two hours on a chimney pot in Mermaid Street. Curtchying into the chimney, like as if he were looking for a sweep!' added the plumber with aroused curiosity. 'Hop across, Tom, and take a look.'

The apprentice scrambled over two intervening roofs, clattering over the tiles.

The starlings who nest in the gables flew out, scolding and screaming; and Mr. Tidler paused in his dance.

The sexton went round into Mermaid Street and watched from the opposite pavement, while the boy climbed upon the chimney stack of the empty house.

Mr. Tidler stuck to his post in speechless indignation; he threw himself into an attitude of defiance, with one wing raised in the air.

When the intruder stooped over the pot to look down—Mr. Tidler rose upon his toes with a hinnying noise, and slapped his wings across the boy's face, knocking off his cap which fell into the chimney.

'He's been and gone and done it!' chuckled the sexton. 'Climb in at the garret window, lad; the catch is broken.'

Tom scrambled cautiously down the roof. Mr. Tidler remained on the chimney pot, uttering angry crows, and puffing out his neck.

Amabella and her son down below were hissing and slapping at the cap, which had fallen on the top of them.

The catch of the old-fashioned leaded window gave way with a push, and the boy stepped down into the garret through the cobwebs.

'Here be corn for sure; but it be shelled,' said Tom, looking round in perplexity at the piles of husks, relics of the supper-parties of the friends of Madam Mouse.

He pulled the sack out of the fireplace. It was followed by a stream of grain and mortar and dirt.

On the top of it came his cap, and Mrs. Tidler and her son, hissing and flapping and dazzled with the sudden return to daylight.

Tom drove the young pigeon into a corner and caught it.

Amabella bounced out at the window. The boy got out and climbed up the roof again, pursued by the two old pigeons, who flew wildly round his head.

'He be a right fat 'un!' said Tom, holding up his prize.

'I loikes pigeon poy!' said the objectionable plumber, leaning over the chimneys of the next door roof.

'He be a beauty to keep in a dove box,' said Tom, stroking the even markings of the feathers—'*I* catched him,' he added sullenly.

Mr. Tidler in desperation dashed at him from behind, and knocked the cap over his eyes.

The boy clutched at the cap, and Toby slipped through his fingers, fluttering down the tiles till he lay in the spouting overhanging the street.

Mr. Tidler alighted on the water spout near him; he cooed and bobbed in wild defiance.

Amabella looked on from the house on the opposite side of the street; she was feeling stiff.

'I be afeared to follow him there; this roof be main rotten,' said the boy.

'Butterfingers!' said the plumber.

Mr. Tidler taught his son to fly in the course of the afternoon. And Amabella exceedingly enjoyed a bath under the town pump.

By the time she had preened and dried her feathers—Toby was down in the road, taking short flights and running after his father, who was beside himself with ridiculous joy. He turned round and round in circles, cooing with his head wrong side up, and his bill on the ground.

They roosted at home in the Ypres Tower that night.

And ever after Mr. Tidler bobbed and bowed devotedly upon the battlements in proud admiration of his wife Amabella—

The opening page of The Faithful Dove as written in the first and second Manuscripts

First Manuscript

There is a town—a little old red-roofed town that I know—a city of gates and walls. It has steep cobbled streets that mount—like the ribs of a crown; to the grey flint church on the summit.

The gold weather-cock glitters in the sunshine; and the pigeons wheel round in short sharp flights. As they turn and tumble, their wings show white against the dark clouds over the sea.

Sometimes on hot harvest days they fly out to the corn fields; but always with an eye on safety and their nests in the Ypres Tower, high up on the walls of the town. And the other eye for the falcons across the marsh at Camber.

But more often they peck about in the grass-grown streets, amongst the cobblestones of the market-place, or in a dusty yard of the flour-mill down by the river.

Second Manuscript

There is a town—a little old red-roofed town, a city of gates and walls. It has steep cobbled streets that go up, like the ribs of a crown; and a grey flint church on the summit.

The gold weather-cock glitters in the sunshine, and the pigeons wheel round it in quick short flights. As they turn and tumble, their wings gleam white against the thunder clouds over the sea.

On hot harvest days they fly out to the cornfields; but always with an eye on safety and their nests high up in the Ypres Tower—And the other eye for the falcons across the marsh at Camber—

But more often they are pecking about in the grass-grown streets, amongst the cobble stones of the market place or in the dusty yard of the windmill by the river.

It is interesting to note that Beatrix Potter liked unusual words, and she used the 16th century 'stoop' for the descent of the falcon on its prey, instead of the more usual 'swoop'. Also, at the end of the second manuscript there is a note about falcons which reads: 'Falconers call the female peregrine "the falcon"; she is much larger than the male bird, who is known as the "tiercel". There used to be peregrine falcons at Camber Castle; I don't think they breed there now; but there are still a few about the chalk cliffs on the south coast.'

Rye Church
'A grey flint church on the summit . . . Mr. Tidler . . .
tumbled into a holly bush in the church yard'

Enid Linder

'The doves asleep upon the house tops'
An inscription on the back reads—'Sleeping Beauty—The doves asleep upon the house tops—H. B. Potter—March 99'. She must have had this picture in mind when writing *The Tale of the Faithful Dove*, for facing page 1 of the first manuscript are German words, which when translated read—'The doves also slept there on the roof'

PART THREE

MISCELLANEOUS WRITINGS

13
Fairy-tales

Fairy-tales

In her Journal Beatrix Potter tells how in July 1894 she spent one hot summer afternoon at Lennel, Berwickshire, reading Chamber's *Rhymes and Fairy-Tales*.

This was no passing interest. Beginning in the nursery at Bolton Gardens, the love of fairy-tales lasted the rest of her life. But it was not only a love of fairy-tales. In the Journal, too, we get glimpses of what the world of fantasy meant to her. The realm of fairyland was part of her secret life. 'I remember I used to half believe and wholly play with fairies when I was a child', she wrote, and for her the 'whole countryside belonged to the fairies'. Hedgehogs were fairy creatures. When the corn escaped mildew it must be because of the work of the fairies. When she sat on Oatmeal Crag near Esthwaite Water and looked down on a cluster of toadstools, they seemed to be fairies 'singing and bobbing and dancing in the grass'. And when she watched the weird dance of the fell ponies which she describes in some of her Fairy Caravan writings, they too were fairy creatures, 'Who had taught them? Who had learned them "dance the heys" in that wilderness?'

Perhaps it was because of this fairy element she infused into the story of *The Tailor of Gloucester* that it became 'my own favourite amongst my little books', as Beatrix Potter wrote in one of her presentation copies.

She often saw incidents too, that happened to her in the light of a fairy-tale. 'Just at the turn to Hawkshead', she wrote 'is an old-fashioned house, and at the gate of the carriage drive was the most funniest old lady, large black cap, spectacles, apron, ringlets, a tall new rake much higher than herself and apparently no legs: she had stepped out of a fairy-tale'. And she also tells how at Camfield Place in her early childhood she used to sit for hours looking out of a window 'into the stable yard and wondering if there was an enchanted Prince below; but he made no sign'.

When she was young Beatrix Potter read fairy-tales; in her twenties she drew pictures to illustrate them; and years later when most of her *Peter Rabbit* books were written, and new ideas were slow to come, she still felt the urge to write, and her thoughts turned to the old favourites—Red Riding Hood, Cinderella and Blue-beard.

Of the four fairy-tales included in this section, two, *The Fairy in the Oak*, and *Llewellyn's Well*, are original, and two are her *own* versions of Red Riding Hood and Cinderella. The first three were written in 1911 or 1912, and Cinderella about 1930.

In Fleet did most of the work; no shepherd could

count surer, I suppose a lamb was missed. If a lamb strayed into the thicket, Fleet saw it omitting pushing it gently towards the flock. While the sheep fed in the open he stretched himself to sleep in the sun. He was a grave quiet dog;

Facsimile from a paragraph in the manuscript of *The Idle Shepherd Boy*, written in October 1911. 'It is a story of the calling Wolf! wolf!' wrote Beatrix Potter, 'it ends all right.'

Several rough drafts of this unfinished story exist, with variations in the text of each; but the point of interest is that in this paragraph Beatrix Potter alternated between ordinary writing and code-writing, even though fourteen years had elapsed since she had used this medium regularly.

The example reads as follows, code-writing being in italics:

'For Fleet did most of the work; no shepherd could count surer, and *never a lamb* was missed. *If a lamb strayed into the thicket, Fleet saw* it and turned it *pushing it gently towards the flock. While the sheep fed* in the open he stretched himself to sleep in the sun. He was a grave quiet dog . . .'

No code-writing appears on any of the other sheets.

A sheet of code-writing found amongst Beatrix Potter's drawings. It is a rough draft of a story promised to two little New Zealand girls, telling of a cockle-shell fairy. In the end, however, they were sent her story of *The Fairy in the Oak*

THE FAIRY IN THE OAK

The story of *The Fairy in the Oak* was a present for two little girls in New Zealand called Kitty and Hilda, and it is believed to have been written in 1911. In 1929 Beatrix Potter rewrote it as the last chapter of *The Fairy Caravan*.

She had originally promised the children a story about a little cockle-shell fairy, and long afterwards this unfinished fairy-tale was found at Castle Cottage, written in code on a sheet torn from an old exercise book. When transcribed it reads:

Peermingle was a fairy—a sea fairy—while the tide was rippling over the sands—but when the little waves had danced away down to the sea leaving miles and miles of yellow sands shining in the sun—then Peermingle was very like any other cockle shell asleep, half buried in a sandy bed.

Peermingle was a very very little fairy, and she had been born in the sea like the fishes, so she could only play and dance as long as waves were by her feet.

The cockles came down the sand banks hop, hop, hop, and Peermingle raced after the tide, along the little wet rivulets, and when a wave ran away too fast and left her stranded, Peermingle shut up snap and was a cockle shell stranded amongst shells and seaweed, and then another wave ran back and splashed over Peermingle, and Peermingle jumped up laughing and clapping her hands and raced another down the shallows after the tide. She was always laughing and singing and dancing as long as her feet were in the water.

All the shrimps and crabs and flounders danced in the tideway with Peermingle. Sometimes she swam up the river that winds across the sands at low tide, and the flounders followed her for they do not mind fresh water, up and up the river to the bridge between banks of seashore where the oyster-catchers cry, up and up to where the bluebells nod over the water and ring their bells to Peermingle, ringle, tingle, tingle.

Peermingle turned back at the bridge and swam down the river to meet the rising tide, laughing and clapping her hands . . .

[There is one more line, with spaces left for words—and then the writing ends.]

In the little note book containing the first version of *The Fairy in the Oak*, the text of which follows here, Beatrix Potter had faintly pencilled the words: 'For 'tis my faith that every flower enjoys the air it breathes'.

The Fairy in the Oak

Written for two little New Zealand fairies—
by promise.

My dear Kitty and Hilda,

This is not the fairy tale which I promised to tell you—that other one was about a little cockle-shell fairy who lived on Lancaster Sands. I know a good deal about her, but not enough yet to finish her story.

This fairy tale here was told to me all complete; only the man that told it to me, did not know that there was any fairy in it at all. Perhaps *you* may say—there is not much fairy either—only a great deal of English history.

James shook his head and said he did not know what to think—He was building a wall in my orchard while he talked to me; this is what had happened at the last place where he had been working. He had helped to take down an enormous oak, the finest tree for miles around—and that oak did not want to leave the place where it had grown.

You have such great tracts of bush in New Zealand, that it is necessary to burn them for a clearing. Therefore you will think the felling of one tree a small matter. But you have seen that we have fewer trees in England; and many are only hedge-row elms.

There is something great and glorious about an English oak. Oaks were held sacred by the druid priests in the days of the ancient Britons; and the Saxons who followed, respected the druid's tree.

Towns with Saxon names such as Oakham and Okehampstead mean the Saxon 'hamlets of the oak'.

William the Conquerer came next, and he ordered a record of all parts of England to be written down in Doomsday Book; and because there were no maps, they must describe the land carefully in writing, and they wrote down objects that stood up far off—a hill, a square church tower, or a very tall tree.

When I was a little girl, my Grandfather had a house in Hertfordshire, and in the field there was an oak tree that is named as a boundary mark in Doomsday Book.

When I knew it, it was split into several parts; my Grandfather bound it together with chains. It was green upon the top in spite of its thousand years. It must have been a notable, outstanding, full grown tree as long ago as 1085.

This north country tree in my story was younger than the Doomsday Oak. It was in its prime in Queen Elizabeth's reign—I know its age by the rings; and by comparison with other, younger trees planted in 1603 by a yeoman named Stephen Green. The man who plants and trains an oak rears for himself a noble monument. Men may forget his name; but the tree grows clean and straight, through centuries, to thank him.

This little oak grew strong and tough, deep rooted amongst rocks, off a corner by the old high road between two market towns. At first the road was but a winding track for pack-horses with their loads.

Then it was widened sufficiently for rough country carts; and still the oak grew green amongst the rocks above. The timber waggons passed below, bearing other oaks to build our ships—old England's wooden walls. But this oak stood out of reach; it grew another hundred years in peace.

Now our ships are made of iron, and iron horses rush along our roads—and the District Council ordered the widening of that corner, and the removal of the rocks and tree, to make the high road safe for motor cars.

Surely it is cruel to cut down a very fine tree! Every dull dead thud of the axe hurts the little green fairy who lives in its heart.

The fairy of the oak had been a peaceful little spirit for many hundred years—but now she was so angry—she nearly killed three men, and lamed a horse.

In the days when the oak was a sapling without any fairy, there were wolves in the woods. The dalesmen hunted them with hounds.

The fairy played under the trees, a wolf ran by; she was frightened and jumped into the little oak tree's boughs.

There she felt so safe and happy, that she stayed, and made it her home. And because it had a fairy—that oak was a lucky tree, and grew straight and tall.

Each of the finest trees in the wood had its fairy as well. There were beech fairies, and birch fairies, alder, pine, and fir fairies, all dressed in green, in the leaves of their own proper tree.

In spring when the trees grow new leaves—each fairy got her a new green gown.

They never went far from the trees that they lived in and loved; only on moonlight nights they came down, and danced on the moss together.

In winter when the trees were cold and bare, each fairy disappeared under the bark, and curled up in the heart of its tree to sleep till Spring. Only the fir and pine fairies kept awake and danced upon the snow; because the pines and fir trees do not lose their needle leaves; and that is why the fir trees sing in the wind on frosty winter's nights.

The oak fairy had danced with the pine fairies under the Hunter's moon, because an oak tree keeps its leaves much later than birch and beech. But the last of the russet oak leaves blew off in a November gale, and she settled herself to sleep.

The oak was enormous, tall and bold; it held up its head against wind and snow, and scorned the wintry weather.

—But alas! the Surveyor of the District Council has no sentiment; and no respect either for fairies or for oak trees—

The pine needle fairies were awake and watched, from the tops of their trees further back in the wood. The pines swayed about in the wind, and moaned and shivered. But the little oak fairy slept through it all.

There was Mr. Thompson and two members of the Highway Board on bicycles; and the Surveyor in a trap; with poles, a tape, the chain links, and the theodolite on three legs. They clambered about the rocks, and measured, and squinted through the theodolite. Then they made marks in note books, and hammered in pegs; got on their bicycles and rode away.

Nothing happened for two months.—Except a gale at Christmas, which blew down an ash. It fell crashing amongst the rocks; its fairy fell out shrieking, and ran up and down the wood, in tattered yellow leaves. She hid herself in an empty bird's-nest; and the wood was silent again.

In January a number of men arrived, they had a small wheeled hut, barrows and a quantity of tools. They set up a sort of camp, and commenced to cut away the coppice, and to blast the rocks.

My friend James had orders to use some of the stone for a new roadside wall—but first the oak must go.

They thought to take it down in a day, but it took them three; it was as hard as iron.

From daylight to twilight of the short winter days, they hacked and sawed. The blows of the axes and hammering wedges woke every fairy in the wood.

And when the oak was part way through—how it did creak and groan! The little fairy within it sobbed and moaned; and cried again and scolded—and grew fierce and angry.

The great tree groaned louder; and suddenly without warning, came down with a roar.

The wood men stumbled helter-skelter out of its way over the slippery rocks. The arms of the tree were broken, and its fairy was stunned and lay still.

Then for another two days the woodmen sawed its branches off painfully, and its head.

Perhaps all the noise in the wood was the grating noise of the saws—perhaps it was the wind sighing in the pines, and the little tree fairies lamenting.

At length the oak was one great smooth trunk, [   ]* foot run of clean timber in the bole without a branch. They turned it over the rocks with levers, and it rolled down into the road.

But roll as it would—the little oak fairy danced with rage on the top of it—The woodmen did not see her; they fastened chains round the oak, and set to hoist it on the timber waggon.

The upper end of the oak began to rise—the little fairy sprang upon it—snap went the chains and knocked a woodman on the head. He was taken away senseless.

The oak lay in the road all night—It all but upset Farmer Dixon's trap. He vowed there was a little creature like a green squirrel, sitting on the trunk, that clapped its hands and jumped in the light of his cart lamp, causing his horse to shy.

In the morning the men came back with double chains. The hoar frost was white

* Beatrix Potter had left a space, intending to put in the length of the trunk.

and slippery; the iron froze in their hands. How the oak groaned and heaved as they raised it! The oak fairy screamed and threw herself against the chains; but she could not break them again.

The thinner end of the oak was raised, and the heavier end—with a last great effort, its whole length lay along the wheels.

Immediately there was another accident—the brake gave way. The waggon was standing on a slippery hill; of its own accord it rushed upon the horses.

The waggoners ran shouting to the horses' heads, and drove them at a gallop, to keep the waggon upright in the middle of the road. One of the woodcutters had a fit. The waggon floundered along, over-running the terrified horses; and the fairy danced and screamed on the great log.

'We got it pulled up in the bottom,' said James. 'We were white and shaking, and the horses in a sweat with fear.'

So far as I remember, after that, they came safely through the woods by Hawkshead Hall. The fairy was tired, and sat huddled on the log. They turned the corner by the walnut tree, sweeping down a length of dry stone wall with the tail board of the waggon.

They took Hawkshead Hill with an extra pair of horses. Six horses strained at the chains, up and up. They gained the top and rested. Five horses were unharnessed, the brake was screwed down hard, to face the steep descent.

Far down below from the valley came a humming sound,—the noise of Coniston Saw mill.

The fairy heard it and understood; she sprang off her poor oak tree, and fled into the woods.

The horse in the shafts took fright, and by way of a last accident, horse—oak—and waggon were overturned. No wonder James said it was very strange, and that he was glad to get away alive.

But there comes comfort after trouble, and usefulness out of pain.

The oak-fairy wandered up and down, homeless. One day she climbed into one tree; another day she climbed into another tree. She always chose an oak tree; still she could not settle to rest.

Whenever a load of sawn timber came back up the road from the saw-mill the fairy came down to the road, and looked at it wistfully. But it was always ash or larch or plane—not oak.

She wandered further afield in springtime into the meadows outside the woods. There was fresh green grass for the lambs in the meadows; and young green leaves in the woods. But no new green gown grew for the oak fairy; her leaves were withered and torn.

One day she sat in a tree top, and the west wind blew over the land. It brought

355

sounds of the lambs and the plovers calling, and rushing sounds of spring floods—And strange unusual sounds from the water-meadows—clear ringing blows upon oak.

'Men do not fell trees in May when the sap is rising. Why does this sound stir my heart and make my feet dance in spite of me? How can I hear cruel nails and hammers and saws upon oak wood—and yet feel glad?' said the Fairy of the Oak.

She came down from the wood, and her feet danced across the meadow, between cuckoo flowers and water marigolds, to the banks of the flooded beck, where men were building a bridge.—A new bridge where none had been before, a wooden bridge with such a span—across the rushing flood; and the straight brave timbers that spanned it, were made of the fairy's oak.

Now she lives there contentedly, and may live there through hundreds of years; for well-seasoned oak lasts for ever—well seasoned by trial and tears.

> Alike in summer and winter, the bridge stands firm and strong;
>> over blue rippling shallows and pebbles—or brown floods racing along.
> The little toddling children, pass by to school, or play;
>> the farm wife with her basket—all take that shortened way.
> The patient plodding horses, bend to the easier road;
>> and Something leads them over, and helps to lighten their load.
> It wears a duffle grey petticoat and a little russet-brown cloak;
>> and that is the end of my story of
>>> The Fairy in the Oak.

LLEWELLYN'S WELL

Although the date of this fairy-tale is uncertain, it was probably written in 1911 or 1912.

On the manuscript are the words 'Made and part written at Gwaynynog, Denbigh'. The story is incomplete towards the end, but Beatrix Potter had made rough notes which indicate her intention for the missing paragraphs. The name of the Well is believed to be imaginary.

Llewellyn's Well

In a little stone house beneath a great chestnut tree dwelt two little Welsh girls, and they were twins. One was called Evadne, and one was called Myfanwy, and their father was a gardener, and his name it was John Jones.

The little stone house was roofed with blue slates; but when the chestnut flowers snowed down in Springtime—then its roof was whitey pink. And when the chestnut leaves rained down in autumn—then its roof was gold and russet.

The garden lay behind the house, inside a mossy red brick wall. It was filled with apricots, apples and pears; and peaches in their season.

In Summer there were white and damask roses, and the smell of thyme and musk. In Spring there were green gooseberries and throstles, and the flowers they call ceninen.* And leeks and cabbages also grew in that garden; and between long straight grass alleys, and apple-trained espaliers, there were beds of strawberries, and mint and sage. And great holly trees and a thicket of nuts; it was a great big garden.

John Jones worked therein and whistled. And very often sometimes while he worked, his wife Morved Edwards Jones locked her house door, and went down the long hill to the town.

And because the hill was long, returning, and the children were two little twins, she left them at home behind her, locked out of the house on the door-step.

'The fire is banked with cinders; the sun shines warm enough. Better the sunny side of the latch, than the burnt side of the fender. Play by the door stone, little daughters, while I take the little pitcher to the well.'

Now the well was a step across the meadow, and a step adown, at the head of a

---

* Emeritus Professor G. P. Jones, M.A., Litt.D., of Witherslack near Grange-over-Sands, writes: '*Ceninen,* as the word was usually written in the 19th century, or *cenhinen* in the reformed orthography of today, is the ordinary Welsh word for a leek. The plural is *cennin* and *cennin Pedr* is a common name for daffodils. I have no knowledge of names peculiar to the Denbigh region, but I imagine that the wild daffodil is most probably the flower to which Beatrix Potter referred. When a boy, I gathered plenty of them in the neighbourhood of Ruthin, not so far away from Denbigh.'

little dell that dipped into a wood; and the well's name was called after Prince Llewellyn. Its water was fairy water. (But the name of the wood was not good.)

The water came out of a limestone bank, and twinkled over a sheet of crystals; it flowed down a wooden runnel into a basin of rough stone. Thence it bubbled and tumbled, soaking through cress and rushes, by a soggy hollow, through the hedge into the thicket. It disappeared into the wood; out of the dancing sunshine, into the silent shadow.

But sometimes when the air was very still there could be heard a tinkling in the wood; and before times of thunder the sound of crackling laughter. The name of that wood was not good.

Now the well was a wishing well. The water came out of the limestone rock— came into the sunshine with a rush and with a dancing, and a noise like tinkling laughter. Then it stopped—stopped while she that had brought a pitcher could count seven.

And then again it came—came with a bubbling and a dancing and a singing, while she that had stood her jug under the runnel could count another seven. Then again it stopped.

So that she that had brought a great pitcher might count seven sevens, or wish seven wishes before that pitcher ran over.

Generations of Welsh children had dabbled their hands in the basin, where the fairy waters danced and bubbled. They had wished for shoes or sweeties or dolls, or a little baby brother out of the wishing well. And older girls and women had wished for many things—things wise or things of unwisdom. Sometimes their wishes had come true, for banning or for blessing. Morved Edwards Jones had wished a wish that had come double. Also there had come to her a good husband, and the little stone house under the chestnut tree.

But now nothing will she wish for except money—money, money—money for fine clothing and for junketing in the town.

Seven times she wished for money on that warm spring afternoon, while the fairy waters bubbled and leapt into her pitcher—

'Money! money! money! Oh, well, weird me money! weird me money; weird me money; weird me money, wishing well!'

Then the waters stopped; and without waiting to fill her pitcher, without a wish for her children, without a thought to her husband—Morved Edwards drew her red Welsh cloak about her, and stepped away across the meadows, leaving her half-filled pitcher at the well. She stepped across the grass, across the silver daisies, and the dusty golden buttercups that gilded the skirt of her cloak—stepped away towards the blue distance where rises the smoke of the town.

The fairy waters leapt into the pitcher; the bubbles that were in the hollow pitcher whispered and mumbled. One bubble murmured to another low down in

the jug—'Weird, brothers, weird! What shall we weird for Morved Edwards?'
And another bubble answered low down—

'I weird money for a curse; I weird by ill comes worse.'

And another—

'I weird her life to trouble, her sheaves to dust and stubble.'

'I weird a curse of gold; I weird a cross, I weird a loss; weird trouble manifold.'

'Weird her age and cold; weird pains manifold.'

'Weird her bowed and bent; weird her tears be spent.'

'I weird her sorrow and sighing; weird her long a-dying.'

Then another little bubble answered—

'I weird her tears be pearls; I weird forgiveness.'

The fairy waters broke afresh out of the limestone rock. They came into the sunshine with a rush and with a dancing and a singing—

'Weird, brothers, weird! What shall we weird for Evadne and Myfanwy? What shall we weird them through the months?'

Then two little bubbles answered—

'I weird they be gentle and holy, like the snow flakes in January.'

'I weird they be white browed and lowly like the fair maids of February.'

And others sang—

'I weird sweet voices clear, March throstle's without fear.'

'Forget-me-not's blue eyes, like April rain-washed skies.'

And another sang in an undertone—

'Like bluebells in the wood, like a bit of blue sky that has come down to play!'

'I weird they be gay, like the white lambs in May.'

The manuscript is unfinished, but according to Beatrix Potter's rough notes the fairies weird for love in June, in some time soon; for *content* in July for *pleasure* in August. The weirds for September and October had not been given; but the fairy-tale concludes:

'I weird for full barns for November. His mercies remember.'

Then a last little bubble sang the verse for December—

'I weird for joy, rest and peace—His mercies never cease—For December—for December—I weird peace!'

Then the fairy waters bubbled over the rim and ran over the pitcher.

LITTLE RED RIDING HOOD

About 1912 Beatrix Potter wrote *her* version of the story of *Little Red Riding Hood*. Many years later she rewrote it as a part of *The Fairy Caravan*, but it was never used. She followed Perrault's original seventeenth-century story, in which both Granny and Red Riding Hood fell victims to the wolf!

In its Fairy Caravan setting, the story is told by Habbitrot, one of the ewes, who 'learnt it from a bird; a swallow who came from France; "Is it old, like your other tales, Habbitrot?" "It is old, and sad," said Habbitrot comfortably. "We are all listening," said the sheep. The mice sat amongst them, where they lay at the foot of the Cherry Tree.'

Beatrix Potter's 1912 version is given here.

Red Riding Hood

Adapted from the French of Charles Perrault

Once upon a time there was a village child who was so pretty—so pretty as never was seen.

Her mother was fair silly about her, and her granny was sillier still.

The good woman her mother made her a little hood of scarlet flannel, and the scarlet set off her bonny black curls like the flame coloured leaves round the heart of a poppy flower—

Wherever she went she wore it; and folks called her 'little red riding hood'.

One day her mother had baked tea-cakes—'Come,' said she, 'come, put on thy little red hood, and trot away to thy Granny's. They tell me that she's poorly. Take her this scone, and a little pat of butter. Run along quick with the basket, and bring me back word how she does.'

Red Riding Hood set off obediently with the basket. Her grandmother dwelt in another village.

The path led over hill and dale, through golden meadow sunshine, and under flickering leafy shadows of the birch trees.

The bog myrtle smelled sweet in the warm sunny glades, and the west wind blew softly through the wood.

It brought a cheerful sound—clink of axes and the voice of woodcutters, singing at their work—

> 'Sing Ash, sing oak, sing charcoal smoke!
> Sing hey the merry gean cherry!
> Lay birk between, for the windward screen,
> —Blue smoke and hazel and copse wood green—
> Sing hey for the woodland merry!'

Another voice far off amongst the trees took up the song—

> 'Here's ash and oak for the broad axe stroke,
> Hey down comes the red gean cherry!'

The cheerful voices died away in the distance. But no one saw little Red Riding Hood.

By the wooden swing gate at the end of the wood, hard upon the open meadow, sat a great grey wolf.

He rested his chin upon the bars of the gate, and he listened to the woodcutters. He was afraid of them. He durst not go home to his bed in the thicket. Neither durst he jump upon Red Riding Hood, when she laid her hand on the swing gate. He had eaten nothing for three days, and his mouth watered when he looked at her. But the woodcutters' jolly voices rang down the wind, and the slow, long, crash of a falling tree—

'Child, where are you going?' said the gaunt grey wolf.

Now Red Riding Hood did not know that it is dangerous to talk to wolves—

'Sir,' said she quite simply, 'I am going to my Granny's. This is a tea-cake that my mother has made, and this is a little pat of butter.'

She lifted the white cloth that was spread over her basket.

'Does she live far off?' asked the wolf.

'Oh, yes indeed,' said Red Riding Hood, 'right across this big meadow, and beyond the mill. It is the last house in the village.'

'Heigh ho!' said the wolf, stretching himself—'I may as well go too, and see her; I have nothing else to do. I'll go by the cart road along the side of the wood. And you shall follow the foot path over the little bridge; let us try which road is shortest.'

The wolf went up the cart road, lippity, lippity, slouching along. But as soon as he had turned the bend of the fence, and was hidden by trees—he laid out his legs and he ran!

The little girl loitered near the gate; she climbed on the railing to gather nuts.

Then she wandered along the foot-path over the meadow, picking wild flowers as she went.

She made a posy for her Grandmother.

And where the foot path climbed the brae, beyond the plank bridge—there were little scarlet wild strawberries among the grass—as red as holly—as red as the hood of little Red Riding Hood.

She gathered them in a dock leaf, and put them in her basket.

At last she reached the high-road, and at last she stepped out faster. But the golden sunshine was very low, and the shadows were long and slanting, before she passed the mill.

Nobody saw her pass.

The wolf had run with all his might along the shorter way. When he came in sight of the mill, he jumped over a wall on to the hill-side above the road.

He slunk along amongst the fern and boulders.

He came down at the further end of the village, behind the old woman's cottage. Through a broken wall and round the wood shed, he slipped between the cabbages and pea-sticks.

His wicked eyes winked at the sun, as he stood in the porch, under the honeysuckle.

He knocked at the door, Tap! tap! tap! very softly with the pad of his foot.

'Who's there?'

'It's your little Red Riding Hood, Granny,' said the wolf in a mincing voice, 'I've brought you a tea-cake and a little pat of butter.'

The poor old grandmother, who lay ill in bed, called out—

'Pull the bobbin and the latch will go up!'

The wolf pulled; the door opened; he crept in.

—And then he made one great spring over the foot of the bed. . . .

The wolf was very hungry; he had had no food for three days.

In a little less than no time there was nothing left at all of Red Riding Hood's Grandmother.

When the wolf had finished, he still felt a little hungry.

He shut the door, put on the poor old woman's night cap, and bed jacket; and he got into bed.

He hid under the blankets, pulling the quilt up to his eyes, and he waited.

After a while someone tapped at the door, Rap-tap-tap!

'Who is there?' said the wolf from the bed.

Red Riding Hood was surprised to hear such a gruff deep voice.

But she thought that her Grandmother must be hoarse with a cold; so she answered—

'It is I, Granny, little Red Riding Hood. My mother has sent you a tea-cake, and a little pat of butter.'

The wolf made his voice as small as he could, and cried—

'Pull the bobbin; the latch will go up!'

Red Riding Hood pulled; and the door came open.

The wolf crouched down under the bed-clothes.

Said he in his hoarse deep voice—'Put the tea-cake and the butter on the dresser. Take off your shoes, and sit beside me on the bed.'

Red Riding Hood took off her little muddy shoes. She scrambled up on to the bed to kiss her granny.

But she was very much surprised when the thing that she thought was her Grandmother pushed back the quilt and blanket and sat up.

'What big strong hairy arms you have got, Granny!' said Red Riding Hood.

'The better to hug you, my dear!'

'What big hairy ears under your night cap!'

'The better to hear you, little Grand-daughter!'

'But Granny—your eyes have turned yellow!'

'The better to see you, my pretty!'

'But Granny, Granny—what big white teeth—'

And that was the end of little Red Riding Hood.

CINDERELLA

There are many different versions of *Cinderella*, but it is generally accepted that the story as we know it today is the work of the French writer Charles Perrault (1628–1703). It was included in his *Tales of Mother Goose* which were published towards the end of the seventeenth century.

Beatrix Potter's version is more than twice as long as Perrault's story, and it gives the setting in great detail. In her rough notes she has listed some of the background details to be described: 'The Palace drowned in sunshine that seemed always afternoon. The royal garden flushed with tulips in box-bordered flower beds; plots of quaint shapes; crowns, crescents, cyphers in clipped box.' She then gives a somewhat fuller description: 'A sun-dial raised on a stone platform stood at the intersection of four broad gravel paths. The broadest, overlooked by row upon row of windows, led from the garden front of the palace straight between the flower beds to a terrace with a stone balustrade above the river. Clear green water in breadth and depth glided swiftly below.'

In her story Beatrix Potter tells of the King's Court and of the court apartments at the palace; of Cinderella's Fairy Godmother whom she called Madame La Fée Marraine; of the Merchant's house in the Place of Linden-trees; and of Cinderella's step-mother and her two step-sisters, Serina and Katinka.

This version differs slightly from the accepted version, for example, the name *Cinderella* is given to the child at her christening, and is not derived from the nickname Cinder-clod or Cinderbottom. Another variation is that Cinderella was told to leave the Ball at a quarter to eleven on the first night instead of at midnight, and at a quarter to twelve on the second night. Also, instead of horses, the coach is drawn by rabbits.

In early drafts the scene is set in the kingdom of Nowara (sometimes spelt Nowharra), in other words *no where*! Curiously, in her later drafts no name appears, and Beatrix Potter has left a space for the name of the kingdom. A further detail which was later omitted is the size of Cinderella's glass slippers—they were $2\frac{1}{2}$!

Cinderella

I

In an old-world town of Europe there lived many years ago a wealthy merchant who had the misfortune to lose his pretty young wife within a year of their marriage. She left behind her a baby daughter. The mother had been a maid of honour at the Court of Nowara. By her dying request the infant was carried to be christened in the Chapel at the Palace where she herself had been married. The child received the curious name of Cinderella.

The merchant had been sincerely attached to his young wife; he was overwhelmed with grief. But he had neither leisure nor skill to manage a household as well as a counting-house, or to rear a crying orphan baby. He married again.

The second wife was a widow of suitable age and station. She was frugal without niggardliness, a skilful housewife respected by her servants and neighbours. She ruled the merchant's home with decorous hospitality and she reared his little daughter through childish ailments and the A.B.C. Above all she inculcated principles of truth, unselfishness, and joy in simple tasks well done, and thereby laid the foundation of a very lovable character. Perhaps she had learnt to teach through experience of earlier failure.

She herself had two self-willed, disagreeable, nearly grown-up daughters. These young persons, offended by their parent's re-marriage, treated her counsels with scant respect and flouted her authority.

The merchant made no attempt to check them. As time went on he became more and more absorbed with business. At length during an epidemic which swept the state of Nowara, the merchant and his second wife died within a week of each other.

I am not well informed about the laws of inheritance in Nowara. Moreover— the Lord Chief Justice, the King and Queen, the Lord High Chamberlain, seven of the sentries and the Court Chaplain had all got influenza too. If the merchant's house and fortune ought to have devolved upon Cinderella—there was no one to assert her childish rights. The Step-sisters were her natural guardians, and they took possession.

II

Snow never fell in the kingdom of Nowara; the sun was always shining. It shone in the springtime on ranks of gold and scarlet tulips; it shone in summer on flaming red geraniums and begonias planted out in shaped flower beds in the royal gardens. The grass plats before the public front of the palace were marked off with white posts from which depended chains painted white. The window sashes and window flower-boxes were white, against warm red brick; and there was a white sentry-box on either side of the portico.

The sentries had the whitest of pipe clayed breeches and gaiters and white facings to their uniforms. The army consisted of eight sentries, a Commander in Chief, a Lord High Admiral, and a band of fourteen musicians, who supplied music at court balls.

Over the portico was the royal coat of arms. And above the red tiled roof of the Palace stables was a white belfry with a clock. The clock played chiming music at the quarters, and it struck the hours with a deep toned bell. Inside the coach entrance there was a large quadrangle surrounded by the rambling buildings of the palace, which covered quite two acres without counting the orangery and the formal gardens.

The state rooms were in the south front. Rows of tall windows looked down upon the garden, where Dutch tulips, Crown imperials, roses and carnations bloomed in season within box edgings. Eleven gardeners tended the flowers; they wore blue aprons and three-cornered hats. Fountains played in the sunshine; quaint sculptured figures stood on stone pedestals and in niches in the orangery, where golden-fruited orange trees grew in green tubs.

The ladies of the court with hooped petticoats and powdered head-dresses walked in the garden with fans in their hands. The youngest Princesses in mob caps and muslin frocks played battledore and shuttlecock and skipping rope on the terrace; and hide and seek in the orangery.

On the east side of the quadrangle was the chapel, a plain building with a fine organ. The royal pew had red curtains. The stables and other offices were on the north side of the quadrangle; a busy scene.

Grooms and stable helpers washed the royal carriages and groomed and exercised the fat cream-coloured horses; while fantail pigeons strutted and cooed on the gravel and flew up to the roof with clapping wings. There was another grass plat with a statuary group and a fountain basin in the middle of the quadrangle, facing the main door of the palace which opened into a marble hall.

The pavement was black and white marble, and the walls of the grand staircase were painted with historical subjects, immense sprawling pictures on ceilings and landings. The state rooms above were full of fine furniture, carved mantelpieces, mirrors and chandeliers. The floors were polished, and very slippery. Nobody ever sat down in the presence of the King and Queen; except by mistake.

In the great presence chamber the furniture was white and gold and the curtains and upholstery were of crimson brocade. Pictures of battle ships and sea fights hung on the walls; and over the fire-place there was a curious dial; a sea-map enlivened with figures of three-decker ships and tritons and whales as big as Sweden and Norway, and points of the compass whereon a long pointer showed the direction of the wind. The hand of this wind clock was worked by a vane upon the roof over-head.

Besides these staterooms, there were numbers of smaller rooms where the Royal Family and household lived very comfortably, crowded cosily into wainscoted apartments. There was the Equerry's waiting room where His Majesty played back-gammon with Major Silverstock. And the Queen's private sitting room where there was a cage of canary birds and her little dog 'Badine' in a basket by the fire, and her tambour frame and spinning wheel. And her dressing room where Mrs. Pincushion the wardrobe woman attired her Majesty, while one lady-in-waiting handed the tippet and long ruffles, and another lady-in-waiting handed the snuff-box and the fan. And the powder closet where Mrs. Puff the court hairdresser piled up her 'head' of powdered curls and feathers while Her Majesty read the newspaper.

'The Palace drowsed in sunshine that seemed always afternoon. The royal garden flamed with tulips in box bordered flower beds; plots of quaint shapes; crowns crescents cyphers in clipped box. A sun dial raised on a stone platform stood at the intersection of 4 broad gravel paths — The broadest, overlooked by row upon row of windows led straight from the garden front of the palace straight between the flower beds to a terrace with a stone ballustrade above the river. Clear green water in breadth and depth glided swiftly below. Coarse fish, chubb and dace and bream broke surface, coming up with stroke of warm tails beneath streaming garlands of water crowsfoot. An orange floated by amongst jetsam. Barges worked up this the towing path alog the further bank. Other barges coming down lowered brown top sails to slide under a white arched stone bridge.

A studious youth walked upon the terrace, short sightedly reading a book.

A pencil sketch of Cinderella's Coach

And there were the Princesses' apartments where the youngest played with her doll and the elder ones were taught by their governesses to play on the harpsichord, to work tent stitch and samplers, to write very beautiful court hand and to learn geography and the use of the globes.

And the gentlemen-in-waiting and the pages in attendance upon the king had a dining room; and the maids of honour had a parlour up two pairs of stairs where they made tea for the king's gentlemen. There were staircases in every passage, and passages to everywhere; a labyrinth of rooms.

Several suites were lent to dowagers. The Lord High Admiral's Aunt had a panelled bed sitting room and powder closet somewhere above the Long Gallery. Fiddlers and a clarionet and trombone played every evening in the Gallery. The Court was very musical. And the court hairdresser's sisters, the Miss Puffs, had an attic on the fourth floor. Other garrets had been appropriated by pensioners, and of course there were innumerable servants; so that a considerable proportion of the inhabitants of Nowara lived beneath the palace roof.

Not even the Lord Chamberlain knew the exact number of rooms nor of inmates. They came and went, uncounted. Some came in by the stable entrance, and the back stairs, like cockroaches, some by the Blue stairs, some by the Green; some the side doors; some by the Portico. Some were even saluted by the sentries.

There was one small erect little old lady who tap tapitted out of afternoons in the sunshine with an ivory-handled stick. She was something of a mystery. She was dressed in a bygone fashion with a ruff, a coif, and a jewelled stomacher, and a quilted skirt. No one knew her age, nor when she had first come to live in the palace. She was known as Madame La Fée Marraine. The sentries saluted her with awe. Even the King and Queen treated her with distinguished politeness and were gratified when she stood Godmother to the youngest prince.

III

Madame La Fée Marraine had been fond of the merchant's first young wife. She was Godmother to the forlorn little baby as well as to Prince Charming. I do not know whether she disapproved of his second marriage; the second wife did not like her, and there was coolness. She ceased to visit the tall red brick house on the Place of Linden-trees.

All the houses on the Place were built of brick; substantial, dignified, mellow with age. In olden days the merchants of Nowara had transacted business in their homes. There were archways through the ground floor of many of the houses; paved entrances built high for the passage of high piled goods, passing through to warehouses at the back. Now the courtyard behind the merchant's house was deserted; only the worn pavement under the arch still bore the wheel marks of the heavy wool waggons.

Grapes ripened on the counting house wall; lilac bushes looked over from the neglected garden, where berry bushes and flower beds were over-run with weeds and great golden pumpkins. There was a tumbledown glass-house in the garden and a summer house with mossy steps where green lizards basked in the sun. The front of the old house was still imposing. A stone canopy over the front door stood at the top of six steps. On either side were wrought-iron balustrades, and torch extinguishers, and ironwork grills protected the half-buried basement windows.

The house looked across a sunny boulevard where the citizens took the air, strolling under the lime trees, or sitting on benches smoking long pipes, and watching the pleasure boats on the blue gliding river. Across the river was a park with big chestnut trees and fallow deer.

Cinderella, leaning out of her attic window, high amongst the twisted chimney stacks, could look along the river front as far as a white stone bridge. Towards the left along the Place she could see a corner of the portico and all the south front of the palace. Rows and rows of windows glittered in the sunshine above the formal garden with its straight gravel walks where the cocked-hatted gardeners wheeled barrows; the fountains played; and the court ladies, attended by gallants with swords and velvet coats, walked on the broad terrace above the river. On the palace roof she could see a gold weather vane; and she could hear the chiming of the clock.

The clock strikes the hour. The royal coach with four fat cream-coloured horses rumbles out under the portico. The sentries salute. A small crowd raises a cheer. Their Majesties go for a drive. The sentries ground their muskets; they talk together and discuss; the porter brings them a pot of beer. The nursemaids and the butcher's-boy gossip and gape at the sentries; the children bowl hoops on the smooth walks between the grass plats.

An erect be-ruffed little figure emerges from the palace. The sentries spring to attention. The butcher's boy slinks away; 'tis said that once an urchin put his tongue out and could not draw it in again until she gave permission. The nursemaids collect their charges and remove themselves.

Madame, tapping with her ivory handled stick paces along the boulevard under the limes, aloof, distinguished beyond her tiny stature, shrewdly observant. The young and giddy step aside behind the lime-trees. The ancient smokers remove their pipes, rise from their green benches, and bow, bare-headed. She paces along the Place, with high-heeled shoes, hoop petticoat, and ruff.

As she passes the merchant's house she hears a sweet girlish voice singing in the basement. The song is interrupted by coarse reproof and sobs. When the step-sisters had finished scolding and slapping, they went upstairs to put on finery. And Cinderella, drying her tears upon a dirty apron, looked up to find Madame La Fée Marraine in the kitchen.

From thence forward her visits became frequent and unaccountable. She did not knock, she appeared. Cinderella became much attached to her Godmother; although the old lady was a bit censorious. She highly approved Cinderella's precocious house-wifely skill in the kitchen; but why was her face always dirty? why did she not hold herself elegantly? (the old lady was erect as a poker) did she know dancing steps? could she play the harpsichord? and oh, why was she always late with dinner (a fruitful cause of scolding).

Cinderella was so sweet tempered that scolding ran off her merry nature like dewdrops off a golden pumpkin. She continued to be unpunctual; but she profited by her Godmother's instruction. She practised curtseys and deportment and steps of the minuet on the kitchen flags while Madame beat time with the ivory handled stick. 'H.m.m. a neat ankle, a tiny foot, but your deportment leaves much to be desired. I will instruct you in the minuet and the court curtsey this evening in the kitchen—'

In came a cross step-sister; 'What are you about, lazy bones? talking to yourself? Get out of the parlour with your mop and duster. Go down to your kitchen and bake macaroons. We expect two ladies and four beaux—gentlemen of the first fashion—to play ombre.* Do not dare to show your smutty face upstairs. Prepare supper in the saloon, with coffee and ices. Bring up the urn when I ring the bell. Away with you, dirty little cinder wench!'

Cinderella ran downstairs. Madame La Fée had already vanished. And while Cinderella practised her steps in the kitchen that evening under Madame's direction, and pointed her toes in the gavotte and minuet under the guidance of the ivory-handled stick—the palace clock took a fit of chiming. And the palace clock chimed and chimed to the perplexity and exasperation of the Court of Nowara. The King ordered the High Chamberlain to run up the belfry and stop the clock. The Queen ordered one of the sentries to right-about-face-quick-march and fetch the court clock-maker who lived in the Avenue of Spectaclemakers. But while the clock-maker was mounting a ladder to the belfry to stop the clock—the clock came to its senses, and struck the hour quite properly. Cinderella had finished her dancing lesson.

IV

When work was done Cinderella played in the high-walled garden behind the house. She never went out into the town because she had no tidy clothes. But often she leant out of the attic window behind the parapet, and looked down on the broad white Place, the lime trees, and the grass plats; leaning out and looking side-ways she could see the portico of the palace. The two sentries on guard in and out of their sentry boxes like red and white toys up and down strutting; the flourish of salute, as the royal coach with the fat coachmen and four fat horses, came out under

* Ombre: a card game popular in the seventeenth and eighteenth centuries.

the portico when the King and Queen took an airing. The butcher's boy and the nursemaids talking to the sentries when the King and Queen had gone out, and presently a small erect lady coming out under the portico, whom the sentries hastily saluted.

Cinderella smudged a towel over her smutty face, fastened her bodice with a pin where a button was wanting, and ran down the long flights of tall stairs at risk of a headfirst fall with a broken-heeled shoe. By the time that she reached the basement, Madame La Fée stood beside the hearth in the kitchen. 'Why were you leaning out of the garret window?' said her Godmother, who saw everything. 'I was looking at the Palace, Marraine—my sisters are going to a ball there tomorrow night—How grand it will be! How I wish I could go.' 'Why not? you are a great girl now; and a pretty girl if you would keep your face clean,' added Madame La Fée as though talking to herself. Even Cinderella began laughing, 'Oh what a funny sight I would be at the royal ball in my dirty, sooty frock.'

Then came a loud knocking at the door—'it is my sisters expecting company, and I have not tea ready'—'unpunctual as usual, naughty girl,' said Madame La Fée—Cinderella fetched a tray of tea things from the pantry to carry upstairs; she passed through the kitchen but Madame was no longer there.

Her step-sisters would scarcely taste tea, and tomorrow they would scarcely taste any meal; they were too excited about the ball to eat. Besides when they tried on their new dresses they could not make them meet. Cinderella had to wash her hands clean and pull the laces, how tightly they were laced! how would they ever dance? and what wonderful 'heads', powder puffs, hair cushions, bows, feather birds! and lace ruffles and bracelets and necklaces—They fidgeted and fumed and squabbled with each other and ordered Cinderella about and rapped her over the knuckles with their fans.

At length they were finished attiring and departed to the palace in two sedan chairs which waited for them at the merchant's door, escorted by two fine young gentlemen, one in a ruby velvet coat and the other in blue, each with a cocked hat.

Cinderella watched them into the sedans, saw the chair men lift the poles and bear them off. She closed the door and crept down to the kitchen and sat down by the cinders. The crickets chirped, the firelight danced—'Oh dear, how I should like to dance just once!' 'So you shall, my child,' said the voice of Madame Marraine. She stood leaning on the ivory-headed stick, erect, shrewd, smiling kindly on Cinderella.

'Oh, Godmother, I should love to—but how can I go?' cried Cinderella. 'Run into the garden; fetch me a large pumpkin; set it down on the floor. Now fetch me four white rabbits from the hutch. So,' said Madame La Fée, herding the rabbits into the centre of the floor. 'Now fetch me the mouse trap.' 'Six mice, all alive, am I to let them out, Godmother?' said Cinderella. 'Do so,' ordered the old lady. 'Fetch me the wire rat trap.' It contained one large fat rat with impressive whiskers. 'Fetch me four lizards from under the flower pot by the apricot tree. Set them down—So.'

Madame La Fée waved her ivory-headed stick. And instead of a pumpkin there was the most beautifullest gold coach, harnessed with rabbits driven by a whiskered rat, attended by mouse link boys and on the backboard hung four lizard footmen. 'Hey presto, out of the door with you,' said the dictatorial old lady, and the coach and four and the link boys and the coachman and footmen were waiting for Cinderella before the door of the house.

Cinderella clapped her hands with delight—'Oh, Godmother! but look at my dirty frock, and the coach is lined with white velvet!' 'Never mind your frock, attend to me Cinderella. I permit and arrange that you shall go to this ball; but listen God daughter and obey me. When the palace clock strikes a quarter to eleven —no matter how merry and pleasant—you must return—punctually—remember,' said Madame La Fée touching Cinderella's frock with her stick. Then no longer was the frock made of dirty brown baize—it was rose-coloured silk, and her Godmother drew from her pocket a pair of glass slippers.

Cinderella got into her carriage, as though in a dream. The grenadier sentries saluted, the carriage rattled under the portico and she was set down at the main door inside the quadrangle. Thanks to the old lady's instructions her deportment was perfect, and before she had time to become shy or feel conspicuous through coming forward alone, Prince Charming who happened to be in the vestibule stepped forward with a low bow, took her hand respectfully and conducted her to dance.

He danced with her repeatedly and took her in to supper. Everybody was agog with curiosity to guess who she was. Her sisters amongst the rest. They could scarcely taste any supper so tightly were they laced and so occupied with staring at her. The Prince took her hand to lead her again to dance—when the clock struck a quarter to eleven. Cinderella curtseyed to him but resisted all entreaties to stay for one more dance—The golden coach took her home, and turned again into a pumpkin. And when the step-sisters at length returned from the dance, a very sleepy, shabby Cinderella was waiting—yawning—to unlace them.

The Court of Nowara was completely puzzled by this apparition of the fair unknown—Where had she come from? who was she? The porters had been unable to extract any information from the discreet mice link men.

The Prince was distracted by more than curiosity; her beauty and sweet manners had so deeply impressed him that he lost appetite. In vain the love-sick Prince questioned the eight grenadier sentries, the link men, the porters. The Queen, concerned, inquisitively questioned the Lord Chancellor; the King conferred with the Prime Minister and Lord High Admiral; no one could give the faintest guess or suggestion.

They did not think of asking Madame La Fée Marraine. The Prince languished and refused a second helping of plum pudding—when an idea came to the Court Chamberlain—'Your Majesties, why not announce another ball? Perchance the fair one may come again to dance?'

And so it happened. The step-sisters put on their finery; the elite of Pumpkin-ville patched, powdered and printed, the ladies in great 'heads,' the gentlemen with pigtails, swords and embroidered waistcoats hied to the second palace ball, with even greater glee and zeal and excitement of curiosity. 'Don't you wish you could go? Dirty little Cinder wench, another pinch of the curling tongs—Come here at once Cinderella, draw up another inch of my laces. Are your fingers clean? Fasten my panniers straight.'

The sedan chair men waited before the door—The step-sisters departed with their beaux. Cinderella crept downstairs to the kitchen. Madame La Fée stood before the hearth. 'Child,' said she, 'you shall go again, but promise to obey my instructions. Leave the Ball punctually at a quarter to twelve. Otherwise you will turn into a dirty kitchen wench.'

Cinderella promised. The pumpkin coach and servants were conjured with a whisk of the enchanted stick. She drove away in splendour.

In the quadrangle of the palace the coach drew up at the broad stone steps where the Prince was fidgeting and fretting—great was his satisfaction when the lacquey footmen opened the door of the pumpkin coach and Cinderella descended. In place of the rose-coloured robe she was attired in a sacque of blue silk and silver tissue. The Prince conducted her to the hall where they danced a gavotte—The King and Queen spoke to her, and were highly satisfied with her modest sweetness. The Prince conducted her to supper and was particularly attentive. It was the general opinion of the company that he would propose during the evening.

The Fiddlers fiddled furiously and sweetly. The Prince was more and more charmed with pretty Cinderella. He led her again to the ball room, the musicians struck up. Cinderella curtseyed to the Prince, he bowed to her and they commenced a minuet. Above the hum of conversation and the sweet-toned humming of the fiddle, there came the chiming of a clock. At first Cinderella thought it was but chiming the quarters—But alack the clock proceeded to strike—At the first stroke of the hour bell—Cinderella suddenly stopped. She listened, scared. At the second stroke she turned and fled from the ball room, running fleetly like a mouse down the broad staircase. She tripped over her ball dress, dropped a glass slipper, recovered herself and ran, hearing more and more strokes of the clock; twelve in all.

No coach awaited her at the door; but as she ran through the quadrangle, there was a rush of mice and a rat and rabbits. Once she paused to take off her remaining glass slipper; she thrust it into her pocket—the pocket of a dirty drab frock! Cinderella got home again, a dirty little Cinder maid, attended by a pumpkin coach too small to carry her, and a troop of lizards and mice and rabbits.

The step-sisters returned later full of conversation. The Prince had been desolated; the palace had been in hubbub. Every corner had been searched for the beautiful unknown, as the sentries denied that she had gone out by the gate. Nobody had passed for two hours except a dirty-looking-like beggarmaid—and some curious contraption of rats. The Prince had picked up the glass slipper, the tiniest and most beautiful little shoe. The foot that could wear it must be fairylike. He vowed he would marry none other than the unknown charmer.

V

All witnesses agreed that the equipage of the Unknown had arrived from the direction of the Place of Linden-trees. That the helter-skelter pumpkin cavalcade had retreated also that way seemed to have escaped attention. But several late loiterers by the river front had seen a magnificent golden coach swinging along the Place with blazing lights. It had not come from beyond, because it had not passed the watchman on the bridge. Neither had it left the walled town after midnight by any of the city gates. All evidence seemed to suggest that some one of the ancient houses might have harboured in its dusty stable buildings an antique gilded chariot of an earlier day.

So to the Place of Linden-trees went the impatient Prince, attended reluctantly by the Lord High Chamberlain, two sentries and four footmen; and determined that the slipper should be tried upon the foot of every unmarried woman in the row. The Lord Chamberlain carried the glass slipper upon a purple velvet cushion. A crowd of idlers and small boys followed the procession.

Great was the excitement amongst the fair ones residing on the Place; heads popped out of windows, as the Prince's footmen thundered at the door knockers. Each house was visited in turn, commencing at the end that was nearest to the Palace.

The first house belonged to an extremely fat widow, who laughed consumedly, and humbly begged to decline the honour of trying to insert her gouty toe into the little glass slipper. Her maids might try. Two were flat-footed and the other one squinted. All the females in the second house had enormous feet. In the third house all were married except mere babies. In the fourth house there was a daughter aged fifteen who very nearly got it on, to every one's alarm, for she was badly pitted with the smallpox.

The Lord Chamberlain became more and more annoyed. He was very stout himself; and it was demeaning to kneel like a shoe-maker and try a slipper upon the feet of young women who were altogether out of the question. The Prince himself was discouraged and sulky, but still obstinately determined to proceed with the trial. The footmen continued to knock at doors, and every lady's heart was in a flutter.

When they reached the merchant's house, the door flew open at the instant of knocking. The step-sisters were revealed upon the door sill, attired for taking the air. They wore black silk mantuas, large white Leghorn straw hats trimmed with ruches and bows of pink ribbon, striped gauze gowns, very full over hoops, pink sashes, and long yellow elbow-length gloves.

They gave little shrieks at sight of the sentries' muskets and the staves of the footmen; although as a matter of fact they had been peeping like their neighbours, and they had opened the front door themselves to conceal the deficiency of not keeping a man servant.

When the Lord Chamberlain explained the business on hand—or on foot—the step sisters were all smiles. They sidled and bridled and curtseying backwards they ushered the Prince into the saloon. Serena the elder seated herself in an arm chair; not without deferential argument as to whether etiquette permitted such freedom in the Prince's presence. But she could not try on the slipper while standing. So she sidled and bridled into the chair and spread her hoop petticoat, and poked out a silk-stockinged foot—not of the smallest size—upon the foot stool. 'It won't go on, M'am,' said the Lord High Chamberlain. 'Let me see. Let me push my toe well in first.' 'Pardon me, Ma'm. I cannot permit pressure. The slipper is made of glass.'

Serena flounced out of the chair; Katinka took her place. 'Oh, the sweet little shoe!' simpered Katinka with a killing sidelong glance at the Prince. But the Prince was taking no interest at all in the proceedings. He was staring in amazement at a very pretty shabbily dressed girl who was standing in the doorway. 'It is useless, madam. It fits neither of you,' said the Lord Chamberlain, getting up from the floor wheezily. 'Your Highness, if it is really your command that the slipper must be tried by *all* the ladies on the Place—we had better be moving.'

'Who is this maiden?' asked the Prince suddenly. 'Our cook-maid. Be off with you!' replied the elder step-sister, losing her temper. 'Stay!' said the Prince, 'let her try on the slipper.' 'Sire!' exclaimed the Lord High Chamberlain. 'What? Her??' exclaimed the step-sisters. Prince Charming began to laugh. He lifted the slipper himself from the purple velvet cushion, and advanced towards Cinderella, bowing low. He took her smutty little hand and handed her to the chair; their laughing eyes met as he knelt before the foot stool. Her foot slipped into the little glass slipper; and Cinderella, smiling and blushing, drew the other little glass slipper from her pocket.

Then—nobody quite knew how—Madame La Fée Marraine stood amongst them, and touched Cinderella's dirty gown with her ivory-handled stick.

The Prince married her within a week, and they lived happily ever after.

14
Tales of Country Life

Tales of Country Life

In 1913 a story by Beatrix Potter called *The Fairy Clogs* appeared in the October 25th issue of *Country Life*, in their section devoted to 'Tales of Country Life'. As it was published a few weeks after her marriage, it was signed H.B.H.

Anderson Graham of *Country Life* selected the story from four which Beatrix Potter had submitted. In his letter of acknowledgement dated October 8th he told her, '"The Fairy Clogs" is a fine little story and I hope to use it in an early number. The others I am returning herewith. "Pace Eggers" is not topical. "The Mole Catcher's Burying" is for a children's paper, and "Carrier's Bob" I do not think quite happy.'

The stores were written during the latter half of 1911, in North Country dialect. They were apparently written on Sunday evenings at Hill Top.

Carrier's Bob, dated August 1911, is believed to have been founded upon fact, for on a slip of paper attached to the manuscript Beatrix Potter wrote: 'The dog was a portrait of old Isaac Brockbank's terrier, the ferryman. It was his inseparable companion. After his death it used to go down to the Ferry—and wait for the boat —and go home looking forlorn.'

In *The Mole Catcher's Burying*, dated 'Sunday 29 Oct. 1911', the farmer, old Jimmy Dacre, lived at Finsthwaite, four or five miles south of Sawrey. He bred shorthorn cattle. Bruce Thompson who knows the neighbourhood well says: 'This is almost a prose poem? I like the way the field-names are brought in: I believe they are the names of the fields at Hill Top.'

Pace Eggers describes an old folk-lore custom. 'It is an admirable description', writes Bruce Thompson, 'of a custom still observed until "between the wars". It was probably a continuous tradition—I saw the play in Hawkshead, Troutbeck, etc.,—but it seems not to have survived except in artificial revivals.'

The Fairy Clogs is by far the longest story. The lake in the story is evidently Windermere, because Esthwaite Water has no islands and is less than two miles long; also, the head of Windermere can be seen from Tock How, but not Esthwaite Water. The story given here has been taken from Beatrix Potter's manuscript, and differs slightly from the edited version in *Country Life*. On the manuscript she has lightly pencilled—'Hill Top Farm Nov. 5. '11, Sunday eve.'

CARRIER'S BOB

Up and down by hill and dale—pitter patter bandy-legged—on before the lumbering coup carts trotted 'Carrier's Bob'. East the gate o'Mondays, north by the fell road Wednesdays, stationways on Fridays and Tuesdays, to the market town on Saturdays—he held the road for seven years and never missed the round.

The carrier walks between the carts; he drives the first horse with long rope reins, his hand is on the headstall of the second.

Slowly, step by step ('Ah Lady, ah Whitelegs!') through hail and shine, through storm and sun. Half way up the hill the horses rest, with a stone behind the wheel of the first cart, and the carrier's foot on the spokes of the second. Then Bob went on, panting, to the top of the brae, and waited. His wise-like golden-brown eyes looked out over woods and ferry, down the long white hill where the horses come zig-zag up. Another rest at the top; then Bob jogged on in front.

He was an unfriendly short-legged prick-eared terrier, with a snap and a growl if you tried to pat him. His harsh coat smelled like damp fire-irons; no dog in a twenty-mile round could leave much mark upon that bristly hide in battle. They might as well bite a door mat. Bob bit the collies on the legs. Whenever they rolled him over, he contrived to roll under the horse; and if any dog were pinched—it was not Bob.

He had a jaw like a brock's; and the badger's broad round feet, with nails worn down to the quick. But the road must be burning hot—or the snow must be drifted to the hubs—before Bob would take a lift under the tilt. The carrier flung him in, pitched and rolled and jolted amongst kegs and soap and sacks. A very few yards was enough; a hairy muzzle poked under the canvas, and Bob tumbled out upon his head.

His place was on the road, twenty yards before, pitter-patter, bandy-legged with tail-flag stiffly flying. And his eye was as sharp as his master's for the fluttering white rag on the gate, that marks a carrier's call. Sharper on the homeward round, after Whitelegs and Lady had stamped and shivered before the 'Hawk and Buckle' while Bob guarded the packages in a biting wind. The old dusty high road is a jolly life in summer; but wind and ice are cruel when the days draw in.

So there came a winter Monday morning when Isaac Simpson did not rise to yoke the horses with a lantern; and Bob lay by the fire, and snapped at the carrier's children's legs. Followed by a Tuesday when neighbour Hawkrigg went station-ways with his own long-cart instead of the carrier. And other strange dark days, when Bob—kicked out of the kitchen—slept in some straw at the bottom of the cart. And then a burying on Saturday; and Bob walked before the carts, filled with friends instead of packages, for the last time through the snow.

The carrier's widow hired handsome Jock Sowerby to hold the gear together.

She looked toward the day when her own white-headed laddie should be a man grown; strong to take the road and drive his father's carts. Jock came to the stable in the morning with a lantern, and he had a tussle with Bob. The man roared with laughter and was sparing with his clogs; but never again would Bob go out with the carts.

Every evening he went half way down the brae, and watched the long steep hill, where the horses come zig-zag up ('Ah, Lady! Ah, Whitelegs!'). Passing farmers in gigs called to him by name; he looked at them silently, with unblinking puzzled eyes. When the carts came in sight at the bend, he got up and went home. In summer he wandered, and was seen upon the roads; but he always took the round on different days to the carts. In autumn he occasionally went rabbiting; always by himself. Perhaps there was not a great deal to eat. Mrs. Simpson would have hungered herself before she would have 'put down' Bob. Still, undeniably, he was another mouth for porridge. In winter he slept much in the stable; but the game-keeper noticed a broad round foot mark in the snow.

Then came a crisis in December. A package had been stolen; and on a Saturday night—Jock Sowerby came back with a new cur dog under the cart. There was a battle in the star-light. The cur dog seemed to be undermost, but perhaps Whitelegs was nipped. Anyway the wheel went over Bob. His agony was very brief; the cart was heavy laden (with Sally Bain's new mangle as a last straw on the top). He died between the wheel, and his own beloved road. And his end was well timed. Mrs. Simpson never fails to tell, with kindly tears, that within another fortnight she must have bought a new dog licence for Bob.

The carrier's children, whose heels he had pinched, held a grand burying. They lapped him in a sheet of the West Cumberland Times; they dug his shallow frozen grave by the wall at the head of the brae; and covered him up with stones. Carrier's Bob sleeps beside the road.

THE MOLE CATCHER'S BURYING

'Little blind brother—little blind brother! heard ye the news? Come up from your digging; come up, bring your shovels; come up in black velvet.'

'What news? what news? what news?' 'Come up from Mill Bottom, come down from Hindsyke, come under the wall by the drain from Stone Ridding. Come in black velvet.'

'The barrel traps are sprung in Stone Ridding.' 'The runs are unstopped from Bowman's wood.' 'The traps are not set in Long Parrock and the Grassings—little blind brother, what news?'

'Old Jimmy Dacre is dying.'

(The moles clap and clash their shovels.)

'Come up from Low ground from Eel house and Green gate. Cross the fields in the twilight; cross the roads, cross the bridge. Bring your shovels, come hurry.'

(More moles come up.)

'Old Jimmy Dacre is dying.'

(The moles clash their shovels.)

'Dying! Dying! The barrel mole-traps are sprung, the saplings are unbent.'

'Eight of my sons hath he snared, Brother Mowdiewarp.' 'Seven of my daughters, Sister Moleskin.' 'Six of mine, Brother Diggory.' 'Five of mine, Brother Delvet.' 'Four of mine.' 'And seven of mine.' 'And eight of mine.'

'My castle did he dig up in Hindsyke; he threw out the oak leaves, and killed my children in the nest.' 'And mine in the Croft, in the long lush grass.'

'And mine in Pudding Carr, amongst the peat. He scattered the black mound, and slew them while they slept.'

'The Mill-pick is furrow-less. We will tunnel it! and throw up heaps!'

'The Long field is harrowed and sown, since we fled to the woods.'

'The worms hold the fields, and the wire worm hath the stubble, since our runs have been stopped; and we stayed in the plantings.'

'The worms have the mastery in the kirk-yard, Brother Mowdiewarp; come up, bring your shovels.'

(More and more moles come up.)

'Come up, come up, blind brothers. There is no moon; I feel the darkness come over the fields by Wilfin Beck. Come over the stony path by the witchit gate at the Fold. Come over the road at Town End.'

(Hundreds of black velvet moles bearing shovels rustle over the road, through the dead leaves.)

'There is a light in Jimmy Dacre's window, Brother Mowdiewarp. I smell the lamp dimly. The door is shut.'

379

'Come up to the kirk-yard, blind brothers; come under the gate with your shovels.'

(The moles swarm under the gate, and stumble over the mounds.)

'Where shall we bury him, blind brother? blind brother? where shall we bury him?'

'Here beside his wife; she died long ago.'

'Dig brothers; dig, dig, dig. Six foot deep and six foot long.

The ground is hard. The worms are hungry. Dig, dig, dig. Dig a grave for Jimmy Dacre; he delved a many pits.'

'My father did he trap in Crook Meadow.'

'My mother did he trap in the Mill Pick.'

'And mine.' 'And mine.' 'And mine.'

'Our fathers, grandfathers and great grandfathers. He numbered his slain by thousands. Their warm black velvet coats were ripped. Their raw red bodies dangled in the wind.'

'Dig brothers, dig. Dig Jimmy Dacre's grave. Throw up the earth; the ground is stony.'

'Four score from Hill Top; four score from Castle Farm; five score from Currier. No more shall the tally mount. The ash saplings are sprung; the traps are unset.'

They dug and they delved; deep, long and narrow. When the sexton came at daybreak, the grave was dug already.

Old Jimmy Dacre is dead.

PACE EGGERS

At dusk when the damp begins to rise, with a smell of white violets—there comes a clatter of clogs up the flagged path through the farm garden. It stops before the door; there is a whispering and tittering. Four shrill treble voices strike up. They sing an old old jingling tune, with a diddle-dum chorus; a tune whose curious haunting lilt, accented on the second and fifth syllable, betokens music much more ancient than the doggerel rhyme which now accompanies it.

The little voices keep good time, and pipe as gaily as the throstle on the ash—

> 'Here's *four* funny *jol* ly boys all of one mind'—
> (their tones proclaim them little girls)
> 'We've *come* a pa *egging*, we hopes you'll prove kind;'
> (the house door opens above their heads and they quaver into giggles)
> 'We hopes you'll prove kind, with your egg and strong beer,
> And we'll come no more pace egging till the next year,
> With the diddle dum dum day, with the diddle dum de dum day.'

They stand solemnly in a row; diminutive figures in long borrowed coats. Three have their faces blacked and wear male attire; the fourth is dressed as an old woman, and carries a basket. She is addressed indifferently as 'Miser' or 'Maggret' or 'Nanny Basket' or 'Bessy Brown-bags' as the case may be. Today's 'Nanny Basket', I regret to say, has borrowed a motor veil; but her correct costume is a high-waisted gown, with a cross-over, sun bonnet, and mittens. These clothes and the reference to Lord Nelson fix the date for the words. But the tune with its old English cadence is probably as old as Queen Elizabeth.

The children sing the first verse together, and the choruses. Each sings her character verse alone, stepping round her companions in a consequential little trot.

> 'The *first* that comes *in* is Lord *Nelson* you see,
> With a *bunch* of blue *ri*bands right *down* to his knee;
> The star on his breast like diamonds do shine,
> And we hope you'll remember its pace-egging time!
> For the diddle dum dum day, for the diddle de dum day!'

Lord Nelson has secured a rosette of blue paper, and a bit of tin for a star. In other respects, he and the next actor are similar in appearance. Both are sooty.

> 'The next that comes in is a jolly Jack Tar—
> He fought for Lord Nelson all through the late war,
> He fought for the King and Lord Nelson so true,
> But now he's come back for old England to view.'

Perhaps 'a pig-tail' was originally this sailor's hair queue, but our children always translate it into a caudal appearance for 'Toss-pot', the comic character—

> 'The next that comes in is old Toss-pot, you see,
> He's a funny old fellow, in every degree,
> He's a hump on his back and he wears a pig-tail,
> And all his delight is in drinking strong ale!'

Toss-pot moves the audience to shrieks of laughter, and turns shy. In ordinary life this figure of fun is little Betty Green. Now her yellow hair is bundled up under a scarecrow cap, she wears her daddy's much-too-long blue trousers, a pillow under her great coat forms a hump, a lamb's tail wags at her heels, her face is smutty. Only her white teeth and roguish eyes betray little Betty.

'Miser' the last character does not sing. She breaks in with a gabble of scolding words, shaking her basket. And finally the whole company with renewed animation sing the concluding and most important verse—

> 'Now ladies and gentlemen that sit by the fire,
> Put your hands in your pockets, it's all our desire!
> Put your hands in your pockets and pull out your purse;
> Come give us a trifle, you'll not be much worse!
> For the diddle dum day, for the diddle de dum day.'

The basket contains eggs, pennies, and other small presents, not forgetting a piece of soap, which will prove useful.

Another party of big lads comes in boldly by broad daylight to act the guizzard's play. They sing the song, but carelessly—The play's the thing.

It must be confessed that our local version is a confused and degenerate one. 'Galatian' has disappeared; and a misguided 'King' George slays Lord Nelson!

There are only four characters, and the leader is obviously mixing up two parts —that of St. George and an opposing champion called 'Slasher'. The dragon is not present; but we hear of him, ungrammatically—

> 'I am him that killed the dragon, and brought him up for slaughter,
> And by that act I won the King of Egypt's daughter.'

After bragging about his wealth and reciting an irrelevant rhyme about mince pies, 'George' (who by the way is adorned with paper feathers as a Red Indian) challenges 'Lord Nelson' to combat. Lord Nelson, also decorated with paper trimmings, responds suitably. This character invariably wears strips of calico bound round his legs; can they be reminiscent of the Admiral's white silk stockings?

After a short noisy fight with wooden swords, Lord Nelson falls. 'Miser', who acts rather well, flings herself beside him, upbraiding King George—'What have you gone and done? You've been and gone and slain mine heir and only son!'

Then one of the little sweeps calls for 'a doctor, a doctor! Five fifteen pounds for a doctor!' Whereupon the other little smutty character announces himself to be a *hatter*, and offers his services, which are indignantly refused by Miser until he explains that he is 'Jack of all trades and Master of None'. Questioned 'where he got his learning?' replies 'By travel.' Further questioned where? answers—'Higgledy piggledy France and Spain, three times round old England, and back again.' 'Anywhere else?' 'Up my grandmother's stair-case, where I found three corner cupboards full of fat bacon. I didn't ask for *fat* bacon! I didn't ask for *lean* bacon; I want what I can cure.' (A pun?) 'What can *you* cure?' Here follows a list of ailments, ending with the assurance that 'if this man has nineteen devils, I can cast out twenty.'

The doctor then gives the recumbent Nelson some highly coloured fluid out of a medicine bottle, which causes him to rise hurriedly; and the play ends with the usual appeal for coin, which 'George' collects in his hat.

The party visits every house in the village, only excepting old Grump's 'where us got a bucket of water last year!'

For our part—in these days of semi-artificial folk-lore revival—we gladly bestow a whole shilling upon this genuine fragment from old times. Rumours of our largesse brings up yet another company of two actors, aged three and five. Their appearance reminds us of Tweedledum and Tweedledee as arrayed for battle by Sir John Tenniel. No amount of prompting will induce them to remember the words; but their encounter with our turkey cock brings down the house.

THE FAIRY CLOGS

Mrs. Hodgson scrubbed the blue flag-stones, because it was Saturday; swisher, swisher, swisher went her scrubbing brush. Mary Feirn, her sister, polished the fire-irons and brass candlesticks. The matting was rolled up; the fender lay on the couch; the coal-scuttle sat in the rocking-chair; and the rest of the chairs and odd-ments reposed upon the kitchen table.

Mrs. Hodgson, on her knees, wriggling backwards towards the door in the course of scrubbing, conversed volubly—about the inferior quality of latter-day storkings—and the rise in sugar—and above all, how much should be kept for cur-ing when the butcher killed the pig? Whether both flitches, or one flitch and a hand? She got to the doorstep at the question of trotters.

She helped herself up by the door-check—stout, capable, with nippy red elbows —and took her pail across the yard to the sack-bound pump. A gale of wind blus-tered her petticoats, and blew wisps of hair about her smiling broad face—'Now mind yourself on that ice, Agnes Ann,' said Mary Feirn, 'the children have made slides something shameful.'

Mrs. Hodgson piloted herself and the pail safely back. The wind blew half a gale from the north; it roared in the ashes; even in the sunny yard the ground was freezing. Out in the field the wintering hoggs trampled disconsolately over frosty grass and pulled at the bushes. Whitey-brown reed beds bobbed and danced and rippled in the sunshine and tearing wind. Beyond them, the frozen lake gleamed like the steel that Mary Feirn was polishing in the doorway.

There had been no wind when the frost began; the lake was frozen from end to end, black, clear, mysterious. The green weeds in the depths showed through the ice as through dusky bottle-glass. Above, in the upper air, Snawfell shone dazzling white against cloudless blue.

'Give us a sup of hot water out of the boiler, Mary; it freezes afore I can get my brush out,' said Mrs. Hodgson.

She proceeded to coat the doorstep with a sheet of ice, and then sprinkled it with cinders, according to the usual perversity of house wives in winter.

'Be the children coming back to luncheon, Agnes Ann?' 'Nay; I gave them a piece bread and blackberry jam to get shut of them. I doubt they've gone to Auntie Meg's.' (But they hadn't.)

Mrs. Hodgson and Mary, having redd up the kitchen, turned their attention to the pantry, conversing still about pig.

Roused by a discovery of cockroaches, and secure in the knowledge that Mathew [sic] was unlikely to return from market till four, they next routed out a recess in the wall beside the kitchen chimney, where he kept a miscellany of treassures. They were rewarded by finding a pair of pliers, long mislaid; and a secret hoard of string; and they upset a bag of shot into the fender.

At two, they took a cup of tea and bread and butter by way of dinner. Subsequently they tidied themselves, and put on the kettle, after another perilous journey to the pump.

They sat down before the fire, to darn the offending stockings. Wind and sun were dropping together; the sticks burnt crisp and crackly.

'Be n't you fidgeted about them children, Agnes Ann?'

'Wait till you have a pair of pickles of your own, sister. 'Tis the one time I'm none fidgeted, in a hard frost. They cannot fall in't water. A plague it is to live with young children beside a lake. Auntie Meg will bring them back at tea time; no fear.' (But she did not; they arrived in state, most unexpectedly at a quarter to three.)

A cart rumbled up to the door—'Save us, that cannot be Mathew? I meant to toast him a wigg. It does not tread like Daisy.'

'Hey, missus! Missus! Come oot there!'

'Good even to you, Mister Carradus; a fine dry frost!' 'Fine, mum,' said old Mr. Carradus, twinkling and rosy, with a drop at the end of his nose.

'And how's Mrs. Carradus?'

'Oo aye, she's fine, thank ye.'

'And the prize heifer; has she calved yet?'

'Fine,' said Mr. Carradus, with an absent manner. 'Aye, aye, a fine frost. 'Tis a roan bull calf.' His eye roamed round the yard, and fixed on Mary.

'This is my sister, Miss Feirn, from Lowthwaite.'

Old Mr. Carradus bowed profoundly, as it were from a hinge on his seat; he winked elaborately at Mary, who collapsed into giggles behind a blue-checked apron.

'And how's the market today, Mr. Carradus? Mathew took a cart of 'taties. In sacks weel happed up, but the silliest idea ever I heard of in such a like frost— They do say 'taties would be up to sevenpence—Hev you been buying a pig, Mr. Carradus?'

The old man was preoccupied in keeping something quiet beneath a blanket under his legs. He looked at Mrs. Hodgson quizzically over his nose, and winked again at Mary. 'Hev you lost two lile bit Herdwicks, Mrs. Hodgson? A lile bit fat ewe hoggie? and a lile bit tup, with a red muffl—He, he, hee!—a red pop at the back of his neck?'

'Ours is popped near and bitted far; and the wintering hoggs is tar marked with a T on the near—'

'Do you mean to tell me you've none *missed* them?' said old Mr. Carradus staring very hard, and keeping down the blanket with his foot. It bulged and broke into lamentations. A fat little girl of three pushed her head out—'Boohoo! I want my dinner—Auntie Mary—boo hoo!'

'I'se coom back. I'se warm,' said a fine little boy of four, struggling up between the knees of old Mr. Carradus, sucking a stick of pepper-mint rock. ('A lile bit Herdwick! we mun punch him on't ear if he strays!')

'Bless us, it's the children,' said Mrs. Hodgson calmly, 'and you taken the trouble to open three gates. But happen you've a message for Mathew?'

'D'ye know where they've *been* to, woman? (a cool hand for sure).'

'To their Auntie Meg's, Mrs Fleming's, at the Riddings. A fine job Fleming's had with your horse he bought at Cockermouth fair—He—'

'Woman!' said Mr Carradus impressively, 'I catched them on the ice at Silver-holme—'

'Get along with you, Mr. Carradus! Which the man tellt him that sellt it—'

'Where? Why, 'tis seven miles by road and four across the water,' said Mary.

'I'm much obliged to you for giving them the pleasure of a lift, Mr. Carradus, from the Pig and Whistle (aside); they loves a trap—'

'Don't mention it, Mum! don't mention it,' said Mr. Carradus, stand-offishly. He bestowed the blanket round his legs—'Good day, Miss Mary! ta tah! lile bit Herdwicks! I wish you good even, Mrs. Hodgson,' said old Mr. Carradus with a grand manner, turning round his horse's head.

As he was driving out of the gate he pulled up, and shouted back—'I'll pound 'em next time, Mrs. Hodgson. I'll pound 'em!'

The joke refreshed him so much that he drove off twinkling.

He had left undone half his own errands, as he passed through the market town, in order to hurry home the little lost lambies to the anxious mother—who had never missed them.

Poor old Mr. Carradus, it was a flat ending to his little 'ro mance'. And none too much time for the long way round of the Lake, with no cart lamp.

His own old woman was sympathetic, and forgave him for forgetting the baking powder, and two other knots in his red cotton pocket handkerchief. It could be got on Monday when neighbour Thompson went in for coal; and he will take back the blanket borrowed from Mrs. Rawlings at Nab Wood—'Tell me about it, Tummas.'

Old Carradus had spied the children crying on the ice behind the shelter of an island, as he jogged along the lake-side road, in the teeth of a bellowing north-east wind.

The gale had brought the little lad's shouts to his none too quick ears. He tied his horse to a gate, and went upon the ice, where he sat down painfully. It was like glass. The difficulty which he experienced in struggling fifty yards against the wind made him more ready to believe the children's story.

According to their confused account, they had 'swimmed' from the top end of the lake—'Swimmed? Skated, you mean, my mannie; 'tis four miles. But right down the wind, for truth. And what might your name be? Tommy Hodgson? Sure the lile one has a look of Mathew. She could niver come four miles; she can hardly toddle. But there's no house this end you can ha' come from, here abouts. Catch hold of my coat tails; I'll take you rightieways.'

He steered the children back with him to the shore, over the last strip of ice. The little roundabout girl in her cloak and petticoats caught the wind like a wherry— 'For sure, they have been blown upon their clog irons like skates. 'Tis a ro mance,' said old Carradus.

Mrs. Rawlings at the first cottage he came to agreed with him, 'There's none children of that age and looks at this end o' the Lake.' She lent him a blanket to cover them. The girl was very sleepy.

He spoke to one or two on the road. One had seen some little dark thing scudding before the wind in the middle of the frozen lake. He had taken it for a dog; but it might easy have been two children hand in hand—'That settles it,' said old Carradus, ''tis a ro mance.'

He told the story to the saddler, and to the grocer; he hurried out of the latter's shop after buying peppermint-rock and forgetting his wife's baking powder. The grocer had suggested that Mathew Hodgson, the father, was in the market, and was for calling him. But Mr. Carradus reflected that Mathew was unalarmed and unaware, whereas Agnes Ann would be distraught and truly thankful. It was flat— very flat—to be received with incredulity. But it was a happy thought to tell her he would put her stray offspring in the pound next time she lost them.

Old Mr. Carradus smiled placidly as his well-sharpened horse picked its way carefully home, by the longer west side of the lake. His own lile bit lambie slept quietly under the frosty grass—cold nor fire nor suffering would never harm her again, a little lass carried off by the fever at seven years old. His eyes had twinkled as he lifted fat little Mary Hodgson into his cart—'But it wears with time; it hurt a while, but it wears. She is safe at rest in the fold.'

Mathew heard the strange story soon enough in the market. He rattled home pell mell in his empty 'tater cart, and burst into the kitchen. He was younger than Mrs. Hodgson; mild eyed, with long-legged shambling gait, and fair hair.

'Hev they come, mother? are they starved? will I fetch Dr. Peter?'

'Dr. Pills? fudge!' said Mrs. Hodgson, fussing about with the tea pot and toasted muffin. 'It's a pack of lies; as if they could run four miles; more partic'lar Polly.'

When a person sets up for a monument of capability and good housekeeping, it is disconcerting to have two children strayed for five hours without ever missing them.

'They're no worse, Mathew,' seeing her man's pitiful anxiety. 'They've had some hot bread and milk, and Mary's laid them on the bed.'

'They could not keep their eyes open, they are that sleepy with the wind. 'Deed, they are no worse, Mathew,' said Mary Feirn.

The father creaked upstairs, to look at them; he came down blowing his nose, and went out again to stable his horse and put the cart away.

He ate his tea rather silently. Mrs. Hodgson said no word about having failed to miss the children. But she apologized for upsetting the bag of shot. Mathew reddened to the tips of his ears. He had never in the course of his married life received an apology from Agnes Ann; he did not quite know how to take it. It seemed prudent to let the matter pass. He lit his pipe.

Little voices were heard overhead. Mrs. Hodgson and Mary were busy cutting out baby clothes upon the cleared kitchen table. Mathew went upstairs, and fetched down the runaways; one on each knee, in the corner of the settle.

How fat they were, how warm and cuddly! Little pink ears and shiny plump cheeks, soft fluffy flaxen hair against his chin and whiskers; and stumpy worn shoes kicking his knees. Mathew hugged them closer.

'It blew—it plew—it plewed!' said Tommy, 'and it tatched her petticoats, and I hung on till her—' 'Tatch em—tatchem! tatchem! Oh, zee pitty fairies!' crowed little Polly.

'Zur was leetle teeny weeny fairies dancing—the beech leaves they was *full* of fairies—they danced wiv us all the way across the lake—' (Fairies?—good angels, that kept them off the spring heads where the wild ducks swatter, and the ice skims thinly.) Mathew shuddered, and hugged them closer.

'Did ye none try to turn back, Tommy?' 'Me *couldn't*, Dada; me went with my legs, and my clogs *swummed* after the fairies!'

'Tis the clog irons, mother; they've slid up the ice before the wind like a sledge.'

Mathew was no quick scholar; neither was Mr. Carradus. It took the latter almost as long to read this heart felt epistle as it had taken Mathew to write it:

> 'Tock How. Janr. 21. 18–
> Sir
>   this is they fuw lins To tell Jas Simpson as A february
> calver Mid sute Yow wantin try him 12 £ Has he as no turnps*
>   yrs respfl
>   M. Hodgson
> p.S. i du Thank yow   (blotted)'

* Bruce Thompson tells us that this somewhat illiterate letter can be interpreted as: '. . . these few lines to tell [you] James Simpson has a February calver [that] might suit [what] you're wanting. Try offering him £12 . . .'

15

Articles for the Press

Articles for the Press

From time to time Beatrix Potter sent contributions to the Press—'Sometimes a letter to the papers about farming or country affairs, which as often as not does not get printed'—we are told. In these contributions she always showed a complete mastery of her subject.

The article on hedgehogs, believed to have been published in *The Field*, is based on experience with her pet hedgehog Mrs. Tiggy-Winkle; while the letter to *The Times* on hawfinches, is in all probability based on observations made at Camfield Place, Hertfordshire. Other articles appear to have been written during World War I, and are associated with Beatrix Potter's work as a farmer.

The text of these articles has been taken from her rough drafts, as it has not been possible to trace the actual articles as they appeared in print.

HEDGEHOGS

Although sufficiently common animals, hedgehogs appear to have been very little studied by naturalists judging by the letters that occasionally appear in *The Field*.

The animal moults about one-third of its spines every spring, the spines being moulted after the rest of the fur. It will be noticed that the fur and spines pass from one form to the other—stiff bristly hair gradating into thin spines at the borders of the prickly jacket. The spines are attached to the skin by a slight knob. I believe that they fall out. I do not think that they are pushed out by a new spine growing in the old socket. This is a point of interest because new spines, grown at odd times to replace broken ones, are I think grown from the old root; and they are white and soft like those of a young hedgehog.

The spines which are grown in the ordinary course of moulting, are dark coloured and hard when they first pierce the skin. They grow very rapidly and cause the animal extreme irritation; it scratches itself with its hind claws like a dog. A few new spines are scattered all over the prickle jacket, but the main crop grows in bands. One season it is along the top of the back, another season in a stripe along either side; I think the animal completes a new coat about every third year, but a few individual spines may stick in for several years longer; but a healthy animal is never without a sufficient coat for protection.

Probably the bald hedgehog described in *The Field* was unable to grow new spines through some physical deficiency; it is no more remarkable than a bald skye-terrier.

The generally received idea that hibernation, like the freezing of water—depends directly upon a given low temperature, is not borne out by intimate acquaintance with the habits of hedgehogs, wild or tame. Their footprints may be seen in the snow, and there is nothing mysterious in the fact.

The hibernating trance is entirely under the animals' own control, and only in a secondary degree dependent on the weather. My tame hedgehog could rouse herself at half an hour's notice at any time, even during severe frost; and conversely she could 'go off' at will on a merely wet day in August, or upon the hearthrug in front of a hot fire.

I have watched the somewhat ghastly process on several occasions. The first time I saw it I administered brandy, being under the impression that the animal was dying. The trick is done by swallowing the breath, like Stevenson's 'Secundra Das' in the *Master of Ballantrae*.

The hedgehog composes itself comfortably, usually after a large meal and an evening of extra liveliness. The idea that it is made drowsy by cold weather is altogether wrong. It closes its eyes and holds its breath, occasionally it catches a breath in spite of itself with a sobbing gasp. The process looks difficult and highly uncomfortable; and the animal is very cross if interrupted. Gradually the involuntary gasps come at longer intervals, and the extremities grow cold and the nose becomes quite dry. In less than an hour the cataleptic state is complete.

When the hedgehog wants to return to the world the process is reversed; the breathing which has been slow and faint during the trance is quickened tremendously. I think I have counted 120 respirations to the minute. The first visible result of this vigorous consumption of air is a wetness of the hitherto dry nose. The heat reaches the paws last.

The waking up is a much slower process than the going off, and the animal is often painfully weak and nervous for several hours.

HAWFINCHES *
1888

Sir,

I notice that a correspondent writes to *The Times* of 6th. inst. to say that he has observed Hawfinches in the Forest of Dean.

This is the first season in which I have seen them in the neighbourhood of Hatfield, Herts, but it did not occur to me that they were particularly rare birds.

They arrived with us on the 23rd. January, a wet stormy day, in company with a flock of Redwings and one Snow-Bunting. The other birds disappeared with the wet weather, but the Hawfinches still remain.

Yarrell† states that they are shy birds, but, though wild at first, they are now

---

* Written in code; see *The Journal of Beatrix Potter*, F. Warne & Co. Ltd., London, 1966.
† William Yarrell, *A History of British Birds*. A three-volume edition 1837–1843, and a four-volume edition 1871–1885.

very bold. I never see them except near the house, and they can be approached within a few yards when feeding on the ground in the shrubbery.

There is a flock of tom birds, and a few old ones always in the garden. I noticed a curious piece of natural economy as regards their food. They are constantly feeding on holly seed. The seed is by no means always under holly bushes, but beneath branches where the thrushes and blackbirds roost, these soft billed birds having eaten the berries but not digested the pips, thus a month since there were quarts of holly seed lying on the grass, washed quite clean by the rain, and apparently in no way affected by the thrushes' digestive organs.

I never saw the Hawfinches eat the fruit in its natural condition, perhaps for the sufficient reason that there was not a berry left at the date of arrival, owing to previous invasion of Mistle Thrushes.

The Hawfinches pick up and shell the seed very rapidly. While on the ground, they move about less than any bird I ever noticed; sometimes one will sit for half-an-hour on the same square foot of turf. I believe they waddle like a starling.

I think it unlikely they will stay to nest (although I have seen one pair generally at a distance from the flock), as the supply of holly seed will soon be finished, and I never see them eat any other food.

When on the wing they are more active, constantly flying from tree to tree, very noisily, and conspicuous on account of their large heads, which give them a top-heavy appearance. When on the wing they swing up and down in their flight in the same manner as a Bullfinch.

WASTED LAND

Sir,

The root of this matter—the impoverished wasted root—is the eternal question of supply and demand. Misunderstanding, contumely, generations of bad times have broken the heart of farming. And farming is the heart of England. When Macaulay's New Zealander stands on the site of Westminster Bridge, there will still be tillers of the soil.

To-day Political economy and Science bestir themselves to proffer help. But without Confidence the farmer will not help himself. Confidence and stability; not inflation. Heaven forbid that another war should bring inflated prices again; famine prices that were begrudged to us, although earned by the labour of girls and old men whilst their lads died in Flanders.

How long did the country remember the farmer? Within very few years, a good sheep could be bought for five shillings. Can political economy build a permanent bridge, a just understanding, between producers and the overwhelming devouring town electorate? That the land is capable of producing more food is a commonplace. But who will guarantee the farmer a reasonable and permanent market?

I ask forgiveness if I bring forward my own farm as an example of what can be produced. Independently I seem to have followed much the same methods as Professor Stapledon, only I have relied more on quality, full quantity of stock and upon its management rather than upon expensive manure and seeds. We both knew the value of lime (which by the way has risen 1/-).

For the last three seasons my sheep farm has reared over one thousand Herdwick lambs and thirty Galloway and crossbred stirks. Its carries a summer population of 2800 sheep and 70 cattle. The farm is 1900 acres, half of it above the 1000 ft. contour, running up to 2500 ft. high crags; there is only 25 acres of mowing grass.

I am now stocking another farm with surplus sheep. Nevertheless I have had sheep for sale this autumn; and I have felt that I am rather swamping the local Fairs.

Farmers could produce far more sheep and cattle than they do at present; but is there any assurance that this increased production will not produce a glut, and another ruinous slump in prices?

OAKS

The spreading oak beloved of painters and poets is mercifully of less timber value than the oak of the woods. Wide-flung ancestral trees of English parks have usually contemptibly short butts compared with the bulk of their branches.

Of course any decent oak timber is valuable; but the cynosure of the wood-monger is the oak that has spindled skyward in a thicket; a long straight trunk of clean timber without a branch. Trunks above 20 ft. are wanted for the under-carriage of railway trucks; no metal has the same strength and resilience, combined.

A good forester will prune any likely seedling that he meets with in a plantation. It is useless to prune branches on a big oak. Even if tarred over, the wound will grow a lip which holds rain water. Hedgerow trees which have been justifiably lopped for the sake of grass or cereals below—seldom make good timber; besides the risk of fence nails.

ACORNS

It is doubtful whether tree-lovers realize the drawbacks of oaks. About every third or fourth season there is an acorn year. In one such an autumn a Kendal knacker collected ten poisoned cattle in one day from farms about Troutbeck and Staveley. The Trust's tenant at Thwaite farm lost three heifers; a money loss of sixty pounds apart from the distress of losing home-bred stock which cannot be adequately replaced.

I asked him could he not keep his cattle in a safe field until birds and sheep had cleared up the acorns? He said he had *no* safe field.

As Thwaite had been bought expressly to save the oaks there was nothing to be done. Had the farm been private property it would have been reasonable to fell single trees which were rendering a whole field unsafe.

Acorns are more dangerous to young beasts than to dairy cows. Horses and sheep seem to eat them with impunity; although *horses* are peculiarly susceptible to poisoning by oak *leaves*. Never fell a field oak in leaf. And if felled in winter bareness—have the twiggy branches burnt, (or given away to cottages in return for removal *if* the farmer *does not want them*. Farm tenant has *first* claim to *firewood*, but you can't force him to clear up).

Some oak trees bear more frequent crops than others. I have never seen many on the large oak opposite Yew Tree Farm: whereas a similar tree at Hill Top is such a perennial nuisance; I wish it would blow down!

Nevertheless—think twice and thrice before you fell an oak. Generations of men and cattle will come and go before its like matures again.

OF TIMBER

There are two points of view in considering trees; the aesthetic, and the commercial. The former consideration may be subdivided into pictorial and antiquarian interest. Ancient yews, old oaks, old Scots fir are incomparably more interesting— more entitled to preservation—than the rapid growing sycamore, or the ash, or the self-grown birch which springeth as a weed amongst the loose wet shale.

Yews: It is disputed whether there is truth in the legend that each farm of the Border country had to grow its quota. 'Spanish' yew is said to have been imported for bows. Be that as it may, the ancient yew trees are primaeval with the ancient farm steads. Happily they do not run much risk (except from modern poisonous sheep dips where they grow below the folds as at Birk How, Little Langdale).

Tenants often cut them hard back, on account of livestock; but yews like hollies can stand hand cropping. The timber of an old yew is valueless; usually 'shaked' and starred; and too hard to be tempting for firewood. Like the Fraternal Four of Borrowdale and the great Yew of Yew Tree Farm—they stand till the inevitable gale. Had I a hollow yew falling to pieces I would put a chain round the trunk—iron hoops off barrels are sometimes used but they soon rust. Yew berries sprout readily.

Of Yew Poisoning: Young yews grow rapidly and are not particularly interesting. If in a position likely to become troublesome—cut them out ruthlessly while still insignificant (this advice applies to any young tree that looks like becoming a nuisance later on—such as a sycamore seedling rooting too near, or under a building; or an ash sapling that will later on push against and sway a fence [or] wall— have them out while they are still insignificant).

Of Timber

Yew poisoning is a disputed subject—On the fells and in the woods the yew is cropped by deer and sheep (likewise rhododendron)—yet lowland farm stock is occasionally poisoned. I do not agree that only certain yews are poisonous. I think it depends on the stomach condition of animals at the time of swallowing.

The worst cases I ever heard of were a drove of hungry bullocks put in for the night on the road to a fair; and a team of brewers horses at a wayside inn near Gloucester. The unicorn horse was lying dead when the dray man came out; the near horse was fatally ill; the off horse had not been able to reach and escaped damage.

Remember that dead brown branches of yew are even more dangerous than green leaves. A farm tenant should look after the lopping of his yew trees; but he should not cut down a sizeable yew without leave. The agent should keep an eye upon roadside yews near houses; at least in the old days of tradesmen's horses it used to be very necessary, and there is still risk to cows, passing home to the byre.

It is not many years since a van horse was poisoned by a yew tree at Grasmere church bridge. And this summer two colts belonging to Mr. Dixon, Low Wray, were killed by eating laurel clippings carelessly left by a gardener on the *field* side of a hedge. Laurels are not usually suspect. But all farm animals appear to have a morbid curiosity and greed for any newly scattered fresh object.

16
Election Work

Election Work
1910

Soon after the publication of *The Tale of Peter Rabbit*, Beatrix Potter made a Peter Rabbit doll for one of the Warne children, and on December 10th 1903 she told Norman Warne, 'I am cutting out calico patterns of Peter. I have not got it right yet, but the expression is going to be lovely; especially the whiskers—(pulled out of a brush!). I think I will make one first of white velveteen painted . . . fur is very difficult to sew . . . I think I could make him stand on his legs if he had some lead bullets in his feet!'

The Peter Rabbit doll was soon finished, and on December 15th Beatrix Potter told Norman Warne, 'I hope the little girl will like the doll—There is some shot in the body and coat tail, I don't think it will come out until the legs give way. Children sometimes expect comfits out of animals, so I give fair warning!' She was wondering whether Mr. Warne could help her to get some of these Peter Rabbit dolls on the market, pointing out that 'there is a run on toys copied from pictures'. 'I made another doll,' she wrote on January 1st 1904. 'I am sure they would sell, people are so amused with it.'

The years passed and nothing came of this idea. Apparently the British toy trade was hard hit by the large quantities of cheap toys which were being imported from Germany; and at that time the Camberwell doll trade was virtually on its last legs. After much searching Beatrix Potter could find no firms who were in a position to take on the manufacture of these Peter Rabbit dolls and so the idea was dropped.

She therefore felt strongly that Free Trade should be abolished and some form of tariff reform brought in; and with the 1910 Election in sight, busied herself with propaganda in favour of tariff reform, which amongst other things was one of the issues of this election.

With this, and other ends in view, Beatrix Potter had various leaflets printed, and drew by hand a number of coloured posters. 'I am so busy over the election,' she wrote, 'my fingers are quite stiff with drawing posters', and by way of comment; 'These posters are good bold practice, I must have made sixty.'

The posters were about 280 mm × 215 mm in size, and dealt with the undesirable effects of Free Trade with Germany. 'Here lies The South London Toy Trade, killed by Free Trade with Germany,' she wrote at the top of one of them—beneath which was a water colour sketch of a British-made doll in a limp condition, and below, a verse of her own composition:

A hand-drawn poster in protest against Free Trade

A hand-drawn poster in protest against Free Trade

When a Workman ain't got any Wages—
Now what is the good of 'cheap' bread?
While you argues and talks and rampages—
Poor Camberwell Dolly lies dead!

The leaflets dealt with her various political views, and in particular with the necessity of introducing tariff reform.

One leaflet, printed by Martin, Hood & Larkin, of Great Newport Street, London, W.C., and signed Beatrix Potter, put forward a number of arguments in favour of tariff reform. Another, printed by Edmund Evans Ltd., of Swan Street, London, S.E., was headed 'The Shortage of Horses', and was an attempt to protect the rights of the many small farmers in Lancashire, of which Beatrix Potter was one.

As a farmer, Beatrix Potter was very concerned about the present shortage of horses and of possible government interference. In a letter to Mr. Wilfred Evans on February 28th 1910, she wrote, 'It is useless to talk to farmers about *dolls*. But if there *is* a subject which enrages us—it is meddling with our horses! (*I* am a one-horse farmer, amongst other trades.) Last autumn we filled in an innocent looking paper, handed by the county police, for a horse census. Everybody thought it foreshadowed a most welcome scheme for subsidising *army remounts*. Last week it came out under cross-questioning in the House of Commons that we have rendered our horses liable to requisition in case of necessity during war. I am as loyal as most people; nobody likes to be tricked. What the Unionists have advocated for a long time is a proper system of reserve horses, earmarked and registered for a very small retaining fee. I would willingly keep a yeomanry horse. But to seize the very scanty stock would bring agriculture to a standstill. Even at a fair price it would be exasperating.' And referring to the present scarcity of horses, she wrote, 'For instance, that sale of bus horses, I am told by two bus drivers that all their best mares were bought by "a foreigner", some discussion whether French or German army agent; but anyhow the mares are gone.'

When discussing the wording of her leaflets with Mr. Evans Beatrix Potter told him with due consideration, 'Of course I could not ask any body to print anything they did not like on reading it over'; she wished the name of the printer to appear on the leaflet. And in regard to the horse leaflet, 'It must not be let out the horse leaflet is written by a *female*. I should give it away as being written by a small farmer in Lancashire.'

To make this horse leaflet attractive, there was on the front page a drawing of two horses standing by a hut, with a valley and hills in the distance, one which Beatrix Potter had drawn at Lyme Regis in April 1904. Also, at the very end of the leaflet was a small drawing of a one-horse hay cart with farm labourers gathering in the hay. 'My writing takes more space than I expected', she said. 'If there is not room for the hay cart—leave it out.'

The leaflet was signed 'Yours truly, North Country Farmer'. 'The chief thing', she told Mr. Evans, 'is clear printing . . . and don't use too cheap-looking paper . . . and please notice my spelling, when I have copied a thing several times I can neither write nor spell.'

After the leaflets were printed Beatrix Potter told Mr. Evans, 'I have posted it to a funny collection of names, mostly from Agricultural Show Catalogues and advertisements of farmers and sales.' She had also written letters of protest to several of the country papers.

In her letter of April 4th Beatrix Potter mentioned still another leaflet, saying 'I think you might let me have 1000 each of the horse and printer leaflets.' The latter evidently dealt with problems such as foreign copyright and import restrictions which faced the printers at that time; and Edmund Evans, who were engravers and printers, and who printed her books, were sufficiently sympathetic to offer to print some of these leaflets gratis.

'I have been writing, after much thought, to Mr. Spurgeon of Cassell's,' wrote Beatrix Potter, 'to ask if he can give the names of any French or German authors who have published for *their own benefit* English translations in U.S.A.? The great difficulty of translations is to get any royalty at all.' And in a further letter, 'I am afraid the book trade by *itself* will never make anything of the United States.'

The following week she informed Mr. Evans that she would be writing to various firms of engravers and paper makers and book binders in the London directory, to see whether any of them would be willing to distribute the printers' leaflet. This they evidently did, for in a few weeks time we are told, 'There seems to have been a fresh run on that leaflet, through the Master Printers—I had a letter via Bedford Street which nearly cleared out my supply here.'

In reference to one of her leaflets—probably the printers' one—Beatrix Potter told Mr. Evans, 'I have posted some with letters, and put C/o Messrs Evans—I don't *suppose* there will be any replies—it is a case of casting bread upon the waters—! but if there are any this week, my address is so uncertain I think it would be best if you would open them. I offered to send more copies gratis to several firms that I believe to be tariff reformers—I wrote to Smiths' that if the leaflets "caught on" and were asked for—we should of course be glad to sell them. One never can tell—nobody expected "Peter" to go off.'

The addressing and stamping of these leaflets presented a problem to Beatrix Potter, who at that time happened to be at the Royal Hotel, Teignmouth, on holiday with her parents. 'My parents' plans are inconveniently uncertain', she wrote.

In this work she was helped by Margaret Hammond, niece of her first governess, and in a letter to Mr. Evans she wrote, 'Miss M. Hammond finds there are more names than I thought. Can you let her have 1000 at 51, Minster Road—instead of 500. I daresay a good many will get thrown away as circulars, but I have instructed her to fold them with the title at the top. The bulk of them will go with a ½d stamp, but I am writing short letters for a number of the big firms, to post with 1d. I think it is worth doing.'

In due course replies were received, and we find Beatrix Potter thanking Mr. Evans 'for forwarding the curious, unexpected bundle of letters—I will answer some of them', she said. 'It is very pleasant to hear that it is appreciated by the Printers' Association.' And a week later: 'Some of the replies are very curious. The man at Carlisle, who thinks he would like a little tariff in places—but not tariff reform all round—rather reminds me of the curate's egg "parts of it are excellent".'

Beatrix Potter did not receive sympathy from all those she approached, and confiding in Mr. Evans, wrote, 'I doubt whether Whitley's post card counts, as it looks to me to be written by a clerk in the bookselling department—but I have been strongly of opinion all along—that those big stores do favour Free Trade—They make an immense profit on German goods, and they have an immense turnover of trash (which is not *really* 'cheap' to the consumer)—because people buy so much rubbish that they need not buy at all—only they think it is a bargain.'

During 1910 Beatrix Potter worked hard at her election propaganda, but after this, she made no further attempt to influence the electorate, and we are told by Margaret Lane that 'the year of this memorable election was long distinguished in conversation by the Potter family as "the year when Bee went into politics".'

EVERYBODY knows where their own shoes pinch. Do you know how much trouble some of us are having with the Foreigner? It is the same all over British trade, large things and small.

A few years ago I invented a rabbit doll which was in demand. I tried in vain to get it made in England. There was not a single British wholesale toy-maker left who could undertake the job. There seems to be one survivor, who makes superior Teddy Bears. My doll is now made by scores in Frau H——'s factory in Germany. She can make it cheaply because German work-people work longer hours and under different conditions to ours. British factories and work-people are restricted—most properly—by the Factory Acts. We are fighting foreign competition with one arm tied, so long as there is no import duty. The London toy shops are choked with foreign toys.

Now the question has reached my books. There has always been very great difficulty about English books in the United States. The States are enormously rich and protected by heavy tariffs. We have no tariff by means of which we might bring the States to reason. They simply laugh at us. My most successful book has been pirated and reprinted by American printers who have never sent me a halfpenny.

The difficulties about "copyrighting" an English book in America are now so very great, that we are obliged to engrave and print *in* America all copies intended for American use. We cannot print them here and send them to America like we used to do; the manufacture and wages belonging to those copies are now lost to England.

It is expensive and troublesome to engrave and print the books in both countries (as we now do). In 1909 there was a serious proposal to print *ALL* copies in future in America, and ship part of them back from America to England for use here.

My publishers and I refused to agree. The American printing is very good; but it would mean a loss of £2,000 a year to British wages.

P T.O.

It is uphill work, trying to help folks who will not help themselves. Why should *I* bother myself about the British workman, if he prefers " Free " Trade ?

The land tax clauses are almost impossible to understand. I have one expensive field which would be liable to the special ½d. on its capital value, an extra 12/5½ per year. At the present rent, and land tax of 7/-, it pays me about 2¼ per cent. on what it cost, and I mend the walls.

If the tax is raised I shall be obliged reluctantly to raise the rent.

I suppose there are 22 Dukes in Great Britain ; but there are hundreds and thousands of farmers and small holders who will suffer by the rise in the taxation of land. I am not a Duke ; I bought that field out of my earnings and savings. Also I have no vote !

My grandfather was Radical member for Carlisle, a colleague of Bright and Cobden. In those days the working man had not the Franchise. It is nonsense to pretend that the old bad days of the Corn Laws can ever come back, now that the people have votes. The working man can safely give Tariff Reform a trial without being frightened by the bogey of dear bread.

Let us have honest British and Colonial goods, even if we have to pay a little more for some of them. We shall at least have the satisfaction of knowing that our money is being spent in British wages.

BEATRIX POTTER.

Printed by Martin, Hood & Larkin, Great Newport Street, London, W.C.

THE SHORTAGE OF HORSES.

On Feb. 25th certain questions were asked in the House of Commons about a **census of horses**. Papers have recently been distributed and collected by the country police. Probably many farmers believed, (as I did,) that the census fore-shadowed some welcome scheme for encouraging horse-breeding, or for subsidising yeomanry remounts. **Such schemes are constantly advocated by Unionist Members.**

On Feb. 25th Capt. Faber (Unionist, W. Hampshire) asked the Home Secretary (Mr. Winston

Churchill) whether the information contained in the recent census of horses compiled by the police was given voluntarily; and if such information would be used for **requisitioning** any of the horses?

Mr. Winston Churchill, Home Secretary, replied that the information contained in the census was given voluntarily by owners. " It was explained to them that the information was required for the military authorities, and would not be used for purposes of taxation; and I believe it was generally known that it would be used by the military authorities to guide them in the purchase of horses, or, **in a great national emergency, in their impressment."**

Farmers are as loyal as most people; and they would welcome a business-like arrangement. But --Is it fair to allow a dangerous shortage of army remounts, with a plan of obtaining them by conscription at a time of crisis and panic?

· No doubt we should be paid for our horses; but **what about our ruined crops?**

Suppose the "emergency" occurred in summer. How should we carry the hay and corn? And every sheaf of British corn would be wanted, if our foreign supply of wheat were interrupted by war.

In old days we might have made shift to save the crops with help of brood mares and young stock. That reserve scarcely exists now. Everybody has parted with the extra mare.

Agriculture would be at a standstill if our working horses were taken unexpectedly by conscription.

In the debate upon the Army Estimates, March 10, Mr. Haldane said that out of 2,000,000 horses, the War Office would require about 140,000. That seems to be one horse out of every 14 or 15. But in actual fact a larger percentage will fall upon farmers, because **farm horses are strongest and soundest.**

It has never been explained what is meant by an "emergency." Does it mean actual invasion? or does it include acute difficulty abroad?

Every one remembers the disastrous waste of money and horseflesh which took place during the Boer war, through want of a proper reserve of seasoned horses. The animals that worked best in S. Africa were colonial ponies, and the London bus horses which dragged the guns. The omnibus companies, and certain large London firms, are stated to have received a yearly subsidy for holding this reserve of bus horses and "vanners." They were subsidised — not "commandeered." Now the London streets are given up to motor buses and French taxicabs, and the London bus men go about with an organ. Another 400 bus horses are advertised for sale this week.

The only persons who are likely to keep horses extensively in future will be hunting men, country tradesmen and **farmers.**

Let these horse owners watch the action of the present Liberal Government. The Opposition constantly press for attention to the dangerous shortage of horses. Mr. Haldane's answers vary from day to day; before this leaflet can be printed he may have changed his plans. If Unionists succeed in obtaining a scheme upon a business basis—let Unionists have the credit.

The present policy is penny wise and pound foolish. **Why has a Liberal Government such a spite against any industry con= nected with Land?**

Yours truly,

NORTH COUNTRY FARMER.

PRINTED AND PUBLISHED BY EDMUND EVANS, LTD., SWAN STREET, LONDON, S.E.

APPENDICES

APPENDIX 1

End-papers for Editions in the Small Format

Warne's first edition of *The Tale of Peter Rabbit* had end-papers with a leaf design on a pale grey background, but at the beginning of 1903, Beatrix Potter began to experiment with end-paper designs on which there were drawings of her animal characters.

In one of her privately printed copies of *The Tailor of Gloucester* two different end-paper designs were roughly sketched out. In the first she drew four corner panels—in one, Peter is holding a closed book, while in another, a little mouse is reading an open book. In the remaining two panels are old Brown, the owl, and Squirrel Nutkin. The panels are linked together with scroll designs, and there is a sketch at each mid-position, showing a pie dish, a cup and saucer, some bags of nuts, and a pair of scissors and reel of thread.

The second design is a rough sketch of the one which was actually used. A third design, intended for *The Tale of Squirrel Nutkin*, consisted of a border of twelve squirrels with a design of nuts between the two uppermost squirrels. In the centre of the page is a cluster of three hazel nuts. Later, this idea formed the basis of the end-papers for *Peter Rabbit's Almanac for 1929*, with rabbits in place of squirrels and a cabbage in place of nuts.

At first Beatrix Potter considered that her end-papers should be uncoloured, and she prepared a finished drawing of the second design, from which a block is believed to have been made, although it was never actually used.

She felt that if the end-paper design were fully coloured and repeated four times, the effect might be somewhat heavy for so small a book—but after giving the matter further thought she wrote to Warnes saying, 'I think if it were kept rather small, or rather light coloured, it would look very nice.'

For this reason the first published pictorial end-paper, Fig. 1, was printed with very delicate colouring; but when used for later printings, and paired off with Fig. 2, the colours were intensified.

In Fig. 1 there is a white cat on the right; and in Fig. 2, to balance the pair, the white cat is on the left.

In September 1904, when *The Tale of Benjamin Bunny* was first published, Fig. 2 was paired off with Fig. 3, in which the cat was brown, and the 'amiable guinea-pig', from one of Beatrix Potter's *Appley Dapply* rhymes, appeared for the first and only time as an end-paper. Beatrix Potter had every intention of finishing off her *Appley Dapply* book of rhymes by 1905, but when Norman Warne died in August of that year, the book was put on one side, and in 1907 when the next end-paper, Fig. 4 appeared, the 'amiable guinea-pig' was replaced by Mr. Jeremy Fisher. On the other hand, the guinea-pig might have been Tuppenny, because at that time Beatrix Potter thought *The Tale of Tuppenny* would be published in the near future.

The various end-papers for the books in the ordinary-size format are shown in Figs. 1 to 14. The end-papers, Figs. 1 to 9, however, are of special interest because by observing the particular animal characters in them, it is possible to form an approximate estimate as to when a particular book was printed. The exception being the case of Figs. 6 and 7, which are the end-papers currently in use.

In referring to her first edition end-papers 'depicting the little animals of the Series', Beatrix Potter wrote, 'you can "place" editions of other books, approximately, by looking at these animals.'

Table 1

INTRODUCTION OF END-PAPERS, FIGURES 1 TO 9

Figure	When introduced	Title of book
1	August 1903	The Tale of Squirrel Nutkin
2	December 1903	The Tailor of Gloucester (2nd printing), and The Tale of Peter Rabbit (6th printing)
3	September 1904	The Tale of Benjamin Bunny
4	September 1907	The Tale of Tom Kitten
5	August 1908	The Tale of Jemima Puddle-Duck
6	July 1909	The Tale of the Flopsy Bunnies
7	July 1910	The Tale of Mrs. Tittlemouse
*8	December 1918	The Tale of Johnny Town-Mouse
†9	December 1918	The Tale of Johnny Town-Mouse

* This is Fig. 6, with a central figure of Johnny Town-Mouse added.
† This is Fig. 7, with a central figure of Timmy Willie added.

Table 2

END-PAPERS USED IN FIRST EDITIONS (SEE FIGURES 1 TO 9)

Title of book	First edition end-papers			
	Front		Back	
	Left hand	Right hand	Left hand	Right hand
*The Tale of Peter Rabbit (5th printing)	Fig. 1	Fig. 1	Fig. 1	Fig. 1
The Tale of Squirrel Nutkin	Fig. 1	Fig. 1	Fig. 1	Fig. 1
†The Tailor of Gloucester	Fig. 1	Fig. 1	Fig. 1	Fig. 1
The Tail of Benjamin Bunny	Fig. 2	Fig. 3	Fig. 2	Fig. 3
The Tale of Two Bad Mice	Fig. 2	Fig. 3	Fig. 2	Fig. 3
The Tale of Mrs. Tiggy–Winkle	Fig. 2	Fig. 3	Fig. 2	Fig. 3
The Tale of Mr. Jeremy Fisher	Fig. 2	Fig. 3	Fig. 2	Fig. 3
The Tale of Tom Kitten	Fig. 2	Fig. 4	Fig. 2	Fig. 4
The Tale of Jemima Puddle–Duck	Fig. 5	Fig. 4	Fig. 5	Fig. 4
The Tale of the Flopsy Bunnies	Fig. 5	Fig. 6	Fig. 6	Fig. 5
The Tale of Mrs. Tittlemouse	Fig. 7	Fig. 6	Fig. 6	Fig. 7
The Tale of Timmy Tiptoes	Fig. 7	Fig. 6	Fig. 6	Fig. 7
The Tale of Johnny Town–Mouse	Fig. 8	Fig. 9	Fig. 8	Fig. 9

* First printing having coloured pictorial end-papers. The next printing had Figs. 1 and 2 end-papers.
† The next printing (still with 1903 on the title page) had Figs. 1 and 2 end-papers.

One of Beatrix Potter's early designs for her pictorial
end-papers

Beatrix Potter's uncoloured pictorial end-paper. A line block is believed to have been made but it was never used

Design 1: First used in August 1903 for *The Tale of Squirrel Nutkin*
(Note the white cat on the right-hand side)
Fig. 1

Design 2: First used in December 1903 for the 2nd
printing of *The Tailor of Gloucester*, and for the 6th
printing of *The Tale of Peter Rabbit*
(Note the white cat on the left-hand side)
Fig. 2

Design 3: First used in September 1904 for *The Tale of Benjamin Bunny*
(Note the cat has changed colour (brown), and the figure of
the guinea-pig has been added)
Fig. 3

Design 6: First used in July 1909 for *The Tale of The Flopsy Bunnies*. This is the end-paper currently in use (Note there is no cat, and the Flopsy Bunnies appear for the first time)

Fig. 6

Design 7: First used in July 1910 in *The Tale of Mrs. Tittlemouse*. This is the end-paper currently in use

(Note there is no cat, and a bee has been added at the top right-hand corner)

Fig. 7

Design 8: First used in December 1918 for *The Tale of Johnny Town-Mouse*
Note that this is Design 6 with the figure of Johnny Town-Mouse added in the centre)
Fig. 8

Design 9: First used in December 1918 for *The Tale of Johnny Town-Mouse*
(Note that this is Design 7 with the figure of Timmy Willie added in the centre)
Fig. 9

End-paper for the first edition of *The Tale of Mr. Tod*

(Used at the front and back)

Fig. 10

End-paper for the first edition of *The Tale of Pigling Bland*
(Used at the front and back)

End-paper for the first edition of *Appley Dapply's Nursery Rhymes*
(Used at the front)

Fig. 11

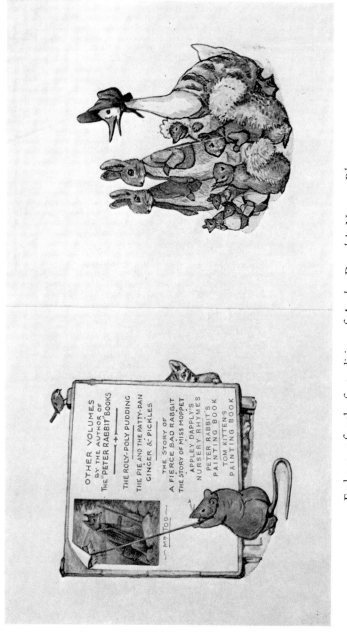

End-paper for the first edition of *Appley Dapply's Nursery Rhymes*
(Used at the back)

Fig. 12

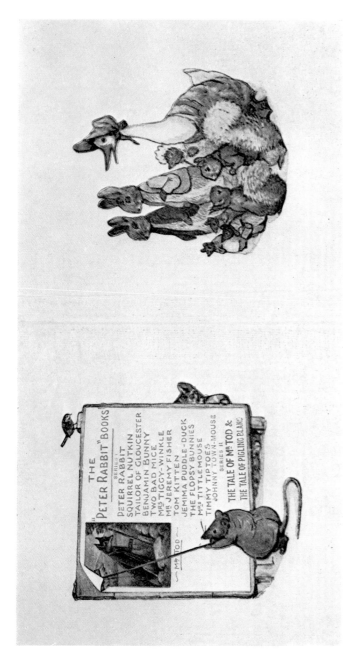

End-paper for the first edition of *Cecily Parsley's Nursery Rhymes*
(Used at the front)
Fig. 13

End-paper for the first edition of *Cecily Parsley's Nursery Rhymes*
(Used at the back)

Fig. 14

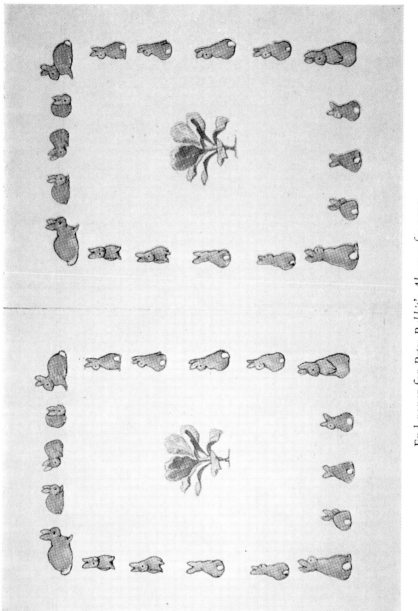

End-paper for *Peter Rabbit's Almanac for 1929*
(Used at the front and back)

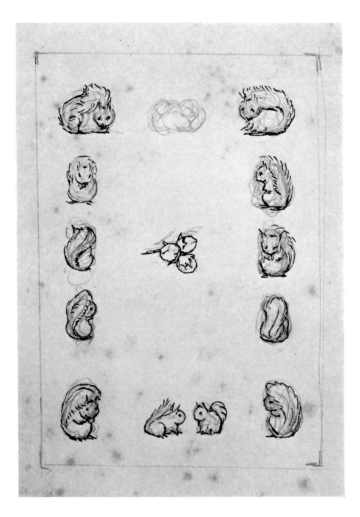

An early design for the end-papers of *The Tale of
Squirrel Nutkin*
(not used)

APPENDIX 2

Page Numbers of Book Pictures

When reference is made to the page numbers of the *Peter Rabbit* books, it is important to know whether the book is an early printing or a more recent one.

In the earlier printings there were more pages, due to some of the pages being left blank—also, in the case of the first four printings of *The Tale of Peter Rabbit*—there were four extra pictures which were removed in 1903 when the coloured end-papers were first introduced.

The corresponding page numbers of the pictures in different printings are shown in Tables 1 to 5.

In these tables the frontispiece has not been mentioned—also, the titles *The Tale of Mr. Tod, The Tale of Pigling Bland, The Story of a Fierce Bad Rabbit, The Story of Miss Moppet, Appley Dapply's Nursery Rhymes* and *Cecily Parsley's Nursery Rhymes* are omitted, as the page numbers of these books are the same in all printings.

Table 1

THE SMALL FORMAT BOOKS

CORRESPONDING PAGE NUMBERS OF BOOK PICTURES

Applying to all the titles listed below, including Peter Rabbit		*The first 4 printings of Peter Rabbit*
Earlier printings 85 pages	*Current printings 59 pages*	*97 pages*
8	8	8
11	11	11
14	12	17
17	15	20
20	16	23
23	19	29
26	20	32
29	23	35
32	24	38
35	27	41
38	28	44
41	31	47
44	32	50
47	35	53
50	36	56
53	39	59
56	40	62
59	43	65
62	44	71
65	47	74
68	48	77
71	51	80
74	52	83
77	55	89
81	57	93
84	58	96

Peter Rabbit	*Mrs. Tiggy-Winkle*	*Mrs. Tittlemouse*
The Tailor of Gloucester	*Mr. Jeremy Fisher*	*Timmy Tiptoes*
Squirrel Nutkin	*Tom Kitten*	*Johnny Town-Mouse*
Benjamin Bunny	*Jemima Puddle-Duck*	NOTE
Two Bad Mice	*The Flopsy Bunnies*	*All pictures are in colour*

Appendix 2

Table 2

THE PIE AND THE PATTY-PAN

CORRESPONDING PAGE NUMBERS OF BOOK PICTURES

Small Format (76 pages)	Large Format (52 pages)	Small Format (76 pages)	Large Format (52 pages)	Small Format (76 pages)	Large Format (52 pages)
7	7	**31**	**23**	**54**	**38**
9	**9**	35	25	57	40
12	11	**38**	**27**	59	41
15	12	41	29	**61**	**43**
17	**14**	**43**	**31**	65	45
21	16	47	33	66	46
24	**18**	49	34	68	47
26	20	51	35	70	48
29	21	52	36	**72**	**50**

NOTE: *Pictures in colour are indicated by heavy type*

Table 3

GINGER AND PICKLES

CORRESPONDING PAGE NUMBERS OF BOOK PICTURES

Small Format (75 pages)	Large Format (52 pages)	Small Format (75 pages)	Large Format (52 pages)	Small Format (75 pages)	Large Format (52 pages)
7	7	35	25	59	41
9	**9**	**38**	**27**	**61**	**43**
12	11	40	29	64	45
15	12	**43**	**31**	67	46
18	**14**	47	33	69	47
21	16	49	34	70	48
23	**18**	51	35	**72**	**50**
26	20	52	36	74	52
28	21	**54**	**38**	—	—
31	**23**	56	40	—	—

NOTE: *Pictures in colour are indicated by heavy type*

Table 4

ROLY-POLY PUDDING

CORRESPONDING PAGE NUMBERS OF BOOK PICTURES

Small Format (76 pages)	Large Format (70 pages)	Small Format (76 pages)	Large Format (70 pages)	Small Format (76 pages)	Large Format (70 pages)
7	1	**31**	**25**	**55**	**49**
9	3	32	26	56	50
10	4	33	27	57	51
11	5	**34**	**28**	**58**	**52**
12	6	36	30	60	54
13	7	37	31	61	55
15	**9**	**39**	**33**	62	56
16	10	40	34	63	57
17	11	41	35	**64**	**58**
18	**12**	**42**	**36**	**67**	**61**
20	14	44	38	68	62
21	15	45	39	69	63
23	**17**	**47**	**41**	**70**	**64**
24	18	48	42	**73**	**67**
25	19	49	43	74	68
26	**20**	**50**	**44**	75	69
28	22	52	46	76	70
29	23	53	47	—	—

NOTE: *Pictures in colour are indicated by heavy type*

Table 5

LITTLE PIG ROBINSON

CORRESPONDING PAGE NUMBERS OF BOOK PICTURES

Small Format (112 pages)	Large Format (96 pages)	Small Format (112 pages)	Large Format (96 pages)	Small Format (112 pages)	Large Format (96 pages)
7	end-paper	47	42	91	79
10	**9**	**48**	**43**	**92**	**80**
13	11	50	44	95	82
17	15	55	49	98	85
21	19	59	53	102	88
28	**25**	**63**	**56**	104	90
31	27	72	64	107	end-paper
34	30	76	67	109	95
38	33	80	**71**	111	end-paper
40	35	83	end-paper	—	—
42	37	89	77	—	—

NOTE: *Pictures in colour are indicated by heavy type, and they face the page numbers given. The American edition, with additional black and white pictures, is not covered by this table*

APPENDIX 3

Notes on First Editions

It is accepted that a book bearing the year of publication on the front of the title page may generally be regarded as a first edition. In a few cases, however, a more definite recognition of an actual 'first' can be made by referring to the information given in this appendix.

Identification of the first printing by means of a dated title is not always possible, because even if the year of publication appears on the front of the title page—which it does in the majority of cases—in many instances there was more than one printing in the year of publication, and the later printings made during that year are sometimes indistinguishable from the first.

In the absence of authentic records of the actual date of publication, the relevant information in the following tables has been based upon

(a) The date when Frederick Warne & Co. placed their order with the printer.
(b) The date when the printer's account was paid.
(c) The date which Beatrix Potter inscribed in her 'author's copies', and in presentation copies of first editions.

The sizes given are the *height* and *width* of the actual page, and *not* that of the cover. Slight variations should be expected, due to guillotining tolerances when trimming the sheets.

While the stated colours of the paper boards are those which are usually found, it is possible that other colours may sometimes have been used—for example, copies of the first edition of *The Tale of Squirrel Nutkin* were specially bound in brown for a very particular customer—Liberty's of Regent Street!

This appendix is intended to help in the identification of first editions of Beatrix Potter's books—in the case of the *Peter Rabbit* series it is based on the English editions.

PRIVATELY PRINTED EDITIONS OF THE TALE OF PETER RABBIT AND THE TAILOR OF GLOUCESTER

The Tale of Peter Rabbit		The Tailor of Gloucester
First edition	*2nd printing*	
250 Copies	200 Copies	500 Copies
December 1901	February 1902	December 1902
In paper boards, pale olive-green (Flat Back).	In paper boards, olive-green (Rounded Back).	In paper boards, pink
Size: 135 mm × 103 mm	Size: 131 mm × 103 mm	Size: 131 mm × 102 mm
	In this printing there are slight changes in the text.	The text is shorter than that of Freda's manuscript, but appreciably longer than the regularly published edition. Illustrations throughout in colour.
Apart from the frontispiece, which is in colour, all illustrations are line drawings, similar in design to the coloured pictures in Warne's first edition.		

EDITIONS OF THE TALE OF PETER RABBIT WITH PLAIN LEAF-PATTERN END-PAPERS

First edition	*2nd printing*	*3rd printing*	*4th printing*
8000 copies October 1902	12,000 copies November 1902	8220 copies December 1902	8250 copies April 1903
In paper boards, grey or brown. Price 1/- *In green cloth, light green or olive-green, with brown lettering, gilt top. Price 1/6 (Believed to have been 2000 copies from the first 8000)	There are no recognizable differences between the first three printings, except that green boards were introduced after the first printing.		The words 'wept big tears' on page 51 of the first three printings have been changed to 'shed big tears' in the fourth printing.

The illustrations are now coloured throughout. In these four printings, the book finishes on page 97. Four of the pictures do not appear in subsequent printings—they include the one of Mrs. McGregor and the pie, also the cover picture. There is no year on the title-page. Size: 139 mm × 104 mm.

* This de-luxe edition was replaced by one having a gilt decorated cloth cover with gold lettering; first introduced in October 1904.

EDITIONS OF THE TALE OF PETER RABBIT WITH COLOURED PICTORIAL END-PAPERS

5th printing	*6th printing*	*7th printing*	*8th printing*
10,000 copies October 1903	10,000 copies December 1903	10,000 copies April 1904	20,000 copies October 1904
A single-page end-paper, Fig. 1, occurring four times. (See Appendix 1)	A double-page end-paper, Figs. 1 and 2, occurring twice. (See Appendix 1)	A double-page end-paper, Figs. 2 and 3, occurring twice. (See Appendix 1)	A double-page end-paper Figs. 2 and 3 occurring twice. (See Appendix 1)

With the introduction of coloured pictorial end-papers, four of the coloured pictures were removed to enable the printer to continue with the same imposition of the sheets. The book now finishes on page 85, as compared with page 97 in the first four printings.

NOTE: In the autumn of 1907 a set of new blocks was made, and two of the drawings are slightly different. On page 68 where Peter is in the wheelbarrow and Mr. McGregor is in the distance hoeing onions, both Peter and Mr. McGregor are drawn to a larger scale. Also, the picture of Mrs. Rabbit pouring out Peter's camomile tea on page 81 is more pleasing than the earlier one. These blocks were in use for six or seven years, after which the old ones were again used.

FIRST AND EARLY EDITIONS OF THE PETER RABBIT BOOKS—1903

Title	Details of First Editions	Details of Publication			Identification of First Editions
		1st edition	2nd printing	3rd printing	
The Tale of Squirrel Nutkin	In paper boards, grey or dark blue. Price 1/- ★In art fabric, flower pattern. Price 1/6 Size: 138 mm × 104 mm	10,000 copies August 1903	10,000 copies September 1903	7500 copies November 1903	The year 1903 appears on the front of the title-page of the first three printings. The difference between the first and third printings is that the title-page of the latter bears the words 'Author of The Tale of Peter Rabbit' under Beatrix Potter's name. It is believed that this change was not made until *after* the second printing.
The Tailor of Gloucester	In paper boards, maroon or dark green. Price 1/- ★In art fabric, flower pattern. Price 1/6 Size: 139 mm × 103 mm	20,000 copies October 1903	6000 copies December 1903	7500 copies October 1904	The year 1903 appears on the front of the title-page of the first two printings. The first printing has a single-page end-paper occurring four times, and the second printing, a double-page end-paper occurring twice. In the art fabric de-luxe edition, some copies have the usual frontispiece, others have the cover picture in its place. Both pictures were printed on one sheet, which was cut in half, and each half used as a tipped-in frontispiece. With this binding there was no cover picture.

★ This de-luxe edition was replaced in October 1904 by one having a gilt decorated cloth cover with gold lettering. Copies having the year 1903 on the front of the title page would have been bound from first edition sheets.

FIRST AND EARLY EDITIONS OF THE PETER RABBIT BOOKS—1904

Title	Details of First Editions	Details of Publication			Identification of First Editions
		1st edition	2nd printing	3rd printing	
The Tale of Benjamin Bunny	In paper boards, grey or tan. Price 1/- In decorated cloth. Price 1/6 Size: 139 mm × 104 mm	20,000 copies September 1904	10,000 copies October 1904	7500 copies March 1905	The year 1904 appears on the front of the title-page of the first two printings, which are believed to be identical. In these two printings, the word 'muffetees' is wrongly spelt on page 15, and reads 'muffatees'. A few years later some of the drawings were mislaid and Beatrix Potter prepared fresh ones. With the exception of the picture where 'little Benjamin Bunny slid down into the road . . .' in which the figure of Benjamin was larger in the new picture, and also a drawing of the cat, in which the tail was made shorter, there was very little difference between the new pictures and the old. The old ones were not used again.
The Tale of Two Bad Mice	In paper boards, red or grey. Price 1/- In decorated cloth. Price 1/6 Size: 139 mm × 105 mm	20,000 copies September 1904	10,000 copies November 1904	7500 copies September 1905	The year 1904 appears on the front of the title-page of the first two printings, which are believed to be identical.

FIRST AND EARLY EDITIONS OF THE PETER RABBIT BOOKS—1905

Title	Details of First Editions	Details of Publication			Identification of First Editions
		1st Edition	2nd printing	3rd printing	
The Tale of Mrs. Tiggy-Winkle	In paper boards, brown or green. Price 1/-. In decorated cloth. Price 1/6. Size: 139 mm × 104 mm	20,000 copies September 1905	10,000 copies November 1905	5000 copies August 1906	The year 1905 appears on the front of the title-page of the first two printings, which are believed to be identical. About 1910 the name 'How Keld' was taken out of the picture on page 20 of the hill-side spring.
The Pie and the Patty-pan	In paper boards, brown, blue-grey or maroon. Price 1/-. In decorated cloth, light blue. Price 2/-. Size: 177 mm × 138 mm	17,500 copies October 1905	8000 copies January 1906	4750 copies November 1907	The year 1905 appears on the front of the title-page of the first printing. The early printings have plain mottled lavender end-papers, which were shortly replaced by an end-paper design featuring a pie and a patty-pan. The cover picture was then changed from a cat in a small circle, to one of Ribby sitting by the fire, in a large circle. In 1930 the title was changed to *The Tale of the Pie and the Patty-pan*, and the book printed in the small format.

FIRST AND EARLY EDITIONS OF THE PETER RABBIT BOOKS—1906

Title	Details of First Editions	Details of Publication			Identification of First Editions
		1st Edition	2nd printing	3rd printing	
The Tale of Mr. Jeremy Fisher	In paper boards, red or grey-green. Price 1/-. In decorated cloth. Price 1/6 Size: 138 mm × 105 mm	20,000 copies July 1906	5000 copies September 1906	5000 copies September 1907	The year 1906 appears on the front of the title-page of the first two printings, which are believed to be identical.
The Story of a Fierce Bad Rabbit	In wallet (panoramic form) Price 1/-. Size: 108 mm × 89 mm (108 mm × 2492 mm open)	10,000 copies November 1906	10,000 copies December 1906	none	On the back of some wallets are the words 'London & New York', and on others 'New York & London'. The former is believed to be the November printing, as the wording corresponds to that on Beatrix Potter's 'author's copies' and on a copy inscribed to Joan Moore. In 1916 this title was first printed in book form. Size: 122 mm × 103 mm
The Story of Miss Moppet	In wallet (panoramic form) Price 1/-. Size: 108 mm × 89 mm (108 mm × 2492 mm open)	10,000 copies November 1906	10,000 copies December 1906	none	On the back of some wallets are the words 'London & New York', and on others 'New York & London'. The former is believed to be the November printing. In 1916 this title was first printed in book form. Size: 122 mm × 103 mm

FIRST AND EARLY EDITIONS OF THE PETER RABBIT BOOKS—1907–1908

Title	Details of First Editions	Details of Publication			Identification of First Editions
		1st Edition	2nd printing	3rd printing	
The Tale of Tom Kitten	In paper boards, grey-green or beige. Price 1/- In decorated cloth. Price 1/6 Size: 138 mm × 105 mm	20,000 copies September 1907	5000 copies December 1907	7500 copies December 1907	The year 1907 appears on the front of the title-page of the first three printings, which are believed to be identical.
The Tale of Jemima Puddle-Duck	In paper boards, grey or green. Price 1/- In decorated cloth. Price 1/6 Size: 138 mm × 104 mm	20,000 copies August 1908	5000 copies October 1908	5000 copies December 1908	The year 1908 appears on the front of the title-page of the first three printings, which are believed to be identical.
The Roly-Poly Pudding	In cloth, bevelled boards, maroon. Price 2/6 Size: 201 mm × 158 mm (In March 1918 there was a large format edition in paper boards)	7500 copies October 1908	5500 copies December 1908	4200 copies August 1913	The year 1908 appears on the front of the title-page of the first two printings. The title-page of the first printing has the words 'All rights reserved)' at the bottom. This was omitted at the second printing. In 1926 the title was changed to *The Tale of Samuel Whiskers*, and the book printed in the small format. (The title was not changed in the American edition.)

FIRST AND EARLY EDITIONS OF THE PETER RABBIT BOOKS—1909

Title	Details of First Editions	Details of Publication			Identification of First Editions
		1st Edition	2nd printing	3rd printing	
The Tale of the Flopsy Bunnies	In paper boards, brown or dark green. Price 1/– In decorated cloth. Price 1/6 Size: 138 mm × 104 mm	20,000 copies July 1909	5000 copies October 1909	5000 copies November 1909	The year 1909 appears on the front of the title-page of the first three printings. The Notice Board in the picture on page 14, of the market-garden scene, is believed to have been taken out soon after publication, as a 1909 copy has been seen without this Notice Board (probably a third printing).
Ginger and Pickles	In paper boards, pale olive green or buff. Price 1/– Size: 177 mm × 136 mm	15,000 copies October 1909	10,875 copies November 1909	10,600 copies November 1910	The year 1909 appears on the front of the title-page of the first two printings, which are believed to be identical. In 1930 the title was changed to *The Tale of Ginger and Pickles*, and the book printed in the small-size format. There are two variations in the coloured pictures. In the large-format edition—in one picture, a biscuit tin has the name 'Carr & Co', while in another picture a box is marked 'Sunlight Soap'. In the small-format edition the names are 'Uneeda' on the tin, and 'Toilet Soap' on the box. (This latter wording also appears in the large-format American Edition.)

FIRST AND EARLY EDITIONS OF THE PETER RABBIT BOOKS—1910–1913

Title	Details of First Editions	Details of Publication			Identification of First Editions
		1st Edition	2nd printing	3rd printing	
The Tale of Mrs. Tittlemouse	In paper boards, blue-grey or cream. Price 1/- In decorated cloth. Price 1/6 Size: 138 mm × 104 mm	25,000 copies July 1910	10,000 copies November 1910	5000 copies November 1911	The year 1910 appears on the front of the title-page of the first two printings, which are believed to be identical.
The Tale of Timmy Tiptoes	In paper boards, brown or dark green. Price 1/- In decorated cloth. Price 1/6 Size: 137 mm × 105 mm	25,000 copies October 1911	10,000 copies November 1911	8400 copies November 1912	The year 1911 appears on the front of the title-page of the first two printings, which are believed to be identical.
The Tale of Mr. Tod	In paper boards (rounded back) grey or buff. Price 1/- Size: 138 mm × 104 mm	25,000 copies October 1912	10,000 copies November 1912	10,000 copies October 1913	The year 1912 appears on the front of the title-page of the first two printings, which are believed to be identical.
The Tale of Pigling Bland	In paper boards (rounded back) grey-green or maroon. Price 1/- Size: 138 mm × 104 mm	25,000 copies October 1913	10,000 copies November 1913	10,000 copies November 1914	The year 1913 appears on the front of the title-page of the first two printings, which are believed to be identical.

FIRST AND EARLY EDITIONS OF THE PETER RABBIT BOOKS—1917-1930

Title	Details of First Editions	Details of Publication			Identification of First Editions
		1st Edition	2nd printing	3rd printing	
Appley Dapply's Nursery Rhymes	In paper boards, pale olive-green. Price 1/3 Size: 122 mm × 104 mm	20,000 copies October 1917	15,000 copies November 1917	9250 copies September 1920	There is no year on the title-page. It is believed that a first edition can be identified only if inscribed as a 'first', or with an inscription dated 1917. (Correct end-papers would indicate a 1917 printing.)
The Tale of Johnny Town-Mouse	In paper boards, brown or grey. Price 1/- Size: 138 mm × 105 mm	30,000 copies December 1918	5000 copies June 1919	5000 copies March 1920	There is no year on the title-page, but the first copies to be printed had the letter 'N' missing from 'London' in the imprint.
Cecily Parsley's Nursery Rhymes	In paper boards, red. Price 1/6 Size: 123 mm × 103 mm	20,000 copies December 1922	5000 copies July 1926	3400 copies June 1929	There is no year on the title-page. It is believed that a first edition can be identified only if inscribed as a 'first', or with an inscription dated 1922 to 1925. (Correct end-papers would indicate a 'first'.)
The Tale of Little Pig Robinson	In cloth, light blue. Price 3/6 Size: 202 mm × 158 mm	5000 copies September 1930	5000 copies December 1930	5000 copies March 1931	There is no year on the title-page. The first printing can be identified by the absence of the word 'reprinted' which appears on the back of the title-page of the next printing.

BEATRIX POTTER'S BOOKS—MISCELLANEOUS

Title	Publisher	First Published	Number Printed	Binding	Size
Peter Rabbit's Painting Book	Frederick Warne & Co.	October 1911	20,000 copies	In paper boards, or limp cloth, olive-green, Price 1/–	209 mm × 180 mm
Tom Kitten's Painting Book	Frederick Warne & Co.	June 1917	5000 copies	In paper boards, or limp cloth, brown. Price 1/–	207 mm × 178 mm
Jemima Puddle-Duck's Painting Book	Frederick Warne & Co.	August 1925	10,350 copies	In paper boards, or limp cloth, grey. Price 1/6	213 mm × 180 mm
Peter Rabbit's Almanac for 1929	Frederick Warne & Co.	September 1928	15,000 copies	In paper boards, buff. Price 1/–	123 mm × 90 mm
The Fairy Caravan	David McKay Company (Philadelphia)	October 1929		In cloth, dark green.	210 mm × 160 mm
The Fairy Caravan (Beatrix Potter's Limited Edition)	First section printed at Ambleside—remaining sections from the sheets of David McKay's edition.	October 1929	100 copies	In grey paper boards, cloth back. (Uncut edges.)	225 mm × 170 mm
The Fairy Caravan	Frederick Warne & Co. Ltd.	July 1952	7500 copies	In cloth, light green. Price 10/6	204 mm × 147 mm

BEATRIX POTTER'S BOOKS—MISCELLANEOUS

Title	Publisher	First Published	Number Printed	Binding	Size
The Tale of Little Pig Robinson	David McKay, Company	1930	unknown	In cloth, dark green. (There are more black and white drawings than in Warne's edition)	210 mm × 160 mm
Sister Anne	David McKay, Company	1932	unknown	In cloth, royal blue.	190 mm × 132 mm
Wag-by-Wall	Frederick Warne & Co. Ltd.	1944	100 copies (numbered)	In cloth, light green.	136 mm × 106 mm
Wag-by-Wall	The Horn Book, Inc. (Boston)	1944	unknown	In buckram, fawn. Price $1.50	155 mm × 110 mm
The Tale of The Faithful Dove	Frederick Warne & Co. Ltd.	1955	100 copies (numbered)	In cloth, light green.	137 mm × 106 mm
The Tale of The Faithful Dove	Frederick Warne & Co. Inc. (New York)	1956	2500 copies / 1500 copies	In cloth, buff. Price $1.50 (First trimmed to the smaller size.)	155 mm × 113 mm / 186 mm × 117 mm
The Tailor of Gloucester Facsimile of the original manuscript and illustrations	Frederick Warne & Co. Inc. (New York)	1968	1500 copies (numbered)	In cloth, black. (Boxed.) Price £8. 8. 0 in U.K.	234 mm × 180 mm
The Tailor of Gloucester From the original manuscript	Frederick Warne & Co. Inc. (New York)	1968	12,000 copies	Price $4.95	
	Frederick Warne & Co. Ltd.	1969	5000 copies	In paper boards, cream Price £1	234 mm × 180 mm

APPENDIX 4

The Beatrix Potter Books

(Published by F. Warne & Co Ltd, unless otherwise stated)

1. The Tale of Peter Rabbit (privately printed, first edition, flat back), 250   1901
   copies, Dec. 1901, followed by a second edition (round back, 200 copies,
   Feb. 1902)
2. The Tale of Peter Rabbit   1902
3. The Tailor of Gloucester (privately printed, 500 copies)   1902
4. The Tale of Squirrel Nutkin   1903
5. The Tailor of Gloucester   1903
6. The Tale of Benjamin Bunny   1904
7. The Tale of Two Bad Mice   1904
8. The Tale of Mrs. Tiggy-Winkle   1905
9. The Pie and the Patty-pan (first published in the larger format)   1905
10. The Tale of Mr. Jeremy Fisher   1906
11. The Story of a Fierce Bad Rabbit (first published in panoramic form)   1906
12. The Story of Miss Moppet (first published in panoramic form)   1906
13. The Tale of Tom Kitten   1907
14. The Tale of Jemima Puddle-Duck   1908
15. The Roly-Poly Pudding (first published in the larger format)   1908
    Later renamed The Tale of Samuel Whiskers
16. The Tale of the Flopsy Bunnies   1909
17. Ginger and Pickles (first published in the larger format)   1909
18. The Tale of Mrs. Tittlemouse   1910
19. Peter Rabbit's Painting Book   1911
20. The Tale of Timmy Tiptoes   1911
21. The Tale of Mr. Tod   1912
22. The Tale of Pigling Bland   1913
23. Tom Kitten's Painting Book   1917
24. Appley Dapply's Nursery Rhymes (first published in a smaller format)   1917
25. The Tale of Johnny Town-Mouse   1918
26. Cecily Parsley's Nursery Rhymes (first published in a smaller format)   1922
27. Jemima Puddle-Duck's Painting Book   1925
28. Peter Rabbit's Almanac for 1929   1928

THE BEATRIX POTTER BOOKS PRINTED IN BRAILLE

(The Royal Institute for the Blind)

Peter Rabbit, Mrs. Tiggy-Winkle, Tom Kitten, The Flopsy Bunnies,   1921
Pigling Bland, Johnny Town-Mouse
The Journal of Beatrix Potter has been tape-recorded by The British   1970
Talking Book Service for the Blind

Appendix 4

THE BEATRIX POTTER BOOKS PRINTED IN i.t.a.

Peter Rabbit, Benjamin Bunny, Two Bad Mice, Mrs. Tiggy-Winkle,
Mr. Jeremy Fisher, Tom Kitten, Jemima Puddle-Duck, Flopsy Bunnies,   1965
Mrs. Tittlemouse
Timmy Tiptoes   1966

THE BEATRIX POTTER BOOKS
TRANSLATED INTO OTHER LANGUAGES

French	Pierre Lapin (Peter Rabbit)	1921
	Noisy-Noisette (Squirrel Nutkin)	1931
	Le Tailleur de Gloucester (Tailor of Gloucester)	1967
	Jeannot Lapin (Benjamin Bunny)	1921
	Poupette-à-L'Epingle (Mrs. Tiggy-Winkle)	1922
	Jeremie Pêche-à-la-Ligne (Mr. Jeremy Fisher)	1940
	Toto le Minet (Tom Kitten)	1951
	Sophie Canétang (Jemima Puddle-Duck)	1922
	La Famille Flopsaut (Flopsy Bunnies)	1931
Dutch	Het Verhaal van Pieter Langoor (Peter Rabbit)	1912
	(published under licence by Nijgh & Van Ditmar's Uitgevers-Maatschappij, Rotterdam)	
	Benjamin Knabbel (Benjamin Bunny)	1946
	Twee Stoute Muisjes (Two Bad Mice)	1946
	Jeremias de Hengelaar (Mr. Jeremy Fisher)	1946
	Tom Het Poesje (Tom Kitten)	1946
	Het Verhaal van Kwakkel Waggel-Eend (Jemima Puddle-Duck)	1912
	(published under licence by Nijgh & Ditmar's Uitgevers-Maatschappij, Rotterdam)	
	De Kleine Langoortjes (Flopsy Bunnies)	1946
	(The following twelve titles have been published under licence by Uitgeverij Ploegsma, Amsterdam)	
	Het Verhaal van Pieter Konijn (Peter Rabbit)	1968
	Het Verhaal van Eekhoorn Hakketak (Squirrel Nutkin)	1969
	Het Verhaal van Benjamin Wollepluis (Benjamin Bunny)	1969
	Het Verhaal van Twee Stoute Muizen (Two Bad Mice)	1969
	Het Verhaal van Vrouwtje Plooi (Mrs. Tiggy-Winkle)	1969

Het Verhaal van Jeremias Hengelaar (Jeremy Fisher) — 1970
Het Verhaal van Poekie Poes (Tom Kitten) — 1970
Het Verhaal van Jozefien Kwebbeleend (Jemima Puddle-Duck) — 1968
Het Verhaal van De Wollepluis-Konijntjes (Flopsy Bunnies) — 1969
Het Verhaal van Minetje Miezemuis (Mrs. Tittlemouse) — 1970
Het Verhaal van Timmie Tuimelaar (Timmy Tiptoes) — 1968
Het Verhaal van Diederik Stadsmuis (Johnny Town-Mouse) — 1969

Welsh
Hanes Pwtan y Wningen (Peter Rabbit) — 1932
Hanes Benda Bynni (Benjamin Bunny) — 1948
Hanes Meistres Tigi-Dwt (Mrs. Tiggy-Winkle) — 1932
Hanes Dili Minllyn (Jemima Puddle-Duck) — 1924
Hanes Meistr Tod (Mr. Tod) — 1963

German
Die Geschichte des Peterchen Hase (Peter Rabbit) — 1934
  (Style 1, English type; style 2, Gothic type)
Die Geschichte von den zwei bösen Mäuschen (Two Bad Mice) — 1939
Die Geschichte von Frau Tiggy-Winkle (Mrs. Tiggy-Winkle) — 1948
Die Geschichte von Samuel Hagezahn (Samuel Whiskers, — 1951
  or The Roly-Poly Pudding)
Die Geschichte Der Hasenfamilie Plumps (Flopsy Bunnies) — 1947
Die Geschichte von Herrn Reineke (Mr. Tod) — 1951

Italian
Il Coniglio Pierino (Peter Rabbit) — 1948

Spanish
Pedrin El Conejo Travieso (Peter Rabbit) — 1931

Swedish
Sagan om Pelle Kanin (Peter Rabbit) — 1948
Sagan om Kurre Nötpigg (Squirrel Nutkin) — 1954
Den lillae grisen Robinsons äventyr — 1938
  (Little Pig Robinson, no illustrations)

Norwegian Fortellingen om Nina Pytt-And (Jemima Puddle-Duck) — 1948

Danish
Tom Kitte (Tom Kitten) — 1946

Afrikaans
Die Verhaal van Pieter Konyntjie (Peter Rabbit) — 1929
Die Verhaal van Bennie Blinkhaar (Benjamin Bunny) — 1935
Die Varhaal van Die Flopsie-Familie (Flopsy Bunnies) — 1935
Die Verhaal van Mevrou Piekfyn (Mrs. Tittlemouse) — 1935

Latin
Fabula de Petro Cuniculo (Peter Rabbit) — 1962
Fabula de Jemima Anate-Aquatica (Jemima Puddle-Duck) — 1965

Appendix 4

Japanese   The following titles are to be published under licence by Fukuinkan-
Shoten, Tokyo

The Tale of Peter Rabbit	1971
The Tale of Benjamin Bunny	1971
The Tale of the Flopsy Bunnies	1971
The Tale of Tom Kitten	
The Story of Miss Moppet	
The Story of a Fierce Bad Rabbit	
The Tale of Squirrel Nutkin	
The Tale of Jemima Puddleduck	
The Tale of Mrs. Tittlemouse	
The Tale of Ginger and Pickles	
The Tale of Two Bad Mice	

INDEX

Index

Index